EBERRON

THE TYRANNY OF GHOSTS

LEGACY OF DHAKAAN / BOOK 3

DON BASSINGTHWAITE

Legacy of Dhakaan, Book 3
THE TYRANNY OF GHOSTS

©2010 Wizards of the Coast LLC

All characters in this book are fictitious. Any resemblance to actual persons, living or dead, is purely coincidental.

This book is protected under the copyright laws of the United States of America. Any reproduction or unauthorized use of the material or artwork contained herein is prohibited without the express written permission of Wizards of the Coast LLC.

Published by Wizards of the Coast LLC

EBERRON, WIZARDS OF THE COAST, and their respective logos are trademarks of Wizards of the Coast LLC in the U.S.A. and other countries.

Printed in the U.S.A.

Cover art by Michael Komarck
Map by Rob Lazzaretti

First Printing: June 2010

9 8 7 6 5 4 3 2 1

ISBN: 978-0-7869-5506-0
620- 25452000-001-EN

The sale of this book without its cover has not been authorized by the publisher. If you purchased this book without a cover, you should be aware that neither the author nor the publisher has received payment for this "stripped book."

U.S., CANADA,	EUROPEAN HEADQUARTERS
ASIA, PACIFIC, & LATIN AMERICA	Hasbro UK Ltd
Wizards of the Coast LLC	Caswell Way
P.O. Box 707	Newport, Gwent NP9 0YH
Renton, WA 98057-0707	GREAT BRITAIN
+1-800-324-6496	Save this address for your records.

Visit our web site at www.wizards.com

Lake Brey
BRELAND
THE MOURNLAND
The Lightning Rail
Kennrun
Gorgonhorn
Skullreave
Olkhaan
Sterngate
Lyrenton
Ghaal River
Rhukaan Draal
ZILARGO
Zarrthec
Volaar Draal
Seawall Mountains
Rheklor
DARGUUN
Arthuun
Torlaac River
The Khraal
Torlaac Moor
Korranberg
THUNDER SEA
N
W
E
S
0
400
miles

Raat shi anaa.

"The story continues."

—Traditional opening to hobgoblin legends.

EVENTS OF WORD OF TRAITORS

As the body of Lhesh Haruuc Shaarat'kor—slain by the traitor Chetiin—was placed in the royal tomb, Geth and his allies faced a dilemma. Although Geth held the throne and the Rod of Kings in trust, a new lhesh would soon be chosen. Any heir, on grasping the rod, would be caught by its curse—memories of the ancient Empire of Dhakaan that sought to make the lhesh into a tyrant and gave the would-be emperor the power of irresistible command.

Yet Geth—immune to both the rod's curse and its power because of his connection to its sibling artifact, the Sword of Heroes—could not simply steal the rod either. Haruuc had made the rod a symbol of the lhesh's sovereignty, and without that symbol, the new lhesh's position would be weakened. With the rod, the new lhesh would lead Darguun into a war with neighboring nations and their allies that it could not win; without it, Darguun would crumble into civil war. In either case, Haruuc's dream of a homeland for his people would be lost.

An answer presented itself with the return to Rhukaan Draal of the cunning gnome scholar, Midian Mit Davandi. Midian proposed that they have a false rod created and present it to the new lhesh. The false rod would remain as the symbol of authority and unity that Haruuc had initially intended, while they smuggled the true rod out of Darguun and dealt with it in safety.

But Makka, the bugbear chieftain overthrown by Geth and the others during their quest for the Rod of Kings, had also arrived in the city intent on revenge. His attempted ambush of Ashi d'Deneith and Ekhaas of the Kech Volaar ended badly, however, and he was forced to flee. Dying from his wounds, he encountered Pradoor, a blind old goblin woman released from the fortress of Khaar Mbar'ost by Geth in a misguided act of mercy. Pradoor, a priestess of the gods of the Dark Six, believed that she was destined to restore their worship to its proper place in Darguun. Healed by her prayers, Makka became her servant and pledged himself to the Fury, the dark goddess of vengeance.

Meanwhile, Ekhaas, Geth, and the young warlord Dagii slipped out of Khaar Mbar'ost and met with Tenquis, a tiefling artificer. Tenquis agreed to create a false rod in exchange for a chance to study lore preserved by Ekhaas's clan. In examining the rod and Geth's sword, Tenquis guessed at something of the rod's hidden properties and of the heroes' intentions. He warned Geth that if they sought to destroy the rod, they wouldn't find it an easy task—such artifacts did not pass out of existence easily.

Leaving Tenquis's workshop, Geth and the others returned to Khaar Mbar'ost only to be ambushed—by Chetiin! To their amazement, he insisted that he had not been the one who had killed Haruuc. On the day of the assassination, he had himself been attacked and left for dead while someone else—likely another hired assassin of his clan, the *shaarat'khesh* or Silent Blades—had stolen his unique magical dagger and posed as him. Ekhaas and Dagii believed him but Geth remained doubtful. Only one of their group could have known words spoken by the assassin over Haruuc's body. If Chetiin's story were true, Midian was the one behind the hired assassin.

Geth, Ekhaas, and Dagii agreed to keep Chetiin's survival from both Ashi and Midian, so that Chetiin would be free to look for further evidence of treachery. The goblin vanished into the night and the three continued on to Khaar Mbar'ost, only to receive another surprise. Valenar raiders had attacked and

destroyed clanholds in the east of Darguun. Moments before his death, Haruuc had attempted to channel the aggression born of the cursed rod into conflict with the elves of Valenar. Although it had seemed that the threat of war had passed with Haruuc's death, the elves still sought battle and had chosen to strike first.

Tariic, Haruuc's nephew and potential heir, roused Darguun's warlords with an impassioned speech demanding the defense of the nation. He appointed Dagii to lead a small force to confront the raiders. Dagii, bound by honor and duty, accepted the command, and Ekhaas was ordered by Senen Dhakaan, the ambassador of her clan, to accompany him and record the story of the battle. They were also accompanied—in secret and at Geth's request—by Chetiin. Geth had investigated details of Chetiin's story and finally had been convinced that it was the truth. Although sending Chetiin away left only Ashi and Midian (his trustworthiness suspect) in Rhukaan Draal, Geth wanted to be certain Dagii and Ekhaas were kept safe.

Soon after, Tariic was chosen as Haruuc's successor. With Tariic's coronation imminent and the false rod in hand, Geth felt confident that their scheme would succeed. He was shaken by the appearance of Pradoor and Makka at the coronation ceremony: Tariic had allied himself with the priestess to secure the support of the people in his selection as lhesh. Geth's confidence was completely shattered, however, when Tariic, taking possession of the false rod during the ceremony, instantly recognized it as a forgery.

While they had all assumed that no one but Haruuc and Geth had ever touched the Rod of Kings, they had forgotten that on the day they had returned to Rhukaan Draal with the rod, Tariic had taken it from Geth and had ceremoniously presented it to his uncle. Even that brief contact had exposed him to the curse. Where Haruuc had resisted the rod, though, Tariic had opened himself to it.

Combined with Tariic's natural ambition and charisma, the rod would be a greater danger than ever. Tariic could not,

however, reveal the rod's forgery without placing his newly-crowned status in jeopardy, and Geth took advantage of this vulnerability to escape the throne room. With guards in pursuit, he fled for his chamber to retrieve the true rod, intending to flee with it. Bursting into his chamber, however, he surprised Chetiin in the act of stealing the true rod.

Stunned, Geth watched as the goblin traitor escaped with the rod, rappelling down the side of Khaar Mbar'ost, just as the guards reached the chamber. Outnumbered, Geth climbed out the window and plunged to the ground. He survived, thanks to his shifter-granted toughness, but was left badly injured. With his allies trapped in Tariic's fortress, he turned to the only remaining person he could trust to hide him, passing out on Tenquis's doorstep.

But at the same time, far away, Chetiin stood with Ekhaas and Dagii in a skirmish against a small group of Valenar. Thanks to Dagii's tactics and the timely use of Ekhaas's *duur'kala* magic, the elves were defeated and the Darguuls discovered that the raiding warbands were only a cover for a larger force: an entire Valenar warclan. Dispatching warnings to Tariic, Dagii commanded his soldiers to make a stand against the Valenar.

Meanwhile, in Rhukaan Draal on the day of the coronation, Ashi had come close to attacking the soldiers sent after Geth, but had been held back by Aruget, a loyal guard assigned to her by Haruuc. Aruget, knowing something of the heroes' secrets, saw that if Ashi had attacked, Tariic would have been within his rights to arrest her. Vounn d'Deneith, Ashi's superior and House Deneith's envoy to the court of Darguun, agreed and kept Ashi isolated for several days. As soon as she deemed it safe, Vounn made arrangements with Pater d'Orien, viceroy of House Orien, to have Ashi magically transported out of Darguun.

While Vounn made her arrangements, though, Ashi was able to meet with Midian for the first time since the coronation. Discovering that Geth had apparently returned and taken to accompanying Tariic everywhere while avoiding them, Ashi

THE TYRANNY OF GHOSTS

and Midian decided that they needed to confront their friend. Their conversation was overheard by Makka, still seeking vengeance and assigned by Tariic to deal with Ashi and Midian without bringing suspicion on the throne. Soon Ashi received a message from Geth arranging a secret meeting on the roof of Khaar Mbar'ost late at night. Though she, Midian, and Aruget were wary, they were unprepared for the attack launched by Makka and "Geth"—in actual fact, a changeling, Ko, ordered to take on Geth's likeness by Tariic in order to hide the real Geth's disappearance.

Aruget managed to get Ashi away. Their escape trapped Midian with Makka, but Aruget would not let Ashi go back, saying only that Midian could take care of himself. In the process of escaping, Aruget revealed that he was more than he seemed. He was not a hobgoblin at all, but another changeling, known to Ashi from previous adventures as a half-elf named Benti—an agent of Breland. Ashi and Aruget fled for the compound of House Orien. However, Tariic had sent a messenger ahead with a notice declaring Ashi a wanted criminal. As Aruget, looking out for himself, vanished, Ashi found herself cornered by Tariic's soldiers and arrested.

The next morning, Dagii's forces engaged the Valenar near the town of Zarrthec. Though Darguul discipline and tactics initially dominated the battle, elven cavalry and war magic soon turned the tide. The Darguuls seemed doomed to fail until reinforcements arrived—*taarka'khesh*, goblin wolf riders rallied by Chetiin and his own wolflike worg mount, Marrow. Devastated, the Valenar fled the field. Victory belonged to Dagii, who used the opportunity to proclaim his love for Ekhaas. In the midst of the battle, however, Ekhaas had received a magical warning from Senen of Ashi's arrest. Ekhaas and Chetiin hurried to Rhukaan Draal followed by Dagii and the survivors of the great battle, the victory march serving as a distraction from Ekhaas and Chetiin's return.

Ashi, to her own surprise, was left unharmed following her imprisonment. A daring attack by Midian freed her, but the

gnome confessed that after being captured by Makka, he'd given her up for his own life and freedom. Worse, he'd also betrayed Geth and Tenquis, having uncovered Tenquis's identity and guessing that Geth had taken refuge with the artificer. The shifter and the tiefling were also Tariic's prisoners.

Encountering Ekhaas on her way to rescue Ashi, they descended deeper into the dungeon and discovered that Geth and Tenquis had been tortured by Tariic in the belief that Geth had stolen the Rod of Kings. Geth hadn't, but before their capture he and Tenquis had devised a way to track the rod and had found its location—Chetiin had somehow hidden the stolen rod in Haruuc's sealed tomb! Although Geth had resisted torture, Tenquis had not. The lhesh's allies were already on their way to the tomb.

Chetiin's appearance drove Geth into a rage, but the mystery of the goblin's apparent treachery was solved as Aruget arrived (also with the intent of rescuing the prisoners). Just as Aruget was an agent of Breland, Midian was an agent of the gnome nation of Zilargo, and the gnomes were manipulating events for their own benefit. Midian had assassinated Haruuc in disguise as Chetiin, when it appeared Haruuc would become a tyrant, not realizing the rod's curse was to blame. He'd donned the disguise again to steal the rod and discredit Chetiin after discovering the goblin had survived his initial attack.

The need to retrieve the rod before Tariic could was more important than Midian's guilt or innocence, however. Slipping out of Khaar Mbar'ost, the heroes hurried to Haruuc's tomb, where they discovered Makka and Pradoor overseeing bugbear workers attempting to break through the tomb's massive door. Midian had previously slipped into the tomb through a natural shaft in the rock, but no one trusted him enough to allow him to go back in on his own. Ekhaas, Ashi, and Aruget distracted Makka and the workers, while Tenquis used artificer magic to open the tomb so that Geth, Chetiin, and Midian could enter and retrieve the rod.

THE TYRANNY OF GHOSTS

But Midian escaped and ran for his own secret entrance to the tomb, betraying them all yet again. Geth, Chetiin, and Tenquis opened the door and beat Midian into the tomb but were unable to retrieve the rod before he began sniping at them with a crossbow retrieved from a hidden cache. Chetiin sneaked up to Midian, and while the goblin and the gnome struggled, Geth retrieved the rod. As he climbed out of the tomb, he was ambushed by Makka, who had returned. Seizing the rod from Geth, Makka and Pradoor rode back to Khaar Mbar'ost and Tariic.

Geth came up with a desperate plan—another assassination. Forced to spare Midian in spite of his continued treachery, they returned to Khaar Mbar'ost and found Tariic, rod already in hand, waiting alongside the warlords of his court to greet Dagii as he marched into the city. Geth and the others worked their way through the gathered crowd until Midian could strike Tariic with a poisoned crossbow bolt, killing him. As the crowd scattered, Geth, Chetiin, and Ashi leaped onto the platform to retrieve the fallen rod—only to find that Tariic had outwitted them. In death, the lhesh's body transformed into that of Ko, the changeling. The rod they had risked themselves to retrieve was the false one. Tariic, the true rod in his grasp, appeared and ordered the assembled Darguuls to seize the traitors.

The heroes found themselves surrounded by Darguul warlords and commoners caught up in the irresistible power of the Rod of Kings. Aruget and Midian disappeared into the crowd. Ekhaas, confronted by Dagii, briefly believed herself rescued, only to realize that Dagii had also succumbed to the rod's power. Tenquis, left beyond the crowd, rode to their rescue, parting the mob with horses for the heroes to ride to freedom.

Or almost all the heroes. Makka—his vengeance long delayed—found himself with a chance to kill a momentarily defenseless Ashi. He attacked, but his killing blow was intercepted by Vounn d'Deneith, who attempted to turn the blade

with the power of her own weak dragonmark. She failed, and Makka's thrust impaled Vounn and Ashi together.

Stunned at their friends' deaths, there was nothing the others could do but flee as Tariic ordered Dagii to ride them down. Away from the crowd, Ekhaas turned to confront her beloved and allow the others a chance to flee, but found herself unexpectedly aided by Senen. Distracting Dagii with a spell of confusion, Senen told Ekhaas to guide the others to refuge with the Kech Volaar and to warn their clan against the dangers of an alliance with Tariic. The heroes fled, vowing to stop Tariic's mad ambition but unaware of what they had left behind . . .

CHAPTER ONE

5 Aryth, 999 YK (late autumn)

The Darguul patrol—two bugbears and six hobgoblins—crept among the trees in near silence. Their armor had been padded to dampen the rattle of plates and mail. Their scabbards had been bound close. They had left their horses behind and placed their feet with care, avoiding sticks and dry leaves and the tufts of crackling, frost-stiff grass left by winter's first breath on the foothills of the Seawall Mountains. They carried no light source and didn't need one—goblin eyes saw as well by night as by day.

In the small camp ahead, four blanket-wrapped forms lay around the dim coals of a fire. The loudest sound in the night was the gentle snoring that came from one of those forms.

The patrol's leader, a hobgoblin with the ceremonial scars of the Rhukaan Taash clan across his forehead, raised a hand, and the patrol halted beside a thick fir tree. The leader studied the camp ahead, then gestured. As the patrol resumed its stealthy approach, two pairs of soldiers split off to come at the camp from south and north.

Hidden among the thick boughs of the fir, Geth saw the patrol leader's ears stand tall and his sharp teeth flash in a grin. The shifter knew what he was thinking: there would be honor and glory in Khaar Mbar'ost for the hero who brought back the heads of the would-be assassins of Lhesh Tariic Kurar'taarn.

Geth could have told the hobgoblin that honor and glory weren't always the rewards of heroes. For the two days since

they'd fled the city of Rhukaan Draal, rage and anguish had festered in him. Anguish for the murders of Ashi and Vounn. Rage at Makka for having killed them. Rage at Tariic and at Pradoor. Rage at Midian Mit Davandi for betraying them yet again. Rage at Aruget—or whatever the changeling Dark Lantern of Breland chose to call himself—for abandoning them.

Rage at himself for thinking he could try to save Haruuc's dream of Darguun as a homeland for the *dar*, the three related races of hobgoblins, goblins, and bugbears. The disaster in Rhukaan Draal was his making.

As the last hobgoblin passed, he tightened his grip on his sword, tensed his muscles—and exploded out of hiding, his roar shattering the silence.

Already on edge, the patrol whirled, and Geth buried Wrath deep in the gut of the first of Tariic's soldiers. The hobgoblin's falling body trapped the sword for a moment. Geth whipped his right arm up to catch on the armored sleeve of his great gauntlet the swift blow of a second soldier. The soldier's blade skittered across black, magewrought steel, then Geth had Wrath free. With a grunt, he sliced at the soldier's legs. The hobgoblin hopped back just in time.

At the fire, Ekhaas and Tenquis rose from their position as decoys. Out of the corner of his eye, Geth saw Chetiin, wrinkled face stained dark for stealth in the night, drop from the shadowed branches of a tree onto a bugbear. The goblin's arm went around the soldier's head, the unexpected weight dragging it back and exposing his throat. A dagger flashed—the ordinary dagger Chetiin sheathed on his left forearm, not the soul-stealing weapon that he kept on his right and that Midian had used to kill Haruuc—and the bugbear groped at the gaping, bubbling wound that opened across his neck. Chetiin kicked away as the sword of another soldier skimmed past him to plunge into the back of his already dying comrade. The dagger flashed again and the second soldier fell with a shriek, clutching at a crippled leg.

THE TYRANNY OF GHOSTS

Geth didn't see the killing blow that ended the shriek. Two of his opponents came at him together and he whirled aside. He blocked one sword with his gauntlet, turned Wrath in his grip, and caught the second in the jagged teeth that formed the back of the ancient blade. A twist of his wrist locked the weapons together. Geth kicked underneath them, driving a foot hard into the belly of the soldier and sending him reeling away. The other soldier tried to catch him off balance with a sweeping blow. Geth threw himself away—or tried to. The blood of the first hobgoblin slid under his feet. He fell to his knees, hand slamming into the gory muck to keep him from pitching forward onto his face. The soldier of Darguun loomed over him and raised his sword high—

—and jerked back as a crossbow bolt punched through his armor to bury itself in his chest. Geth reared up and slashed out with Wrath, shearing through chain mail, thick padding, and flesh. More blood soaked the ground. Geth rose and spared a glance for the source of the bolt. Tenquis cranked back the string of a crossbow for another shot while Ekhaas, sword out, moved to meet two more soldiers.

The hobgoblin who had led the patrol snarled and lunged for Geth. Most *dar* swords were forged in the same traditional style, millennia old, as Wrath—heavy blades sharp on one side and deeply serrated on the other, their broad ends slightly forked but not pointed. They were weapons for hacking and chopping and slashing but not for thrusting. The patrol leader, however, carried a human sword, narrow tip ground sharp. Geth jerked to one side as the sword darted at him, stepped inside the hobgoblin's extended reach, and punched him hard in his flat-nosed, sharp-boned face. The hobgoblin's ears sagged, his eyes rolled up, and he toppled backward.

Near the fire, the soldiers who faced Ekhaas hesitated. Half of their patrol was dead, and their leader was down. Geth saw them glance at each other, weighing the option of retreat.

Ekhaas didn't let them decide. She thrust out her free hand and sang a burst of song that cracked and popped with wild

energy. Brilliant light flared from her palm, bright at a distance, blinding close up. As the soldiers yelped and squinted, Ekhaas struck. One soldier went down with a bloody gash from shoulder to navel. The other got his sword up, parrying Ekhaas's in a clang of metal. The two hobgoblins traded blows back and forth—until Ekhaas suddenly jumped clear. The soldier held his next strike, confused.

Then Chetiin slipped in front of him and thrust his dagger up under the soldier's ribs. The soldier's confusion drained away into the shock of death. Chetiin pulled his dagger free, and the hobgoblin sank to the ground.

The soldier Geth had kicked in the stomach, the last one standing, stared in dismay at the devastation inflicted so swiftly on his patrol. Still wheezing and hunched over, he turned and fled.

Tenquis raised his crossbow and whispered a word. Blue light flared, lighting the dark skin of his face. He pulled the trigger of the crossbow, and the bolt leaped away in a hissing blue streak—

—that missed. It hit the trunk of a tree and stuck there, crackling and spitting sparks. The soldier ducked and kept running.

He took perhaps six more strides before a shadow seemed to separate itself from the night and leap on him with a terrible snarl. Teeth flashed as they closed on the back of the hobgoblin's neck. Powerful muscles bunched and shook the soldier like a toy. The snap of his neck was loud. Marrow tossed the soldier away, then sat back on her haunches and licked her bloody muzzle. Chetiin's big, black, wolflike mount had caught up to them on the first day of their flight. Chetiin had been evasive about whether the worg had found them on her own or if he had somehow summoned her. Geth hadn't pressed the question. One more ally was one more ally. Silence returned to the night.

"Better?" Ekhaas asked Geth as she wiped her sword.

"Not really, no," he said as he straddled the unconscious leader of the patrol, and slapped the hobgoblin.

THE TYRANNY OF GHOSTS

His eyelids fluttered open. Geth put Wrath across the hobgoblin's throat, steadying the blade with his gauntleted hand. "How many patrols are in the hills?" he asked in Goblin. The words were awkward, his accent thick—Wrath's magic might allow him to understand the language of the *dar*, but it didn't enable him to speak it.

The soldier's ears flicked as the others gathered around. His eyes darted between Geth and Ekhaas, with side trips to Chetiin and the dagger still in his hand, and to Tenquis, running fingers along his crossbow. Geth pressed down a little on Wrath to encourage a swift response. The soldier's eyes widened and came back to him.

"Lhesh Tariic ordered the Gold Hand battalion into the foothills under the command of Daavn of Marhaan."

Geth glanced up at Chetiin. The goblin gave a nod of approval.

Senen Dhakaan had told them to seek refuge in Volaar Draal, stronghold of the Kech Volaar—southwest of Rhukaan Draal. But Tariic, whatever else he might be, was no fool. Traveling south with a *duur'kala* of the Kech Volaar among them would have given away their destination. So they'd turned their flight from Rhukaan Draal to the northwest instead, hoping that the lhesh would believe they sought to reach Marguul Pass and Breland beyond it.

If Tariic had ordered one of his most trusted advisors into the mountains, their ruse had worked—maybe too well. A battalion's worth of patrols searching the hills . . .

Geth looked back down at his prisoner. "Did you signal another patrol that you'd found us?" he asked.

Desperate guile stirred in the soldier's face as he tried to think of an answer that would save his life. Geth pressed a little harder with Wrath. "*Doovol*," he said. Truth.

"Daavn commanded it."

Fresh anger twisted in Geth. He leaned hard on Wrath's blade. Sharp metal with the weight of a shifter behind it sliced

through the hobgoblin's throat. The patrol leader barely had time to look surprised before the sword crunched through bone and his head separated from his body.

It wasn't as good as killing Tariic, but it was good enough. Geth rose. "More patrols coming," he said.

"*Khaavolaar*," Ekhaas said between her teeth. "I should have finished Daavn when I had the chance at Haruuc's tomb."

"Regret is the blade that wounds over and over again," said Chetiin. "We haven't come to the end yet."

"The farther we go, the longer the journey back to Volaar Draal will be."

"We don't need to go farther." Moonlight glittered on the golden orbs of Tenquis's eyes, from the gold flecks in the polished horns that grew back from his brow, and on the short spikes that edged his chin like a goatee. "We can lay a false trail northward for a short distance from this spot and leave our fire smoldering in the morning. The smoke will draw other patrols here—the deaths will enrage them, and they'll follow the most obvious trail. Vengeance blinds hobgoblins."

Ekhaas's grimace became a narrow glance, but Chetiin nodded. "It will work." Ekhaas turned her glare on him. The old goblin just spread his hands. "He is right. It is how *ghuul'dar* will react. Tenquis would make a good *golin'dar*."

Ghuul'dar and *golin'dar*—the ancient Goblin words for hobgoblins, the mighty people, and goblins, the quick people. Not just quick for their speed, but also their cunning. Geth was glad that Chetiin was on their side and not, as he'd thought after Haruuc's death, an enemy. "That sounds like a plan," he said, "but we should at least make a show of hiding the bodies. It would seem odd if we left them out in the open." He jerked a thumb over his shoulder. "There's a gully back there. I'll go find their horses—"

Marrow interrupted with a growl and a whuff. Her reddish eyes flashed in the firelight, and she turned to disappear into the night. "She says she'll deal with the horses," translated Chetiin.

THE TYRANNY OF GHOSTS

Geth looked after the worg, then shrugged and sheathed Wrath. As Chetiin and Ekhaas moved to deal with the other fallen soldiers, he reached down and took hold of the patrol leader's body by the ankles, ready to drag the decapitated corpse into the undergrowth.

Tenquis stayed close. "He died too easily," he said. "You should have let me talk to him."

Geth followed his gaze down to the head and body of the soldier, then glanced back up at the tiefling. His gut clenched, anger and sorrow coming back as if they would never leave him. The feeling almost choked him. "Maybe I should have."

"Next time." Tenquis seized the hobgoblin's head by its lank black hair and held it up so that he could stare into the vacant eyes. Blood dripped from the severed neck, spattering fallen leaves at Tenquis's feet. The tiefling stood looking at the head for a long moment, then spun around sharply and hurled it off into the darkness. It crashed through dry branches like some great clumsy bird before hitting an unseen tree with a solid *thunk*. Tenquis bent and hooked his arms under the dead soldier's arms to help Geth carry the body.

Chetiin wasn't the only one Geth was glad to have as a friend rather than as an enemy.

"Tenquis," he said, "why are you doing this? Why are you still with us? You didn't know Ashi. You met her—what? Three times? The only reason you even came to Tariic's notice is because you created the false Rod of Kings for us."

Tenquis, still bent over, hands under the soldier, twisted his neck to look up at Geth. "And because you came to me for help when your plan fell apart around you."

Heat burned in Geth's cheeks. "And that. I'm sorry."

"Remember what Chetiin said about regret being the blade that wounds? Tieflings have a saying too: choices are a sword sharpened on both ends. I chose to help you. Apology accepted, but you're not the one to blame."

He heaved the soldier's torso up off the ground, holding it

away to avoid smearing himself with blood. Geth started walking backward, leading the way toward the brush-screened gully that would serve as an open grave. "You're not a part of this."

Tenquis showed needle-sharp teeth. "Tariic made me a part of it. Because of him, everything I had, all of my research, is gone except for what I managed to stuff in my pockets." His breath wheezed from exertion as he spoke, but he managed to tap his chin against one shoulder, indicating the long, labyrinth-patterned vest that he wore. The garment was magical, its pockets unnaturally capacious. Geth had seen Tenquis slide a long iron pry bar into one pocket creating only a slight bulge in the fabric. "Because of him, my—"

His face hardened, and his mouth closed tight, cutting off the words, but Geth knew what he'd been about to say. In addition to sharp teeth, eyes of gold or black or red, and heavy horns, tieflings had another feature that betrayed the bargain that their sorcerous ancestors had struck with infernal powers in ages past—a thick, sinuous tail. Because of Tariic, Tenquis's tail was only a scarred stump, a reminder of what Haruuc's nephew had been willing to do to gain the Rod of Kings.

They pushed past bushes and reached the edge of the gully. Neither of them spoke as they swung the patrol leader's body into the shadows. Geth listened to the snap and crash of branches below. It was like the crackling of fuel in the fire of his anger. Grim determination settled over him as they turned back to the scene of the ambush.

"Maybe we shouldn't be going to Volaar Draal," he said. "Maybe it's time to stop running. If Tariic thinks we're headed for Breland, we can go anywhere we want. We can go back to Rhukaan Draal. He won't be expecting an attack." Geth's gut tightened. "We can end this."

Tenquis frowned. "How? Without Ashi, you're the only one who can stand up to the power of the rod."

"All the more reason to go back," said Geth. "I'm going to carve the price of her death out of Tariic's heart."

THE TYRANNY OF GHOSTS

"Geth." Tenquis grabbed his arm and stopped him. The tiefling faced him eye to eye. "I want to see Tariic pay for what he's done, but charging back to Rhukaan Draal isn't the way. Volaar Draal can provide us with more than just sanctuary. Haruuc learned about the Rod of Kings from the stories preserved by the Kech Volaar. We may be able to find a way to stop Tariic in the vaults of Volaar Draal."

He dropped his voice and added, "We need to rest and plan first, or we'll fail. Tariic will win, and who will avenge Ashi then? There's an old Dhakaani proverb that goes *'Khaartuuv kurar'dar, mi shi morii'dar.'* "

Geth's hand rested on Wrath's hilt, and the magic of the sword translated the Goblin words. He spoke them back to Tenquis. "To avenge the dead, remain among the living."

Tenquis nodded. Geth clenched his jaw. "We're going back, though," he said. "When we have a solution, we're going back."

Tenquis smiled at him, the tips of his teeth showing past his lips. "I wouldn't be here if we weren't."

CHAPTER TWO

7 Aryth

Ashi d'Deneith stood on the dais of the throne room of Khaar Mbar'ost, stared out over the mob of Darguul warlords, and remembered another moment, just a week shy of four months earlier, when she had stood on a similar dais. The occasion had been the arrival of Tariic, ambassador of Darguun and nephew of Lhesh Haruuc Shaarat'kor, in Sentinel Tower, home fortress of House Deneith. Ashi had been waiting to perform for Tariic, her mentor Vounn d'Deneith's firm hand restraining her eagerness.

But Vounn was dead. Ashi stood at the left hand of Lhesh Tariic Kurar'taarn in his fortress, restrained by the threat of a sharp knife.

And yet she was still performing.

Drums beat slowly as two guards marched down the central aisle of the throne room. They dragged a gruesome burden behind them—the corpse of a bugbear with every scrap of skin flayed away, from foot to face. The thing had been laid on a mat of coarse burlap to keep it from leaving a trail of blood across the floor, but even so, red smears—and the turning heads of Darguul warlords—marked its progress through the room.

The guards brought the corpse to the foot of the dais and stepped aside so that Tariic could look down on it. He did, then looked to the crowd. "This was Makka," he said, "who shamed me by murdering a guest and an ally and by nearly doing the same to another." He spoke formal Goblin but Ashi understood

it easily—Ekhaas had taught her the language. Tariic looked to his right. "Pradoor, is this just?"

The elderly goblin priestess whose prayers had dragged Ashi back from sharing Vounn's fate glanced with disdain at the tortured corpse of her former servant. Or rather seemed to stare with milk-blind eyes that saw more than they had any right to. "It is just, lhesh," she answered.

Tariic turned and looked at Ashi. "Ashi d'Deneith, does this cleanse the honor of Darguun in the eyes of House Deneith?"

Ashi stood straight and spoke, also in Goblin, the words that were required of her. "It does, lhesh."

"Then let this thing be taken from our presence," Tariic said, his words rising. "Take it through the streets, and throw it in the dust beyond the city. Let all Darguuls know Makka's fate and let them learn from it. For I am Lhesh Tariic Kurar'taarn, and their honor belongs to me!"

Cheers and applause—predominantly goblin applause, an open hand slapped against the chest—filled the throne room. The guards gripped the burlap cradling Makka's corpse and dragged it back up the aisle. The nearest warlords leaned out and spat on the corpse as it passed. Cheers and applause settled into the buzz of any crowd.

Ashi's hands clenched into fists. Tariic looked up at her from the throne. "Well done, Ashi," he said in the human tongue. "Be patient."

For anyone else in the great hall, the words would have been a command. Tariic held the Rod of Kings, braced casually against his knee, in his right hand. Ashi felt the power of the artifact try to take hold of her—and felt it skitter aside like a blade against armor as it encountered the power of the dragonmark that patterned her body. Maintaining the power of the mark that shielded her from the rod's influence had become her new discipline. On each of the four days since Vounn's death—and, very nearly, her own—she'd risen with the sun, reached into herself, and drawn up the clarity of the mark's protection.

THE TYRANNY OF GHOSTS

She gave Tariic a thin smile. "You can convince everyone in this room that what happened was Makka's fault alone, Tariic," she said quietly, "but Breven d'Deneith is beyond your reach."

Tariic's ears just twitched, and he looked back out to the waiting crowd. He lifted a hand, and half the warlords, thinking he was pointing to them, started calling his name. He indicated Ashi, and there was a smattering of renewed applause. In the gallery above the hall, the envoys of the dragonmarked houses and the ambassadors of the nations beyond Darguun looked down on her with nothing but pity. Pradoor's voice rose in an ear-pinching cackle unmoved by Makka's harsh death.

"They would welcome the Fury's kiss if you suggested it, lhesh!"

Ashi's stomach twisted, but she kept her face still. By rights those in the throne room should have glared at her with hatred or at the very least mistrust, not offered her applause. Only six days ago, she'd been part of an attempt to kill a king. Every one of them had witnessed it. In any other nation, she would already have been executed as an assassin. The Rod of Kings had changed that.

The rod—and Vounn's murder and her own near death at Makka's hands. She could still feel the sword, her own grandfather's honor blade, in her chest and the weight of Vounn's body against hers. She suppressed a shudder.

Tariic had needed an explanation for what had taken place. Why had former friends attempted to so publicly assassinate him? Why had a member of his entourage attacked and killed two highly placed members of House Deneith? The answer to one question would have revealed the powers of the Rod of Kings to the world; the answer to the other would have destabilized any confidence other nations or the dragonmarked houses might have had in his reign. And yet, Ashi had to admit, Tariic had brilliantly turned both events to his benefit.

The rod's powers of command could be subtle, it seemed, as well as overwhelming. Tariic had spoken, the Rod of Kings

in his hand, and earlier reports rushed out of Darguun by means magical and mundane were recanted. In the minds of the warlords, envoys, and ambassadors, Geth and the others had become traitors intent on upsetting the fragile reign of the new lhesh and destroying Darguun—never mind that they'd all been hailed only weeks earlier as the saviors of the nation. Makka had become one of the traitors, trying to destroy the vital relationship between Darguun and House Deneith. Ashi—her role in the attempt virtually erased—was a lucky survivor and Vounn an unfortunate martyr.

Makka's execution in the dungeons of Khaar Mbar'ost had been as much about reinforcing Tariic's lie as it had been about honor or justice. She should have felt satisfaction at the bugbear's death, but all she felt was a sharp fear. Every morning when she renewed her own protection against the Rod of Kings, she offered a silent prayer to unnamed powers that Geth, Ekhaas, Chetiin, and Tenquis were far from Tariic's reach.

Soon she would be too. Tariic might hold her as a "protected guest," but even he wouldn't dare keep her in captivity if the patriarch of House Deneith, Darguun's greatest ally among the nations and powers of Khorvaire, demanded her return. No matter what false reports emerged from Darguun, Ashi knew that Breven d'Deneith would be suspicious. Her house would look after its own, and she would be free to take the truth out of Darguun. The powers of Khorvaire would learn of Tariic's ambitions and the danger he posed to them all.

She lifted her head, raising her chin defiantly. It only earned her more applause from the warlords and even a bit from the ambassadors. Ashi couldn't think of a time she'd ever felt more isolated.

Yet there were a few who understood the situation, even if they didn't dare speak of it. Senen Dhakaan looked down from the gallery, though never directly at Ashi. The ambassador of the Kech Volaar had risked much to deliver a message of hope—Ashi had woken one night to whispered song, the magical

THE TYRANNY OF GHOSTS

communication of the *duur'kala*, and the news that Ekhaas and the others were on their way to Volaar Draal. Out in the crowd of warlords, Dagii of Mur Talaan stood in a place of honor. The gray-eyed and gray-haired—in spite of his young age—warlord hadn't tried to speak to her, and Ashi knew he couldn't without sacrificing his own freedom. He understood the effect of the rod and probably hated every action that its influence forced on him, but there was little he could do. Even if he hadn't been directly involved in the attempt on Tariic's life, Tariic knew that he'd been involved in the plot to substitute a false rod for the true Rod of Kings. But Dagii was also a hero, victorious in battle against the elves of Valenar. The warlords and people of Darguun loved him. Even with the power of the rod at his command, Tariic would have been hard-pressed to find a good excuse to execute a popular hero. Dagii lived—so long as his loyalty never wavered. Friends who stood close at hand, but they might as well have been in distant Sharn.

She thought of the changeling she knew both as Aruget, a hobgoblin guard, and Benti Moran, a half-elf, but who was actually an agent of Breland. He'd vanished after the assassination had failed, saving his own shifting skin. Maybe he'd made his way back to Breland. Maybe news of the danger brewing in Darguun was already abroad in the world.

Then why did the ambassador of Breland laugh and chat as if there were nothing wrong?

"Do you see something that interests you, Ashi?" asked a voice from her left.

She was staring, she realized. She forced her gaze away from the gallery and down to the speaker, a gnome with bright eyes and a shock of pale hair. Midian Mit Davandi had once been a friend, a scholar of the great Library of Korranberg joining them on their quest for the Rod of Kings, but then his true nature had shown itself. An agent for the gnome nation of Zilargo, neighbor of Darguun across the Seawall Mountains, he was the true assassin of Haruuc, a crime widely laid at the feet of

Chetiin. Midian's many treacheries were also the reason that their attempts to keep the Rod of Kings from falling into Tariic's hands had failed. He'd paid the price, though. When Ashi had returned to consciousness after Pradoor's prayers had healed her, she'd found Midian was also Tariic's captive.

Unlike her, however, the gnome had no protection against the Rod of Kings. Later that night, Tariic had made her watch as he demonstrated his mastery over the rod's power. He'd broken Midian with words. The agent of Zilargo had become a loyal servant of Darguun, and Tariic knew everything that Midian knew.

Officially, Midian was Tariic's royal historian. Unofficially, he was Tariic's assassin—and the sharp blade at Ashi's back. Her dragonmark could block the rod's influence, but it wouldn't stop a poisoned dagger.

"Vounn should be up there," she said, nodding to the gallery.

"If Vounn were up there, you wouldn't be down here," Midian replied without a trace of irony. Ashi wasn't sure he even remembered his former allegiance to Zilargo. For a moment, she considered reaching out and touching him. With an effort of will, she could channel the power of her dragonmark perhaps twice in a day, but no more. Surely it would break the hold of the rod over Midian, at least temporarily.

And if it did, what then? She was surrounded by enemies. Even reaching for Midian could be a risk. The friendly scholar was only a mask. Midian was like a cornered rat. Just putting out her hand could provoke him, and her act of protection would result in a slash from Midian's poisoned dagger. Ashi kept her hands to herself.

"Have you spoken to Esmyssa lately?" she asked instead. The ambassador of Zilargo stood near the front of the gallery.

A smile flickered across Midian's face. "I tell her what she needs to know."

Tariic's assassin and his mouthpiece to Zilargo. Ashi glanced at the lhesh and found him watching her with glinting, clever eyes. She looked away again just as Razu, the old hobgoblin

THE TYRANNY OF GHOSTS

mistress of ceremonies who stood by the throne room door, rapped her staff on the floor. The crowd fell silent.

A human man appeared in the wide doorway and walked with a measured pace down the throne room's central aisle. Ashi knew him: Viceroy Redek d'Deneith, a thin and leathery man whose long service to House Deneith in Darguun had been supplanted by Vounn's arrival as special envoy to the court of Haruuc. Normally his place was at the Gathering Stone, the Deneith compound and training center two days' journey outside of Rhukaan Draal. With Vounn's death, however, he'd once again become the most senior member of the house in Darguun. He stopped before the dais and bent his head to the lhesh.

"Who comes to the court of Lhesh Tariic Kurar'taarn?" asked Tariic, returning to Goblin as he raised his voice.

"Redek of Deneith, son of Kain, comes. He brings a message for Lhesh Tariic from Baron Breven d'Deneith."

Tariic sat back in his throne. "Speak," he said.

Ashi felt a prickle across the back of her neck. Tariic was calm. Too calm for someone on the verge of losing his prized prisoner. Her eyes darted back to Redek as he produced a folded piece of heavy paper. Holding it high so that all could see, he broke the seal. Pieces of blue wax, the color favored by Breven, scattered across the floor and Redek read in Goblin:

"To Lhesh Tariic Kurar'taarn—greetings.

"Since the time of Cail d'Deneith, House Deneith and the dar of the territory that is now Darguun have enjoyed the strongest of relationships. House Deneith values the support of the lhesh of Darguun and hopes that the lhesh values our support as well.

"In the wake of the tragic death of our envoy, Vounn d'Deneith, we thank you for your condolences and what we trust will be the swift delivery of justice to the one responsible. We thank you also for the care that you have shown members of our house remaining in Rhukaan Draal. Violence is a regrettable danger in our world. Vounn d'Deneith served her house with honor and in her last days worked to bring Deneith and Darguun closer.

"We do not wish to see her legacy wither. It is our wish that Vounn's aide, Ashi d'Deneith, remain with your court—"

Ashi stiffened and drew a sharp breath. In the attentive silence of the throne room, the sound was loud. Redek paused to look at her, but Tariic gestured casually with the Rod of Kings. "Continue," he said.

Redek's eyes went immediately back to his letter.

"It is our wish that Vounn's aide, Ashi d'Deneith, remain with your court as a sign of the faith we hold in the relationship between our house and your nation. Redek d'Deneith will be responsible for the operations of House Deneith in Darguun, but it will fall to Ashi to see that the bond between Darguun and Deneith grows ever more cordial and profitable.

"May your reign be long and glorious—Breven, patriarch of Deneith."

Redek folded the letter and bowed low to Tariic, but Ashi barely registered the gesture. One thought filled her mind. Tariic had known what Breven's letter would say. No wonder he was calm. No wonder he'd allowed Redek to read it openly. Somehow he'd been in communication with House Deneith.

Then a second revelation broke over her like a blow to the head: She wasn't leaving Darguun. Breven wouldn't be bringing her home. Her belly clenched. She felt sick.

While she stood, stunned, Tariic rose. He wore a smile, his sharp teeth bright against deep red-brown skin. "We acknowledge Breven d'Deneith for the honor and respect that he shows Darguun. I mourn the death of Vounn but embrace Ashi as Deneith's new envoy." He turned to her. "How do you greet this news, daughter of Deneith?"

Deep inside Ashi, the part of her that had once been a savage hunter of the Bonetree, the most feared clan of the Shadow Marches, rose up. She wanted to strike Tariic down. Tear open his throat with her bare fingers. Snatch the Rod of Kings from his grasp and beat his face in with it.

But she didn't. Another part of her, the part that had been

THE TYRANNY OF GHOSTS

Vounn's reluctant student in the ways of civilization, pushed her anger aside. Attacking Tariic would solve nothing—she'd be dead before he was. Ashi bent her head.

"It is an honor," she said, her voice tight, "that I did not expect."

Tariic's smile grew just a little wider, and he spoke through his teeth at a pitch only she could hear. "Of course you didn't." He looked out over the gathered warlords and up at the watching ambassadors and raised his arms. "Hail to Deneith and Darguun!"

Shouts and applause filled the throne room. Ashi watched Redek bow again, face shining in innocent triumph as if he had just achieved the pinnacle of his career.

ⓞ ⓞ ⓞ ⓞ ⓞ ⓞ ⓞ

There was another message, one just for her.

I know what happened. I do not want to know why it did.

By your actions you have cost House Deneith the life of a valuable servant in Vounn d'Deneith and nearly severed the connections that she worked to strengthen. The bonds between Deneith and Darguun are not just pretty words to be spoken at ceremonies. The mercenaries hired to Deneith by the lhesh of Darguun are worth more than the life of any member of this house—including that of a bearer of the Siberys Mark of Sentinel.

You are fortunate that Lhesh Tariic understands the demands of politics and economy and sees that Darguun benefits more from fighting with Deneith than fighting against us. He is more understanding to accept your continued presence in his court than I would be.

Remain in Rhukaan Draal. Carry out Vounn's mission to Darguun and you may be redeemed. If you are found beyond the borders of Darguun before that day, however, you are excoriated.

—Breven

Ashi ground her teeth together so hard they hurt. To be declared an excoriate was to be exiled from a dragonmarked house, the worst punishment the members of the great houses could inflict on one of their own. In the distant past, it had been both a symbolic and a literal severing of connections; the offender's name would be stricken from the rolls of the house and the dragonmark that swirled over her skin cut away. Ashi had heard rumors that a secret gallery in the heart of Sentinel Tower held grisly relics of those nameless excoriates who had been expelled from Deneith in ancient times. Excoriates were no longer flayed alive, but for many dragonmarked, to be cut off from their house, the source of much of their identity, was still a terrible punishment.

Ashi had lost her identity before, when she abandoned the Bonetree Clan for House Deneith. The threat of taking away her connection—already tenuous—to Deneith held little power over her. What hurt more was Breven's accusation. *By your actions, you have cost House Deneith the life of a valuable servant in Vounn d'Deneith.*

He might as well have written, *You killed Vounn.*

Ashi raised her head to glare at Tariic. "What did you tell him?"

Seated in the best chair in the chambers she had, until only a few days before, shared with Vounn, Tariic gave a thin smile. "The truth, of course. That when Geth and Chetiin moved to seize the Rod of Kings, you were with them. That in a misguided attempt to protect you, Vounn put herself in the path of Makka's blade as he tried to defend me—"

"That's not the truth!" Ashi snarled. The heavy paper crumpled in her fist, and she drew back her arm to hurl it at Tariic.

A massive hairy bugbear hand caught her wrist and squeezed. Ashi hissed in pain. The paper ball fell. The bugbear—one of three who surrounded her, loyal servants who had been deafened to preserve secrets spoken in their presence—glanced at Tariic,

THE TYRANNY OF GHOSTS

who gestured casually. The bugbear's grip eased. Ashi slipped her hand free. Her wrist throbbed, but she refused to give Tariic the satisfaction of seeing her rub it.

He ignored her discomfort anyway. "It's all the truth that Breven wants to hear. He knows that by blaming poor, faithful Makka, we preserve the fiction that Deneith is blameless. Kings make their own truth, Ashi."

"Breven isn't a king."

"He holds your life and obedience in his hands. He has the power to command armies. He brokers deals with nations and places envoys in the courts of monarchs." Tariic's ears twitched. "Breven could seize power with half-a-dozen commands. I guarantee you that he's thought of it. He probably thinks about it every day. Breven and I are more alike than you think."

The crumpled letter had rolled close to his boot. He stretched out and kicked it back at Ashi. "You're to stay at my court under pain of excoriation, yes?"

Ashi clenched her teeth again. "How did you talk to Breven?" she asked through them.

"The gnomes of House Sivis—unlike the gnomes of Zilargo—take their neutrality very seriously. They were happy to relay my messages to Sentinel Tower for their customary fee. As you've seen, the dragonmarked houses generally listen when money talks." His ears twitched a second time. "Although, it was your friend Pater d'Orien who opened the channels to Breven. Did you know that when he used his mark to teleport away from Khaar Mbar'ost after Vounn's death, he went to Deneith instead of his own house?"

Anger flared again in Ashi as she realized there was one friendly face she hadn't seen in the gallery of the throne room. She would have lunged for Tariic, but the bugbears reacted swiftly. All three of them grabbed her, leaving her struggling against thick, muscular arms. Tariic just sat back. "Calm down, Ashi. You don't have to worry about Pater. I . . . talked to him when he returned to Rhukaan Draal, that's all." He tapped the

Rod of Kings against his knee for emphasis. "I know he had nothing to do with your plot."

"Then where is he?" Ashi asked through the cage of muscle.

"Safe in the Orien compound, sticking close to his wagons and horses. Do you think I'm so weak that I need every foreign dignitary attending my every word? Besides, he's no more a challenge to me now than Midian. Or you."

"Or Geth?"

That wiped the smug look from Tariic's face. "He and the others will be found. Chetiin. Ekhaas. Even the Brelish changeling. I know where they're headed. It's only a matter of time. Every route into Breland is being watched, from the Marguul Pass to the humblest mountain path."

Ashi did her best to keep her expression neutral, hiding her elation. Tariic thought Geth and the others were heading to Breland? Then they would be safe in their haven at Volaar Draal. And if Aruget was with them, so much the better!

Tariic must have mistaken her stony silence for an attempt to hide another emotion. His lips curled in renewed smugness. "Afraid for them, Ashi? Shouldn't you be afraid for yourself?"

The bugbears had dragged her upright again. Ashi raised her head and glared down at Tariic. "I don't think so. If I'm to be House Deneith's new envoy to your court, you can't very well keep me prisoner. You may have made a deal with Breven, Tariic, but you've traded away some of your hold on me."

This time, though, the lhesh's expression didn't waver. Ashi felt unease reach into the pit of her stomach. "If you do anything to me—"

"I wouldn't think of it, daughter of Deneith," said Tariic. His words sounded like a serpent's hiss. He raised his voice slightly. "Midian!"

The outer door of the chamber opened. Ashi twisted her head around enough to see the gnome enter. Before the door closed, she saw hobgoblin guards outside—Tariic's honor guard, plus a trio of guards she didn't recognize. The unfamiliar guards wore

ornate, polished armor as if ready for some ceremonial parade. Two of them looked back at her curiously. Both had the forehead scars of the Rhukaan Taash, Tariic's clan.

They vanished as Midian closed the door. He made an elaborate, mocking bow. "Lady Ashi."

She offered him no reply, but he didn't wait for one. He glided up to Tariic and went down on one knee as he offered a square wooden box to the lhesh. "House Cannith sends its highest regards."

Ashi's unease grew. House Cannith bore the Mark of Making. Their artificers were capable of creating all manner of wonders—and dangers. The box was featureless, offering no clue of what it contained. Tariic flipped it open.

Nestled against black velvet inside was a pair of polished silver wrist cuffs.

In the moment that she stared, Tariic gestured. One of the bugbears holding her wrenched her right arm out straight. She gasped in surprise and started to pull back, but Tariic was quicker. Snatching up one of the cuffs, he closed it around her wrist just above the bugbear's meaty hand. The delicate clasp closed with a deep *clack* that was louder than it should have been.

"Now the other one," said Tariic, gesturing again. Midian, grinning like an idiot offered him the box once more.

The bugbears didn't have the advantage of surprise a second time. Ashi screamed fury and fought them, but together they were far stronger than she. Her shoulder throbbed as a bugbear twisted her arm away from her body, then came a second deep *clack* and the faint pressure of the matching cuff on her wrist.

Then the bugbears let her go.

The release came so suddenly that Ashi stumbled before catching herself and dropping into a crouch, ready for whatever might come next. But the bugbears were already backing off— one favoring a shin that she'd stomped on, another cradling an injured hand and glaring at her—while Midian tucked away the empty case and Tariic returned to his chair.

For a moment, the hobgoblin's back was to her. Rage surged inside her. She leaped at him.

Cold so intense it burned seized her, turning her leap into a sprawl that ended at Tariic's feet. The snarl on her lips became a hiss of agony, then a choke as her arms went numb. Ashi forced herself onto her knees and stared at the wrist cuffs. Frost coated the bright metal. Around the cuffs, her skin had already started to turn white as it froze. The blue-green lines of her dragonmark stood out in colorful contrast.

"The emperors of Dhakaan presented similar creations to those they wanted to keep on a short leash," said Tariic calmly. Ashi wrenched her eyes away from the cuffs to glare at him. "They can't be broken or removed except by me," he continued. "Left long enough, the cold will kill you, but frostbite will ruin your fingers and then your hands before that."

He murmured a word under his breath, too low for Ashi to hear, and the cruel cold vanished. Her pride couldn't stand up to the release and the feeling of warmth—she slumped back on her heels, chest heaving in relief. Tariic sat forward.

"Breven may believe that the threat of excoriation is enough to keep you in Rhukaan Draal, but I don't. Travel north of the Ghaal River or south of the city's edge, and the cuffs will be activated. Try to attack me, and they will be activated. I promise you I won't turn them off a second time. Do you understand?"

Ashi drew a deep breath and stood up. "Won't it look suspicious if the envoy of House Deneith is found frozen to death, Lhesh Tariic?" she asked, holding her head high.

"Accidents happen, Lady Ashi. Don't worry, you'll have an escort to keep you safe." Tariic raised his voice again. "Warriors, enter!"

The door opened for a second time, and the Rhukaan Taash warriors Ashi had glimpsed entered the chamber. They fell into a perfect line behind her, heads up, hands on the hilts of their swords. All three hobgoblins were young and in prime fighting

THE TYRANNY OF GHOSTS

condition, their armor bright, their eyes alert, and their ears tall and straight. Ashi had no doubt that they were the most skilled and loyal in Tariic's clan.

"Trusted warriors to ensure that you are able to go about your duties as envoy untroubled," said Tariic. He gave her a hard look. "And only your duties. One of them will accompany you at all times."

The cuffs prevented her from leaving Rhukaan Draal, but the presence of the guards would keep her from causing trouble within the city. She would be a prisoner in Khorvaire's largest prison, a puppet moved by Tariic's strings. Ashi clenched her teeth and for a moment the temptation to attack Tariic again made her pulse throb in her ears. If she was fast enough . . .

But the part of her that Vounn had trained from a barbarian of the Shadow Marches into a lady of House Deneith held her back. Attacking Tariic would kill her. Patience would keep her alive.

Ashi bent her head with stiff dignity. "Your kindness is appreciated, lhesh."

Tariic hadn't been expecting that. His ears went back and his thin lips pulled away from sharp teeth as he considered her. At his side, Midian, too, looked suspicious. "Tariic, she's up to—" he started to say.

The hobgoblin silenced him with a gesture of the Rod of Kings. "She does what is commanded of her. I would do the same." His ears flicked. "And I would search for my opportunity later."

He lifted the rod and pointed it at the three guards. "Warriors of Rhukaan Taash," he said in Goblin, "you will report any unusual or suspicious activities by the envoy of House Deneith to me. No bribes or tricks will prevent you."

Ashi saw a flickering in the eyes of the guards as the power of the rod forced the command upon them. The hobgoblins beat their fists against their chests in salute and said in unison, "*Mazo, lhesh!*"

DON BASSINGTHWAITE

Tariic nodded in satisfaction and rose from his chair, stepping close to Ashi. "You can't stop me," he murmured.

"Are you certain?"

"Yes," he said with a smile, then moved past her. "Oraan, you have the honor of first duty. Give Lady Ashi the present you carry."

"*Mazo*," the young warrior said again. He took a step forward and reached behind his back to produce a sword sheathed in a plain scabbard. He offered it to Ashi.

It was the honor blade of her grandfather, the sword that had been the first clue—even before the manifestation of her dragonmark—that she carried the blood of House Deneith. It was the sword she had lost to Makka. The sword that had killed Vounn and almost killed her. Ashi stared at the weapon but did not reach for it.

"You see how certain I am," said Tariic. He turned away and walked out the door, gesturing for the bugbears and the two other hobgoblin warriors to follow. Midian was the last one to leave, sliding past Ashi like a weasel.

"The Rod of Kings teaches power," he said. "Tariic will be an emperor. It would be better for you if you recognized that."

She didn't move. The gnome left, closing the door behind him. Oraan still stood with her sword held out to her, a final taunt from Tariic. Slowly the despair that Ashi had held off began to creep back into her, eating away at her anger and defiance until she was almost ready to admit that Tariic *had* won.

The opening of the door broke the moment. Oraan twisted around. Ashi looked up. Framed in the doorway was a hunched old bugbear woman with an armload of firewood. She froze under the combined gaze of Ashi and the warrior, then hefted her burden and nodded silently toward the fireplace. Oraan grunted. "Be quick."

The old servant bobbed her head and entered, bumping the door closed with a hip as she came through. Oraan returned his gaze to Ashi. "Take Lhesh Tariic's gift, Lady Ashi. It is an honor that he—"

34

THE TYRANNY OF GHOSTS

Wood clattered as the servant dropped her burden. Oraan turned again, ears going back, mouth opening in anger.

The slim dagger that the old bugbear had concealed among the sticks of wood punched through his throat and up under his jaw, pinning his mouth closed. His eyes went wide. "Catch him!" ordered the servant in a tone that was harsh but quiet. She shoved hard on the dagger and twisted. Oraan went limp.

Ashi reacted without thought. She stepped sharply around the dead warrior and grabbed his corpse under the arms. The old bugbear kept her dagger pressed tight into the wound, stemming the worst of the blood, as her other hand grabbed the honor blade before it could fall to the floor. Her voice rose in an uncanny imitation of Oraan's—"Clumsy fool!"—then dropped back into the broken cackle of age—"Forgive me, *chib*!"

Anyone outside the door would have thought two people were speaking. The bugbear looked at Ashi with sharp black eyes, then let her take the full weight of Oraan as she stood straight and her features began to flow like wax. Aged female bugbear servant became a vital, young male hobgoblin warrior. Oraan, alive and well, faced her.

Except it wasn't Oraan, of course. Ashi sucked in her breath. "Aruget?"

The changeling flicked hobgoblin ears. "You're not alone, Ashi."

CHAPTER THREE

9 Aryth

On the fourth day after their skirmish with Tariic's soldiers, Ekhaas began recognizing landmarks. Not in the way that she knew landmarks across a vast swathe of the continent of Khorvaire—from the ramshackle streets of Rhukaan Draal to the towers of Sharn to the dangerous wilds of southern Droaam—but in a much more familiar way. There in the distance was the white mountain Gim Juura. Closer, the weathered remains of a slim spire stood against the sky, the ruins of Bran'aa, where ancient seers had watched the stars in the Age of Dhakaan. Closer still, the steep depths of the valley they skirted, a cursed place where the ancestors of her clan had once trapped and slaughtered raiding rivals during the Desperate Times that had come after the fall of the great empire.

A sense of ease and belonging rose inside her. She sat up a little straighter in her saddle. "We're in Kech Volaar territory."

Geth roused himself from a weary doze, opening one eye to look around. "How much longer until we reach Volaar Draal?"

"Just after noon."

"Are there patrols?" asked Tenquis.

A hawk burst up from the trees on the hillside above them and flew southwest. Ekhaas bent her lips in a smile and flicked her ears. "Yes. We'll be expected."

The territory claimed by the Kech Volaar was not large. With every valley slope they crossed and every mountain flank

they rode around, Ekhaas's sense of familiarity increased. Kech Volaar was one of the smallest of the clans that held true to the traditions and glories of Dhakaan. Other Dhakaani clans, like the militaristic Kech Shaarat might try to defend larger territories, but the strength and wealth of her clan was in the ancient lore preserved in its vaults and in the stories of its *duur'kala*. *Kech Volaar*, meant "Word Bearers," and Ekhaas had never imagined a life that did not center around the venerated heritage of Dhakaan.

Never, a small part of her said, until now.

It was difficult to believe that only a week ago she'd been watching Dagii of Mur Talaan command an army against Valenar raiders in defense of Darguun. The gray-eyed young warlord's cunning tactics, combined with Chetiin's timely rallying of the wolf-riding cousins of his clan and her own songs of inspiration, had turned what might have been a massacre of *dar* into a rout of the elves. It had been a triumph for Darguun.

And flush with triumph and the excitement of battle, Ekhaas and Dagii had faced each other and expressed the love and respect that had grown between them, exchanging endearments of *taarka'nu*—wolf woman—and *ruuska'te*—tiger man.

He'd replaced some of her love for her clan. Every familiar place she saw reminded her that he wasn't there with her. He had a sense of *muut* and *atcha*, the twin imperatives of duty and honor that held *dar* society together, that would have impressed even an elder of the Dhakaani clans.

It had impressed her. Her ears drooped a little at the thought of him.

The last time she had seen Dagii, the light of intelligence and honor in his eyes had been dimmed by the fanaticism inspired by the Rod of Kings. That betrayal hadn't been his fault—only the influence of Aram, the Sword of Heroes, and the shield of Ashi's powerful dragonmark could have offered protection from the rod's power—but it still struck her like a knife in the belly.

THE TYRANNY OF GHOSTS

"Dagii will be fine," said Chetiin from beside her. Ekhaas's ears rose again as she gave the old goblin a sharp stare. Chetiin gave her back a thin smile, his head with its cobweb-fine hair bobbing slightly in time with Marrow's loping gait.

"It's not a difficult guess," he said. "Among the clans of the Silent Folk, death has its own language. You have the look of mourning someone who is absent rather than someone who is dead. Dagii is the only one I know who fits that description. But don't worry about him. Tariic has more to gain by keeping him close than by imprisoning or killing him. After his triumph over the Gan'duur rebels and victory in the Battle of Zarrthec, Dagii is a hero to the people."

"Legends are full of lords and kings who set aside inconvenient heroes."

Chetiin bent his neck in acknowledgment. "I will not argue legend with a *duur'kala*. But don't give up on Dagii. The absent return more readily than the dead."

⊚ ⊚ ⊚ ⊚ ⊚ ⊚ ⊚

As the sun reached its zenith, they emerged onto a stone-paved road winding up into the mountains. The road showed its age in worn stones and moss, but Ekhaas knew that it was even older than it seemed. Even the oldest stone was a replacement for a stone that had been there before, the newest a replacement for a replacement for a replacement. When Volaar Draal had first been established, there had been no road. The early Kech Volaar had hidden themselves away alongside the lore that they guarded, but as the clan had grown stronger, hiding had given way to display of their heritage.

They rounded the final bend in the road, and Volaar Draal was revealed.

Geth's wide animal eyes opened even wider. Tenquis reined in his horse so sharply, it almost reared up. Even Chetiin's eyebrows rose and he signaled Marrow to pause for a moment.

Ekhaas's chest felt tight as pride rose up in her. "Volaar Draal," she said. "In the human tongue, the 'City of the Word'. Called *Niianu Raat*, Mother of Stories, among its children and *Skai Duur*, the Great Dirge, among those who have tried to seize it."

Beyond its final bend, the road entered a steep-sided valley cradled in the arms of the mountains. Ancient stories told how, when the Kech Volaar had first come, the valley had risen to a sheer wall of naked rock, and a cleft in the wall had been the only opening into the refuge of the Word Bearers. But that cleft had become a great gate and the wall of rock transformed, carved away as if Volaar Draal had waited within the mountain since the birth of the world for the hands that would reveal it.

Four mighty spires stood above the valley like the blades of massive swords, edges turned to meet whoever or whatever came against them. The bulk of the city lay within the mountain, the precious vaults deep below it, but this was the face that Volaar Draal presented to the world. From slits within the walls, archers could command the area before the spires. Hidden behind sliding panels of stone, powerful ballistae and catapults could sweep the entire valley. Master strategists had a hand in creating the stronghold of the clan, but the lore of Dhakaan had guided the masons who brought it forth from the rock. As harsh and functional as the spires were, there was a cruel majesty in their proportions. Volaar Draal was like a warrior defending himself in battle with a heavy blade—enemies who attacked the City of the Word were promised death beneath its walls.

"Horns of Ohr Kaluun," said Tenquis. "It's incredible." He glanced at Ekhaas. "*Daashor* constructed this."

Ekhaas saw a thin smile flicker across Geth's face. "You must be feeling better," the shifter said. "You're talking about *daashor* again."

"You think I would come to Volaar Draal and not ask about them?" Tenquis asked. He looked back to Ekhaas. "You promised me tales of the *daashor* in payment for crafting the false Rod of Kings. While we're looking for a way to stop Tariic and the

rod, I'd be happy to take whatever lore about the *daashor* that's stored in the vaults."

Ekhaas's ears flicked. The *daashor* had been the artificers of the Empire of Dhakaan—and more. Wizard-smiths of astounding ability, they had forged wonders that were the stuff of legend even before Dhakaan's fall. The Sword of Heroes and the Rod of Kings were the creations of just one *daashor*, the legendary Taruuzh. In many ways, the *daashor* were the counterparts of the *duur'kala*. The magical music of the dirge-singers manifested almost entirely in women of the goblin races; the craft of the wizard-smiths in men. Ultimately, music had proved more lasting than craft—the traditions of the *duur'kala* had survived the Desperate Times, while the lore of the *daashor* had faded away, scattered in crumbling tomes and ancient carvings that the dirge-singers could not access. Some knowledge persisted, handed down among masons and smiths, but such magic was less than the shadow of what the *daashor* had practiced.

Until he had agreed to help them, Tenquis's life had been devoted to the rediscovery of the lost lore. Who knew? Perhaps a modern artificer, even one who was not a *dar*, could find more meaning in the ancient writings than a *duur'kala* could. But . . . "The vaults are vast, Tenquis. The Kech Volaar have been collecting the lore and artifacts of Dhakaan for thousands of years. The archivists who tend the vaults maintain a list—the Register—of everything placed in them, but even it's massive."

"Even better."

Ekhaas sighed and urged her horse back into a walk up the road toward the great gates. "Just don't do anything stupid. The vaults contain the treasures of my clan, and the Kech Volaar don't like trespassers."

Three ranks of guards stood before the gates, all dressed in armor that had not changed since the days of Dhakaan. Linked plates provided strength and mobility. Spikes at strategic points provided weapons even if a warrior should be unarmed. Flared

helmets protected vulnerable necks while still allowing openings for large and expressive ears. A Dhakaani legion on the attack would have looked like a wave of steel. As the travelers approached, the guards moved in response to some unseen signal, their ranks splitting to open the way into Volaar Draal.

One of the guards, a red insignia of rank on his helmet, stepped forward and thumped his chest in salute. "Ekhaas *duur'kala*," he said in Goblin, "you are expected. Tuura Dhakaan summons you. An escort comes for you and your . . . companions."

It was impossible to miss the dip in his ears or the way his eyes flicked over Geth and Tenquis as he said it. Ekhaas knew exactly what he was thinking: *chaat'oor*. It was the Goblin word for humans and the races descended from them, like shifters and tieflings, that had come to Khorvaire after the fall of Dhakaan. Loosely translated, it meant "outsider." More specifically, it meant "defiler." Ekhaas's own ears went back. "Treat them with respect, *lhurusk*. Their names will be sung alongside the heroes of the *dar*."

"Then you move in honored circles," said a familiar voice from the shadows of the gate. "Walking with heroes and summoned by the leader of our clan. Perhaps a humble lorekeeper isn't enough of an escort for you," A hobgoblin woman dressed in a black wool robe and a red leather girdle tooled with angular designs walked out between the parted ranks of the gate guards. "*Saa*, Ekhaas."

Ekhaas felt her face flush hot. "Kitaas," she said. She bit the name off, hating the sound of it. "You're our escort?"

Kitaas inclined her head, ears twitching. She looked at Chetiin and Geth, ignoring Tenquis. "Chetiin of the Silent Blades, and Geth, wielder of Aram, the Sword of Heroes. I am honored to greet you."

Chetiin returned her nod. So did Geth, although a little more slowly. Ekhaas saw the stirring of curiosity, then a flash of recognition in his eyes. Kitaas turned to lead them into the gate and as they rode after her, the shifter leaned close to Ekhaas and whispered in the human language. "I recognize that

THE TYRANNY OF GHOSTS

girdle. In Rhukaan Draal, you used an illusion to disguise me as a woman—you said you had to choose someone familiar." He nodded toward Kitaas's back. "She's your sister!"

"In the way that a dagger is sister to a sword," she told him.

Inside the gate, goblin stablehands came to take their mounts. One approached Marrow, but the worg snapped at him. Chetiin slid to the ground and she ran back out the gate, drawing yelps of surprise from the guards as she slipped among them.

"She will remain outside to find her own shelter and prey," Chetiin said to Ekhaas.

"As she wishes," said the archivist.

The others dismounted as well and unloaded their meager gear. Tenquis looked at Kitaas with interest. "You're one of the keepers of the vaults of Volaar Draal?" he asked.

Kitaas glanced at him with the same disdain the gate guards had. "I understood that tieflings had tails."

Tenquis's face went hard, and he self-consciously twitched the back of his long vest to cover the mutilated stump. Ekhaas bared her teeth and snapped back at her sister before he could. "Don't antagonize my friends, Kitaas."

"*Ban*," said Kitaas. She gave Tenquis a haughty look. "I am adjunct to Diiteshm the High Archivist of Kech Volaar."

"It means that she may call herself a 'humble lorekeeper,' but she isn't," Ekhaas said. She met Kitaas's glare with one of her own. "You recognized Geth and Chetiin."

"Senen Dhakaan makes regular reports. We are not isolated from events in Rhukaan Draal." Kitaas folded her hands across her girdle, but her ears stirred languidly, and the ghost of a smile crossed her lips. "Those events are what Tuura Dhakaan wishes to speak to you about."

* * * * * * *

Beyond the inner gate stretched the echoing length of the Great Passage, the final approach to the City of the Word.

Kitaas didn't slow her stride for the weary travelers. Soon she was a dozen paces ahead of them. Geth moved closer to Ekhaas. "What's between you and Kitaas?" he asked quietly.

Ekhaas kept her eyes on her sister's back. "That's not your concern."

"You don't think it might be? She's the assistant—"

"Adjunct," Ekhaas snarled.

"I don't even know what that means. Is this High Archivist she works for in charge of the vaults? Maybe we want to stay on her good side."

"It's years too late for that," she said curtly.

Geth took the hint and fell back a pace to let her walk in silence. Distant sounds flowed through the shadows—the clash of weapons and the stamp of boots as warriors trained, the haunting song of a far-off *duur'kala*, the rhythmic ringing of hammers against anvils—and again Ekhaas felt a pang that Dagii wasn't with them. She would have liked to introduce him to the sounds of Volaar Draal. And to the sight of the city, gleaming in the darkness as they emerged from the Great Passage.

But Geth, Tenquis, and Chetiin paused in awe, and at least that was something.

Close-packed ranks of homes, halls, and workshops filled the floor and crept up the walls of the vast cavern where early Kech Volaar had once sought refuge. From windows and posts, sparks of dim white-green ghostlight glimmered. Against the shadows of the cavern, the lights resembled the dense brilliance of the Ring of Siberys in the night sky. Monuments rose in silhouette, and the sounds of life filled the still air. Ekhaas felt a rush of pride in the hidden beauty and grandeur of Volaar Draal.

Kitaas didn't even slow down. While not quite so chaotic as the streets of Rhukaan Draal, the way through the Home Cavern was twisting, narrow, and filled with *dar* going about their business. Ekhaas gestured for the others to keep up and hurried after Kitaas, who said nothing to her and just kept walking. Ekhaas

THE TYRANNY OF GHOSTS

couldn't help noticing that the way opened up before her sister.

"Do they respect you or the robe of an archivist?" she asked boldly. Kitaas didn't answer, but her ears went back a little. For a moment, the satisfaction of a well-struck blow warmed Ekhaas—then Geth nudged her.

"We're attracting attention," he muttered.

Ekhaas glanced over her shoulder. Where they had passed, ugly expressions and flattened ears followed as Kech Volaar stared after Geth and Tenquis. Kitaas, she realized, had deliberately taken them along one of the city's busiest streets. "Ignore them," she said. She thought she heard a satisfied chuckle from Kitaas.

"Is this going to make it difficult to keep our being here secret from Tariic?" asked Geth.

"Most Kech Volaar never leave sight of Volaar Draal," said Ekhaas. "Those who do don't talk much about clan matters. We're safe."

"What about them?" asked Chetiin. He pointed ahead with a slight, concealed gesture. Ekhaas looked.

The blocky shape of the Shrine of Glories, the seat of the Kech Volaar's leadership, rose before them. Clustered at the foot of the stairs that swept up to the entrance was a group of six armored hobgoblins. An outsider less knowledgeable than Chetiin might have mistaken them for Kech Volaar, but Ekhaas saw instantly that they weren't. The armor they wore was even heavier and more archaic than that of the guards at the city gate—and here in the heart of the city, they were the only hobgoblins wearing armor at all. The emblem of a sword was displayed on their helmets, and Ekhaas knew that if they got close enough, she'd see the emblem repeated in brands on their cheeks.

Kech Shaarat.

Ekhaas grabbed Kitaas and shoved her into the cover of an alley. Her sister let out a curse, but Ekhaas put a hand over her mouth. "What are the Blade Bearers doing here?"

45

Kitaas pushed her hand away. "They come under compact of peace to speak with Tuura Dhakaan. It's no business of yours."

"We can't let them see us." It was possible that the warriors of the rival clan wouldn't recognize the significance of Geth's presence in Volaar Draal, but they were far more likely to tell stories of what they'd seen to someone who might. "We'll go in the slaves' door."

Kitaas's ears went back at the suggestion. "You go too—"

A flash of anger broke over Ekhaas. Seizing her sister's wrist, she twisted her around with an arm behind her back, and Kitaas's words broke off in a soft cry. Ekhaas pushed her bent arm higher. "The slaves' door," she ordered and pushed Kitaas deeper into the alley.

Kitaas hissed but marched on.

The slaves' door of the Shrine of Glories was far less grand than the front entrance, but there was no one here to see them except for a startled old bugbear who bent low as they passed. Once they were inside, Ekhaas released Kitaas. "Where's Tuura?"

"The Hall of Song."

Ekhaas flicked her ears. "We'll have cover at least." Geth glanced at her, eyebrows raised. "It was designed after the audience chamber of the Dhakaani emperor," Ekhaas added. "There are pillars everywhere."

Pillars, she realized when they reached the hall, that reminded her uncomfortably of the woods where Tariic's men had ambushed them. Like trees, the thick columns of stone gave them cover but also blocked their line of sight. Functionaries and petitioners lurked in the shadows like thieves. Ekhaas wished they still had Marrow with them.

She heard the flowing water of Tuura Dhakaan's voice before she saw her. "The truth of the matter is that Ruus Dhakaan wishes to exploit the connections that the Kech Volaar have made with the leaders of Darguun."

Ekhaas's ears flicked upright. She saw Chetiin's big ears twitch as well and knew he'd recognized the name too. Ruus

THE TYRANNY OF GHOSTS

Dhakaan, leader of the Kech Shaarat. Ekhaas caught Kitaas's arm. The archivist scowled but held her position.

The voice that answered Tuura was also a woman's though not so musical—the speaker had not undergone training as a *duur'kala*. "The Kech Volaar's connections were with Haruuc Shaarat'kor. You have no connection with Tariic Kurar'taarn yet. In fact, we have heard that you delayed negotiations of your alliance with Darguun."

Tuura sounded irritated as she answered, "A matter of tradition and prudence, Riila Dhakaan, not a sign of weakness. We respected the period of mourning for Haruuc, and while there was still competition among his potential heirs, approaching one of them would have been foolish. Even now, Tariic may hold the throne of Darguun, but he has yet to prove himself."

"Prove himself? Does such a thing matter?" A man's voice this time. Ekhaas's ears rose higher. She leaned forward and saw the speaker between the pillars. He was big, even for a hobgoblin. The steel breastplate of his armor had been hammered into the visage of a snarling demon, and the hilt of a massive sword projected over his shoulders. His features—long ears, flat nose, square chin, and angular cheeks beneath branded swords—had a sharpness that spoke of an ancient and closely bred bloodline.

The woman, Riila, who stood just slightly ahead of him, also carried the sword brand of the Kech Shaarat on her forehead. Her features were so similar to the warrior's that they might have been brother and sister. She didn't wear heavy plate armor, but instead a suit of light scale mail beneath the blue-edged mantle of a diplomat traveling under a compact of peace. Though her ears flicked in anger at her companion's outburst, she recovered quickly.

"Through his choice of a general, Tariic won a victory over the elves of the Valaes Tairn, ancient enemies of Dhakaan. If that does not prove his ability, at least it shows he has potential. Through cunning, he also survived an attempted assassination."

Riila's ears flicked again. "An assassination we are told one of the Kech Volaar was involved in."

Ekhaas would have shrunk back into the shadows, but Geth put a hand on her shoulder, steadying her. A figure previously hidden by a pillar leaned forward in a raised chair, and Ekhaas caught a glimpse of Tuura Dhakaan. The leader of the Kech Volaar carried more lines in her face than the two envoys combined. Her eyes, however, were as keen as a hunting bird's, and her words were just as sharp. "The actions of one are not the actions of the clan. If they were, the Kech Shaarat would not be here. We meet under ancient oaths of honor. I'd advise you not to break them."

While her warrior companion fumed in silence at the rebuke, Riila bent her head. "As you say, Tuura Dhakaan. Still, this is not the time for the Dhakaani clans to stand alone or apart. Tariic respects the past, perhaps even more than Haruuc did. He wields Guulen, the Rod of Kings, with confidence. Ruus Dhakaan believes that the Kech Shaarat and the Kech Volaar together—our strength and numbers combined with your lore—could help Tariic bring about a new era of empire."

"Riila Dhakaan and Taak Dhakaan speak the truth," added a dusty voice, and Ekhaas saw the movement of a black wool robe behind Tuura. She recognized the voice—Diitesh, the High Archivist whom Kitaas served. "An alliance with Haruuc offered us the chance to spread the lore and tales of Dhakaan across Darguun. Joining with Tariic and the Kech Shaarat could see the glory of Dhakaan spread across—"

"I have matched wits with Ruus many times," said Tuura, cutting off the archivist. "I didn't realize he had become such an optimist." She looked down on Riila. "Ruus Dhakaan guides your clan with aggression. He has conquered two lesser clans by force. He knows he can't take the Kech Volaar by the same means, so he pursues a strategy of friendship. Perhaps he will attempt the same with the lhesh of Darguun. My answer is no. The Kech Volaar will not ally with the Kech Shaarat in this—or

THE TYRANNY OF GHOSTS

any other—matter. If Ruus truly wishes to find favor with Tariic, let him do it himself."

The warrior of the Kech Shaarat, Taak, twisted his face and started to speak, but Riila silenced him with a gesture. She gave Tuura a cold look. "You put your clan in the path of the Kech Shaarat."

"The path of the Kech Shaarat is not so wide as Ruus thinks it is." Tuura sat back and disappeared from Ekhaas's sight. "You may go."

Riila inclined her head, though there was nothing of deference in her bearing. Without another word, she turned and walked away. Taak didn't even bend his neck to the leader of the Kech Volaar but whirled and stalked after Riila.

"That was ill-considered, *chib*," said Diitesh, almost too softly for Ekhaas to hear. "We might have turned this to our advantage."

"Whose advantage, Diitesh?" Tuura asked. "When Ruus Dhakaan pours wine, I check for poison. You might want to remember that." She raised her voice. "I know you've returned, Kitaas. Bring them forward."

There was no hiding from an elder of the *duur'kala* in her own court. Ekhaas straightened and started forward, but Kitaas pulled her back and went ahead of her, bending her head low. "Diitesh Dhakaan, Tuura Dhakaan, I obey your commands. Here are the travelers recently arrived at the gates of Volaar Draal."

Ekhaas ground her teeth at her sister's manner, then moved forward with Geth, Chetiin, and Tenquis at her back. Tuura's face was impassive as they approached. Behind her, though, Diitesh gaped in open shock at the sight of outsiders brought into the heart of Volaar Draal. The High Archivist had a pale complexion, yellow like the dust of Rhukaan Draal, and the flush that rose in her face turned it the color of mud. She glanced at Kitaas as she took a place beside her, then leaned close to Tuura again. The leader of the Kech Volaar silenced her with a flick of her fingers.

Ekhaas bent her head in a deep nod before meeting Tuura's gaze. "Mother of the dirge, I claim sanctuary—" she began.

"Do not speak, Ekhaas." Tuura looked down at her with eyes that were suddenly filled with anger. Shock shivered through Ekhaas, and she closed her mouth sharply. Tuura ignored her discomfort. "You heard my conversation with the emissaries of the Kech Shaarat. I do not like being placed in a position to defend attempts by members of this clan to assassinate potential allies. Do you understand that?"

Ekhaas nodded again. Tuura sat forward, and her voice dropped into a whisper more terrible than any shout. "Then why did you do it? And why by the blood of the Six Kings did you bring your fellow assassins to Volaar Draal?"

Diitesh made a noise like a boiling kettle. "Sanctuary!" she spat. "For *chaat'oor*!"

"Diitesh!" said Tuura. The High Archivist fell silent. Tuura looked back to Ekhaas and the others. "Just by coming here you put the Kech Volaar in danger."

Anger at the accusation rose inside Ekhaas, pushing aside shock and dismay. She raised her head to look Tuura in the eye. "Tariic thinks we've run for Breland. Kech Volaar would be in greater danger if we hadn't come. Mother of the dirge, we carry a warning for you." Ekhaas stood straight. "Tariic cannot be trusted. Make an alliance with him and the Kech Volaar will be dragged down along with Darguun under Tariic's rulership."

This time Diitesh snorted and leaned forward to hiss in Tuura's ear. "Tuura, this is nonsense! They're trying to turn us against an ally who could restore the empire!"

But Tuura's eyes were on Ekhaas. Her ears, which had been folded back flat against her scalp, rose slowly. "Where does this warning come from?"

"From our own experience—and from Senen Dhakaan. She aided our escape."

"You dragged her into this?" Diitesh said harshly. "Where is your honor, daughter of the dirge?"

THE TYRANNY OF GHOSTS

"It was Senen's suggestion that we come here," Ekhaas snapped.

"Then why didn't she send the warning in one of her reports?" Kitaas leaped into the argument like Diitesh's echo. "She has used her magic to sing reports to us of your disgrace. Why didn't she warn us directly?"

"Maybe because she believed that a warning from our mouths would carry more weight than one sent by magic."

Diitesh bared her teeth. "And she said nothing in her reports because she believed the word of traitors would be respected above the word of a trusted emissary?"

"She said nothing," Tuura said with unexpected calm, "because she knew that she was being watched."

Ekhaas's gaze darted back to her, a retort to Diitesh's argument fading on her lips. Tuura sat back in her chair. "Senen's reports of late have been unusually circumspect," she said, "but she is adept at hiding brief messages within them. One message said that she was being watched and could not report all that she wanted to." Tuura rested her chin on her hand and looked again at Ekhaas. "Another said that I would receive advice and would be wise to accept it."

Ekhaas felt a burst of elation, but she bent her head humbly. "I urge you to heed her words."

"And perhaps," Tuura added, "you can shed light on another of Senen's hidden messages. Is there a reason she would feel it was important to tell me that Tariic holds the younger daughter of Deneith?"

Ekhaas stiffened. The younger daughter of Deneith? Ashi. Ashi was Tariic's prisoner. But if she was his prisoner, that meant—

At her side, Geth drew a sharp breath. "Grandmother Wolf, Ashi's alive!"

The elation she'd felt before turned into radiant joy. Ekhaas fought to stay calm as she raised her head. "I think that message was meant more for us than you, Tuura Dhakaan. Thank you for it."

51

She watched Tuura consider each of them, even Tenquis. Then the leader of the Kech Volaar turned back to her.

"If Tariic doesn't suspect that you are here," she said, "I see no harm in granting sanctuary to you and your allies, so long as they respect the customs of the Kech Volaar."

"Tuura!" Diitesh's voice rose sharply. "They are *chaat'oor*. They have no place in—"

"Remember *your* place, Diitesh!" Tuura stood up and turned to face the High Archivist. She was nearly a handspan taller than the other woman and in her anger looked even taller. "Your *muut* is to the archives. My *muut* is to the clan. If there is a danger to Volaar Draal, it must be examined. I know Senen. She would not do this lightly. You may return to the archives, Diitesh." Tuura looked to Ekhaas. "We will find a place we cannot easily be overheard, and I will hear your whole story, Ekhaas *duur'kala*."

But Ekhaas's joy was already turning to a sickening knot in her belly as Diitesh and Kitaas glared at her over Tuura's shoulder. Geth had suggested that they try to stay on Kitaas's good side—but it was too late for that with both the High Archivist and her adjunct angry with them, and that wasn't going to make her next request any easier.

She swallowed her pride. "Actually, Tuura Dhakaan," she said, "there is something else . . ."

As she made her request, the knot in her stomach grew tighter, Tuura's expression grew harder—and the smile that grew across Diitesh's pale face became gloating.

CHAPTER FOUR

16 Aryth

Song, half-heard, surrounded Geth as he returned to himself. Visions, half-remembered, of a distant time and place were already fading in his head. He had a lingering memory of a hobgoblin woman, a *duur'kala* and an empress. A name came to him: Mekiis Kuun, fourth in the line of heroes who had wielded Wrath in the time of the Dhakaani Empire. At the back of his mind, the sword's presence tickled him with something that felt like pride in the ancient heroine.

His throat was dry. "*Iinanen*," he croaked in Goblin. Thirsty. There was no response, only a rising chatter of voices that replaced the song. Geth opened his eyes. "*Iinanen!*"

One of the crowd of archivists and *duur'kala* that packed the room glanced over at him, then picked up a metal cup and thrust it at him without taking her attention off the expanding argument. Shifting Wrath from its position at his side, Geth pushed himself up from the couch where he lay. Cold mushroom tea. He drank it anyway, then scanned the crowd for the yellow face of the High Archivist.

"Diitesh," he called, "are we done?"

Diitesh broke away from a conversation to look at him as if he were a piece of furniture that had inconveniently learned to talk. "There are questions," she said. "Where was the palace where Emperor Okaat Baaz courted Mekiis Kuun? When did she lay the Sword of Heroes aside—"

"I've told you before. I don't know. Wrath doesn't remember things like that."

The insolent growl silenced that babbling crowd. Geth glared at them, though mostly at Diitesh, and stood up. His legs felt loose and weak after lying on the couch all day. "We're done," he said. He gathered Wrath and walked for the door.

Behind him, the archivists and *duur'kala* started talking again, his presence—or lack of it—irrelevant.

Ekhaas was waiting for him outside. "Who were you today?"

"I don't want to talk about it." He looked at her. Ekhaas's eyes were red and squinting. "Did you find anything?"

"What do you think?"

Geth just grunted and sheathed Wrath.

Diitesh's permission for access to the vaults and the records of the archivists had come with a price. Only Ekhaas would be permitted to search the massive Register for references to the Rod of Kings and only if Geth agreed to share the memories of Dhakaan contained within Wrath. An exchange of knowledge for knowledge. Diitesh had presented the proposition as if it were the fairest deal in the world—but then for her, it was. Not even Tuura Dhakaan could have granted them access to the vaults over the High Archivist's objections.

For the week since they had arrived in Volaar Draal, Geth had spent his days in a dream as *duur'kala* songs drew out the nebulous memories, while archivists scribbled down his words. Unlike the Rod of Kings, the touch of the Sword of Heroes was light on his mind, providing inspiration but no more. Not usually, at least. Under the influence of the *duur'kala* magic, the memories flowed right through him, leaving him with nothing but vague recollections and a headache. At least Diitesh had been true to her word—though perhaps too true. Ekhaas had access to the Register but no one to help her search it. Finding something to help them stop Tariic and the rod could take months. At least, Geth was sure, as long as it would take Diitesh to ransack the memories of the sword.

THE TYRANNY OF GHOSTS

He wondered sometimes if they might not have been better off staying on the run in the mountains. And not just because of Diitesh's antagonism, either. He looked up into the darkness above Volaar Draal as they emerged onto the streets of the city. "I need to get outside, Ekhaas. I need to see the sun and the moons."

Ekhaas's ears twitched. "You know we can't. Being granted sanctuary doesn't mean you can come and go whenever you want. By our tradition a host honors her guests, but guests have their *muut*—their duty—to the host."

"I just want to step out of the gates," he protested. "It's not like we'd run into Tariic's patrols."

"It doesn't matter. Tuura has told the gate watch not to let us pass. I think she's worried we'd go off and try to rescue Ashi." She looked at him sideways. "Don't pretend you wouldn't."

A growl rose up Geth's throat, but he bit if off with clenched teeth. Learning Ashi was alive had been a mixed blessing. She was still Tariic's prisoner—and he felt helpless because there was nothing they could do about it. Rescuing Ashi wouldn't help them stop Tariic, and it would certainly cost them their access to the lore of the Kech Volaar.

"No new information from Senen?" he asked. Ekhaas shook her head. Her ears flicked back as she did, and Geth knew she wasn't thinking just about Ashi. One of Senen's reports had made a passing reference to Dagii but no more than that. Was he still an ally or was he under Tariic's power?

If he was controlled by the Rod, he wouldn't have been the only one. Senen had also mentioned Midian's appearance as Tariic's royal historian. Geth would have expected the gnome to flee for Zilargo. He couldn't believe Midian remained at Tariic's side of his own free will. For that matter, they couldn't even trust that Senen's will was her own, though her continued warnings that she was being watched at least suggested it.

"I hate this," he said. "There has to be something more we can do."

Ekhaas's ears went even farther back. "I know. If I had an archivist to help me with the Register—or even another *duur'kala*—I might at least be able to find the right place to start."

"No other *duur'kala* will help you?"

Ekhaas made a face. "They don't want to cross Diitesh. And to be honest, they're all more interested in you right now."

"It's nice to be wanted," Geth said dryly. "Do you want to duel?"

One of the discomforts of Volaar Draal was passing the time—he and Tenquis weren't exactly welcome in the gathering places of the *dar* city. Ekhaas and Chetiin, of course, blended in with the other goblins, hobgoblins, and bugbears, but a tiefling and a shifter stuck out like . . . well, like *chaat'oor*. There was no shortage of private dueling circles in the city, however, and Ekhaas had started joining Geth in them, fighting away the tension that gathered during the day. Occasionally Chetiin fought with them as well, though neither of them could land a touch on him unless he permitted it. Tenquis abstained entirely, preferring to sit beside the ring and read. Diitesh might have blocked him from access to the wonders of the vaults, but he'd sought out the smiths and masons of the Kech Volaar. Against all expectations, he'd even managed to make contacts among them and was busy learning what he could of half-remembered *daashor* traditions from their techniques and borrowed scrolls.

Ekhaas, though, only shook her head at the invitation to duel. "I can't keep up with you," she said. "I need a rest. Let's go look for Tenquis. He's probably still with the smiths."

"He isn't."

Geth almost jumped at the sound of Chetiin's scarred voice. His hand went to Wrath, and he whirled around, looking for the goblin. He found him crouched in the shadows below the statue of some unnamed Dhakaani hero, calm and undisturbed. "Boar's snout," Geth said. "What are you doing?"

"Waiting for you." Chetiin stood up. "Tenquis hasn't been visiting the smiths of Volaar Draal."

THE TYRANNY OF GHOSTS

"What's he been doing then?" asked Ekhaas. "Where did he get those books?" Her ears rose. "Why have you been following him?"

Chetiin actually looked slightly ashamed for the first time since Geth had known him. "I wasn't following him. I came across him yesterday when I was coming back into Volaar Draal."

"Chetiin!" said Ekhaas in protest.

"The *shaarat'khesh* come and go as they please," the old goblin said stubbornly. "I wanted to speak to Marrow."

"Was it nice outside?" Geth asked.

"The air was as sharp and clear as a knife made of glass."

"You still broke the terms of sanctuary." Ekhaas looked around them as if Diitesh might be lurking nearby, ready to pounce on this violation.

"Ignore that. As I was coming back into the city, I came across Tenquis. I was mistaken when I said he'd make a good *golin'dar*. He has no talent for stealth. He wasn't in the smiths' quarter of the city, though. Today I followed him to see where he went."

"And?"

"Proof requires more than words," said Chetiin. "Come with me."

◉ ◉ ◉ ◉ ◉ ◉ ◉

Chetiin led them to a building on the other side of Volaar Draal that seemed mostly deserted, with only scattered ghostlights glimmering in the narrow windows. Geth raised an eyebrow to Chetiin, but he just shook his head and ushered them inside. The corridors were empty and smelled mostly of damp stone.

"What is this place?" Geth asked Ekhaas softly.

"Unused apartments," she said. "The clan grows and shrinks. Buildings fall in and out of common use."

Chetiin gestured for silence, then pointed up a flight of narrow stone stairs. They moved, the goblin as noiselessly as

a shadow, hobgoblin and shifter as quietly as possible. Two floors up, Chetiin pointed around the corner of a landing into another corridor. Geth eased his head around the corner. Light shone around a door, and he could just make out voices. One of them might have been Tenquis's, but he wasn't sure. He mimed approaching the door to Chetiin, who nodded. Walking softly, Geth stepped into the corridor and slipped up to the door.

It was Tenquis, speaking Goblin. From the cadence of his voice, it sounded like he was reading something. Geth gripped Wrath's hilt, and the words became clear.

"—rebellion among the nobles ultimately cost Saabak Puulta, *marhu* of Dhakaan, fifth lord of the Second Puulta dynasty, his life, but many of the nobility of the empire died along with him. Though Saabak Puulta's successor, Giis Puulta, lavished favor on a chosen few, the empire would never be strong again. On the Stela of Rewards that he erected before his fortress of Zaal Piik, it is recorded that this was the time when *muut* was broken." Tenquis paused, his voice thin with amazement. "Horns of Ohr Kaluun."

"Indeed," answered another voice. "Records from the era of the Rebellion of Lords are sparse. It was a shameful time, but the Stelae of Rewards that emperors and generals of Dhakaan erected as memorials to those they deemed heroes are a rich source of information. Here is the final piece of the puzzle, though—and if you ever doubted your decision to approach me, then don't, because I am the only one who could have brought you this."

The second voice was familiar. It belonged to a woman, probably a hobgoblin, and Geth had a feeling that with just a few more words, he would recognize her. Ekhaas, apparently, needed no time at all. Her ears went back flat. Her skin flushed dark. In three swift steps, she spun around Geth and kicked the door. It slammed open.

From over a table covered in books and scrolls and loose pieces of age-darkened paper, two faces stared back at them in surprise. One was Tenquis. The other was—

THE TYRANNY OF GHOSTS

"Kitaas!" snarled Ekhaas. "What are you doing here?"

For an instant, both the artificer and the archivist simply looked startled. Then Kitaas rose imperiously. "I, my sister, am recovering the heritage of Dhakaan while you seem intent on denying it!"

Ekhaas bared her teeth. "What are you talking about?"

Geth felt a whirl of confusion. After Kitaas's greeting when they had arrived in Volaar Draal, he wouldn't have expected that she and Tenquis would exchange polite words, let alone meet in secret. The only thing he could really understand was why Chetiin had insisted they see this for themselves. He wouldn't have believed it.

A scowl flitted across Tenquis's face, and he stood as well. "Get out!" he said. "Just get out and leave us alone."

Ekhaas and Kitaas had locked eyes, however. "You travel with a store of knowledge you don't even recognize," said Kitaas. "This one understands the lore of the *daashor* better than our own smiths"—she pointed at Tenquis—"and archivists will record Kitaas as the one who bargained to bring it back."

"You called him *chaat'oor*," Ekhaas said. "Which is he, then? A defiler of Dhakaan or a guardian of its lore?"

Geth looked to Tenquis in surprise. The tiefling's face was taut with frustration. "I traded some of my knowledge for access to records from the vault," he said. "There's nothing wrong with that."

"Records from the vaults?" Ekhaas strode up to the table and snatched up a scroll. "Kitaas, you took records from the vaults?"

Kitaas's ears flicked. "Don't question my *muut*. I am adjunct to the High Archivist. The secrets of the *daashor* are worth showing a few minor histories to a *chaat'oor*."

"We can talk about this later," said Tenquis. He turned golden eyes to Geth. "Please just go now!"

The hair on Geth's arms and the back of his neck rose. There was more than just frustration and anger in Tenquis's voice. There was anxiety too. Maybe even outright fear. He genuinely

59

needed them out of there. "Ekhaas," Geth said, "we should go. This isn't the right time—"

The *duur'kala* wasn't swayed. She looked at the scroll in her hands. "The life of Taruuzh?" Her glare moved from Kitaas to Tenquis. "I've been struggling on my own to learn about the Rod of Kings and you've been here learning about the rod's maker with *her*." Ekhaas flung down the scroll. "Is all of this about Taruuzh?"

Kitaas froze. Her eyes darted to Tenquis, and her ears went all the way back.

"No," said Tenquis. His voice was soothing, but he took a step away from her and held out his hands. "No, Kitaas. This isn't what you think."

"Isn't it?" asked Kitaas, baring her teeth—then she grabbed a curl of paper from the table and bolted for the door.

"No!" Tenquis spat. "Stop her!"

Geth leaped. Kitaas tried to duck past him, but he got his arms around her and wrestled her to the ground. She drew breath, ready to shout. Geth freed one hand and slapped it over her mouth, then yanked it away with a hiss as she sank sharp teeth into his fingers. He grabbed a fold of her black robe, forcing it into her mouth and holding it there as a makeshift gag. Kitaas's eyes blazed at him.

Her hands writhed underneath them. Geth heard the tearing of paper.

"Get her up!" Tenquis came hurrying around the table. Geth twisted around, turning Kitaas over. Scraps of paper fluttered away. Tenquis cursed and scooped them up. His face flushed dark. "Mercy of the sorcerer-kings!" he cursed as he bent down to pry the last pieces from Kitaas's fingers. "Well done, Ekhaas. You couldn't have just left us alone?"

She looked at him in amazement. "What were you doing?" she asked.

The tiefling's teeth showed stark white against his skin. "What you couldn't. Getting an archivist's help." He got the

THE TYRANNY OF GHOSTS

last bit of paper away from Geth's prisoner and stood. "I'm sorry, Kitaas, but she was right."

Kitaas shrieked into her makeshift gag, thrashing with new energy. Geth tightened his hold on her as he stared up at Tenquis.

* * * * * * *

"I could tell after your first day with the Register that you weren't going to get anywhere," Tenquis said. "It was obvious that Diitesh was playing you. If you were going to find anything, it would be by pure chance, and how long would that take? I've done this sort of research before. You needed help. I decided to get it by pretending to search for additional *daashor* lore."

The tiefling stood at the table, his back to them in anger as he picked through the scraps of paper Kitaas had shredded and struggled to piece them together. Geth exchanged glances with Ekhaas and Chetiin. They both looked like he felt—stunned at Tenquis's initiative. "Why didn't you tell us?" he asked.

Ekhaas spoke at the same moment. "Why Kitaas?" More properly restrained with rope drawn from one of Tenquis's magical pockets, her sister squirmed and hissed.

Tenquis raised his head and finally looked around. His eyes went to Geth first, and he looked a little shamed. "Maybe I should have told you," he said. "But you've been spending time with *duur'kala* digging into your mind. And if I'd told you, Ekhaas, what would you have done?" He dropped the paper scraps and turned fully to face them. "I could have traded some of what I knew about the *daashor* to any archivist, but that wouldn't have been enough. Your people are too devoted to their sense of duty. You and Kitaas gave me what I needed. A chance to recover lost lore *and* steal glory from you was more than she could resist."

Kitaas gave another muffled curse. Geth watched Ekhaas's face flush, then go pale, then flush again. Her lips pressed tight

together and her ears pulled back. "My sister despises me more deeply than she despises *chaat'oor*. I am flattered." Kitaas hissed again. Ekhaas ignored her.

"If she even suspected it was some kind of trick, she would have had us thrown out of Volaar Draal," said Tenquis.

"She still can. More so, now." Ekhaas took a deep breath. "Let's hope it wasn't all for nothing. I'm sorry we interrupted you, Tenquis. What have you found?"

"Ah." A smile spread across Tenquis's face—one that reminded Geth too much of a schoolmaster from his childhood—as he gestured for them to join him around the table. "You've been searching the Register for mention of the Rod of Kings. I couldn't be that direct. If I wanted Kitaas to believe that all I wanted was more information about the *daashor*, I couldn't approach the rod directly. So I told her I wanted to start my search with the great Taruuzh. He may have created the Rod of Kings and the Sword of Heroes, but he created other wonders as well."

"The first grieving trees," said Ekhaas. "Fortresses. What about them?"

"We've been so focused on the rod and the sword that we've ignored something else. When you, Geth, and Dagii brought me the rod to study, you told me a story about the creation of it and the sword."

Ekhaas's ears flicked and her eyes narrowed. "The Rod of Kings or *Guulen*—'Strength' in the human language—was created by Taruuzh *daashor* from byeshk ore he mined himself out of a vein he named *Khaar Vanon*, the Blood of Night. He forged the Sword of Heroes, *Aram* or 'Wrath,' from the same ore. That's how we were able to find the rod in the first place. Geth recovered the sword from the ghost fortress of Jhegesh Dol and *duur'kala* songs reawakened its connection to the rod."

"But that's not the story you told me that night," said Tenquis. "You left something out. There was a third artifact, wasn't there?"

THE TYRANNY OF GHOSTS

Ekhaas blinked. "*Muut*, Duty, the Shield of Nobles, but legends say it was shattered as the Empire of Dhakaan slid toward the Desperate Times—"

Her ears rose sharply. Geth felt his belly twist as he saw the same thing she must have. Even Chetiin's wrinkled face stretched tight with surprise. On the floor, Kitaas's shrieks and curses faded into silence. Tenquis nodded at all of them and spoke what they were all thinking. "I said once that artifacts like the rod aren't destroyed easily, but if the Shield of Nobles could be shattered—"

"So can the rod!" Geth growled. "How?"

Tenquis grimaced. "I don't know."

Hope bled out of Geth, but the tiefling shook his head. "I don't know *yet*," he said quickly, "but that's what I was working with Kitaas to try and figure out. She thought I was just trying to track down the history of another of Taruuzh's creations."

Kitaas let out another screech, this one descending into deep choking noises. For a moment, Geth thought she had sucked the gag into her mouth in her struggles. When he checked on her, though, he found her weeping with helpless rage. He looked at Ekhaas but she turned her face away and said to Tenquis, "But Taruuzh has been studied for generations. What did Kitaas bring you? We heard something about a Stela of Rewards and the Rebellion of Lords during the Second Puulta dynasty."

"Taruuzh has been studied by *duur'kala* and archivists," Tenquis said, "not by artificers. You talk about things in metaphors of song and music. We talk about things in metaphors of crafting and alchemy. So did *daashor*." He picked up a brittle scroll. "This is an account of Taruuzh's creations written by a later *daashor*. 'And the shield of Taruuzh was sundered by the golden ones of Dhakaan when they fell in the fifth great transformation of thunder returned. The second of the artifacts of the Blood of Night passed beyond this sphere, marking the beginning of the end of Dhakaan.'" Golden eyes looked up. "Does that make any sense to you, Ekhaas?"

63

Her face twisted. "Some of it. The artifacts of the Blood of Night would be the rod, the sword, and the shield. And the shield was shattered as Dhakaan collapsed."

"Although when this was written, the author believed that the shattering of the shield was the beginning of the end, not just a part of it." Tenquis traced the lines of faded text with a fingernail. "The important bit is what he says about who broke the shield and when they did it. In alchemy, gold is the highest state of common being, a state as close to perfect as possible without magic or divinity. 'Golden ones' are people of a perfect state. Today we might say they were great thinkers, but among the Dhakaan, they were more likely to be nobility."

"Not the emperor?" asked Geth.

"Emperors were more than common beings," Ekhaas said, her ears flicking rapidly. "In legends they're compared to gems or metals even more precious than gold."

Tenquis nodded. "So nobles broke the shield as they fell, which Kitaas"—there was a moan from their prisoner—"identified as a reference to the Rebellion of Lords when the nobles of Dhakaan rose up against Saabak, the fifth emperor of the Second Puulta dynasty for a brief time during the late empire. The passing of power from one emperor to another could be seen as a great transformation."

"And *puulta* is an old word for the noise of an army on the march, like thunder," said Chetiin. "The fifth transformation of thunder returned—the fifth succession of the Second Puulta dynasty."

"Which led us to what you heard when you broke in. Kitaas knew of a history of the late empire that had a very specific reference to Saabak Puulta. She brought it to me today." He tapped an open book with the end of the scroll. "It confirms what's in the scroll!"

Ekhaas's face tightened. "Don't be so certain. Let me see that." She picked up the book and, marking the page with her finger, looked at the title and author. Her expression turned

THE TYRANNY OF GHOSTS

grim. "Shaardat the Elder. No wonder Kitaas knew it. Archivists adore Shaardat's interpretations."

"So?"

"*Duur'kala* might cling to tradition, but Shaardat wallowed in it." Ekhaas set the book down. "I knew I'd heard the expression 'the time when *muut* was broken' before. It survived Shaardat, and it means the nobles rebelled against their duty—their *muut*—to the emperor and to the people of the empire." She shook her head. "I'm sorry, Tenquis. Whatever is written on Giis Puulta's Stela of Rewards, it's talking about the breakdown in social order, not literally about the Shield of Nobles."

Geth watched Tenquis's mouth open and close as he tried to find a counter-argument, but Chetiin answered before he could. "What if it isn't?" the old goblin asked thoughtfully. "Stories can contain mistakes that are transmitted across generations. The scroll talks about the shield. Shaardat may have misinterpreted what was written on the stela."

Tenquis's eyebrows rose. Ekhaas answered grudgingly. "It's possible. But even if she did, what does it tell us other than when the Shield of Nobles was shattered?"

"Perhaps there's more written on the Stela of Rewards."

"I've never heard of the fortress of Zaal Piik before. I have no idea where it would have been located."

An idea burst over Geth. "But maybe Kitaas did." He turned back to the paper that Kitaas had tried to destroy. "Tenquis, when Kitaas said she'd brought you the final piece of the puzzle, is this what—?"

He didn't need to finish the question, and Tenquis didn't need to answer, because Kitaas went mad with fury. Shrieking behind her gag and writhing against her bonds, she threw her body across the floor like some grotesque worm. Geth and Chetiin hopped out of the way. Kitaas hit the legs of the table hard enough to send books sliding around. One fell onto the scroll—the brittle rolls cracked and split. Another threatened the torn page, but Tenquis caught it. Geth reached down and

grabbed Kitaas by the back of her robe, ready to drag her to a safe distance.

Ekhaas stopped him. "No, keep her close," she said coldly. "She might be useful." She bent over the bits of paper.

Restraining the still struggling archivist with one arm, Geth looked too. Although Kitaas had done severe damage to the page, a few large pieces were still intact. Tenquis had managed to piece several more sections together. The entire page was covered in the dark, angular characters of Goblin script. Geth gripped Wrath's hilt with his free hand. *Show me,* he willed the sword.

Wrath translated spoken Goblin for him with no special command, but Geth had discovered early in his possession of the blade that it could also allow him to read the language. The characters on the page didn't change to his eyes, but in his mind they shifted suddenly from meaningless scribbles to real words.

The page was a list of artifacts. *A Tome Bound in Dragonhide. The Reliquary of Waroot Gar. Seven Blades of Shaarat Kol. A Talon Found in Aarlak.* Each was accompanied by a description, some longer, some shorter.

"This is a page from the Register," said Ekhaas in amazement. She stared at her sister. "You stole a page from the Register and were willing to destroy it rather than let me see it."

Kitaas's ears went back. Her eyes blazed rage. A shiver ran through Geth. He almost pushed Kitaas away from him, but just then Tenquis gave a gasp. "Horns of Ohr Kaluun!" He laid several scraps of paper together and lifted his hands away. "It doesn't matter where Zaal Piik is, Ekhaas. The stela is here in Volaar Draal!"

Kitaas hissed again and kicked out at the table. Geth wrapped both arms around her again and dragged her back. Ekhaas looked between the torn page and her sister. Tenquis ignored them, studying the paper with a fascinated intensity. " 'The Reward Stela of Giis Puulta,' " he read aloud. " 'Carved of white stone and commemorating the allies of Giis Puulta in his ascension as the sixth *marhu* of the Second Puulta dynasty.

THE TYRANNY OF GHOSTS

Collected by Baaen Dhakaan in ruins below the Hammerfist Mountains in the years 2310 since the fall and 1246 since the founding. Transported to Volaar Draal. Displayed before the Shrine of Glories until the years 3675 and 2619, then placed by the Gallery of Dogs in the Vault of the Eye.' " He looked up, his face fallen. "The stela is in the vaults."

Frustration rose in Geth. "Grandfather Rat is laughing at us. We find a possible clue to stopping Tariic, and we can't get to it." He glanced at Ekhaas. "Diitesh isn't going to let us enter the vaults."

"Then we won't ask her permission." Ekhaas raised her head, expression grim but ears standing tall. "We don't have a choice. We've already broken sanctuary. When Tuura Dhakaan finds out what's happened here, she'll be bound by honor and duty to throw us out of Volaar Draal. If we don't act now, we're never going to get a chance to examine the stela."

"And how do we get into the vaults?"

Ekhaas turned to face Kitaas. Geth felt the archivist stiffen in his arms, her anger becoming alarm at the icy distance in Ekhaas's eyes. "My dear sister will help us," she said.

CHAPTER FIVE

16 Aryth

The entrance to the vaults of Volaar Draal was a wide maw, cast into shadow by pale ghostlights hung beneath deep eaves. It was an unfriendly building, jealously guarding the secrets it had swallowed over the centuries.

No guards stood beneath the ghostlights, though. None lurked in the shadows. From the cover of the nearest building—a good fifteen paces across a dark-flagged plaza—Ekhaas stood with Geth and Tenquis and watched the massive doors.

"I can't believe it isn't guarded," murmured Tenquis. His quiet words were at odds with his appearance. Disguised by illusion with her magic, he wore the face and body of a bugbear.

"There are always archivists inside," Ekhaas told him, "but they don't need guards outside. Intruders would need to pass the gates of Volaar Draal and then the entire city if they wanted to reach the vaults. And none of the Kech Volaar would dare to trespass without permission."

"You're going to."

The words were a twisting knife. Ekhaas scowled at him.

"Quiet," said Geth. Cloaked, like Tenquis in the illusion of a bugbear, he didn't take his eyes off the doorway. "I think I saw Chetiin." He pointed. "There was movement just below the light on the left."

"There's a bat lurking there. You saw it." Chetiin's voice emerged from the shadow just at Geth's elbow. The shifter

jumped, and even Ekhaas felt her heart leap. Chetiin gave a wry half-grin of amusement at his own stealth. "There are no traps, no warning magic," he said. "Nothing to stop us entering."

Ekhaas nodded. "Remember to walk like bugbears until we're past the archivists inside," she told Geth and Tenquis. Two shaggy heads bobbed. Chetiin simply faded back into the shadows once more. Ekhaas braced herself for what she was about to do and stepped out into the plaza.

The unfamiliar length of Kitaas's black robe tangled around her legs almost immediately. She twitched it free and strode on with as much arrogance as she could muster. How her sister managed to walk in the garment every day was beyond her, but at least it was bulky enough to conceal her own clothes underneath.

Kitaas slept beneath the table in the room where they had confronted her and Tenquis. Her towering anger had been no match for Ekhaas's song. Soothed by the magic, she would sleep through the night. She'd been frightened at the end of their confrontation. Ekhaas could only imagine what Kitaas had thought she might do, but all she'd really wanted was her robe. Kitaas would have enough to worry about when she woke in the morning. The thought of Kitaas trying to explaining her actions to Diitesh gave Ekhaas a warm, satisfied feeling.

It was almost enough to quiet the doubt that pulled at her.

When did I stop feeling what she feels? Ekhaas wondered. When did I stop defending the sanctity of the vaults and the honor of the Kech Volaar?

Not so long before she would have been beside Kitaas in challenging any suggestion of *chaat'oor* entering the vaults, the one thing they might have agreed on. Instead she stood with the defilers. What they did was bigger than honor or family, she told herself. It was a duty to the future of the goblin people. Her *muut* to the *dar*.

And yet a small part of her could only think one thing. *Kapaa'taat.* Lowest of the low. Traitor.

THE TYRANNY OF GHOSTS

Ekhaas clenched her jaw and marched on across the plaza.

Beneath the eaves of the building, it was possible to better appreciate just how massive the doors of the vaults were. Three times as tall as a hobgoblin and solid stone—yet when Ekhaas laid a hand on one, it swung open as easily as the door of a cottage.

She passed into the hall beyond with her head up and her stride brisk, concentrating on projecting an air that she belonged there. It worked—or perhaps the archivists they passed were really as absorbed in their own thoughts and conversations as it seemed. In any case, they ignored her and her shambling "bugbear" escort. Ekhaas allowed herself a thin breath of relief as she reached the inner doors—wood this time—at the far end of the hall and glanced back at Geth and Tenquis.

"Whatever happens," she said, "don't say anything. Chetiin, are you ready?"

His answer seemed to come from out of nowhere. "I'll be where you need me if anything goes wrong."

The hinges on the inner doors were as perfectly balanced as those on the outer door. They made no noise as Ekhaas pushed the door open and stepped through into a round room with a towering ceiling and walls lined with books. Massive books, as tall as Ekhaas's forearm was long, on shelves that rose up into the shadowed heights. The Register of the vaults. Ekhaas wondered which of the volumes was missing a page.

At the room's center stood a round desk of age-darkened wood. Within its confines sat a withered archivist bent close over one of the volumes of the Register, checking it against loose pages of parchment. The old hobgoblin looked up at the entry of Ekhaas and her escort and her drooping ears twitched. She squinted at them, her eyes almost disappearing into the wrinkles of her face.

Blind at a distance. Perfect. Ekhaas made a ritual gesture of respect—fingers pressed to breast then to forehead—then forced her voice down into her sister's rough register. "I am about the High Archivist's business."

She wasn't as accomplished a mimic as Midian, but the imitation was close enough, especially when Diitesh's authority was invoked. The elderly archivist returned the gesture of respect with some haste, though her squinty eyes remained on Geth and Tenquis.

"The High Archivist's business," Ekhaas added, "requires strong arms. They are fools. The wonders of the vaults will be meaningless to them."

"All will one day know the glory of Dhakaan," said the old archivist. "May you find what you seek, sister." She bent back to the Register.

Aware of every breath that she took, Ekhaas marched past the desk to where a series of high arched doorways led out of the round chamber. Some opened onto stairs down into darkness, others to stairs up, a few onto level passages. Rods tipped with the dim glow of ghostlight stood in stone jars beside several of the doorways. Ekhaas gestured imperiously for Geth and Tenquis to retrieve a pair, using the delay while they did to locate the archway she wanted. When they returned to her side, she set off without hesitation down a flight of worn stairs.

Just before she passed out of sight of the chamber above, she glanced back. The old archivist hadn't raised her head again. Ekhaas let out a slow sigh of relief.

"Well done," said Chetiin softly. Ekhaas looked down to find him walking beside her as if he'd been there the whole time.

The stairs continued to descend, switching back and forth at regular intervals until they emerged into a short hallway with more arched doorways. Satisfied that they were deep enough that sound wouldn't carry back to the chamber above, Ekhaas stopped and pulled off Kitaas's entangling robe. Able to stride freely once more, she turned to Geth and Tenquis and sang a few rippling notes. The illusion that had disguised them faded away like ink washed with water. Tenquis in turn spoke a word and touched hands to his long vest, drawing Ekhaas's sword out of one of its magically expanded pockets.

THE TYRANNY OF GHOSTS

Geth, however, cocked his head to the side. "Shhh," he hissed.

They all froze instantly, Tenquis with the sword half out of his pocket, Ekhaas reaching for it, Chetiin with a hand ready to draw his dagger. Ekhaas strained her ears—and heard nothing.

"What was it?" she asked Geth.

"I thought I heard a song in answer to yours."

"An echo." Ekhaas hung her sword around her waist, then took one of the glowing rods. "Tenquis, help me." She raised the rod so that its light shone on the symbols carved beside one of the doorways—three circles of varying sizes, the largest containing a stylized axe, the next a fist, and the smallest a spindly-stalked mushroom. "We need to find a circle with a vertical line down the middle of it, like a cat's eye. That marks the way to the Vault of the Eye."

Ekhaas moved on to the next doorway. There was only one symbol here, a circle with its inside hollowed out to present an open surface. She tapped it with the end of the rod. "The first keepers knew from the experience of the Desperate Times how easily knowledge could be lost, so they created a system of guiding people through the vaults that needed only basic knowledge and logic."

Geth stared at the circular symbol and frowned. "How basic?"

"Something anyone would be familiar with, something that wouldn't change over time—"

"The moons of Eberron," said Tenquis from the other end of the hall. His voice held the excitement of discovery. He leaned close to the symbols on the nearest doorway. "This one with a double ring is Olarune, the Shield, isn't it? And this one with the pockmarks looks like Vult. And one that looks like an eye would represent Lharvion."

Ekhaas moved on to the next doorway. "We have older names for them, but yes. Each vault carries the name of a moon and each moon has a symbol." She pointed to the carvings on the first

73

door. "The dark spots on the face of Eyre reminded the *dar* of an axe. Zarantyr is the chief's moon because it's the most dominant. Dravago is the mushroom moon because it glows lavender like a certain kind of cave fungus."

"That's not exactly basic knowledge," Geth complained. "How is anyone but a goblin supposed to know that?"

Ekhaas turned to look at him. "Nobody but goblins are supposed to be down here."

"I've found the Eye," Tenquis called. They joined him beside a doorway that opened onto another flight of stairs. Once again there were three moon symbols beside the door, the slit eye of Lharvion carved at a medium size with a diameter as long as Ekhaas's thumb.

"What do the sizes of the symbols mean?" Chetiin asked.

"The number of vaults we pass through if we take this passage." She tapped a repetition of the hollowed out circle, the largest symbol beside the doorway. "First the Vault of the Night-Sun—Barrakas, the brightest moon—then the Vault of the Eye."

"What's the symbol for returning to the surface then?" asked Geth.

"There isn't one. You have to remember the way you came. Don't worry—I will."

Geth bared his teeth as they started down the stairs. "Grandfather Rat, it would be easy to get lost forever down here."

"I imagine," said Chetiin, "that was part of the first keepers' plan."

At the bottom of the stairs was another passage with more arched doorways, but only one interested Ekhaas: the one with the symbol of the moon Barrakas carved prominently over its peak. Her heart racing, she raised the ghostlight rod high and stepped through.

The walls of a cavern, roughly polished but still natural rock, spread off to either side. She could feel the space that opened up around her, but even goblin vision wasn't sufficient to see distant

THE TYRANNY OF GHOSTS

walls or ceiling through the darkness. The two ghostlights they carried were barely enough to illuminate a fraction of the cavern. That fraction was more than enough, though. The treasures of her clan surrounded them.

The statue of a hobgoblin woman, half-sized but perfectly detailed, watched them from a plinth. Ekhaas recognized a tribute to Jhazaal Dhakaan, the legendary *duur'kala* who brought six kings together to forge an empire. Beside the small statue rested a colossal head, worn into anonymity by exposure to the elements. A rack of spears, their shafts preserved by some magic but still so old that the wood was warped and crumbling. A chest, propped open with the ends of scrolls peeking out from under the lid. Another chest, this one tightly sealed, the attempt at security making Ekhaas wonder what secrets it contained. A suit of armor large enough for a bugbear but of the wrong proportions and crafted from sheets of stone and cloudy crystal rather than metal.

Tenquis stepped up to examine the armor—and froze, staring off into the darkness, before Ekhaas could speak. The stump of his tail stiffened. Hand on her sword, Ekhaas stepped quickly to his side.

Where ghostlight faded into darkness stood a horrific figure the size and shape of a lean hobgoblin but with horrible pits where eyes should have been. Thick tendrils hung like hair from its head and two tentacles reached over its shoulders above outstretched arms. Tentacles, tendrils, and arms were motionless though. The thing was dead, skinned and mounted like a hunting trophy centuries ago.

"A dolgaunt," said Ekhaas. "At the height of Dhakaan's power, Khorvaire was invaded by the forces of Xoriat, the Realm of Madness. The leaders of the invasion were the daelkyr. Some of their troops they brought with them from Xoriat. Others they crafted from the creatures of Eberron." She leaned closer to the eyeless face, feeling a sickening thrill from being so near. "It's said the first dolgaunts were made from hobgoblins."

"Why is it here?" Tenquis asked.

"History holds many lessons. Dhakaan won the Daelkyr War, but the war broke the empire. Whole cities were destroyed or corrupted. And even with the daelkyr defeated, their creations were still a danger."

"*Are* still a danger," Geth corrected her with a growl. He turned away from the dolgaunt. "Let's keep going."

A path led through the vault, winding among the treasures of ages like a forest trail among ancient trees. Where the path branched, tall iron markers with the moon symbol of the Eye pointed them on their way. Ekhaas could have stopped a dozen times to marvel at the artifacts that the Kech Volaar had accumulated, items slowly crumbling even as the Word Bearers tried to preserve them. A sense of time kept her going, though. Kitaas would wake eventually, and they had to be out of Volaar Draal—or at least out of the vaults—before then. They'd stopped at their quarters long enough to gather their gear and ready their packs for a fast flight. Once they were finished in the vaults, they would not be lingering in the city.

She felt a sudden pang of sorrow. What they were doing might save Darguun, but she would never be allowed to see these sights again. For the sake of the future, she was closing herself off from her past.

Ekhaas pressed her lips together and drew down her ears, trying to suppress the thought. She kept her eyes open, though, drinking in everything around her—until the cavern simply ended in empty space, the edge of a great chasm cutting through the rock.

"*Khaavolaar.*" Ekhaas slowed as they approached and studied the chasm's edge. It seemed stable. In fact, an old gantry of heavy timbers stood right at the edge. Ekhaas looked up and saw that the void of the chasm extended above them, too, a vast natural shaft. She had no idea where the shaft opened above them, but she could guess at its use. "This must be how particularly large artifacts are brought down into the vaults."

THE TYRANNY OF GHOSTS

"Something like a big stone stela couldn't exactly be brought down all the stairs we took, could it?" said Tenquis. A final iron marker was planted at the edge of the chasm. He strode right up to it and leaned over, holding out his rod. "There are stairs going down the wall of the shaft," he announced, then stretched a little farther. "I think I can see—"

His words were cut off in a sudden choking breath as he started to topple forward. Arms wheeling, he fought for balance.

Geth was behind him in an instant, grabbing the back of his vest and hauling him onto solid ground. The ghostlight rod wasn't so fortunate. It slipped from the tiefling's grip and plummeted into the chasm. Chetiin stuck his head over the edge and watched calmly as it fell. After a moment, he drew back. "About a hundred paces, maybe a hundred and twenty to the bottom."

Geth glared at Tenquis, who had the decency to look ashamed as well as frightened. "Sorry," he said. "I'm still getting used to not having a tail to balance me. Thank you."

"Try not to do it again," Geth said.

The loss of one rod made the darkness around them seem that much thicker. Ekhaas didn't relish the idea of climbing down the old stairs of the vault without better illumination. Fortunately, that was something she could take care of. Handing the last rod to Geth, she reached into herself and drew up a song. It was a simple magic, but useful; as her song rippled out, blossoms of light unfolded on the air in three floating globes.

Geth stiffened. "There!" he said. "You hear that?"

This time she did hear it—an echo to her song. Except that it was more than an echo. It was similar to her song, but darker and more of a counterpoint. The globes of light flickered like candles in a wind—but then the song was gone and the lights were steady.

Geth, Chetiin, and Tenquis all looked to her. Her ears went back. "Stay alert." With a flick of her fingers, she directed the globes to hover over her, Tenquis, and Geth, then cautiously led the way down into the shaft.

DON BASSINGTHWAITE

Ekhaas didn't normally have a problem with heights, but being suspended on the stairs as they switched back and forth along the wall of the gloomy void was unnerving. The dim glow of Tenquis's dropped rod seemed slow to draw near, and she half-convinced herself that she could still hear that eerie echo of her song over the sound of shuffling feet.

Then Chetiin, leading the way as the most surefooted of them, called back, "The shaft ends."

They were still well above the fallen torch. Ekhaas sent a globe of light drifting forward to Chetiin. It shone briefly on the rock wall of the shaft . . . then nothing. The shaft wall arced away, leaving the stairs to hang suspended in the air.

Just ahead of them, an arch curved above the stairs. On it was the symbol of a circle with a slit down the middle.

"Welcome to the Vault of the Eye," said Ekhaas.

Tenquis, still shaken by his near fall above, squeezed the narrow rail of the stairs so hard his knuckles turned pale. "Your ancestors couldn't have built the entrance at floor level?"

Seemingly undaunted by the dark space around them, Geth moved ahead to where the stairs emerged beneath the ceiling of the vault and leaned out over the rail. "It would be easier to know where we were going if we could see from up here," he said. He looked back at Ekhaas. "Can you make a brighter light?"

Her ears flicked. "I can," she said. "I'm not sure I should. Those echoes came when I sang magic."

"Maybe you can sing the spell softly?"

Ekhaas pursed her lips for a moment, then walked carefully forward to what she hoped was a good position. She drew a slow breath, let it out just as slowly, then drew another and sang a soft note. In her mind, she focused on building the song gradually, bringing it forth like dawn creeping across a mountain valley. Gray half-light first, then a pearly pink glow. Ekhaas held the song there for a moment, listening for the strange echo, but

THE TYRANNY OF GHOSTS

there was nothing. She let the magic flow again and pearly glow became red blush—then finally golden light flowed into the Vault of the Eye as if the sun itself had risen beneath Volaar Draal. The song faded into silence.

And there was still no hint of an echo. Ekhaas breathed easily and looked down.

Twenty paces below them, the artifacts of the Vault of the Eye spread out in a chaotic jumble. Her guess that the shaft had been used to lower large artifacts into the vaults seemed correct—massive statues, incredibly preserved war chariots, and huge chunks of masonry that must have been dragged away from Dhakaani ruins spread out around a clear space at the bottom of the shaft. The main vault was actually smaller than she'd expected, certainly smaller than the Vault of the Night-Sun, but the number of paths that led through the stored artifacts looked like the web of a very large spider. Passages and crevices opened in every wall of the vault.

"Grandfather Rat," muttered Geth. "It's going to take a long time to search through that."

"Maybe not," said Ekhaas. The Register entry had said that the stela was carved from white stone. Most of the collected artifacts below were the gray of weathered stone, or black or red, the colors typically favored by the *dar* for monuments. But across the vault, her conjured light reflected from a sliver of white nearly hidden behind a black obelisk.

"There," she said.

Once they were on the floor of the vault, the sense of vast space Ekhaas had felt above was replaced almost instantly by a feeling of being crowded by the large artifacts that towered over her. She pushed the sensation away, though, and hurried along the path that looked to lead most directly to the sliver of white. It turned and branched, but she used the black obelisk as a guide. Soon it loomed ahead of them, dominating the view ahead, until the path twisted around it. White stone flashed as they rounded the obelisk, then grew—and grew.

DON BASSINGTHWAITE

The Reward Stela of Giis Puulta was taller than the obelisk that had hidden it. It rested in a deep hollow in the floor of the vault, and while nearly a quarter of its full height was below the level of Ekhaas's feet, the rest of it towered the height of three tall hobgoblins over her head. The stone was a dazzling white that would have shone like a beacon under true sunlight. Ancient masons had cut it into a slab as wide as her outstretched arms but not even as deep as the blade of a shortsword. It was no wonder the effort had been made to transport it to the vaults—most such stela would have cracked into pieces over the centuries. At the top of both sides of the stela was an inscription in Goblin:

GIIS PUULTA
Emperor of Dhakaan
Sixth lord of the Second Puulta dynasty
rewards those who served him against the Rebellion of Lords.

Below the inscriptions, text carved in letters a finger's-length high marched down the two faces of the stela. Ekhaas's ears twitched back. There were dozens of names on the stela, each with a description of deeds performed and rewards granted, some with carved pictures and symbols as well. There was no telling where the historian Shaardat had found the passage regarding the breaking of *muut*.

"What now?" asked Geth.

"We read," said Ekhaas. "The bright light will last a little longer. The globes will last as long as we need them." Stepping into the hollow, she slid carefully down to the wide plinth that was the base of the stela and read the lowest—and smallest—line of text. "Banuu who cared for the mount of the emperor is rewarded with the slave who was the daughter of the lord of Em Draal." She grimaced and tilted her head back to stare up at the height of the stela. "We start at the top. I'll take this side. Tenquis, you take the other."

THE TYRANNY OF GHOSTS

"Is there anything in particular we should look for?" the tiefling asked, circling the monument.

"A longer passage of text, I imagine." Ekhaas grabbed Geth's hand as he reached down to help her up the side of the hollow. "Maybe something that puts the events of this rebellion into context—"

"I've found it."

Ekhaas twisted around so sharply, she almost fell back into the hollow. Geth's grip tightened, though, and she regained her feet. "What?" she called over her shoulder.

"I've found it. It's the first inscription on this side, right at the top. Whoever Tasaam Draet was, he was definitely more important than Banuu the stablehand."

She stumbled a second time. Geth and Chetiin both glanced at her, but she ignored them. Suddenly her stomach was twisting in knots. "The name on the inscription is Tasaam Draet?"

"Yes." She heard Tenquis mumble as he skimmed the text on the stela, then he read aloud in Goblin, "Tasaam Draet, who found *atcha* in this time when *muut* has been shattered is embraced as a brother to the emperor. The name of Draet will be inherited by his line. He is further rewarded with the fortress of Suud Anshaar and given the care of the symbols of *muut* forfeited by those lords whose treachery he has ended."

"*Khaavolaar*," Ekhaas said, half to herself. Geth raised his eyebrows in curiosity.

"Who was Tasaam Draet?" he asked.

"A butcher," said Ekhaas. "An avenging spirit. Children of the Dhakaani clans are told to obey their *muut*, or Tasaam Draet will come in the night and drag them down to the depths of Khyber. As we age, we learn to see him as something of a folk hero. According to more reliable stories, he was a real person, a commoner raised to the rank of a lord by the emperor and empowered to bring down any noble who dared rise against the imperial throne in the last days of the empire. He's reputed to have exterminated at least three noble lines—maybe more. The

stories say that the wails of those dying in his fortress of Suud Anshaar could be heard a night's journey away."

Geth wrinkled his nose. "And you call him a folk hero?"

"You invoke a trickster rat as a folk hero. The *dar* invoke a devoted warrior." Ekhaas shrugged and continued. "Tasaam Draet was so powerful, so full of *atcha* in his service to Dhakaan, that the last forces of the daelkyr made a target of him. One day travelers to Suud Anshaar found it utterly empty of life, with only a lingering taint of madness to hint at what had happened. Suud Anshaar was abandoned as cursed, and Tasaam Draet became a legend. It's said that the ruins of Suud Anshaar still stand deep in what's now the Khraal Jungle, the cries of those who died by Tasaam Draet's hand still echoing in the night. *Raat shan gath'kal dor*—the story stops but never ends."

"That doesn't shed any new light on the shattering of the Shield of Nobles, though," said Chetiin somberly. "Or on whether the inscription refers to *muut* as the shield or as the duty of nobles."

"Or maybe it does," said Tenquis, still on the other side of the stela, "Ekhaas, come look at this."

She went around the hollow, Geth and Chetiin following her. Tenquis looked up at the stela. He pointed and said, "There's the inscription." His hand moved lower. "What's that below it?"

Symbols carved into the stone ended the text in praise of Tasaam Draet—three rings with stretched slashes along the outside, like a sword blade bent into a circle with the notched edge out. Ekhaas knew them. In fact, she had recreated them on a battle standard for Dagii's army before the Battle of Zarrthec. "They're *shaari'mal*," she said. "The tearing wheels. They're an ancient symbol of Dhakaan."

"There's something written under them," said Tenquis.

Ekhaas squinted. There was something written there, the letters smaller than the surrounding text, almost too small to

THE TYRANNY OF GHOSTS

read from a distance. She thought she could make out one word though. *Shield*.

"We need to get closer," she said. "Chetiin, can you climb it?"

He looked at the stela and shook his head. Geth growled. "Then we stand on each others' shoulders," the shifter said. He rolled his shoulders, then climbed down into the hollow and put his back to the stela. "Tenquis first."

"Wait." Tenquis dug into one of the pockets of his vest and produced a piece of fine folded paper and a stick of charcoal. He gave them to Chetiin. "Lay the paper over the inscription, then rub the charcoal over it. It will make an impression of the inscription that we can take with us."

"I know how to make a rubbing," the old goblin said. "Try not to fall out from under me."

Geth crouched down. Tenquis stepped onto the shifter's bent knee, then carefully up onto his shoulders, facing the pillar so that he could brace himself against it with his hands. Geth gripped Tenquis's ankles and stood up slowly, breath hissing out between his teeth. When he stood straight, he paused for a moment to let Tenquis adjust his balance, then let go of him and reached down to make a stirrup of his hands for Ekhaas.

She put one foot into it and pushed off from the ground with the other. For a perilous moment her feet joined Tenquis's on Geth's shoulders. Then she grasped the tiefling's shoulders, wrapped one leg around his waist, and climbed up over his back. He groaned and breathed even harder than Geth had.

"Easy," Ekhaas whispered. "You can do it." She got one knee on his shoulder, then the other. His horns made the maneuver difficult.

"Just hurry," he wheezed.

She put her palms against the cool stone of the stela, digging her fingertips into the shallow grooves of the carved letters—*Muurazh who led the defense of the dungeons is rewarded with two swords from the emperor's hand and land before the walls of Zaal Piik*—before drawing up one foot . . .

At the bottom of their pile, Geth lurched suddenly. Ekhaas grabbed onto the stela, as did Tenquis below her. Geth gasped as he tried to recover, and without thinking, Ekhaas sang.

It was a reflexive action, with less magic about it than inspiration. She sang strength and steadiness, focus and will. Geth sucked in a great breath and managed to stand straight once more. So did Tenquis—she could feel him grow steadier under her, and she seized the opportunity to climb all the way up onto his shoulders.

But with the song came the echo, and this time it was distinctly louder and more insistent. And when she stopped singing, it persisted as if it had taken on a life of its own.

"Ekhaas!" said Geth through his teeth.

"I know." She ducked her head and peered under one arm at Chetiin. "Up!"

The goblin swarmed over Geth, then Tenquis as easily as if he were climbing a tree. When he passed over Ekhaas, she barely felt it. Then he was on her shoulders—and cursing.

"This is worse than from below," he said. "The angle is wrong."

The haunting song had drawn closer in just a few moments. It had changed, too, Ekhaas realized. It wasn't just one voice singing anymore. It was several, blended into an eerie chorus. It took all of her will not to turn her head and look around. "Chetiin," she said, fighting to stay calm, "can you climb from—"

Before she could finish, the summoned light that had lit the vault flickered and vanished. Darkness cloaked the cavern beyond the glow of her drifting orbs. The chorus seemed to grow stronger, and even the orbs flickered briefly. Tenquis hissed between his teeth.

"Don't move!" Ekhaas snapped. "Chetiin, how much farther?"

"A dagger's length. Hold still." One foot left her shoulder and planted itself on top of her head. Ekhaas stiffened her neck as

THE TYRANNY OF GHOSTS

Chetiin changed his perch as easily as if he were a bird. Ekhaas heard paper slapped onto stone and a rapid rubbing sound.

"Hurry," said Geth, his voiced strained. She felt him shift, trying to hold their weight.

"I almost have it," said Chetiin. Ekhaas counted heartbeats. One. Two. Three. Four—

"Done!" Chetiin said.

"Jump!" Geth gasped, and an instant later his support dropped out from under them. Ekhaas felt Chetiin's weight leave her head. She heard Tenquis yelp again and the unseen chorus rise as if in excitement. Guessing at where the edge of the hollow had been, she tried to push off from Tenquis's shoulders, from the stela, from anything that would push her away from the collapse.

It almost worked. Her back slammed into the slope of the hollow, driving the wind out of her. Her legs came down across someone else's back. For a moment, all Ekhaas could do was lie still, staring at sparks of light that had nothing to do with her floating globes and everything to do with a hard impact.

At least it was quiet. The haunting chorus was gone. The vault was silent.

A small shadow hovered over her. It touched her face and then—none too gently—slapped her. Ekhaas blinked and sucked in air. She rolled over—all of her limbs obeyed her and there was no sharp pain, which was a good sign—and glared briefly at Chetiin before looking down at the body under her legs. It was Tenquis. She felt a surge of relief to see that he was also rolling over. She looked for Geth and found him on his hands and knees at the base of the stela, chest heaving from exertion. She started to rise and go to him, but Chetiin grabbed her.

"No," he said. "Look!" He spun her around so that she faced up and out of the hollow.

It took her an instant to recognize what she saw. Six figures stood looking down at them. Six hobgoblin women wrapped in

tattered lengths of linen. Six hobgoblin women as thin as bones, their flesh translucent and shimmering with its own cold light.

One of them raised a skeletal hand and pointed at her. "Trespasser," she said in Goblin, in a voice that seemed like an echo of a song. "Thief. Defiler!"

CHAPTER SIX

16 Aryth

"No!" Ekhaas staggered to her feet. What were they? Some kind of spirits, but she'd heard no stories of ghosts in the vaults. "We're not thieves. I'm not a trespasser. I'm Kech Volaar." She thrust a hand back at Geth—Chetiin was urging him and Tenquis to their feet. "He bears Aram, the Sword of Heroes. He is worthy—"

"Defilers," said the ghost again, and this time the others echoed her in a hiss like a bow drawn across the strings of some otherworldly instrument. "Defilers! *Defilers!*"

The word rose into a crashing wave of song so powerful it almost drove Ekhaas back down to her knees. With it came a wave of shame and despair. She *was* a thief and a violator of these sacred vaults. She was a traitor to her clan. To her race. To all of the *dar*.

Somewhere behind her, Tenquis cried out, and Geth shouted her name. Ekhaas squeezed her hands into fists and ground her teeth together. No, she was neither thief nor traitor; none of them were. Face down as if she were walking into a blizzard, she breathed in through her teeth, then raised her head, and sang back at the ghosts.

She chose an anthem of Dhakaan, a song that spoke of need and valor. Her voice clashed with the chorus of the ghosts like a lone warrior taking on a squad of swordsmen. For a moment, the two songs struggled against each other, then the song of the

ghosts rose in strength and volume, pushing Ekhaas back. She staggered under the power of it. The glowing figures drifted forward, shrouded feet not quite touching the ground. Ekhaas clenched her fists, laid her ears back, and focused both her will and her voice.

Her song rose over the ghosts', hung in the air, then slashed down.

The ghosts' song vanished into silence. The spirits went with it, like a candle snuffed out or a chime muffled. The Vault of the Eye was still and—except for the heaving of her breath—silent once more.

It was so sudden that Ekhaas almost stumbled. Could she really have defeated the phantoms so easily?

Then, far off, she heard their song rise again. The ghosts had been dispersed but not destroyed.

"Horns of Ohr Kaluun," said Tenquis. "What are they?"

An idea had sprung into Ekhaas's head as she sang against the ghosts. "*Duur'kala*," she said, her voice rough from the effort she'd put into her song. "Long ago, we were buried in the vaults. But I had no idea . . ." She turned. "Chetiin—the inscription?"

The goblin was helping Geth to his feet, but one hand dipped into the front of his shirt and produced a piece of paper that was dark with charcoal. Ekhaas slid back down the slope of the hollow and snatched it from him. The paper was badly creased and the charcoal had been rubbed over it in haste, but it carried a clear imprint: part of the description of the reward given to Tasaam Draet, two of the three notched rings, half of another, and the words that had been inscribed beneath them.

THE NOBLES OF DHAKAAN NO LONGER HAVE A SHIELD TO HIDE BEHIND, FOR *MUUT* IS IN THE KEEPING OF TASAAM DRAET.

Her heart leaped. References to the shattering of *muut* and to a shield for nobles couldn't be a coincidence.

"What does it say?" demanded Geth.

Ekhaas read the inscription aloud. The shifter looked confused, then understanding flashed in his eyes. "The shattered

pieces of the Shield of Nobles," he said. "Tasaam Draet had them. His fortress—you said the ruins still stood. It could still be there."

Ekhaas nodded. "It's the best hope we've had so far!" Her ears twitched with the desire to climb back up the stela and see if anything else was recorded on it—

Another voice joined the ghostly chorus, this time from a different direction in the darkness. Far more than six ancient *duur'kala* had been buried in the vaults. Ekhaas swallowed her curiosity, roughly folded the paper once more, and stuffed it into a pouch on her belt. "We have to go."

They circled the stela and climbed up the side of the hollow closest to the path through the Vault of the Eye. Ekhaas paused briefly on the edge, watching and listening, then gestured for the others to follow. The echoing chorus of the ghosts was drawing slowly closer, and, she suspected, in greater numbers than they'd initially confronted. Would the ghosts follow them? She hoped not—they'd seemed attracted to her songs, which meant that their best weapon against the spirits would only draw more of them. If she didn't sing, maybe they would converge on the stela, and she and the others could slip away.

She moved as fast as she dared, trying to reverse the way back to the great shaft and the precarious stairs up to the Vault of the Night-Sun. Artifacts she'd made a point of marking in her mind looked strange from the other direction and under the thin light of the drifting globes. More than once, she had to turn around and walk backward to render them familiar. And always she was alert for the unnatural shimmer or approaching song of a ghostly presence. A dim glow appeared ahead, and her first instinct was to press herself into the shadow of a statue in case she could hide from the spirit. It took her a moment to realize that it was the ghostlight rod that Tenquis had dropped.

They'd made it back to the stairs. Ekhaas stepped out into the open, scanned the area one last time, then gestured for the others to go up the stairs ahead of her.

The chorus of the ghosts, muted, remained distant. As they reached the spot where the stairs met the ceiling of the vault, she looked back out onto the darkness, searching for the glowing forms, but there were none.

"Ekhaas!" rasped Chetiin. She whipped around. The others stood just below a narrow landing in the stairs, the first of the switchbacks as the stairs ascended. Ekhaas leaped up the last few stairs to join them.

Ahead of them was the arch over the stairs that marked the Vault of the Eye. Floating in silence beneath the arch was another *duur'kala* ghost. It watched them like a sentinel. Slowly a skeletal hand rose to point at them. A shroud-wrapped jaw opened—

"No," said Tenquis. "Not this time." His hands vanished into pockets on his long vest. One drew forth a slim wand. The other emerged with a pinch of silvery dust squeezed between his fingers. Taking a quick step forward, Tenquis flicked the dust at the ghost as his wand wove an arcane pattern.

For an instant Ekhaas smelled a sharp tang on the air, then the pinch of dust blossomed into a cloud around the ghost. Tiny flashes of lightning erupted in a miniature storm that lit up the ghost's translucent form from within.

It didn't even give the phantom pause. As song emerged from its gaping mouth, it swooped forward and stroked a hand along Tenquis's face in a gesture that seemed almost gentle.

There was nothing gentle in Tenquis's reaction, though. The tiefling staggered as if he'd been struck hard. He might have collapsed backward down the stairs if Geth hadn't been there to catch him. As the ghost pressed forward, Chetiin slipped past them, a dagger in his hand. Ekhaas caught the flash of the blue-black crystal embedded in the weapon's gray blade. It was the dagger he kept sheathed on his right forearm, the one called Witness that would trap a creature's soul when it struck a killing blow. But could it affect something that was already dead? The ghost swiped at Chetiin. He moved aside with graceful ease. The dagger darted out.

THE TYRANNY OF GHOSTS

And passed through the spirit with no more effect than Tenquis's spell. Chetiin's face tightened, and he slid away from another blow. "Ekhaas..." he said.

There was no choice. Ekhaas reached into herself and sang a counterpoint to the ghost's song. Ekhaas thought she saw a look of surprise on the ghost's withered face. It struggled, trying to match Ekhaas's song, but alone its hollow voice was no match for hers. The spirit twisted in on itself and vanished like a wisp of smoke.

But down in the vault, the chorus surged with renewed energy, a pack of spectral hounds on the trail. Ekhaas grabbed Tenquis's arm and helped haul him to his feet. His skin was cool to the touch, and his golden eyes were wide.

"Can you climb?" she asked him. He nodded. "Then do it."

The descent of the stairs along the shaft had been unnerving. The climb back up was grim, step after step, staying ahead of the song that pursued them. At first they raced, taking the stairs as quickly as they could. It couldn't last. Chetiin ran lightly, and Geth bounded on, his stamina extended by shifter-granted toughness, but Ekhaas and Tenquis tired. Every step became a cliff to be scaled. Ekhaas's legs and throat burned. After a time, Geth looked over the stair rail and back down the shaft.

"They're coming," he said.

"I can tell," said Ekhaas. The ghosts' song had swelled until it echoed in the shaft. "How fast?"

"Slow." He grimaced. "But they won't get tired."

"At least they're not flying," said Tenquis.

Geth dropped back to climb with them. "You've used magic to help us march faster before," he said to her.

She'd thought of the spell, too, and dismissed it. "They're drawn to my songs. We'd only have to fight more of them."

"Not if you can make us faster than they are."

Ekhaas pressed her lips together for a moment—then nodded. "Stay close," she warned.

She'd sung spells in battle many times. She'd sung spells in stealth. She'd sung a spell to inspire an entire army and

had almost turned the tide of a battle. Somehow, though, summoning up a song as she climbed the long stairs seemed harder than anything she'd ever done before. Her chest already ached at every breath. Darkness and the weight of a mountain pressed down around her. The angry spirits of ancient *duur'kala* pursued her, and the lives of three of her friends depended on her magic.

And yet she felt a strange flush of satisfaction as she focused her will and sang. She might never be welcome among her clan again, but she was doing something no Kech Volaar had dared to do before. If she and the others could break free, the tiny piece of knowledge that she carried might be the key to saving a nation.

Slapping her hands to set the rhythm and stomping down with every footfall to reinforce it, Ekhaas let the magic flow out of her. She didn't try to sing against the chorus of the ghosts this time. Instead she sang *with* it, as if their song were a wind and she were a boat running before it. Her climbing pace quickened. So did the others' as the magic swept them up. The stone steps raced past beneath them until it seemed as if even the floating globes that she had conjured for light might have trouble keeping up.

And if the chorus of the ghosts grew even stronger in response to her song, it just pushed them along a little faster. The whole shaft echoed and rang with the power of the songs sung within it.

Then they were breaking over the edge of the shaft like a wave breaking on a beach. The transition from racing up the stairs to running across the floor of the cavern made Ekhaas stumble a bit, but she recovered without losing the cadence of her song. They ran on, a little more slowly as the rough floor forced them to watch their steps and the twisting paths among the artifacts once again forced Ekhaas to try and recall the way through the vault back to the stairs that would lead them to safety. Which way to turn at the iron markers? Here left. There right.

She didn't even notice that the ghostly song they'd left behind in the shaft had been renewed until Geth shouted. She

THE TYRANNY OF GHOSTS

felt the hard grip of his gauntlet on her shoulder, thrusting her aside. A shimmering mask of death, mouth open in song, eyes sealed by untold ages, whirled past her. The ground seemed to rise up and slam into the entire length of her body.

The rhythm broke. The song ended—and another wailing song, angrier than ever, took its place. Ekhaas sucked in a gasping breath and rolled over, looking for the others. Tenquis and Chetiin hung back, wand and dagger at the ready, as they peered off into the darkness, but Geth . . .

Geth stood with Wrath drawn and poised. Before him, one of the ghosts swayed back and forth as if looking for an opening in his defense. Its fingers stroked the air. Its song sank down and wavered like a breeze.

It struck.

But Geth struck faster. Wrath spun in his grasp, cutting a sweeping arc through misty arm and insubstantial body. Radiance like fading twilight burst from the purple byeshk, the ancient magic of the blade biting deep. The ghostly *duur'kala*'s song rose in an inharmonious screech as the phantom crumpled in on itself and vanished. It was different from the way the ghosts slid away in reaction to her songs—there was a finality about it. This ghost would not be returning.

Geth shook cobwebby threads from Wrath's blade and grinned at Ekhaas, showing all his teeth. "At least we know Wrath can hurt them."

"Getting out is still a better option." The songs of more ghosts rose from all sides, converging on them. The ghosts had been the same ones that had pursued them from the Vault of the Eye or they might have belonged to the Vault of the Night-Sun—Ekhaas had no desire to find out. She spun around, trying to regain her bearings. They stood at an intersection of paths. The one carrying the moon symbol of the eye marked the way they had come. The way back to the stairs lay along . . .

She spun around again. And cursed. *"Khaavolaar!"*

"Which way, Ekhaas?" asked Chetiin tightly.

"Straight ahead!" said Tenquis. "I remember passing that war chariot."

Ekhaas looked down the path ahead. She recognized the war chariot, too, but they hadn't seen it from that angle before. She looked right, then left, then glanced at Geth. He shook his head.

"Go with your gut," he said.

She turned and plunged down the path on the left. She heard Tenquis curse behind her. "That's not the way!"

"It is!" Ekhaas snapped, then jumped back as another ghost came drifting out from behind a tall plinth, its song already merged with the others. Ekhaas heard Geth cry out, but the spirit swept down on her faster than she could move. A song swelled in her throat, and she sang back at it, wiping it away.

The chorus of ghosts swelled in response.

"I told you, not that way!" Tenquis started down the center path past the war chariot.

"There are ghosts everywhere, Tenquis," said Geth. He grabbed for the tiefling's arm, dragging him to a stop. "We need to follow Ekhaas's lead."

"And where has that gotten us? We're lost!"

Doubt whirled in Ekhaas's head. Was she heading the right way? Maybe Tenquis was right. The song of the ghosts went all the way through her, making it harder to think. The voices of her friends were almost drowned out by it.

Almost but not quite. "You're both wrong," Chetiin said harshly. "Blood of the clans, I don't know why I bother with you clumsy, stupid tallfolk."

For a moment, his words wiped away the song of the ghosts. Ekhaas turned to stare at her friends. She'd never heard Chetiin speak that way. Even if she suspected that was sometimes the way that the *shaarat'khesh* felt, she knew that he was too tightly disciplined to permit those feelings to show. Something was wrong. Geth and Tenquis had never argued like this before. And when had she ever felt such crippling doubt?

THE TYRANNY OF GHOSTS

The song of the ghosts had changed, she realized abruptly. The spirits weren't just mindless apparitions bent on punishment. There was a cunning about them. Earlier the ghosts had hit them with waves of despair and shame. That had failed so their attack had become more insidious, planting doubt and mistrust, turning them against each other.

Ekhaas drew two slow breaths, calming herself and shutting out the argument among Geth, Tenquis, and Chetiin. She listened to the song, trying to grasp the harmonies of it, the rise and the fall. Then she drew a third breath and sang.

The effort brought a fire to her chest. Her throat burned, but she forced herself to sing anyway. She didn't waste energy pouring strength and volume into the song—this wasn't a battle that would be won quickly. The ghosts had changed their tactics. She needed to change hers as well. She made her song bright and cheerful, a reminder of unity and hope. They would escape. The ghosts would not stop them.

Doubt fell away almost immediately, like a heavy pack stripped from her shoulders. She straightened, turned to the others, and extended her magic over them. The release from the ghosts' song was visible in their faces. Geth and Tenquis blinked and looked at each other in surprise, as if their fight had been something happening to other people. Chetiin's face tightened, expression wiped away, and Ekhaas could guess the shame he felt for what he'd said. She reached out to all three, gesturing urgently for them to follow her. Without the influence of the ghosts misleading her, she was certain that she'd chosen the correct path—and she had an uncomfortable feeling that the ghosts knew it too. Their song rose, clawing at the defenses she'd raised.

She denied them. It took all of her concentration to sing as she walked. Geth moved up to walk beside her, Wrath gripped tight in his hand, his eyes alert. Ekhaas didn't look back to see what Chetiin and Tenquis were doing, but she could feel them close behind. She could see the ghostly *duur'kala* all around

them, though. They drifted among the artifacts of the vault, hollow eyes upon her. Some of them whispered between the notes of their song.

Defiler. Thief. Traitor.

She could block the magic of their song, but it was harder to ignore the simple malignance of their words. She poured herself into her own song, reminding herself of why she was doing this and for whom, but the fate of Darguun and vengeance against Tariic seemed like distant things. Even if Tariic was defeated and Darguun saved, the Kech Volaar would not take her back. She would be alone.

No. A face rose in her mind—a gray-haired, gray-eyed young warlord who called her "wolf woman" and who shared his honor with her. She wouldn't be alone because she would have Dagii.

A ghost hissed with sudden rage and lunged at her. Geth intercepted it, lashing out with Wrath. The wisp of a shroud fell to the ground and faded away.

Ekhaas kept walking and singing. She could feel sweat cold on her forehead and through her hair. Where were the stairs?

Then she spotted the nightmare figure of the stuffed dolgaunt and felt a moment of hope. Beyond the creature's unmoving tentacles stood the strange armor of stone and crystal. Beyond that, the monument to Jhazaal Dhakaan. And beyond that . . .

A line of ghostly *duur'kala*, spectral flesh even more decayed than that of the ghosts who harried them. The dark arch of the stairs leading up out of the vaults pierced the wall just behind the silent ghosts, but it might has well have been leagues away. There was an air of tremendous age about the spirits, and Ekhaas knew, somewhere deep in her gut, that in life these *duur'kala* had been among the first to store their secrets in the vaults, had been the first to dwell in Volaar Draal, had perhaps been the first to call themselves Kech Volaar.

And they hadn't yet joined in the chorus of their sisters.

Geth saw them too. "Tiger's blood," he murmured. He turned and looked behind them. "They're all around us, Ekhaas."

THE TYRANNY OF GHOSTS

One of the ancient *duur'kala* raised a withered hand.

The chorus of the ghosts ended. For a moment, Ekhaas sang alone in the dark, her song thin in the sudden silence. The ancient *duur'kala* stepped forward. Ekhaas braced herself for their song, her own trailing off into a whisper. Geth raised Wrath, ready to attack. In unison, the old ghosts opened their mouths—

—and instead of singing, they drew breath.

It was like being caught in a gale that pulled at her rather than pushed. Ekhaas felt the air sucked right out her lungs. She choked and struggled to catch her breath, but there was no air to breathe—it rushed past her into the gaping mouths and bottomless, undead lungs of the ghosts. Dark spots filled her vision almost instantly. Tenquis wheezed and stumbled against her. Geth lifted Wrath and charged but only managed a couple of steps before his legs buckled and gave out. Ekhaas struggled to stay on her feet, fighting panic as she tried to think of some defense.

Nothing came, and still the ghosts consumed the air of the vaults. Ekhaas's eardrums popped, and sounds became muffled and distant. Her vision became more dark than bright. Even the glowing specters became shadowy silhouettes, outlined by what seemed a brighter glow from behind them.

A glow that came from the archway. A glow with figures— real, solid figures—in it.

"By the glory of Dhakaan, cease!" The throbbing in Ekhaas's ears rendered the ringing words as hollow echoes. "I speak for the Kech Volaar. Great mothers of the dirge, cease!"

As her vision dimmed to darkness, Ekhaas saw Tuura Dhakaan and, at her side, the black-robed figure of Diitesh. The High Archivist had her arms raised, a curiously carved block of stone clutched in her hands. "I hold the Seal of the Eternal Bond!" she screamed, trying to match Tuura's rolling tones— and failing. "Great mothers, cease. The vaults are safe."

However weak Diitesh's command might have been, it was effective. The terrible pull ended. Air rushed in to fill the

vacuum. Ekhaas drew in a shuddering breath and blinked, trying to clear the spots from her eyesight so she could see what was happening. The ancient ghosts had turned to regard Tuura and Diitesh and the handful of others who stood behind them. Guards, Ekhaas saw, and archivists. They huddled back, leaving only Tuura and Diitesh to face the ghosts. Diitesh raised the thing in her hands again.

"Go!" she commanded. "Begone."

Tuura's voice became more soothing. "Great mothers, you do your duty. Return to your rest." She bent her head before the ancient ghosts, and, after a moment, they returned the gesture.

Then they were gone, fading back into the shadows and all of the ghosts along with them. When Tuura looked up, her eyes were squarely on Ekhaas. They narrowed. Her ears flattened, and her lips pulled back in anger.

Ekhaas's heart sank.

A figure moved out from among the soldiers and archivists and took up a position at Diitesh's side. Scorn and triumph twisted Kitaas's face. "As I told you," she said to Tuura.

The leader of the Kech Volaar said nothing, just flicked one finger. Before Ekhaas and the others could even stand, they were surrounded. Again.

CHAPTER SEVEN

17 Aryth

Tariic wanted to break her spirit. Ashi knew it from the way he watched her. Whenever they were in the same room, his eyes were on her like the eyes of a dragon. *There is no escape*, said that gaze. *Your resistance only makes the wait more interesting.*

The possibility that he might succeed frightened her. Usually the sickening dread of it went away each morning as the renewed clarity of her dragonmark's power settled over her mind. On the days that it didn't, she did her best to ignore the possibility. Tariic wanted to see her proud and angry, like a great cat pacing the confines of a cage. Ashi found it easy to give that to him. She stalked the halls of Khaar Mbar'ost, fury surrounding her like a cloud. Even her hobgoblin escorts took to following a pace or two back. Everyone else slipped out of her way, finding somewhere else to be. When she was called on to perform the duties that Breven d'Deneith had placed upon her, she performed with detachment. What did it matter? Warlords and clan chiefs were all under the spell of the Rod of Kings anyway. They cared about the bond between Darguun and Deneith only as much as Tariic told them to.

No one commented on the bright silver cuffs she wore. No one except Pradoor.

"I'm told you have been presented with jewelry," the old goblin priestess had cackled when Ashi had come across her one afternoon. "Come here. Let me touch them and feel the cool metal."

Ashi had been tempted to let her feel the cool metal in a blow across her withered face. The cuffs prevented her from attacking Tariic, but would they prevent her from attacking his associates? She'd restrained herself, though. Anything she did would find its way back to Tariic. Let him think he'd won this small victory. She'd held out her arm and let Pradoor run gnarled fingers over the silver.

On rare days she ventured out of Khaar Mbar'ost. If anyone noticed that she did so only under the hard gaze of the warrior Oraan, they didn't say anything.

It was surprisingly easy to stop thinking of Aruget as "Aruget" and to take up calling him Oraan. His personality had altered along with his face—in imitation of the true Oraan, she supposed. It was difficult even in their private conversations to get him to acknowledge his former identity. "Why did you come back?" she'd asked him once. "Tariic knows you're a changeling. Midian told him everything."

"Tariic knows Aruget was a changeling and a Dark Lantern of Breland. Someone like that would have fled back to his masters. That's what Tariic will expect. Will he think of looking for another changeling under his nose? I've never met Aruget. I had nothing to do with him."

The first time they left Khaar Mbar'ost, they were followed. "Don't look," Oraan had said as they walked down one of Rhukaan Draal's busy, twisting streets. "Midian's on our trail."

Ashi had made no effort to evade him or even to pick him out of the crowd. The whole day's expedition was only a show anyway. She wandered the streets, strolled through Rhukaan Draal's infamous Bloody Market. The city had changed in the short time since Tariic had taken the throne of Darguun. Under Haruuc, all manner of races had walked shoulder to shoulder with *dar* in the streets. They were still there—elves, halflings, humans, dwarves, even an occasional warforged or eladrin—but they walked with caution while the goblins, hobgoblins, and

THE TYRANNY OF GHOSTS

bugbears carried themselves with a pride that bordered on arrogance.

"Tariic doesn't need to use the Rod of Kings for it to have an influence," she'd remarked softly. She glanced sideways at Oraan. "Don't you feel it?"

"I feel it," he said, almost without moving his lips. "But unless he gives me a direct order, I can resist it."

"I could protect you from it."

"No. Better that my reactions are genuine. If Tariic suspects anything, he'll act. He has to believe he's cut you off from allies and has you in his power. Head down to the river and look across it. Let Midian see you pining for escape."

The next time Ashi saw Midian and Tariic together, they both seemed triumphantly jovial. The next time she and Oraan left Khaar Mbar'ost, they were trailed again, but not by Midian. The third time they went out into the city, they weren't trailed at all.

○ ○ ○ ◎ ○ ○ ○

A thin fog had risen from the river overnight and settled over the city. From her window, Ashi could see Rhukaan Draal only as a ghost of itself, gray and damp under a weak sun that struggled to break through the clouds. She would have enjoyed going out anyway, but when Oraan entered her chambers to begin his turn as her guard, his eyes flicked meaningfully to her boots.

She straightened. "I will go walking today."

The distaste that wrinkled his face and curled his ears seemed startling genuine. "I obey the lhesh's command," he said sullenly.

They weren't followed. Ashi's trips out of Khaar Mbar'ost had apparently become innocuous in Tariic's eyes. Still, Ashi waited until the red fortress had become an indistinct shape in the mist before she asked Oraan, "Where are we going?"

"To inspect potential mercenaries."

She let the mysterious answer pass. Guided by signals from Oraan—who still checked the thin crowds behind them for signs of pursuit—they followed a winding route through the streets. Ashi would have been entirely lost except for the smell of the river growing slowly stronger as they walked. The buildings around her were unfamiliar. This wasn't an area of the city she had visited before. She heard a sound she recognized, though— the clash of weapons, of warriors training.

It came from the other side of a high, featureless wooden palisade that Oraan followed. Whatever the structure was, they seemed to be on the back side of it. Then a narrow door emerged from the fog and with it the figure of a hobgoblin warrior. A warrior she recognized, though she had never met him in person.

Keraal, warlord of the rebellious Gan'duur clan until Dagii had defeated him and who came to serve the young lord of Mur Talaan, glanced at her without surprise, then moved out of her way. The chain that he had adopted as his personal weapon and that he carried wrapped around his torso clanked softly, but he said nothing.

"Enter," said a familiar voice from behind her. Ashi looked over her shoulder to find Aruget wearing Oraan's armor. The changeling had changed his face as they walked. He flicked his ears at her. "We're expected."

The door opened onto a short hall with several closed doors. The place smelled of sweat and close living. Aruget took the lead, climbing a flight of stairs to an upper floor and knocking on a door at the top. He paused, then knocked again.

The door opened to reveal Dagii. His ears, already standing high, twitched. "Blood of Six Kings. Ashi, it's good to see you again!"

Goblin etiquette frowned upon touching except between family members in private, but the relief Ashi felt at seeing a friendly face was so powerful that she almost threw her arms around Dagii. She'd glimpsed him frequently in Khaar Mbar'ost,

THE TYRANNY OF GHOSTS

but there had always been a distance between them, an awareness of Tariic's attention. Ashi suddenly almost felt free. She managed to hold herself to a smile and a deep nod of her head as she passed through the door. Dagii returned both and even nodded to Aruget before closing and bolting the door.

The room at the top of the stairs was a combination briefing room and bedchamber, as if a field commander's tent had been moved indoors. Wide windows had been shuttered, but from beyond them she could once again hear the sounds of warriors training. She could guess where she was—the barracks of the Iron Fox company, the remains of the army that Dagii had led against Valenar raiders in the Battle of Zarrthec.

Dagii wasn't the only one in the room, though. Ashi started as Senen Dhakaan rose from a chair to greet her. "Lady Ashi."

Ashi looked from her to Dagii, then came to rest on Aruget. "How—?"

"Careful work and patience," he said. "What did you think I'd been working toward? It's going to take more than two of us to bring down Tariic."

"It will likely take more than four." She took Aruget's arm and drew him close. "Do they know?"

"That I'm an agent of Breland?" His lips pursed slightly and she understood the warning. *Say no more.* "Yes. Tariic's ambitions pose a danger to all of us."

"We've met with Aruget before, Ashi," said Dagii. He took one of the chairs. He motioned for the others to sit as well. "He brought Senen and me together. We wanted to include you from the beginning, but he made us see that the time wasn't right."

"If Tariic suspects anything, he'll act," Ashi said. Oraan's words to her. She looked between Dagii and Senen again, feeling a comfort she hadn't felt in days. "Has there been any news from Geth and Ekhaas?"

Senen shook her head, offering Dagii the same apologetic glance she gave Ashi—of course, Ashi realized, he would be waiting for word from Ekhaas as well. "They reached Volaar

Draal and were granted sanctuary. That's all Tuura Dhakaan told me. She's wary of raising Tariic's suspicions as well."

Ashi grimaced. "So we're all paralyzed by fear of what Tariic might do?" she asked. "How are we supposed to stop him if we're too afraid to act?"

Senen's ears lay back at her challenge. Even Dagii frowned. "Every battle requires a strategy. Every strategy requires intelligence. We begin by gathering intelligence. Before we do anything, we need to know exactly what Tariic is up to." He leaned forward and pulled around a map of Darguun so that Ashi could see it. "Tariic doesn't trust me like he used to, but I've managed to learn a few things. Here's Zarrthec"—he pointed to a dot on the map, then moved his finger and traced the long wavering line of Darguun's eastern border—"and this is the Mournland. The Valenar elves who survived the Battle of Zarrthec fled east. We didn't attack their camp in the Mournland, so we can assume it's still there. With the airships of House Lyrandar to supply them, the surviving Valenar could rally and attack again. Tariic has been increasing the presence of troops along the border of the Mournland against that possibility."

Ashi studied the map. "That seems surprisingly sensible for Tariic."

"It might be," said Aruget, "except that I have contacts with the warriors and scouts of the army and they haven't reported any sign of Valenar returning from the Mournland."

Ashi suspected that the changeling had simply donned a new face and done some eavesdropping. She kept that idea to herself however. "Have they scouted the Valenar camp?"

Aruget shook his head. "The mists that form the border of the Mournland are unpredictable—no scout has managed to relocate the Valenar camp to confirm whether it still exists. Either we're being fooled by the mists, or the elves have returned to Valenar—in which case there *is* no enemy."

Ashi considered the map again and a mad idea occurred to

THE TYRANNY OF GHOSTS

her. So mad it might have occurred to Tariic himself. "Could Tariic be planning a counterattack on Valenar?" she asked. The stretch of the Mournland that lay between Darguun and Valenar was relatively narrow. A madman or a tyrant might try marching a force through the nightmare landscape.

"Not even Tariic would be that crazy," said Dagii. "It would be a massacre. Any troops that survived the Mournland would be easy prey for the Valenar on the other side. Besides, his forces are spread out, not concentrated for a swift strike east. And there's more." He nodded to Senen, who took up the thread of evidence.

"I've heard it spoken in Khaar Mbar'ost that Tariic is demanding tribute of the Ghaal'dar clans of the lowlands and of the loyal Marguul tribes of the mountains." Her ears flicked. "Tribute in the form of coins and gems."

The disgust in her voice was biting. Ashi waited for her to explain further but there was nothing. The ambassador of the Kech Volaar sat back as if she'd already proved her case. Ashi raised an eyebrow. "In the Five Nations, that's called taxes."

"But it's not how things are done among the *dar*," said Senen. "Tribute is paid in service or possibly goods, not with money. That is the way it has always been."

"Maybe Tariic is trying something new."

"At the same time he clings to the old?" asked Dagii. "He levies warriors from the clans as well. With the power of the Rod of Kings behind him, no one in the assembly of warlords says no."

"He spent a lot of money buying popularity among the people after Haruuc's death. Maybe he's trying to replenish the treasury," Ashi suggested. "He must have debts."

"He doesn't pay them," said Senen. "His creditors meet with him and go away with full smiles but empty hands."

Ashi wrinkled her nose. "The rod again. What's he doing with the money then?"

"Deneith isn't the only dragonmarked house he courts favor with."

"But Deneith is the only house interested in what Darguun

has to offer—" She broke off as she realized what Senen was really saying. "He's *buying* from the other houses."

"And they seem to appreciate the business," said Dagii. "Tariic needs money because he might be able to control the local viceroys and envoys with the rod, but the lords of the houses beyond Darguun would notice if debts went unpaid. But we haven't been able to find out what he's buying. We need someone who can move among the viceroys."

"Me," Ashi said. Her part in the gathering of intelligence fell into place. "I'm not exactly in demand at the enclaves of the other houses right now, though."

"You underestimate yourself," said Senen, leaning forward. "The viceroys inquire after you. Vounn's murder is still the subject of much speculation and—forgive my bluntness—no one was closer to her at that moment than you."

A vague feeling of nausea swirled at the back of Ashi's throat. "You want me to use Vounn's death to get close to the representatives of the other dragonmarked houses."

"It sounds dishonorable to her memory," Dagii said, "but it is for a greater good. I think Vounn might have approved."

Ashi gave him a hard glare. Aruget's ears dipped. "There are other ways, Ashi. All you need to do is find out what Tariic wants from the other houses—and you are the one of us with the best chance to do it."

She turned her glare on the changeling. "You brought me here to ask me this?"

To her surprise, Aruget looked to Senen and Dagii. Senen sat stone-faced. Dagii's ears flicked, then flicked again. "Not entirely," he said. "If we could have, we would have waited longer. But we had to move today. Something happened last night."

It was probably a mark of how much time she'd been spending around hobgoblins that she almost felt as if her ears perked up. "What?"

Dagii rose and went over to the shuttered windows. Easing one open just a little way, he gestured for her to look outside.

THE TYRANNY OF GHOSTS

The window overlooked a wide yard of beaten earth. At first glance, she saw only ranks of hobgoblin soldiers performing drills while others practiced combat in small groups. Across the courtyard, she recognized the standard of the Iron Fox. There was another standard beside it, though—an upright sword blade mounted within a ring at the end of a pole. But if there was a second standard on display . . . Ashi looked at the soldiers in the yard again.

There were two groups, she realized. They trained together, but not as comrades. In fact, one of the groups appeared to be thoroughly dominating the other in every combat and at every drill. The losing soldiers looked like those she was familiar with seeing around Rhukaan Draal—warriors from disparate clans united in a military company. Many of them wore the sign of the Iron Fox.

The dominant soldiers were different. They were subtly bigger. They were better armed and armored. They had a unified look, as if they'd all received the same training since they were young. Since they were *very* young, judging by the way they fought and moved. Many of them bore brands on their faces that resembled the sword blade standard.

"Kech Shaarat," said Senen softly from over Ashi's shoulder. "Warriors from another of the Dhakaani clans. They arrived last night."

"Tariic instructed them to take quarters here with the Iron Fox," Dagii said. "They claim that they're here to aid the patrols against the Valenar." He closed the shutter.

"Are they?" asked Ashi.

"Fight the Valenar? Perhaps," said Senen. "Patrol under the command of lowland clans? Never." Her ears bent. "Something is going to happen. That's why we needed to talk to you today. Will you do it, Ashi? Will you find out what Tariic wants with the dragonmarked houses?"

"Will you do it for Vounn's memory?" asked Dagii.

Ashi's jaw tightened. "I will."

DON BASSINGTHWAITE

Aruget didn't want to stay at the barracks too long, and they left quickly. On the street, he became Oraan once more, reassuming the demeanor of a resentful guard escorting his willful charge on a damp morning. For appearances, Ashi continued her walk down to the river's edge before turning back to Khaar Mbar'ost. The wandering gave her time to think. How best to approach the viceroys of the other dragonmarked houses? If Senen was right—and she probably was—they would be eager to gossip with her, but Ashi was certain they would also be tight-lipped about their dealings with Tariic. Approaching one before the others would also raise their suspicions and close their mouths. She needed a way to greet all of them casually at or around the same time.

The opportunity came more easily than she had hoped. As she turned the corner of the hallway outside her chambers, she found two figures waiting for her. One was another of her escorts, Woshaar, ready to take over the duty of watching her—Oraan nodded to him, released her into his care, and departed without even glancing at her. He played his role flawlessly.

The other was a goblin wearing the red corded armband that indicated his service to the lord of Khaar Mbar'ost. "Lhesh Tariic sends a message to Lady Ashi d'Deneith," he said. "There will be a feast tonight in the hall of honor. You will attend."

The command drew out a flash of anger, even if the feast was the answer she was looking for. The viceroys and envoys would attend, and she could move among them without her conversations seeming out of place. She bit back her anger. "Tell Lhesh Tariic I am honored," she said.

"He does not wish a reply." The goblin bowed and departed.

Ashi's anger burned a little higher. She turned on Woshaar. "I require hot water and a bathing tub. Demand them of the next servant that passes."

THE TYRANNY OF GHOSTS

She had the satisfaction of seeing a startled expression on the guard's face before she marched into her chambers and slammed the door behind her.

When she had first come to House Deneith and Vounn, one of the house's most talented ambassadors, had begun the task of turning a barbarian hunter of the Shadow Marches into a proper lady of Deneith, Ashi had chafed at her mentor's lessons. Particularly those on dress and style. What was the use, she had thought then, of knowing which kinds of sleeves and collars were in fashion, or of knowing that yellow didn't suit her complexion? Understanding the value of what Vounn taught her had come slowly. Too slowly maybe, Ashi suspected. She'd eventually made her peace with Vounn, and they'd found a respect for each other, but there were some things Ashi hadn't really found a true appreciation for until after Vounn's death. The value of masking her true emotions. The necessity of submitting to demands in the short term with an eye on the future.

The potential power in her own appearance.

She emerged from her chambers as the sun set, striding past Woshaar without pause. Her escort fell in close behind her, and turning her head slightly, Ashi caught him giving her surreptitious glances. He seemed to carry himself with more pride than she'd seen before as well, as if suddenly she was worth keeping watch over. He wasn't the only one whose reaction changed at the sight of her. Servants looked away from her, turning their faces to the ground. Hobgoblin warriors whom she recognized from their service around Khaar Mbar'ost glanced at her, and then looked back and stared. She passed a warlord, Iizan of the wealthy Ghaal Sehn clan, on his way to the feast and deep in conversation with another clan chief. Iizan actually paused, mouth closed, eyes wide, to watch her go by. Ashi raised her head and swept on, up the broad stairs of Khaar Mbar'ost to the hall of honor, the vast chamber that ran from one side of the fortress to the other.

She wore the clothes that Vounn had given her for their first presentation to Haruuc only three months before. A gown

suitable for a feast in the Five Nations would do little to impress the goblins of Darguun, so the outfit resembled a parade uniform with polished boots, trim trousers, and a cropped jacket bearing the crest of House Deneith in silver thread. Her sword hung from a belt likewise trimmed with silver. But tonight the Darguuls weren't the only ones she wanted to impress, and Ashi had taken more care with her hair than she'd ever taken in her life. Washed and brushed, it shone like old gold. She'd pulled it back in a style that was stern but not severe. Commanding, Vounn had called it. Ashi had even raided the small pots of cosmetics her mentor had left. The patterns of the dragonmark that curled over her cheeks made rouge ridiculous, but a light hand with powders around her eyes gave her gaze a startling intensity.

She was a lady of Deneith, and none of the envoys of the other dragonmarked houses could dare deny it.

Ashi paused in the doorway of the hall of honor just long enough for those near the door to get a good look at her—and for her to scan the vast room for familiar faces. The hall was crowded. A long table ran much of the hall's length, taking up space, but even so there were more bodies present than could have sat at it. That was tradition at hobgoblin feasts, she'd learned. Important guests sat and were served. Less important guests lingered on the fringes.

She spotted Pater d'Orien and Dannel d'Cannith. They would make a good place to start her inquiries. Ashi took a goblet of wine from a passing servant and moved into the crowd to join them.

She didn't get far. A hand reached out from among the shifting bodies and caught the hem of her jacket. "You've put an effort into looking your best tonight, Ashi," said Midian.

Disgust mingled with fear raced through her, but she kept it from her face. Did Midian somehow know what she was up to? Had the puppet already told his master? Ashi forced herself to answer. "Tariic commanded my presence, and I am the face of Deneith in Rhukaan Draal, aren't I?"

THE TYRANNY OF GHOSTS

She poured acid into the words as if her appearance was just some attempt to defy Tariic's power. It seemed to work. Midian's eyes narrowed briefly, and he gave a mocking little bow.

"Your clothes complement your bracelets," he said. "I'm sure people will be asking about them all night."

"Blood in your mouth, Midian."

"Now, now. No need for obscure Shadow Marches insults, as colorful as they might be." He took her hand. "There are people you need to meet."

"I don't think so." Ashi tried to take her hand back.

Midian clung to it like a clam to a rock—not with any particular strength but with a determined attachment. "I do. You're the face of Deneith after all."

Ashi threw a glance at Woshaar, standing poised in her shadow, and briefly wished Oraan were the one with her tonight, then realized how pointless that would be anyway. In a room full of witnesses, Oraan would do nothing to betray himself. He would do the same thing as Woshaar—follow blank-faced as Tariic's royal historian dragged her off into the crowd. She caught another glimpse of Pater d'Orien and Dannel d'Cannith watching as well, probably jealous of the special favor she was being shown.

Ashi gave in and let Midian lead her. She'd have another chance with Pater and Dannel. This might even give her a better chance to talk to them. They'd want to know whom she had met. Through the crowd, she caught the eye of Dagii and, a moment later, Senen. The gaze of the ambassador of the Kech Volaar slid over her without acknowledging her presence, but Dagii's gaze lingered for just an instant. His lips pressed tightly together, and his ears flicked back.

Danger.

Ashi's belly tightened even as Midian brought her to a stop beside a knot of unfamiliar hobgoblins kept apart from the members of Tariic's court not so much by physical space as their own haughty presence. Warlords and clan chiefs moved around

the strangers like a pack of dogs around new and stronger interlopers, watching but not yet ready to approach. As if he stood outside of any forces of status, Midian spoke directly to the two hobgoblins at the center of the knot, a massive male whose armor bore the face of a demon and a woman wearing a blue-edged mantle. Both carried sword-shaped brands on their foreheads.

"Lady Ashi d'Deneith," said Midian in Goblin, "meet Taak Dhakaan and Riila Dhakaan of Kech Shaarat."

CHAPTER EIGHT

17 Aryth

Humans, in Midian's experience, tended to imagine themselves as if they were looking in a mirror that extended from their waist to about a handspan above their eye level. They never really considered what they might look like when seen from outside—particularly from below—that point of view. Hobgoblins, used to dealing with goblins, tended to be more aware. But humans, no matter how frequently they took the time to look a gnome in the eye, usually forgot that a gnome looked back.

"Introduce Ashi to the Kech Shaarat," Tariic had said. "See how she reacts."

"Lady Ashi d'Deneith," said Midian, "meet Taak Dhakaan and Riila Dhakaan of Kech Shaarat."

He watched Ashi closely, watched the little muscles under her jaws that most humans weren't even aware of, as she looked over the representatives of the Kech Shaarat. Those muscles twitched, just slightly. Reaction to Riila and Taak's names then, Midian wondered, or just to their presence as Kech Shaarat?

The latter, he decided, as Ashi slowly bent her head to the hobgoblins. If she knew the names, her neck would have been stiffened by fear or maybe disdain. It wasn't. The nod was cautious, deep enough to indicate respect, not so deep as to suggest submission.

She was in for a surprise.

Riila responded with a nod so shallow it was almost an insult. Taak didn't even nod at all, but just looked Ashi over as

if he were evaluating a horse. Whatever he saw seemed to give him some satisfaction, because he snorted and said, "You would give me a good fight, Ashi of Deneith."

Ashi's eyebrows rose, then drew together. Her hand dropped to her sword. "Name the place, and I'll meet you there," she answered with surprising savagery, meeting strength with strength. Midian almost found himself admiring the strategy.

Taak didn't exactly smile, but a certain respect seeped through his arrogant expression. His ears flicked just slightly. "I had heard House Deneith lets others do its fighting for it."

"No hand wields my sword but mine," said Ashi.

An uneasy feeling crept up Midian's back, and he looked around. Others nearby had started to notice the confrontation. Not that a dozen similar exchanges hadn't already happened around the hall. Challenges and posturing weren't uncommon whenever hobgoblins gathered, but none of the previous exchanges had spilled over into actual violence. Those involved knew better. But a warrior of the Kech Shaarat and a human of Deneith . . .

Tariic had wanted Ashi introduced to Taak and Riila. He didn't want an open fight. Trying to find soothing words, Midian edged a little closer, fingers stiff and ready to deliver a numbing poke if words weren't enough.

Riila, however, spoke before he could. "Taak, stand down! Respect our host."

Her tone left little doubt about who was in charge. Taak didn't seem to resent the reprimand. His ears flicked again, more vigorously this time. His thin lips twitched as well, and he tipped his head to Ashi in the tiniest of nods.

Riila moved in to take his place. "Taak honors you," she said.

"And I honor him," said Ashi. "The skill of the Kech Shaarat is legendary." Her hand finally left her sword. Onlookers turned away with an audible grumble of disappointment. Midian let his fingers relax.

Only to tense them again as Ashi asked, "What brings Kech Shaarat to Rhukaan Draal?"

THE TYRANNY OF GHOSTS

The question was innocent—but something in the way it was asked brought Midian's eyes back to Ashi's face. Still hard from confrontation, it revealed nothing. Fortunately, neither did Riila's, though Midian caught Taak's quick glance at his counterpart. Riila ignored it and answered smoothly, "We come to celebrate Lhesh Tariic's victory over the elves of Valenar, ancient enemies of Dhakaan. We extend the friendship of the Kech Shaarat to a great leader of the *dar*."

Someone less attentive might have missed the suspicion that flickered across Ashi's face—but Midian saw it and alarm crept up his back again. Maybe she knew something after all. Delicate as a spider testing its web, he said, "Kech Shaarat are frequently in Rhukaan Draal, Ashi. We saw Kech Shaarat bladedancers in the arena during Haruuc's funeral games."

Ashi looked down at him. There was calculation in her eyes, and Midian felt an answering stir in his guts. Maybe Ashi could stare down Taak, but a game of deception wasn't one she was going to win. He smiled sweetly at her.

"You're right," she said after a moment, and looked back to Riila. "They fought very well too. But I didn't mean you or a handful of bladedancers. I was out in the city today, and I saw quite a number of Kech Shaarat. Are you all here to celebrate victory over the Valenar?"

For a moment, their little group seemed like a bubble of silence among the noise of the hall—then Taak snorted again. Loudly. He gave Ashi a huge grin. Riila smiled, too, though she showed fewer teeth doing it. Midian even found himself smiling. The game was over before it had begun.

"Ah, Ashi," he said and it was difficult to keep the purr out of his voice. He felt almost ridiculous for having worried about what she might or might not know. Ashi's face turned red beneath her dragonmark. Her mouth opened briefly, then pressed into a narrow line. Midian took her hand, holding tight when she would have pulled away. "You worry about entirely the wrong things."

DON BASSINGTHWAITE

As if the gods had decreed its timing, the butt of a staff struck against the floor near the door. Midian couldn't see her through the crowd of taller figures, but he heard Razu, the mistress of rituals, call out, "Lhesh Tariic Kurar'taarn comes!"

The entire crowd turned to the door in unison. Any noise that had filled the hall before was like a whisper compared to the thunder of voices calling Tariic's name and fists thumping against chests in salute. Midian thumped his chest, too, and if there was some small part of him that said that this wasn't right, that a Zil shouldn't be cheering for the ruler of Darguun, he didn't hear it over the din.

The crowd parted as Tariic entered the hall, and allowed Midian to see him. Tariic wore formal regalia—the spiked crown of Darguun, a heavy cloak of tiger skin, polished armor of brass-chased steel—and carried the Rod of Kings high. Midian felt the rush of awe he experienced whenever he saw Tariic. In his head, he knew it was the power of the rod that lent the lhesh his majestic presence, but it didn't matter. Maybe once he had served the Trust, the sharp blade of Zilargo's government, but not anymore.

His new master raised his hands, acknowledging the crowd, then searched the hall. His gaze settled briefly on Midian—the gnome stood straight and proud under his regard—then moved on to stop on those behind him. Tariic gestured with the rod, and the crowd opened farther, clearing a wide space before the lhesh.

"Riila Dhakaan of Kech Shaarat," Tariic said. "Taak Dhakaan of Kech Shaarat. I welcome you to Khaar Mbar'ost."

He had already welcomed the emissaries earlier in the day, of course. Midian had been there, privileged to witness a much quieter but perhaps even more important meeting. What happened here was just a formality and a bit of pageantry. As Riila and Taak put fists to their chests and bent their heads to Tariic, Midian squeezed Ashi's hand.

Tariic motioned for Taak and Riila to join him. They went forward, eyes wide with adulation. No matter what illusion of free

THE TYRANNY OF GHOSTS

will they might present, Midian knew they were already under Tariic's spell. When the pair stood before him, Tariic looked around at the crowd in the hall.

"Warlords of Darguun!" he said. "Honored guests from beyond our borders! It gives me great pleasure to announce that the excellent warriors of Kech Shaarat have chosen to join us in battle against the elves of the Valaes Tairn. Even now, the first company of their infantry—the finest warriors known since the fall of Dhakaan—are in the city. Soon they will travel east to take key positions among Darguun's own soldiers." He paused, a fine bit of effect. "But warriors are not all that the Kech Shaarat bring us. Riila Dhakaan, speak."

Riila raised her head, her ears standing tall. "Lhesh Tariic, we bring news of the traitors who made an attempt on your life. We know where they are."

The thrill that precedes triumph brought a lightness to Midian's belly. He looked up at Ashi. She stood like a statue, all emotion wiped from her face. Vounn had trained her well. There were some reactions, though, that were impossible to conceal. Ashi's fingers were cold in Midian's grasp. He rubbed her hand gently and felt her stiffen, but she didn't try to pull away.

"Where?" asked Tariic, his voice low but clear in the silence of the hall.

"They hide with the Kech Volaar, granted sanctuary in Volaar Draal."

Whispers and growls of surprise rose like a wind, but Tariic's snarl broke above them. "Senen Dhakaan, stand forward!"

Midian found the ambassador of the Kech Volaar easily—those who stood around her pulled away, leaving Senen isolated. For a moment, there was shock on her face, then it was wiped away. Midian saw her eyes dart to the nearest exits from the hall, but they were blocked. Guards positioned by Tariic stood ready for this moment. Senen's gaze went back to Tariic, then she stepped out to face him.

"The claim of the Kech Shaarat is absurd, lhesh," she said

bluntly. "Why would the Kech Volaar jeopardize their relationship with you? My clan shared a relationship with the throne of Darguun before the Kech Shaarat came crawling out of their caves to lick up the blood of your victory."

Taak growled and bared his teeth. Midian was certain he would have drawn his sword and struck at Senen except that Riila caught his arm. "Our word is true, lhesh," she said. "Not all Kech Volaar stand against you. Our information comes from one who sends you her deepest respect."

Dismay broke through the ice in Senen's eyes. "Who makes up such lies?" she demanded.

Tariic spoke before Riila could. "Do not answer." He appeared calm, but Midian had seen his reaction when Riila and Taak had first presented their news to him. The lhesh had taken the day to master his emotions. His control made his presence seem that much larger—the hall of honor could have been empty except for him and Senen.

"Ekhaas, who was in your service, stood with Geth and Chetiin when they tried to take my life," he said slowly, "and the Kech Volaar have long had an interest in the Sword of Heroes that Geth bears." He raised the Rod of Kings. "I had not thought that the clan that helped Lhesh Haruuc find this great relic of lost Dhakaan would turn against me, but perhaps seeing it in the hands of a true ruler was too much for Tuura Dhakaan."

He leveled the rod at Senen Dhakaan. "By the blood of the Six Kings that you claim to honor, speak the truth, Senen Dhakaan. Do the traitors who sought to kill me hide in Volaar Draal?"

It seemed to Midian that he heard an echo in Tariic's words. *Tell me everything, Midian* . . . He swallowed hard, fighting to keep his secrets from spilling out, but this time the power of the rod wasn't directed at him. Senen faced Tariic and, without an instant of hesitation, said, "Yes."

Horror rose in her eyes as the word emerged from her mouth. Roars of anger erupted in the hall. It was difficult to hear Tariic

as he shouted another question. "And you hid this from me? Answer!"

Rage replaced horror. Senen drew a ragged breath and spat, "Yes!"—then opened her mouth even wider, the first note of song rolling up from of her chest.

Midian's gut flipped. The song of a *duur'kala*! But Tariic was ready. "Be silent!"

The order was forceful enough to bring quiet to the entire hall. Senen closed her mouth so suddenly that her eyes bulged, and she gagged on the song sealed in her throat. Tariic pointed the rod at her again and said, "Do. Not. Move."

Senen went still. Tariic allowed silence to linger in the hall for a heartbeat more before he spoke again. "Pradoor, I will listen to the teachings of the Six."

Pradoor, standing in Tariic's shadow the whole time, stirred. "Lhesh," she said in her high, thin voice, "the gods of the Six speak to this in many ways. The Shadow decrees that a slave who conceals knowledge from her master has stolen that knowledge from him. The Mockery prescribes that the hand that steals shall be struck off. The Fury demands that vengeance suit the offense."

"*Ta muut*, Pradoor." Tariic looked back to Senen, his eyes running over her body before pausing at her belt where a knife was sheathed. Once again, he let silence take hold. Midian could feel the crowd in the hall holding its collective breath, waiting for the lhesh to pronounce his judgment. And finally . . . finally . . .

"Senen Dhakaan," said Tariic, "take the knife at your belt and cut out the tongue that dared hide knowledge from me."

The unnatural stillness that gripped Senen vanished, replaced by a straining as she fought to resist the command. Tariic thrust the Rod of Kings at her. "*I said, cut out your lying tongue, Senen!*"

Senen's hands seemed to move of their own accord, the right snatching the knife from its sheath, the left reaching past lips

and teeth to pinch the red muscle of her mouth and stretch it taut—

Memories flowed unbidden out of the dark places of Midian's mind. Memories of himself in Tariic's chambers, a captive only a short time after he had tried to take the lhesh's life. Memories of writhing on rich carpets as Tariic stripped his knowledge, his identity, from him. *You serve me now, Midian. You serve Tariic. Zilargo is nothing to you. You are not worthy to kiss the ground I tread.* Pradoor, watching and cackling. Tariic's deafened bugbear servants holding Ashi and forcing her to watch as well. Tariic himself, hated—and adored.

If he'd been able to take up a knife, Midian would have leaped across the hall of honor and driven it into Tariic's eye socket, the same way he'd killed Haruuc.

No. He would rather have plunged the knife into his own eye. Another memory: ripping a knife through his own belly and offering the bloody blade to Tariic. Tariic laughing. *You live by my kindness, Midian. You will do as I say, now and forever.*

Midian crawled to him through a pool of his own blood and kissed his boot, and in return Tariic gestured for Pradoor to go to him. *Stop the bleeding.*

"Stop the bleeding, Pradoor."

Memories folded like a piece of black paper, disappearing back into the shadows. Senen was on her knees, hands limp at her side, mouth bloody, knife and severed flesh on the floor before her. Pradoor was feeling her way forward, milky eyes staring at something only she could see but that brought a smile to her withered face. Tariic . . .

Tariic stood triumphant, his gaze sweeping the hall. "Let her be returned to Volaar Draal!" he said. His voice rang like a battle cry. "Let her be a message for the Kech Volaar to consider. Let them weigh whether they will please me and surrender those they shelter. Let all consider"—he thrust the Rod of Kings into the air—"the justice delivered to those who defy Lhesh Tariic Kurar'taarn!"

THE TYRANNY OF GHOSTS

The roar of the crowd was all-embracing. Even the representatives of the Five Nations and the dragonmarked houses looked at each other and nodded as if in agreement that yes, the lhesh of Darguun was justified in what he had commanded. Midian looked up at Ashi and found her still staring at Senen as Pradoor murmured prayers over the broken *duur'kala*.

Awareness of intense pain filtered into his brain. Ashi's fingers had tightened on his in a crushing grip. Midian drew a hissing breath through his teeth and grabbed for her arm, poking hard in just the right spot. Ashi grimaced and her grip loosened. Midian jerked his hand free and flexed aching fingers.

"You couldn't have done anything," he said. "Not with your dragonmark, not without it. She was doomed. You should thank Tariic for his mercy in sparing you a similar fate."

Her eyes narrowed. He smiled at the unspoken admission. She knew about the Kech Volaar. Of course, she did. And she knew that they knew it. He gave her a graceful bow.

"Maybe we can discuss it when I get back," he said. "I have to meet someone. Tariic has a little errand for the two of us—just in case the Kech Volaar don't find the right answer to the message that he's sending. A surprise visit to some old friends, if you will." He ran a hand over the hilt of his dagger.

Ashi stiffened and drew her lips back from her teeth—a shockingly savage expression in someone dressed with such elegance—but Midian was already slipping back into the cheering crowd and out of the hall of honor. He followed the edge of rumor as word spread through Khaar Mbar'ost of what had just taken place. A moment in his room was all he needed to change courtly clothes for traveling gear. His companion in Tariic's errand was already waiting for him in the courtyard when he reached it, their packs ready along with a horse.

He hadn't wanted aid in the errand. He'd argued to Tariic that he was capable of dealing with Geth and the others by himself. That it was a point of pride. That it would be easier

DON BASSINGTHWAITE

to slip into Volaar Draal if he were alone. Tariic had overruled him. "Geth, Chetiin, Ekhaas, and Tenquis will die," he'd said. "Get yourself into Volaar Draal, then call on Riila and Taak's informant. It shouldn't be difficult to find her. If she wants to show her respect for me, she can help you get him"—he'd thrust the Rod of Kings at Midian's companion—"into the city as well. Until the traitors are dead, you're allies. I command it."

The command had been unnecessary. Midian might have protested, but he would have done whatever Tariic asked. He crossed the courtyard to his new ally.

"It's done," he said, reaching into his pack and drawing out a silver horseshoe. Tariic would gather an escort of soldiers—he probably already had one waiting—to see Senen safely returned to Kech Volaar territory. They would ride ahead of the escort, an unseen vanguard. Midian threw the horseshoe to the ground and spoke a word. The horseshoe bounced twice in perfect rhythm, then suddenly there was a white pony cantering in a circle around them. Midian whistled. It came to him. He mounted and looked up at his companion.

The big bugbear with the serpentine symbol of the Fury, dark goddess of vengeance, carved into his chest glowered down at him. He looked considerably more alive and angry than someone who had supposedly had the skin flayed from him should have.

"Tariic commands this, but I don't like it," Makka growled, tamping the butt of the trident that was his chosen weapon against the ground. He hadn't escaped Tariic's wrath at the death of Vounn d'Deneith entirely—he was pale from imprisonment in an isolated cell below Khaar Mbar'ost—but he was in better shape than the anonymous bugbear who been put in his place to satisfy the vengeance of House Deneith. "The wolf does not run beside the hound. I swore revenge against you as well as the others for turning my tribe against me."

Midian met his gaze without fear. "After what you did, Makka, you should be glad Tariic finds you more useful as his

THE TYRANNY OF GHOSTS

hound than as a sop to keep Deneith quiet. If it had been my choice, you would have been a naked corpse rotting outside Rhukaan Draal weeks ago."

He turned his back on the bugbear and rode for the gate.

CHAPTER NINE

22 Aryth

As they approached the edge of Kech Volaar territory, the soldiers—seven strong hobgoblins and three burly bugbears—escorting Senen started getting skittish. First one, then another glanced around at his companions, until they were all looking at one another. Finally the leader of the expedition put his ears back and muttered something. Within moments, they had all turned and were galloping away in full retreat.

Midian sank a little farther back into his hiding place among the trees and watched them go. He was fairly certain that Senen, swaying in her saddle, head hanging down on her chest, was barely even aware they had left. Two nights before, Midian had crept into the escort's camp after the soldier who was supposed to be on watch duty turned his attention to the stars and moons overhead. Senen's skin had been hot. He strongly suspected that Pradoor had done no more than close the Kech Volaar's wounds with her prayers. Infection and fever had set in—probably Pradoor's twisted intention all along.

But Senen's fever suited him too. The more confusion there was over exactly what had happened to her when she arrived in Volaar Draal, the more time he'd have to get Makka into the city and approach his targets. They would be busy cursing Tariic, ignorant of the assassin in the shadows behind them.

Geth would be the first to die, he'd decided. Then Chetiin.

Below, Senen crossed some invisible boundary, and the Kech Volaar patrol that had been lurking among the underbrush—Midian had spotted them immediately, even if Tariic's soldiers had only guessed at their presence—emerged. The sudden appearance of the great mist-gray leopards that were their warmounts startled Senen's horse, but the scouts surrounded it swiftly and slid Senen out of the saddle. They were too far away for Midian to hear their words, but the anger that showed on their faces told him all he needed to know. A messenger falcon was dispatched and a warning horn blown in a series of trills. Two members of the patrol bore Senen deeper into Kech Volaar territory, and a third rode off to track the fleeing escorts. A fourth, the one with the horn, waited where he was. Midian waited too.

Geth first, then Chetiin. Then Ekhaas—she'd irritated him from the moment they'd met with the way she clung to *duur'kala* lore. Tenquis would be almost an afterthought.

The sun moved a handspan across the sky, and two more Kech Volaar patrols appeared. With their cats prowling around them, they conferred with the remaining member of the original patrol, then all of them moved off in the direction the escort had fled. Midian didn't hold out much hope for the soldiers' escape—or their swift deaths. He waited until the Kech Volaar patrols were well away, then wriggled out of his hiding place and made his way back to his own unwanted companion.

"The way's clear," he said.

Makka just glowered at him and swung back into the saddle of his horse. Midian ignored the bugbear's bad temper and mounted his own white pony. With patrols in the area either absorbed with Senen's plight or consumed by righteous wrath in their pursuit of Tariic's soldiers, the way to Volaar Draal would be relatively clear. Just in case it wasn't, they stuck to the trees, following the path from under cover as it transformed into an ancient road in the Dhakaani style.

Geth, then Chetiin. Then Ekhaas and Tenquis.
Then Makka.

THE TYRANNY OF GHOSTS

The first night into their journey, Midian had looked across a small campfire, watched Makka sharpening the tines of his trident, and realized that Tariic's command of alliance had a flaw. *Until the traitors are dead, you're allies.* But once they were dead? Ah. Midian wondered if the omission had been deliberate, if Tariic wished to rid himself of one or more potentially troublesome underlings.

He suspected that Makka had realized the same thing. The bugbear kept stealing glances at him when he thought Midian wasn't looking. One way or another, four bodies would become five before Tariic's errand was over, and Midian intended to be the one going back to Khaar Mbar'ost.

He waited until he felt Makka's gaze on him, then turned sharply. He had the satisfaction of seeing Makka twitch in surprise, his nostrils flaring. Midian gave him a wide, insolent smile. Makka's eyes narrowed, then he smiled back, a cold smile that was all teeth. Any doubts were erased in Midian's mind. Makka knew that their enforced alliance had a limit.

But the bugbear's smile lasted only a moment before turning into a deep frown as he raised his head and sniffed at the wind. Midian's smile faded as well. "What is it?"

Makka's big, stiff ears cupped slightly. "Something dead."

They rode even more carefully. Soon Midian could smell the sick-sweet odor of death too. A little farther and they found the source of the stench bound naked to a branching wooden frame—a goblin grieving tree—erected where the road descended into a steep-sided valley shadowed by the towers of Volaar Draal.

Midian slipped from his horse and, staying low, crept around to the front of the tree. The body had been there for no more than a few days. Blood had run down the victim's left side and dried there from a wound that had been opened under her arm. She had lingered on the tree, but not too long before bleeding to death. Her head had been bound into place. The last thing she'd seen would have been Volaar Draal.

There was a sign, the words carved in Goblin. *She betrayed her clan and her* muut. *She dies with no name.*

"Well, this changes things." he said under his breath. He returned to the cover of the trees. "Makka, see if you can track down a lone scout or a small patrol. We need to find out what happened here."

◉ ◉ ◉ ◉ ◉ ◉ ◉

17 Aryth – five days earlier

At Tuura Dhakaan's order, they were thrown into a cell—at least Geth assumed it was a cell. The only light was a thin line around the door, a glowing thread in an echoing darkness. Their prison was vast. Without proper light he had no desire to go exploring.

"Where are we?" he asked.

"Gath'atcha," said Ekhaas. Her voice was rough, strained by her long song in their escape from the vaults. "It means 'without honor.' It is a place of punishment. Kech Volaar who break the traditions of the clan are sent here for a period of time."

"They'll hold us here?" asked Chetiin.

"Hold us, yes," said Ekhaas, "but only until Tuura Dhakaan decides what to do. What we did was more serious than the deeds of most who are sent here."

She tried to keep her voice steady, but even through the trained tones of a *duur'kala*, Geth could hear her fear and dismay. "Don't worry," he said. "Tuura will understand."

"There's nothing to understand, Geth. Breaking into the vaults goes beyond any concern she might have about Tariic or the Rod of Kings."

"If we tell her about Tasaam Draet's fortress and the shattered shield—"

"It makes no difference."

Her voice actually broke. Geth tried to find her in the

THE TYRANNY OF GHOSTS

darkness, but his hands found only air. "Grandfather Rat. Can you sing us another light?"

"I can make a little light," said Tenquis. Geth heard rustling as the tiefling searched the magically capacious pockets of his long vest, then the swish and gurgle of liquid being shaken in some kind of vessel. The sound stopped for a moment, then started again, more vigorous this time.

"Stop," Ekhaas said wearily. "There's no light in Gath'atcha. It's an ancient magic. The only illumination lies on the other side of the door in Volaar Draal."

"A lesson for those imprisoned," said Chetiin. Of all of them, only he sounded calm.

"Can you get out of here?" Geth asked him.

"I might be able to," said the old goblin. "I could get away when we are released. But I would be leaving you behind."

"If it comes down to that, you should do it."

"I will."

No hesitation, no trace of self-sacrifice. Once again, Geth was glad Chetiin was a friend rather than an enemy. "They didn't take our weapons," Geth said. "We could try fighting when they open the door. We may all be able to escape."

"When they open the door," said Ekhaas, "there will be twenty warriors of the Kech Volaar on the other side with *duur'kala* to back them up. There's the whole of Volaar Draal between us and freedom. They left us our weapons as a sign of disdain. We can't escape, Geth."

There was silence for a moment, then Tenquis spoke. "You say 'they' like you don't belong with them anymore."

"I don't," said Ekhaas. "Exile from the clan is the least I can expect."

"What about the rest of us?" said Geth.

She didn't answer him. "I said, what about the rest of us, Ekhaas?" he asked again.

Her voice came hollow out of the darkness. "Go to sleep, Geth. There's nothing else you can do right now."

There was a finality in her words that killed any thought of a reply. Silence settled into the darkness. Geth stood where he was for a long moment, then stretched himself out on the cool stone floor and stared into nothing. His hand came up to touch the polished black stones of the collar around his neck—an artifact of the Gatekeeper druids that had been the dying gift of his friend Adolan. Sometimes that collar grew cold or hot when he was in danger or needed guidance.

Just then it was no cooler than the air and no warmer than his skin.

They'd gained a clue to the destruction of the Shield of Nobles and a possible way to destroy the Rod of Kings, only to find themselves locked up like thieves. A bad end, Ado, he thought.

* * *

The Kech Volaar came for them around what Geth's belly told him was noon the next day. When the door of Gath'atcha was opened, he was surprised to find that Ekhaas's expectations of their escort were wrong.

There were actually thirty warriors waiting for them.

The Kech Volaar said nothing, just waited for their prisoners to emerge, then formed up behind them, guiding them with the bulk of their presence. After a night in the darkness, even the dim lights of Volaar Draal seemed bright. Geth found himself blinking as they were marched through the streets. In another city, crowds might have shouted abuse at them or maybe hurled stones and filth. The hobgoblins, goblins, and bugbears of Volaar Draal, however, watched their passage in silence. Geth thought he could feel the cold anger and disdain in every stare. He almost wished someone *would* shout or throw something.

Volaar Draal held its breath, waiting for them to be judged.

Their escort guided them to the blocky shape of the Shrine of Glories. Geth half expected to be taken around the

THE TYRANNY OF GHOSTS

back and in through the slave entrance they'd used before, but the warriors took them up the sweeping stairs that led to the main entrance. They emerged not into the pillared Hall of Song but into a chamber that reminded Geth uncomfortably of an arena. Tiered benches rose above the isolated floor, each seat filled by a harsh-faced older hobgoblin. Elders of the clan, Geth guessed immediately. On the broad platform of the lowest tier, seated in a high stone chair, was Tuura Dhakaan. Diitesh and Kitaas stood just behind her on one side; a hobgoblin warrior wearing heavy armor, an axe slung across his back, stood on the other.

"*Khaavolaar*," said Ekhaas. "That's Kurac Thaar. He's the warlord of Kech Volaar."

"I didn't realize the Kech Volaar had a warlord," said Tenquis.

"He stands at Tuura's side when important decisions are made." Ekhaas pressed her lips together for a moment, then added, "When there's an execution, he carries it out."

The thirty escorting warriors saluted Tuura and withdrew. Heavy doors boomed shut behind them, leaving Geth, Ekhaas, Chetiin, and Tenquis alone before the elders. Geth was reminded uncomfortably of vultures perched on trees, waiting for a wounded beast to die and become carrion.

The room was silent for a long moment before Tuura, looking down on her prisoners, finally spoke. "Ekhaas *duur'kala*, you will speak for your companions. You stand in this chamber because you have broken not only the terms of the sanctuary granted to you, but the laws and traditions of the Kech Volaar. You assaulted another member of your clan. You entered the vaults without permission and by stealth." Her ears flicked back. "And you took those not of this clan—two of them *chaat'oor*—into the vaults along with you. Is this the truth?"

Ekhaas raised her head. "Mother of the dirge, it is the truth."

A murmur of disapproval ran around the gathered elders. Diitesh and Kitaas glanced at each other with smug expressions.

Tuura's face hardened, and an edge of rage crept into her voice. "What are the punishments prescribed to Kech Volaar for these transgressions, Ekhaas?"

Geth saw Ekhaas's ears tremble just slightly. Her words were steady, though—steadier than he could have managed. "These are the punishments, handed down by the earliest Kech Volaar and drawn from the traditions of the great empire, that are taught to children of the clan. Who strikes without sanction another member of the clan, whether with weapon or hand or magic, will pass time in Gath'atcha. Who enters the vaults of lore without sanction will pass time in Gath'atcha or may be exiled from the clan. Who guides—"

Her voice finally caught, but she swallowed and recovered. "Who guides those not of Kech Volaar into the vaults will be judged a traitor to Kech Volaar and will die without a name."

There were no murmurs this time. Once again Tuura waited before she spoke. "And what are the punishments prescribed by tradition to outclanners?"

"An outclanner who strikes one of the Kech Volaar may be struck in return without fear. An outclanner who enters the vaults of lore will die."

Geth's stomach turned. He glanced urgently at Ekhaas. On the *duur'kala*'s other side, Tenquis hissed her name. "Ekhaas—"

"You have no voice here, *chaat'oor*!" thundered Kurac Thaar from Tuura's side. "Be silent."

Geth glared at the armored hobgoblin, but Ekhaas caught his shoulder, turning him away. "Easy," she said softly, then turned her face back to Tuura. "These are the punishments dictated by tradition, mother of the dirge—but by tradition, we shouldn't be speaking at all. By tradition, my companions and I should be dead already."

Tuura's ears flicked. "One has spoken on your behalf."

She sat back, and Geth saw Ekhaas's eyes go wide, then narrow. She—and he—looked to Kitaas, but Ekhaas's sister seemed as startled as they did. Tuura paid no attention to them

THE TYRANNY OF GHOSTS

or to her. "The High Archivist," she said, "proposes a different punishment."

Diitesh? Geth watched the pale hobgoblin nod to Tuura as another wave of whispers passed through the elders. Kitaas had passed beyond startled to thunderstruck. She grabbed Diitesh's sleeve and spoke into her ear. Diitesh just shook her head and gestured for her to step back.

Ekhaas held her gaze on Tuura. "What punishment?" she asked.

"You came to Volaar Draal seeking sanctuary from Lhesh Tariic. You will be returned to Lhesh Tariic to face his judgment."

There were mutters of confusion among the elders, but Geth also heard murmurs of approval. Chetiin's scarred voice echoed in the chamber. "Tariic's judgment will also be death."

Kurac Thaar drew breath, but Tuura gestured for him to hold his tongue. "Death in Volaar Draal or death in Rhukaan Draal. The honor of Kech Volaar is satisfied either way," she said.

A vague sense of hope stirred in Geth. It would take time to get to Rhukaan Draal. Even under heavy guard, there was a chance that they might be able to escape—certainly a better chance than if they were to be executed in Volaar Draal. But another thought tugged at him. Why would Diitesh of all people propose a deal like that, a break from tradition? What did she gain by sending them back to Tariic?

Except—He looked up at Tuura and Diitesh. "And the Kech Volaar," he said in his thickly accented Goblin, "will gain Tariic's favor by turning his enemies over to him."

"Sometimes such things must be considered," said Tuura. "You should understand—you sat on the throne of Darguun as Haruuc's *shava*."

"Geth, don't," whispered Ekhaas. "This is our way out of Volaar Draal."

She'd seen the same thing he had. He shook his head though. He couldn't let go of his suspicions. And he knew it wasn't just him—he could feel a stirring across his connection with Wrath.

The Sword of Heroes didn't share memories with its wielder in the way that the Rod of Kings did, but it had been created to inspire. A hero did more than fight. A hero questioned.

"We brought you a warning about Tariic when we came, Tuura Dhakaan." As he spoke, his accent faded—the work of Wrath. Geth could feel it putting a hero's words into his mouth. "Do not trust Tariic. Our lives are worth more than his favor."

"Close your mouth!" Kurac roared, driven beyond tolerance. "I said that *chaat'oor* have no voice here—"

Fury caught Geth. "You will respect me, *taat*! I am the bearer of Aram. I hold the honor of the name of Kuun." He drew Wrath, the twilight blade a dull shadow in the dim light. "Fight me, and test your *atcha*!"

Kurac's hand went to his axe, but before he could draw it, Tuura said sharply, "Kurac!"

He froze. Tuura rose to her feet, her face as dark as a thundercloud. "Perhaps Tariic is not to be trusted," she said. "But I have *muut* to my clan. As it has been since the Age of Dhakaan, I lead them and I protect them. I stand between them and forces greater than ours. When Haruuc ruled Darguun, I saw the potential in an alliance with him."

"Tariic isn't Haruuc."

"Even if all that you have told me about Tariic is true, I must consider Kech Volaar. Diitesh offers a way to make the lhesh of Darguun a friend instead of an enemy while punishing those who break our traditions. Two armies fight one battle."

Geth looked at the High Archivist. "I have been told that the archivists guard the history and traditions of Dhakaan," he said. "Aren't you breaking traditions by handing us over to Tariic instead of allowing our deaths here?"

"Geth!" Tenquis said in a low, strangled voice, but his exclamation was almost drowned out by mutters of discontent that made their way around the benches of elders. Apparently Diitesh's suggestion wasn't as popular as it might have seemed.

THE TYRANNY OF GHOSTS

Tuura looked around at the dissenters, but Diitesh raised her head high.

"I have said before that Tariic holds the hope of restoring the Empire of Dhakaan, just as he holds the Rod of Kings," she declared. "He respects the traditions of the ages and restores those that Haruuc stripped away. This is the time the Kech Volaar have waited for. Our legacy is upon us. We must support him!"

As many elders slapped their chests in approval as had raised their voices in dissent. Many of them, Geth noticed, wore the black robes of archivists. He spoke over the noise. "The same argument she used, Tuura Dhakaan, when the Kech Shaarat sought to draw you into an alliance under Tariic."

The applause faltered. Tuura's eyes whipped back to Geth. "The Kech Volaar might ally with Tariic," she said, "but we will not bow before him. That is why I rejected the approaches of the Kech Shaarat."

Diitesh's ears went back. "If Tariic Kurar'taarn is the emperor returned, it is the *muut* of all Dhakaani clans to follow him."

Geth bared his teeth, feeling the full power of the sword flowing through him. He felt powerful, one hero standing before the assembled elders of a clan, fighting a battle as dangerous as if he stood in the path of an army. "Which is it?" he asked. "Will you follow Tariic or not? I tell you that if you send us back to him—or execute us here—the Kech Volaar *will* bow before him. Tariic's power is irresistible. He doesn't need the Kech Volaar, but if you give yourselves up to him, his ambition will consume you."

He paused to look over the crowd of elders, at Tuura and Kurac, at Diitesh and Kitaas, all staring at him in consideration or in anger. At Ekhaas, Chetiin, and Tenquis, likewise caught up in the words of a hero. He felt Wrath's approval and let his voice rise until it rang from the walls and ceiling of the room. "We seek a way to stop Tariic, and we may have found it in the vaults of Volaar Draal, among the knowledge safeguarded through the

ages by the Kech Volaar. If you're willing to break with tradition by leaving our fate to Tariic, consider instead leaving Tariic's fate to us!" He thrust Wrath triumphantly into the air—

"No!" Kitaas pushed past Diitesh to point a trembling finger at him. "By the Six Kings, don't listen to him. They mean to destroy the Rod of Kings! They intend to destroy an artifact of Dhakaan!"

All faces turned to Kitaas. The silence that fell over the chamber was shocking—then the tiered room seemed to explode as every elder present tried to shout louder than the next. "Kill them!" one voice shrieked out above the others. "Kill them where they stand!" Even Tuura looked stunned at the revelation.

Geth felt the pinnacle of triumph crumble under him. The magic of Wrath's power vanished like a winking spark, and the sword almost fell from his hand as he stumbled back. Ekhaas caught him. "Tiger dances!" he gasped. "What—?"

"The Kech Volaar collect history, remember?" Ekhaas said through clenched teeth. She pushed Geth back onto his feet and grabbed for her own sword. "There's one crime worse than breaking into the vaults."

"They didn't know? Why didn't Kitaas tell them before? Why didn't she tell Tuura?" Geth heard the doors of the chamber open as the guards outside responded to the noise within, but he couldn't help looking back to the lowest tier of benches—

—just in time to see Diitesh turn and slap Kitaas. "By the Six Kings, I said hold your tongue!"

They weren't the only ones to see it. Tuura Dhakaan's voice howled over the din of the elders. "Diitesh! You knew about this?"

The elders closest to the leader of the Kech Volaar fell silent instantly. Kurac Thaar, ready to leap to the floor of the chamber with his axe raised high, paused in midstep. The guards rushing into the room stopped where they stood. Diitesh's already pale

THE TYRANNY OF GHOSTS

face turned even paler as she whirled around. For an instant, terror showed in her expression, then was wiped away as she struggled to compose herself.

"Let them go to Tariic, Tuura," she said. "They'll die just as surely."

Tuura's ears went back. "I wouldn't have even considered it if I knew. You held it back from me."

"I wanted to tell you, Tuura Dhakaan," Kitaas blurted. "She wouldn't let me."

A flush crept back into Diitesh's face at her adjunct's betrayal, but she kept her eyes on Tuura. "Kill them, and send their bodies to Tariic, then. But you're missing an opportunity to prove your allegiance to him."

"The Kech Volaar don't need to prove anything to the lhesh of Darguun." Tuura pointed at Geth and the others. "They betrayed us. They are ours to deal with as we see fit. Tariic—"

As Tuura spoke, Geth felt a touch on his leg. "Be ready to run," Chetiin said softly. Geth nodded very slightly, tightened his grip on Wrath, and shifted his weight. The door of the chamber was open. The argument between the leader of the Kech Volaar and her High Archivist provided a distraction. If they chose their moment carefully, they might have a slim chance of escape.

"—can remain ignorant of their fate for the rest of his life!"

Diitesh's features twisted into a mask of anger. "Tariic already knows you've given them sanctuary!"

In spite of himself, Geth flinched. On the benches, all of the elders had fallen silent. Tuura drew a sharp breath. "You—"

"You are blind, Tuura," said Diitesh. "I *see*. When you dismissed the offer of the Kech Shaarat, I went after Riila Dhakaan and spoke to her. When the Kech Shaarat swear allegiance to Tariic as emperor, the Kech Volaar must stand with them or die." Her lips drew back from her teeth. "If you won't embrace the legacy of Dhakaan on behalf of our clan, someone else must. Tuura Dhakaan, I challenge your leadership of the Kech Volaar!"

DON BASSINGTHWAITE

Tuura's eyes opened wide. Without waiting for a response, Diitesh reached into her robe and pulled out a battered black box. She flicked open the lid and spoke a word of magic.

The sound of it echoed for a moment, then seemed to transform into a kind of sleepy hum. A heartbeat later, the hum had become a drone that filled the chamber. As Geth watched, as elders scrambled to get away from an impending battle, three glittering, green wasps as long as a finger rose up from the box. The dim light of the chamber flashed on lean, crystalline bodies formed of knuckle-sized gems fastened together with wires of gold. It shone through wings that threw off splashes of rainbow color as they blurred. Diitesh backed away, leaving the wasps hanging in the air.

Tuura narrowed her eyes and spat, "Your challenge is accepted!" She drew a sharp breath—and sang.

The drone of the wasps rose and broke into a thrumming dissonance. Tuura choked as if her song had been forced back down her throat. She reeled backward.

"*Kapaa'taat!*" Kurac Thaar jumped forward—Geth didn't know what the rules for such a challenge were, but it didn't seem like the warlord was going to let them get in the way of his axe. Diitesh just flicked a finger, though, and one of the wasps darted at him. Kurac swatted, but it skimmed easily around his axe.

It struck like an emerald flash, swooping at his unprotected neck and seeming to do no more than touch it before leaping away. Kurac staggered, clapped a hand to the place he'd been stung, then pitched forward. He hit the ground in a clattering of armor that seemed to go on and on as his body twitched and danced.

"*Duur'kala* have always led the Kech Volaar," Diitesh called over the drone of the wasps. "They have songs and stories of the great empire, but the vaults hold so much more. Tools. Armor. Weapons of all sorts—some of them intended to counter *duur'kala!*" She flicked her fingers again, and the wasps buzzed around Tuura, toying with her as the leader of the Kech Volaar drew a sword.

"Now!" said Chetiin.

THE TYRANNY OF GHOSTS

It was difficult to tear his eyes away from the duel before him, but Geth did. He spun around and ran for the door of the chamber. The guards who'd spilled inside were staring too. Their reactions were slow. One cried out and grabbed for him. Geth swung Wrath in an arc that opened a gash across the guard's side. Ahead of him, Chetiin darted between two guards, spinning to slash at their legs as he went. Ekhaas didn't draw her sword or try to sing a spell but just lashed out with fists, elbows, and knees at any guard who got in her way. Tenquis—

Tenquis wasn't there. Geth twisted around, sliding to a stop.

The tiefling hadn't moved, though he had drawn his wand. He stood watching the wasps, head moving to follow their darting flight as they evaded Tuura's flailing sword. "Tenquis!" Geth shouted.

Tenquis paid no attention to him. But Diitesh did. Her head turned, and she scowled. One hand still pointing at Tuura, she gestured with the other at Geth.

One wasp broke off from the others and flew at him in a green streak. "Tiger!" Geth cursed. He stumbled back, raising both Wrath and his great gauntlet as if they would be enough to protect him.

Tenquis twisted and brought his wand up. For a moment, the tip of the implement tracked the wasp, then Tenquis stabbed at the air. A golden spark flashed from wand to wasp—and the wasp rattled off Geth's gauntlet like a handful of pebbles. It hit the ground at his feet, a motionless collection of crystals.

Diitesh's eyes seemed ready to bulge out of her head. They darted from Tuura to Tenquis, then she gestured with both hands at once. One of the two remaining wasps darted at Tenquis. The other plunged at Tuura.

Tenquis stabbed with his wand, and another golden spark engulfed the wasp coming at him. The thing's body hadn't even dropped to the ground before his wand was following the wasp that bedeviled Tuura. Tenquis took aim and stabbed the air for a third time.

The golden spark that leaped from his wand was as bright as a miniature bolt of lightning, but instead of thunder, it only brought silence. The last wasp fell, its crystal wings still. Tuura looked at it, then up at Diitesh. The High Archivist took a step backward, hands raised, fear on her face.

Tuura's voice rose in a sharp, harsh song, and between one step and the next, Diitesh froze. She didn't move, she didn't blink. Tuura dropped to one knee beside Kurac Thaar's still twitching body and sang again, softly this time. He relaxed immediately, her song dispelling whatever poison the wasp had injected into him.

Geth glanced over his shoulder. One of the guards had Ekhaas in his grip, but neither of them were struggling. Both, along with all the elders in the chamber, were watching Tuura. Geth gestured, and Ekhaas slid away from the guard, returning to him. Moving slowly, they rejoined Tenquis. As ever, the tiefling's pupilless gold eyes were difficult to read, but Geth thought he saw a certain satisfaction there. A moment later, Chetiin joined them as well, though Geth could have sworn he'd made it out of the chamber entirely.

"You could have escaped," he murmured to the goblin.

"I still can."

Tuura stood up from beside Kurac. The warlord's chest rose and fell in an easy rhythm. He seemed to be asleep. Tuura looked at Tenquis. "How?" she asked.

"*Duur'kala* know how to counter the magical songs of another," Tenquis said. "*Daashor* of Dhakaan knew how to still another's creations—at least temporarily." He nudged one of the wasps where it lay near his feet. The crystal wings stirred feebly. "Put them back in the box. That should render them inert." He returned Tuura's gaze. "By Dhakaani tradition, you owe me."

Tuura's ears went back. "I don't need to ask what you want in return." She turned around and seated herself in her stone chair. "*Lhurusk!*"

THE TYRANNY OF GHOSTS

An officer among the guards flinched, then stepped forward. Tuura pointed at Geth and the others. "They are to be escorted from Volaar Draal and shown out of Kech Volaar territory in whichever direction they choose. If they ever attempt to approach Volaar Draal again, they are to be killed."

"*Mazo*!" The guard saluted her. Tuura looked back to Tenquis. The tiefling bent his head to her. Tuura's gaze continued on to Ekhaas.

"Ekhaas, daughter of the dirge," she said, "you are cast out of Kech Volaar. You have no *muut* to us. We have no *muut* to you. Your story ends."

Geth saw Ekhaas's amber eyes flick once to Kitaas before they went hard and distant. She turned sharply, putting her back to Tuura, the elders, and her sister. Geth thought he saw Kitaas's mouth open for a moment, only to close before anything could emerge.

Then a bugbear guard stepped in front of him, cutting off his view, and gestured curtly for him to turn as well.

◎ ◎ ◎ ◉ ◎ ◎ ◎

They were out of Volaar Draal more quickly than Geth would have thought possible. Guards stood over them in their quarters while they gathered their packs, then marched them up the long passage from the city to the gates. Goblin stablehands were still saddling their horses when they arrived, but the gate guards had already marched aside in preparation for their departure. Just beyond the gates, Marrow waited like an independent shadow in the sun.

"How did she know to be here?" Geth asked Chetiin.

The *shaarat'khesh* elder just spread his hands and shrugged.

The guard officer whom Tuura had commanded to see them out of Volaar Draal approached Tenquis. "Which direction will you be traveling?" he asked.

Tenquis looked at Ekhaas. Ekhaas looked at Geth.

There was only one place to go. "Suud Anshaar," he said quietly. "The ruins of Tasaam Draet's fortress. We need to see if there's anything there."

"The Khraal Jungle, then," said Ekhaas. "Southeast on the other side of Darguun. But we can't ride straight across the country. Tariic will be looking for—"

"He'll think we're here," Chetiin reminded her.

She smiled briefly, then looked to the guard officer. "We travel southeast."

He didn't react. Her smile faded. Tenquis repeated her instructions, and the officer nodded and went away. Stablehands brought their horses over. They mounted up and rode into the sunlight. A Kech Volaar patrol on mist-gray leopards prowled out of the gate behind them.

"I'm sorry, Ekhaas," Geth said.

"Don't be." Ekhaas's voice was harsh. "It could have been worse."

"What will happen to Diitesh then?" Tenquis asked her as they made their way up the road and out of the valley. The *duur'kala* didn't answer him, but Geth caught Tenquis's eye, then nodded to a gang of goblin workers assembling a treelike frame beside the road at the valley's edge.

"Something worse," he said.

CHAPTER TEN

They followed the foothills of the Seawall Mountains for several days before descending into the lowlands. Once out of the mountains, it was an easy matter to keep their distance from the scattered farmholds and clanholds of southern Darguun. They traveled through a landscape that was mostly barren, studded here and there with ancient ruins from the age of Dhakaan, but also with the remains of much more recent habitation by the humans of the vanished nation of Cyre. Charred, smashed, and overgrown, the rubble of Cyran farms and villages gave mute testimony to the upheaval the region had seen only thirty years before. This was the land where Haruuc had started his revolution before sweeping north. This was the land where the dream of Darguun had been born.

For the first time in her life, Ekhaas rode past the ruins and felt no pull to investigate them or learn their stories. As much as she tried to conceal the wrenching pain in her spirit, she couldn't fool herself. She wasn't entirely successful in fooling the others, either. As she exchanged watch duties one night with Geth, the shifter paused before sliding into his bedroll.

"It can't be easy leaving your clan and your family," he said.

She held her head high. "My clan exiled me, Geth," she said, "and I don't have a family anymore." The words came out too harsh. She tried to soften them. "I know what you mean. I wish Ashi was here. She knows what it's like to lose a clan."

"She found a place in Deneith. You'll find your place too." Geth pulled his blankets up over himself. "You already have a family in us."

She couldn't help snorting. He turned to look at her, his eyes reflecting the firelight like an animal's. "I could tell you a dozen stories where someone says just that," she said.

"And what happens in them?"

"Usually everybody ends up dead."

Geth propped himself up on one elbow. "Goblin stories can be bloody depressing. Did you know that?"

"*Raat shi anaa.* 'The story continues.' " She sat back against the trunk of a scraggly tree. "Sleep well, Geth."

"Stay alert, Ekhaas." He lay down again. Within moments, his breathing had fallen into an easy, regular rhythm. Ekhaas leaned her head back and looked up at the moons, closer to her than Volaar Draal.

4 Vult

Two weeks after leaving the towering gates of the City of the Word behind, they passed into the village of Arthuun. The contrast was . . . striking to say the least, Ekhaas thought. The gates were formed of massive, rough-cut logs hung from walls that were themselves a mix of dressed stone and improvised patches. Tenquis, staring at the walls as they rode through the gates, simply shuddered.

"I'm no mason," he said, "but I could do better than that."

"It stands up and keeps things out," said Geth. "I think that's all the people here are interested in."

Ekhaas was inclined to agree with him. Built on wet ground between the broad Torlaac River and the green wall of the Khraal Jungle, Arthuun was a ramshackle place. Like most of the villages and towns in Darguun, it was cobbled together from the ruins of an earlier Cyran settlement and rough structures thrown

THE TYRANNY OF GHOSTS

up by its new Darguul inhabitants. Arthuun seemed to have a particularly transient quality, as if people and buildings alike were just passing through on their way somewhere else.

Fortunately, there were enough non-*dar*—mostly ragged, tough-looking humans, but a few half-elves and one grime-stained warforged as well—on the muddy streets that no one paid much attention to Geth and Tenquis. Ekhaas had worried that Tariic might have put a bounty on their heads and circulated their description across Darguun. If such a description had reached Arthuun, it didn't show. Marrow drew more looks than they did, mostly of deep unease and healthy respect. The worg seemed to enjoy the attention, and when they found a grubby building that advertised itself as an inn, she lay down on the porch, putting herself on display like some disconcerting sculpture.

"Be careful," Chetiin warned her. "These are hard people. Bite them and they'll bite you back."

Marrow just whuffed and thumped her tail against the porch boards.

The innkeeper who came hustling across the common room to meet them was a halfling. Although a certificate by the door proclaimed the inn approved by the standards of House Ghallanda, Ekhaas had her doubts that any member of that dragonmarked house had ever set foot in the establishment.

"Two rooms," Geth told him, "and information. We're looking for a guide, someone who knows the Khraal." He flipped the innkeeper a silver coin.

The halfling plucked it out of the air. "You want a hunter, then. Any of them that carry grinders will do." He pointed to a rusty sword hung on one wall in a feeble attempt at decoration. The blade was wider than Ekhaas's palm, but shorter than a typical sword and sharpened on only one edge, more like a farmer's implement than a fighting weapon.

"Grinders?" asked Tenquis.

"Swing one of those against jungle vines for a morning, and you'll know why." The innkeeper pointed to another wall,

this one hung with a spear. "You see a hunter carrying one of those, he hunts across the river in the moors. You see someone carrying both weapons, you walk away—he doesn't know what he's doing."

"If you were traveling into the Khraal, who would you want leading the way?" Geth asked him.

The halfling squinted and looked them over, then said, "Tooth. He's a bugbear. You'll probably find him at the Rat's Tail over by the east wall."

"Tavern?" said Geth. The innkeeper just smiled. Geth grunted and tossed him a second silver coin, then a third. "The last one's for meat," he added. "Take it to the worg on the porch."

They found the Rat's Tail without difficulty. It turned out to be less of a tavern than a kind of open-air drinking hall, the "walls" made of reed mats rolled up to allow the humid air of the village to circulate. Under the roof, though, it was as busy as any tavern Ekhaas had been in, with many of the same features: arguments, gambling, and drunkards.

Only one of the bugbears in the place wore an enormous fang more than a handspan long around his neck. Chetiin confirmed his identity with a harried goblin server just to be certain. It was Tooth.

He sat at a table, playing some sort of dice game with several other *dar*. Ekhaas studied him as they approached. His thick hair was streaked with pale stripes, and one of his big ears was ragged, a good-sized chunk apparently bitten out. His dark, glittering eyes seemed half-hidden by heavy lids—from beneath which, she realized as they got closer, the hunter was watching them.

They paused a few paces from the table. Tooth's eyes flicked back and forth between them and the dice. Finally he gave a slight nod, then announced in Goblin, "Last throw for me." His voice was a rumble. He scooped up the dice, shook them, and rolled them across the tabletop.

One of the hobgoblins crowed in victory and swept up a small heap of copper coins and shiny odds and ends. Bugbears

THE TYRANNY OF GHOSTS

and hobgoblins thumped their chests at each other. Tooth stood up, and Ekhaas saw that he was surprisingly short for a bugbear, no taller than she was. He was massively muscled through the shoulders and chest, though, and when he picked up a belt from which two broad-bladed grinders dangled, she could easily picture him wielding the tools as weapons.

"You want to talk to me," he said.

A statement, not a question. Ekhaas took the lead. "Yes," she said. "Do you speak the human tongue?"

Tooth glanced at Geth and Tenquis, then said in that language, "I do."

"Good." They'd decided there was no need to reveal the magic in Wrath unless they had to. "We want to hire a guide to take us into the Khraal."

He must have already assessed and judged them as fit to venture into the jungle because he didn't hesitate before asking, "Where exactly?"

Ekhaas found an empty table and gestured for him to sit down. Tooth joined them without comment. Ekhaas leaned forward, dropping her voice. "Have you heard of the ruins of a place called Suud Anshaar?"

With generations of mothers using it to frighten their children, the name of Tasaam Draet was common enough among the Dhakaani clans. The tales of his downfall and haunted fortress were more esoteric, though, and Ekhaas didn't know how well the legends might be known among the lowland Darguuls.

Tooth just narrowed his eyes. He looked like he might spit. "The Wailing Hill," he said. "Yes, I've heard of it. I've never laid eyes on it, but hunters tell stories."

"You know where it is?"

"I know to stay away from it. Anything that howls when it shouldn't is warning you not to get any closer." Ekhaas thought he might sit back, then, and declare their conversation over. But he didn't. "They say people have come looking for it before. Hunters take them in—good hunters who know the

Khraal—but nobody comes out. Packs of varags live in that part of the jungle, and *they* don't go near the place."

"What are varags?" asked Geth.

"Savages related to hobgoblins the way shifters are related to lycanthropes," said Tooth. "Completely fearless—usually."

"When was the last time someone came looking for Suud Anshaar?" Ekhaas asked.

Tooth shrugged. "Before Lhesh Haruuc, before Arthuun belonged to us. Back when humans picked at the edge of the Khraal." He looked them over again. "If you want to go there, it will cost you."

"You'll take us?" said Tenquis. "After all that?"

A grin showed all of Tooth's sharp teeth. "Hunters tell stories. If I get you there and come back, I'll be a legend." He lowered his voice. "This is my deal: For what you pay me, I swear by Balinor's blood to take you to Suud Anshaar, but I'm not going in. I'll wait for you, guide you back, but if you don't come out of the ruins, I'm leaving."

Ekhaas understood immediately. If Tooth returned from Suud Anshaar—even if it was as the sole survivor of a doomed expedition—his reputation would be made. She looked to the others. Chetiin and Tenquis nodded, the tiefling a little more slowly than the goblin. Geth grinned.

"I like him," he said with a nod at Tooth.

"Agreed then," said Ekhaas.

Tooth's grin grew even wider. "Good. Now let's talk about how much I'll charge you—"

"We're inflexible on that," said Chetiin. He held out a small fist. "But I believe this should do." He opened his fingers to reveal three sparkling straw-colored topazes.

During their journey across Darguun, they'd realized that while they had some money between them, it wasn't enough to persuade a guide to take them deep into the jungle in search of cursed ruins. Fortunately, Chetiin had the answer. Unraveling the stitching of his belt, he'd revealed a tiny, portable treasure.

THE TYRANNY OF GHOSTS

"For emergencies," he'd said as he sewed the leather back up.

The grin on Tooth's face faltered, his eyes going wide in its place. Chetiin closed his fingers again. "When do we leave?" he asked. "Sooner is better."

⬤ ⬤ ⬤ ⬤ ⬤ ⬤ ⬤

Rain came down heavy on a night as black as a traitor's soul. Deep eaves shielded the windows of the Talenta Hospitality, letting cool air circulate into the busy common room. Lanudo's guests for the night had finally abandoned the dubious shelter of the open-air taverns for somewhere a little more protected—the halfling circulated through the crowd, making certain that the guests whose rooms leaked worse than usual got extra beer. Sufficiently drunk, they wouldn't mind the additional damp in their beds.

He happened to be near the door when it opened to admit two figures. Late for travelers, Lanudo thought, but he'd never turned away potential guests before—and on such a miserable night, he could charge extra for a corner in the common room. He turned to greet them.

The greeting caught on his tongue.

The bigger of the two figures was a bugbear, bareheaded to the rain and looking as if he'd barely noticed the storm. There was a sprawling scar on his chest, a crude outline of a woman with the tail of a snake and outstretched wings. The sign of the Fury.

The smaller figure wore a magewrought cloak that shed water like a duck's back. Lanudo expected to find a goblin underneath, but the figure threw back the cloak's hood to reveal the smiling, nut-brown face of a gnome. Bright eyes fixed on him.

"Ah, innkeep," said the gnome. "Tell me you can spare us going back out on a night like this. My name is Midian Mit Davandi, historian to the court of Lhesh Tariic Kurar'taarn. We're trying to catch up to some colleagues: a hobgoblin

duur'kala, a shifter, a tiefling, and a goblin mounted on a black worg. Quite a distinctive group. I wonder if you might have seen them."

The gnome's manner was friendly, and a lilt in his voice implied that Lanudo would be doing him a huge favor by helping him locate his friends. Lanudo's gut told him differently. Midian's bright eyes were hard with a sharp cunning. His smile was cold. The bugbear didn't smile at all. One hand gripped the shaft of a heavy trident, fingers rubbing the wood. The other hand rested on his belt, uncomfortably close to a dangling clump of reddish hair and orange-brown flesh. It came to Lanudo that he'd been in Arthuun too long if he was able to recognize the scalp of a hobgoblin on sight.

He doubted very much if the gnome and the bugbear were merely trying to catch up with their "colleagues." A better man than him might have tried to throw them off the trail.

A better man than him wouldn't have lived long in Arthuun.

"You've missed them," he said. "They stayed a night but rode out two days ago, heading into the Khraal. They didn't say anything about where they were going in front of me, but they hired a guide, a hunter named Tooth. When he met them here, he looked like he was ready for a substantial expedition. If you want to know more than that, you should go to a tavern called the Rat's Tail and ask there about what Tooth was up to."

Midian raised his eyebrows. "Refreshing honesty. I appreciate that. Would the Rat's Tail still be open tonight? No? How are your rooms, then?"

"Leaky and wet," Lanudo said bluntly, "but I'll give you the same rooms your colleagues stayed in if you want to search them."

"Splendid," said Midian. "How much?"

Lanudo charged him the same he would have on a dry night and, as the pair of them went upstairs, resolved to sleep in the bed of the handcart that the cooper three doors down kept behind his shop. Just to be safe.

THE TYRANNY OF GHOSTS

12 Vult

A week after they left Arthuun, they heard the first shrieks in the night. Ekhaas sat beside their small fire and listened to the screams and wails as they rolled back and forth in the darkness. The jungle played tricks with distance. With rare exceptions, when a ridge or outcropping rose above the canopy and gave them a view of the green horizon, their world was limited to a hundred, maybe a hundred and fifty paces in any direction. The shrieks had the same thin quality as distant thunder, but they could have been much closer.

"Suud Anshaar?" said Tenquis.

"Varags," answered Tooth. "We're on the edge of their territory now. Another day, then we'll hear the Wailing Hill."

"Is it possible the howls that are supposed to be Suud Anshaar are really just the howls of varags?" Geth asked.

"All of the hunter legends say there's no mistaking the wails of Suud Anshaar for the cries of anything alive." Tooth stirred the fire, then sat back. "Gives us another story, Ekhaas. Something to listen to besides varags."

Though they'd tried to use false names at first, Tooth had figured out who they were within a day of leaving Arthuun. Word of events in Rhukaan Draal had filtered down to the south of Darguun after all. Tooth didn't ask them for their version of the story, though—some sort of unspoken hunter's courtesy, Ekhaas suspected. Maybe the bugbear had his own secrets.

And Tariic hadn't, as they'd feared, put a bounty on them. Without a reward, Tooth didn't have any incentive to turn on them. Rhukaan Draal was a long way away and the people of Arthuun had other things to worry about besides who ruled in Rhukaan Draal. As Tooth had put it, "Haruuc was a good *chib*. He traveled south sometimes. He paid attention to us. They say he hunted in the Khraal when he was a young warrior. This

Tariic—what do we know about him? What's he done? We hear stories of a victory in battle against the Valenar, but the stories don't say that Tariic fought personally."

With varags howling in the distance and Suud Anshaar only a couple of days' travel away, Ekhaas felt emboldened. "Tooth," she said, "how would you like to hear the real story of the Battle of Zarrthec from someone who was there?"

The bugbear cupped his big ears in interest. Ekhaas sat a little closer to the fire, closed her eyes, drew a deep breath, then opened her eyes again. "*Raat shi anaa*—the story continues. The sun rose on a battlefield covered with tattered fog, where an army of Darguun waited for an ancient foe . . ."

As the story of the battle, of Dagii's cunning and his warriors' bravery unfolded, Tooth sat up straighter and leaned forward until he might have fallen in the fire if he had lost his balance. Tenquis and Geth, who already knew the story, and Chetiin, who'd also been there, sat forward too. Even Marrow raised her head to listen, especially at the point where she and Chetiin arrived leading reinforcements of *taarka'khesh*, the wolf-riding cousin clan of the *shaarat'khesh*. Ekhaas downplayed her own part in the battle—how she'd rallied Dagii's troops with her songs—but she couldn't in all modesty leave it out entirely.

By the time she finished, eight of the twelve moons had risen, and the shrieks of the varags had moved even farther away. ". . . and with the last of the elves fleeing back to their hiding place in the Mournland, Dagii mounted the command hill and took up the *Riis Shaari'mal*, the ancient battle standard of Dhakaan under which he'd fought, waved it for his surviving warriors to see, and proclaimed the battle a victory. *Raat shan gath'kal dor*—the story stops but never ends."

Tooth sat back, his breathing as quick as if he'd just fought the battle himself. His open hand slapped his chest in appreciation. "*Paatcha*, Ekhaas! Now that's a story—and your Dagii sounds more worthy of respect than Tariic could ever be. I'd like to meet him."

THE TYRANNY OF GHOSTS

Ekhaas leaned back as well. Her blood sang with the euphoria of a story well told, and her heart ached—in a pleasant way—for Dagii's absence. "If we're successful in Suud Anshaar, maybe you will some day," she said.

Tooth's eyes flashed in the firelight. "I haven't asked why you're going there," he said after a moment. "You hired me to get you there, not to take you inside, so I've held my tongue. But I'm curious. The stories say that the ruins have been untouched since before the fall of Dhakaan and that they hide a fabulous treasure. Emeralds as big as a goblin's fist. Pearls as big as mine. Gold coins the size of dinner plates—"

"Nothing like that," said Ekhaas. "I think the hunters of the Khraal have been making stories up. I suppose there could be a treasure in Suud Anshaar, but I haven't heard of one. What we're looking for is different, the remains of something that was broken long ago."

"All this way for something broken?" Tooth snorted. "Are you even sure it's there?"

The question brought back doubts that had plagued them all the way from Volaar Draal. Was one cryptic reference on a stela really enough evidence to venture into jungle ruins? They'd had less evidence when they had gone searching for the Rod of Kings for Haruuc, but they'd also had Geth and Wrath. *Duur'kala* songs had woken the connection the rod and the sword shared through their origin, allowing Geth to find the way. The shifter still felt that connection—he could draw Wrath and point the way to the rod in Rhukaan Draal without hesitation. He had no sense of the shield or its shattered fragments, though. Maybe because it was broken. Maybe because new songs were needed. Maybe because the fragments of the shield no longer existed in Suud Anshaar or anywhere else.

Ekhaas pushed back the doubt. After Volaar Draal, if they didn't have hope of finding something in Suud Anshaar, they had nothing. *She* had nothing. "Absolutely certain," she said.

Tooth shook his head, but then looked at Ekhaas hopefully. "If do you see any treasure, could you bring some back to me? Just to prove that I was here, of course."

"Of course," said Ekhaas.

The sun rose the next day to the kind of sticky, mist-shrouded morning they'd come to expect in the Khraal. They set off early, Tooth leading them with even more care than he normally did. About mid-morning, with the mist burned away, he paused to sniff the air, then cautiously pulled aside a big fern. Behind it were the gnawed and broken bones of a jungle boar—several boars, Ekhaas realized—all heaped up together. The bones were several days old, but there was a foul tang in the air that had nothing to do with rot.

"Varags," said Tooth. "They piss on the remains of their kills."

"There's not much left for a scavenger to pick over," observed Geth.

"They don't piss on the remains to spoil them. They do it to mark their pack's territory."

Geth bared his teeth. "They sound more like animals than goblins."

"They are more animal than *dar*," Tooth said. He glanced sideways at Ekhaas. "There's an old legend that the Dhakaani used magic to breed them out of hobgoblins and dire wolves."

"That's just a legend," said Ekhaas stiffly. "Legends also say that before the rise of Dhakaan, hobgoblins bred bugbears as warriors and goblins as slaves."

"Didn't they?" asked Tenquis. "I'd heard that they did."

Ekhaas gave the tiefling a dark look. So did Chetiin.

Marrow, sniffing around the bones, squatted beside it and sprayed her urine onto the stinking heap. Tooth noticed what she was doing too late to stop her. "No!" he snarled. "Balinor's blood, if they come this way now, they'll know we were here."

The worg snarled back at him, and Chetiin clarified, "She says that if they mark their territory with scent, they'll already

THE TYRANNY OF GHOSTS

know we were here when they come this way. Now they'll also know this pack has a strong female with them."

Tooth grimaced. "That isn't likely to help. Keep going and stay alert. Varags spend most of the day sleeping, but when they hunt, they're almost silent."

The sun rose to its apex, and the stifling heat of the morning became oppressive. They saw and heard nothing more of the varags, though once or twice Ekhaas thought she caught a whiff of varag urine. Tooth's wariness was contagious. Ekhaas found herself tensing up and frequently had to force her body to relax. Geth didn't so much walk as prowl, hand never far from Wrath's hilt, the hair on his neck and forearms as visibly ruffled as Marrow's coat. Chetiin all but vanished into the undergrowth, invisible unless one knew where to look for him. Tenquis held his wand at the ready, twitching it at every unexpected noise or motion.

The end of the undergrowth was so sudden, it was startling. One moment they were among trees and ferns, and the next they were stepping out onto the hard surface of an ancient Dhakaani road. Trees grew together overhead, the canopy turning the road into a tunnel. In spite of its age, the road had survived remarkably well. The black paving stones had mostly remained level, and few plants broke through between them.

"The last landmark," said Tooth. "Stories said there was a road running through the jungle to Suud Anshaar." He looked to Geth and Ekhaas. "We can follow it and be there faster, but we're more visible."

"We're not entirely silent when we have to chop our way through the jungle, either," Geth pointed out. "Follow the road."

Tooth answered with a tight nod and moved off into the gloom.

"We always seem to walk roads the Dhakaani laid down," murmured Chetiin as they followed. "Here. On our journey to Darguun as we rode up to the Marguul Pass. In the Seawall Mountains when we sought the Rod of Kings. Even the road

to Volaar Draal—built by Kech Volaar in imitation of the Dhakaani. We're chasing the empire."

"Everywhere we go, Dhakaan was there before us," said Ekhaas. "It stretched from one side of Khorvaire to the other. From ruins in the Endworld Mountains in the east to Yrlag along the Grithic River in the west; from Ja'shaarat, the city that forms the foundations of Sharn, in the south, and north to—" She shrugged. "There are legends that say *dar* reached the Frostfell during the height of Dhakaan's power. We live with the ghosts of the empire."

"And under the rod's influence, Tariic would re-create it." Chetiin walked a few paces in silence before adding, "Do you think such a thing would be so bad?"

Ekhaas's ears flicked. "For most of my life," she said, "I have been devoted to the memory of the empire. As Kech Volaar, I wouldn't have wanted anything more than the glories of Dhakaan reborn. But the cost?" She spread her hands. "Even with the power of the Rod of Kings behind him, Tariic would face a battle with every other nation of Khorvaire."

"The rod pushes him, shows him how an emperor ruled," said Chetiin. "He doesn't see the world as it is anymore, only as it was. Without the rod—without Tariic . . ."

Geth, walking ahead with Tenquis, looked back at them. "Are you seriously talking about a new empire?" he asked incredulously.

"A dream doesn't die so easily, Geth," Ekhaas said. "Dhakaan is with *dar* every moment, every day, and"—she stamped the surface of the road—"everywhere we go. The reminders of our past surround us. They are us. The Dhakaani knew *muut* and *atcha*. They had *duur'kala*. They gave birth to the *shaarat'khesh*. Some records in the vaults of Volaar Draal suggest that the oldest of the lowland Ghaal'dar clans like the Rhukaan Taash, the Gantii Vus, and the Mur Talaan might have origins in companies within the imperial armies."

"Six thousand years ago when the empire fell!"

THE TYRANNY OF GHOSTS

"It's hard to break from the traditions of millennia. The legacy of Dhakaan marks our lives in ways we can't control. Honor and duty bind us. We don't just live with ghosts—we live under the tyranny of ghosts." Ekhaas let a crooked smile emerge onto her face. "Just because I don't believe a return to the Age of Dhakaan is possible doesn't mean I don't still dream about it."

"Haruuc could have done it," Tenquis said suddenly. "I'm no goblin, but I would have followed him."

"*Cho*," agreed Tooth. The bugbear had also slowed to listen to their conversation. "Haruuc could have. If the Last War had ended differently—"

He didn't have the chance to finish his speculation. Some change in the rising heat of the afternoon brought a sluggish breeze to stir the leaves along the side of the road. Marrow's head snapped up and around, her nostrils flaring, a growl rumbling from her throat. Chetiin whirled. "Varags!"

The wind-stirred bushes behind them exploded.

CHAPTER ELEVEN
13 Vult

Geth ripped Wrath from his scabbard, but their attackers were already on them. They moved fast. Very fast. He caught only a brief glimpse of hairy brown limbs before the first of the varags was on him. He barely got his gauntlet up in time to block the creature's strike. A heavy grinder like Tooth's but much older, the blade worn to a curve by long sharpening, went scraping across the black metal. Geth struck back, but the varag slid aside with frightening speed. His blow found only air.

Then it was past him and whirling to attack again. Geth turned, keeping it in his sight, and finally got a good look at the creature. The varag's face resembled a hobgoblin's, with flat nose and thin lips, but stretched out and thrust forward almost like a muzzle, its teeth sharp and prominent. Flat, heavy horns grew across its brow almost like armor. Its long, powerful legs had the backward bend of an animal's. Its arms were almost as long as its legs and when the varag turned, it hunched forward to pivot around one clawed hand. Rough leathers wrapped a body that was as tall as a bugbear but much leaner, like a hungry wolf.

The varag howled as it lunged a second time—a battle cry, Geth realized as Wrath translated words barely recognizable as thick, guttural Goblin. "Blood and meat! *Blood and meat!*"

The ancient grinder battered Geth's gauntlet again, but this time Geth twisted his hand and grabbed the varag's arm as the blade skittered away. He stepped into the varag's charge,

ducked, and heaved. The shrieking creature—no matter that it spoke, used a weapon, and wore clothes, Geth couldn't think of it as anything other than a beast—hurtled over his shoulder and crashed hard into the ancient stones of the road. Its words cut off with a clashing of teeth. The impact would only stun it for a moment. Geth moved in, Wrath raised and ready to chop down.

Long feet with claws even heavier than those on the varag's fingers raked at him. Geth jumped back, but the claws still caught him a blow across the belly, shredding his shirt and tearing into his skin. The wounds were shallow—deeper and it would have been his guts instead of shreds of cloth sagging to the ground.

Geth wanted to look and see how the others were doing. He could hear the sounds of their fighting, but he didn't dare take his eyes off his attacker. The varag was too fast. As it twisted to its feet and grabbed for its grinder, Geth reached into himself—and shifted.

Some shifters manifested claws or fangs or a burst of speed when they drew on the power of their lycanthrope ancestors. Geth's gift was sheer toughness. He felt the sense of invulnerability that shifting brought burning in his blood, toughening his skin, making his already thick, coarse hair even thicker. The gashes across his belly closed themselves into angry scars. He sank back into a crouch, sword and gauntlet raised.

The varag hesitated, as if it could sense the change in him. As if it knew that he had become a little more like it. The creature paced back and forth, hunched over on three limbs, its nostrils flaring as it breathed in his scent. Geth peeled back his lips and snarled at it. The varag growled in return and came at him.

Geth leaped to meet it. They came together hard, but this time Geth caught the grinder on the back of Wrath. He twisted the twilight blade, and the deep teeth on the sword's back caught the grinder, locking it in place. The varag howled and raked at him with the claws of its other hand, but all they did

THE TYRANNY OF GHOSTS

was add to the shreds that hung from Geth's shirt and vest. Geth drew back his right arm, curled his gauntleted hand into a fist, and drove it hard into the varag's face.

Bones crunched and the varag staggered back, blood welling up from the imprint of Geth's knuckles. Geth didn't let up. He stayed on top of the varag, holding the lock on its grinder, pounding away with his metal-encased fist. The thing's howl of anger turned to one of pain and confusion. It let go of the grinder and turned to run.

Geth lunged and slashed with Wrath. The edge of the sword sliced into the meat of the varag's leg. It folded instantly. The varag pitched forward, arms flailing. Geth didn't give it a chance to recover. He struck hard and fast. Wrath bit deep into its shoulder and halfway through its neck.

A savage growl and a terrible, short scream brought him around, fear for his friends rising in him. The growl was Marrow, though, and the scream a varag—she had it on the ground, her massive jaws around its throat. As he watched, she twisted her head and ripped. The varag's throat tore out in a spray of gore. Marrow threw her bloody muzzle back and howled her triumph.

Geth raised Wrath to the sky and howled with her.

Around Ekhaas and the others, the last two varags hesitated in their whirling, blurring attacks. One was already bleeding from a deep wound; the other bore the smoking scars of acidic fumes—one of Tenquis's spells. Geth caught the glance that passed between them.

They were going to break, he realized, and if they ran, there would be no catching up to them. They would escape, and all the varags in the area would know there was two-legged prey to be had—if they didn't already.

"Stop them!" he spat, but Tooth was already moving. With a stationary target, he swung his grinders as easily as if he were chopping jungle growth. The wounded varag was caught off guard. One arm came off at the elbow and went flying into the undergrowth. The other came off at the shoulder and hit the

ground with a meaty thump. A third stroke of Tooth's grinders took off the creature's head.

The final varag turned and ran. Tenquis flicked his wand at it with one hand, hurling a small metal sphere with the other—in the same moment that Ekhaas's voice rose in song.

The sphere burst against the varag's back. Thin yellow-green vapors, churned by the dissonance of Ekhaas's song, billowed up around the fleeing creature. The varag wailed, clapping hands to its ears while squeezing its eyes shut, but it was too late. It stumbled away from the vapors and crashed to its knees, then slumped over. Its hair was already curled and black from the acid, the skin underneath already burned raw. Blood trickled between the fingers that still clutched its ears.

"Four of them," said Chetiin. "Four of them against six of us. They don't hold back."

"I told you they're not afraid of anything," Tooth said hoarsely. "We were lucky it was only four. *Maabet*, we're in trouble. Other varags will find the corpses. They'll track us. If we can get out of their territory, we might be safe."

Geth grabbed his arm. "We can't turn back now."

"You saw how fast varags move. Once they start tracking you, there's no outrunning them. Even leaving their territory may not stop them, but it gives us a chance. We can let them quiet down, then come back."

"Then Suud Anshaar is safer," said Ekhaas. "You said varags don't go near it."

"That only makes it safe from varags," Tooth growled. He pulled free from Geth and pointed up the old Dhakaani road. "That will take you right to the Wailing Hill. Or at least it's supposed to. We've got a deal. I'll wait for you at the other end of the road at noon, when the varags are mostly asleep, for three days. If you don't come back, I'm heading back to Arthuun."

"You'll be on your own," Geth said.

"Might be better." Tooth turned and started trotting down the road, moving with surprising silence for someone as big as he.

THE TYRANNY OF GHOSTS

The sudden shrieks of varags from that direction—not close but not so distant either, and not hunting calls, but more like a pack skirmish—made him pause. Marrow growled something.

"She says," called Chetiin, "that if she was hunting, she'd follow prey on its own before she followed prey in a group."

Tooth looked down the road, then back up at them. "Blood," he grumbled—then came back to them. "But I'm not going into the ruins, just waiting for you outside them."

Geth could have smiled at that, but the knot of fear that the howls produced in his own belly wouldn't let him. "Done," he said and started along the old road again.

The others fell in alongside him. Tooth looked at Ekhaas and Tenquis. "Any magic you have that might slow them down would be helpful."

The *duur'kala* and the artificer glanced at each other, then Ekhaas shook her head. "No," she said, "but I can help us move faster."

She started to sing again, the song low but rhythmic. The magic caught at Geth's feet, strengthened his legs, and eased the breath in his throat. Soon they were moving at a running pace, even though they still seemed only to be walking. He wasn't sure they'd be able to outrun varags if the creatures gave chase, but at least they wouldn't be as easy to catch.

He kept Wrath in his hand and ready.

The sun had moved a double handspan across the sky when shrieks and howls broke out behind them. The varags had become more active as the heat of the day had passed and Geth had almost gotten used to the distant barks and short screams. The sound that rose from behind them was different, though. It was angry. It was vengeful. It was hungry.

Geth knew what it meant—and he knew he didn't have to say it to the others. The bodies of the varags they'd fought had been found. In unspoken agreement, they all picked up their already magically enhanced pace. The angry howls faded, and the only sound on the thick, hot air was Ekhaas's song. Slowly the

jungle birds found their voices again, and soon her song blended into theirs.

Tooth looked grim. "They'll hunt in silence now," he said. "Some will come up the road behind. Others will come through the trees. Those are the ones we'll have to watch out for."

The growth around them had changed. They'd entered a region of tall trees with a thick canopy that shaded and stunted smaller plants. The landscape was more open, and they could see a greater distance into the jungle. If varags did approach them through the trees, they'd be able to see them coming—hopefully. Plants weren't the only things on the jungle floor. Here and there, vine-choked ruins rose out of centuries' worth of fallen vegetation. Crumbling walls, heaps of squared stones, the shapes of buildings, all of them with the familiar designs of Dhakaani style.

"Are we there?" Geth asked Tooth. "Is this Suud Anshaar?"

"No," the bugbear said. "These ruins have no name. There are places like this everywhere in the Khraal. But we're getting close. The land is rising." He grimaced. "And the sun is setting."

Geth looked up to the canopy. Under the gloom of the trees, it was easy to lose track of the day. The green-tinged bright spot that was the sun had actually vanished from among the leaves, dipping down below the branches to throw irregular beams of brightness among the tree trunks. Where the light failed, shadows were deep; where it penetrated, the brilliance was dazzling.

Something in the middle distance flickered across one of the bars of light.

Geth's breath caught in his throat. A bird? An animal? No, the jungle had gone quiet again.

"Varags," he growled, tightening his grip on Wrath's hilt. "They're pacing us."

Tooth cursed quietly, followed Geth's gaze, then cursed again. Ekhaas looked, too, and her ears flattened back. Tenquis scanned the shadows. "Where?" he demanded, wand already raised.

THE TYRANNY OF GHOSTS

Two more beams of sunlight flickered, and the tiefling cursed as well. Chetiin hissed suddenly, however. "They're letting themselves be seen," he said. "It's a distraction. Watch the other side!"

Geth swung around and peered into the jungle on the other side of the road. With the light playing across them, the trees and ruins were better lit. Nothing moved there. "I don't see—"

The attack came from above, launched from one of the lowest branches of the great trees. From the corner of his eye, Geth saw a swinging blur. There was no time to cry out as a varag gripping a long vine hurtled down into their midst. The creature howled just before it struck, a shocking sound. Powerful legs kicked out—at Ekhaas.

She fell hard, her song ending in a gasp of surprise. The magic faltered so suddenly that it left Geth—left all of them—reeling for an instant. The varag twisted on its vine, swinging around for another howling pass. Geth staggered, fighting to find his balance, and slashed by instinct more than intent. Wrath bit into flesh, the howl rose into a shriek, and the varag lost its grip on the vine. The creature hit the ground and rolled, arms and legs flailing. Marrow snarled and bounded after it.

Geth left the varag to its end beneath the worg's jaws and went to Ekhaas. She was struggling to sit up, the heavy leather of her armor torn by the varag's foot claws. Her breath came harsh. Geth took her hand and helped her up. "Are you—?"

"It knew what it was doing!" she gasped. "Just run!"

It knew what it was doing . . . the varag had deliberately targeted Ekhaas. Geth's head snapped up and around.

The varags that had been pacing them in the middle distance were already racing directly toward them. There were more, too, swarming out of hiding places in the deep shadows.

"Rat!" He released Ekhaas to stand on her own. Tooth, Tenquis, and Chetiin had seen the danger too. Chetiin gestured sharply at a ruined wall, a defensible position that would keep the varags off their backs. Geth nodded and turned to it, but Ekhaas grabbed him.

"No, run!" she said. She pointed along the road. Geth looked—

—and saw what she'd seen ahead while he'd been staring into the jungle to the side. Perhaps four long bowshots away, the red-gold sunlight shone where the road emerged from the trees and started to climb the slope of a hill.

Suud Anshaar? There was no time to wonder. The protection of the ruined wall was dubious, their six no match for the advancing number of varags. "Run!" he ordered and led the way.

The varags abandoned silence when they saw their prey break. Their howls and shrieks filled the jungle, and once again, Wrath translated the thick words for Geth. *Meat! Blood! Flesh!* He tried to block them out and concentrate on sprinting for the sunlight ahead.

The road gave them a slight edge—the varags were forced to contend with the underbrush in their pursuit. Even as thin as it was, it slowed them down just a little. Geth could hear them tearing through bushes, ferns, and clutching vines. He stole a glance over his shoulder and wished he hadn't. The varags came on in bounding leaps, jumping over obstacles and running like animals on all fours. Marrow barked a challenge at them as she ran, but Chetiin had thrown himself onto her back. He leaned down close to her shoulders, whispering in her ears and keeping her on the road.

The bright end of the road drew closer. The undergrowth grew thicker at the jungle's edge, but not so thick that Geth couldn't see through it. There were ruins out there, big and blocky. Nothing to set them apart from the ruins they'd seen elsewhere in the jungle except that here the trees hadn't taken hold.

Between one ragged breath and the next, he wondered what kind of place could exist for centuries in the middle of a jungle but not be taken over by it.

On his right, Ekhaas ran with long strides; on his left, Tooth had abandoned the stealth he'd shown earlier and charged forward like a bull, eyes fixed on the end of the road. Tenquis . . .

THE TYRANNY OF GHOSTS

Tenquis was slowing, stopping as he fumbled in a pocket of his long vest. Geth spun back and grabbed for him. "Keep up!"

The tiefling wrenched his arm away. His golden eyes were blazing. "I can buy us time!"

The first varags were drawing closer. Geth could see the spittle that flecked their lips. He cursed and readied himself for a fight, but Tenquis had his clenched fist out of his pocket. Silvery dust, a whole handful, glittered as he flung it into the air. Tenquis gestured with his wand and the dust streamed away to spread into a thin, sparkling cloud.

The lead varag raced into it, two more of his pack close behind him.

Lightning flashed as if Tenquis had conjured a storm cloud. It danced from silvery dust to the first varag to the second and the third, then back again, leaving the creatures twisting and yelping. A fourth varag entered the cloud and was jolted as well. Others following behind slowed warily.

"Now run!" Tenquis said and leaped into motion. Geth stayed with him. The varags let out another howl as they saw their prey fleeing, and Geth heard their crashing progress resume, but the charge had been broken. Up ahead, the others had reached the edge of the trees and stood outlined by sunset's light. Ekhaas stepped forward, and her song swelled. Geth almost felt the bright and rippling notes wash over him, touching him as they passed. Once again, the varags howled. He risked a glance back.

Glittering golden motes drifted on the air, settling slowly to cover the ground, plants, and at least one of their pursuers. The varag was scrubbing at its eyes and shrieking in confusion. "Bright!" Wrath translated. "Too bright!"

The other varags knew better than to enter another sparkling cloud. They were already flowing around it, but again they slowed. Geth put his head down and ran hard for the end of the road. He could hear the varags' rapid footfalls. He thought he could hear their breathing. He didn't turn around again. Ahead,

167

Ekhaas and Chetiin were shouting encouragement, even as they stepped back into the fading light. Marrow was howling intimidation. Tooth had both of his grinders ready. Thirty paces . . . twenty . . . ten . . .

A varag shrieked with triumph directly behind him. The sound was like a knife. Geth clenched his teeth and whirled, lashing out with Wrath even before he'd locked eyes on his enemy. A lucky strike—the twilight blade slashed across an outstretched arm. It caught on bone, pulling the varag off balance and dragging a scream of pain from the creature. There were more varags close behind though. Geth met their howls with a roar of defiance and raised Wrath again. Somewhere at his back, Tenquis shouted his name—

Roar, howl, scream, and shout were all lost in the wail that rolled through the gathering night. There was an eternity of agony in that wail. It was high and weirdly echoing, the tones of it clashing with every other sound like the edge of a blade scraping against armor. It sent a shiver along Geth's back and raised every hair on his neck and arms. Conflicting instincts fought inside him—turn and face the source, or flee instantly without looking back.

The varags' howls turned to short-lived screeches. They slid to a stop, claws digging into the ground and scrabbling across stones. The creatures seemed to freeze for a moment—then the wail came again and they were turning as fast as they could, fleeing silent back into the night. Even the one Geth had wounded and the one Ekhaas's song-conjured dust had blinded fled as best as they were able, stumbling and hobbling, mewling like pups.

The wail faded and did not come again.

Geth turned around slowly. The others were standing and staring silently up the road beyond the jungle wall. Without speaking, Geth went to join them.

Suud Anshaar—there could be no doubting the identity of the ruins that rose above them like a crown set on top of a

low hill. The bloody light of the setting sun washed over the ancient fortress, and for a moment Geth could imagine it had been constructed not of stone, but bones. The ruined walls had the curve of hips and femurs, the fragmented towers the broken appearance of ribs, cracked and smashed to extract the marrow. On the surrounding slope lay massive tumbled stones, fallen over time from the hilltop and rolled downhill by their own weight, as if they sought to escape this haunted place.

Just as he'd seen while running, no trees adorned the naked ruins, only a few hardy vines and dry, scrubby bushes. Even those faded before they got anywhere near the broken walls of the fortress.

"The wail," he asked Ekhaas quietly, "a ghost? Many ghosts?"

"I don't know what it was. It doesn't matter." Her ears went back, and her jaw tightened. "We're going in."

Geth looked to Tooth. "Do you want to wait for us here?"

The bugbear's eyes flicked between the bony ruins and the dense fringe of the jungle. "Maybe I'll wait under the walls instead."

This time, Geth couldn't help smiling as they followed Ekhaas up the last stretch of ancient road.

CHAPTER TWELVE

27 Aryth

Tariic's summons came more than a week after Senen's mutilation and exile. Ashi had been expecting it, and she told herself that it was just coincidence that it came at a time when Oraan was not her guard. Tariic couldn't know the changeling's identity—could he?

Woshaar was the guard who delivered her to the throne room of Khaar Mbar'ost. He saluted his lhesh, then retreated. The great door of the chamber, a titanic slab of dark wood, slid down behind him, sealing Ashi in.

Tariic looked down on her from the blocky throne of Darguun, the Rod of Kings in his hand, a look of distaste on his face. "You're a scab, Ashi. You itch, you're ugly, and I want to tear you off and be rid of you."

She remembered the first time she'd entered the throne room. It had been her and Vounn's formal presentation to Lhesh Haruuc Shaarat'kor. The hall had been crowded with Darguun's warlords and clan chiefs, the walls hung with banners depicting their many crests. It had been night, and a mantle of shadows, emphasized rather than dispelled by scattered everbright lanterns, had rendered Haruuc powerful, proud, majestic, and mysterious.

Tariic had chosen to summon her by day. The sunlight that streamed through the tall windows behind the throne glowed around him—his presence was blinding. There were no warlords

or emissaries today, only Pradoor beside him on the dais and his three deaf-mute bugbear guards to the side.

The crests of the clans, Ashi realized, had been removed. The only banner that remained showed the black silhouette of a spiky crown above a purple bar. The crown of Darguun over the Rod of Kings. The symbol Tariic had taken as his own.

Ashi raised her chin and met Tariic's gaze. For the last week, Tariic's actions and Midian's parting words—*a surprise visit to some old friends*—had eaten at her, yet without Senen's aid, she'd had no way of warning Geth and Ekhaas that the gnome was on their trail. Oraan had kept her in her chambers, partly to avoid additional suspicion from Tariic, partly, she was certain, to give her rage time to cool. It hadn't.

"If I'm a scab," she said, "that makes you a bleeding wound."

Tariic's ears went back. He slammed the rod down onto the arm of the throne. "I am lhesh! You owe me respect!"

Ashi didn't flinch. "I owe you nothing," she said. She raised her hands, letting the sunlight flash on the silver wrist cuffs. "Feel free to take back these beautiful trinkets, if you want."

His ears went back even farther, and he hissed a word between his teeth. The bracelets grew chill, then cold. Ashi kept her face hard and her eyes fixed on Tariic. If Oraan had been there, she knew, he would have counseled patience, a smile, dissembling words. Senen and Vounn would have done the same, but where had dissembling gotten them?

The skin around the cuffs turned white. Pain tingled in Ashi's fingertips and climbed her arms. She kept her eyes on Tariic even as cold tears blurred her vision. When she could taste ice in the back of her mouth, she finally bent her head.

"*Atcha'rhu*," she said in Goblin. Your honor is great. It was a fight to keep her voice from trembling.

Tariic smiled benevolently and whispered again. The cold ebbed immediately. The fire in Ashi's belly only burned hotter. "You are merciful, lhesh," she said.

The bite of the comment seemed lost on Tariic, but maybe he

THE TYRANNY OF GHOSTS

believed he was. He sat back and gestured with the rod. "I have questions," he said. It was a command, not a request, but Ashi spread her aching hands in silent invitation. Tariic snapped his fingers. "Pradoor."

The old goblin priestess crouched down beside the throne. Craning her neck, Ashi could see that a rough arc of symbols had been drawn on the floor around her. Pradoor reached out and, with a certainty that was eerily at odds with her clouded eyes, let a handful of powder sift over coals in a metal bowl. Smoke rose around. Pradoor breathed it in and began chanting the words of a prayer calling on the gods of the Dark Six to separate lies from truth. Ashi felt Pradoor's magic brush against her, a sensation like questing hands on her mind.

They found no grip, though—the power of her dragonmark protected her against more than just Tariic's commands. While it shielded her, her mind was a blank page to all forms of divination and magical domination. Tariic had underestimated her. The fire in her belly grew a little more.

Pradoor didn't seem to notice anything amiss in her spell. The chant faded. "Ask your questions, lhesh," she croaked.

Tariic's gaze hadn't turned from Ashi. "How long have you known Geth and the others were in Volaar Draal?"

She thought quickly. "I found out when you did—when Senen confirmed it." She let hate fill her voice, disguising the secret triumph she felt.

"*Nu kuur doovol*," said Pradoor. "She speaks the truth."

Tariic's eyes narrowed. "Does she?"

Ashi wrinkled her nose and spat, "I do! How was I supposed to find out, Tariic? I haven't had any contact with Senen. Your guards saw to that."

"She speaks the truth."

"Senen sang messages to Volaar Draal," said Tariic. "If she could do that, she could sing a message anywhere in Khaar Mbar'ost."

"She didn't sing one to me," Ashi snapped back. She folded her frost-numbed arms across her chest.

"She speaks the—"

"Just tell me if she lies, Pradoor!" roared Tariic. The old goblin's blind eyes opened wide. She froze for an instant, then slowly bent her head. Tariic's gaze came back to Ashi.

"Have you had contact with Dagii of Mur Talaan, then?"

"No." A shiver of real fear crept across Ashi's shoulders. If Tariic suspected Dagii, if he questioned him, he'd learn everything. She kept her voice firm. "Why would I jeopardize a friend after what you did to Senen?"

"Maybe you had contact with him before Senen's treachery was revealed and punished."

Ashi offered a silent prayer for the warlord's safety. "I didn't."

Tariic's eyes darted to Pradoor, but the priestess remained still and silent. He rested his chin on his fist and stared at Ashi. "The changeling who posed as Aruget?"

"I don't know where he is." The questions were too close. Her dragonmark might foil Pradoor's spell, but Tariic was no fool. If he saw through her lies, they would all unravel. She had to turn the conversation back on him.

"I want to ask you a question," she said. "In the hall of honor, when you *tortured*"—she put a hard emphasis on the word, but Tariic made no reaction—"Senen, Midian told me you were sending him on an errand. I think you sent him to try and kill Geth and the others." She drew himself up. "Did he succeed?"

Tariic flicked his ears lazily, prolonging the answer. A fear that she hadn't expected built in Ashi. Midian couldn't actually have done it, could he?

"Yes," said Tariic finally.

Her heart dropped. No . . .

Beside the throne, Pradoor's expression tightened, and her face turned toward Tariic for an instant. The lhesh didn't notice, but Ashi did. Tariic was lying—Pradoor's spell had caught him! She felt her heart start beating again.

No, Ashi. She could almost hear Vounn's voice. *Tariic told*

that lie for a reason. Show people what they want to see, and they'll believe it. Ashi swallowed her hope. She seized her despair and held onto it. She dredged up all her memories of loss—Vounn's death, the death of her father, the realization that she was nothing more to House Deneith than an asset to be traded on—and hugged them close. Under such a burden, it was easy to crumble. Her shoulders went slack. Her breath stopped, then returned fast and shallow. Tears rose in her eyes.

She blinked them away—she'd never let Tariic see her cry, not for any reason.

And he was watching her, measuring her reaction. She found it easier than ever to hate him. "Do you have any more questions?" she asked harshly.

Again he paused before answering. "Those are all—for now." He had the thin smile of a merchant who'd just come out on the better end of a bargain.

"Then if I may leave you," Ashi said, taking refuge in formality, "I have duties to House Deneith that I must see to."

She didn't wait for an answer, just bent her head once, then turned and marched to the throne room door. It was still closed, but she stood facing it, staring at the dark wood with her back to Tariic. After a long while, she heard the lhesh shout, "Open the throne room!"

As soon as the creaking door had risen high enough, she ducked under so quickly her appearance startled Woshaar, and the guard had to run after her. Ashi didn't look back at him. She walked to her chambers with her head high and her expression hard, a mask to hide the racing energy inside.

Tariic had made a mistake. It was up to her to take advantage of it.

⚫ ⚫ ⚫ ⚫ ⚫ ⚫ ⚫

Oraan's turn as her guard came that evening. No sooner had Woshaar walked away, than Oraan stepped into her chambers,

closed the door, and hissed, "What were you doing? What were you thinking? You could have given us away!"

In the chair that had been Senen's, Ashi glared back at him. "I didn't exactly go looking for Tariic. He summoned me."

"And what have I been telling you? Keep your head down and your voice quiet. All of Khaar Mbar'ost has been talking about your visit to the throne room. They say you came out looking like Tariic had slapped you. Tariic's saying it was a reaction to bad news from House Deneith." The changeling stood straight and crossed his arms, his ears flicking just like a real hobgoblin's. "Tell me what really happened."

Without getting up, Ashi did. Oraan's ears went lower and lower. By the time she had finished, his lips had pulled back from his teeth. "You were lucky," he said. "*We* were lucky."

"Have you talked to Dagii lately?" Ashi asked. "I know Tariic hasn't questioned him, but has he done anything to him?"

Oraan gave her a sideways glance, as if the question puzzled him. "I'm keeping my distance. I haven't talked to Dagii, but I've seen him. Tariic has been forcing him out to more public appearance—rallies, speeches by the warlord who brought Darguun triumph over the Valenar, that sort of thing. He's using him to keep the people at a frenzy. I wouldn't want to be an elf in Rhukaan Draal right now."

"Have you found out anything more about what the Kech Shaarat are doing here or why Tariic has been dealing so heavily with the dragonmarked houses?"

"I said I've been keeping my distance. This isn't the time to draw attention."

"We're going to have to risk it," said Ashi. "And you can start by making contact with Dagii. We need to know more about whatever he might have learned in the last week."

Oraan's ears stood straight. "Not at the expense of revealing ourselves, we don't! Tariic's already suspicious. An agent who's caught is no good to anyone. We need to keep our heads down more than ever, move slowly—"

THE TYRANNY OF GHOSTS

"No." Ashi looked up at him. The rage that had simmered inside her since she'd left the throne room rose to a boil. "I've had enough of moving slowly. One of my friends is dead because of Tariic. Another one will never sing again. An assassin is hunting others. I've had enough. I want to stop Tariic, and hiding in my chambers isn't going to make that happen."

Oraan bared his teeth again. "Listen to me, Ashi," he growled. "You've been *very* lucky so far, but this isn't a game for amateurs. Midian may be gone, but anyone could be eyes and ears for—"

Ashi stood up and thrust her face into his. "When do I stop being an amateur, Oraan? When Geth, Ekhaas, Chetiin, Tenquis, and Dagii—and maybe even you—are all dead? When I have no allies left? I can't just put on another face and become someone else. I only have one life. You've got the King's Citadel of Breland behind you. I don't even have the support of my house anymore." She poked a finger into the middle of his chest. "Whatever Tariic is planning, I'm going to find out."

He grabbed her hand and pushed it away. "Ashi—"

Ashi twisted her hand in his grasp, grabbed onto his wrist, and wrenched his arm around. Surprise crossed the changeling's face, and he tried to twist back, but Ashi had grown up wrestling the other children of the savage Bonetree Clan. She kicked Oraan's feet out from under him as he turned, and went down with him as he fell, pinning him under her.

Hunter of the Shadow Marches. Lady of Deneith. She was a child of both worlds—why deny either?

"Dagii and Senen asked me to find out what Tariic wants with the dragonmarked houses," she said in Oraan's ear. "I'm going to. You can help me, or you can get out of my way."

She turned him loose and stood back. Oraan lay on the floor for a moment, then rolled over and looked up at her. He smiled, a grin without any humor or warmth at all.

"Welcome to the game," he said. "Where do you want to start?"

She was ready for him. "A week ago, I could have followed the advice Senen gave me—trade on the other houses' curiosity about Vounn's death. I think that source of interest will have been overtaken by Senen's mutilation now." Ashi sat down. "Vounn always said that the essence of diplomacy is using what people want to get what you need. The only thing I've got right now that the other houses would want is a direct line of communication to Tariic."

Oraan's ears stood straight as he rose. "You don't exactly have Tariic's favor."

"The other houses don't know that." Ashi lifted her chin. "As far as they know, I'm still Deneith's special envoy to Darguun—Tariic made that clear, didn't he? And he honored me today with a private audience to deliver bad news. I must be in his good graces."

"But the dragonmarked houses are already doing fast business with Tariic. How can you offer the viceroys a closer connection than that?"

"You don't understand the mindset of the houses," said Ashi with a smile. "They'll always want more. Special treatment, secret information, whatever they can get to give them an advantage." She sat back in her chair. "We should start with Redek d'Deneith. Baron Breven put him in charge of day-to-day Deneith operations in Darguun. I think it's time I found out what my own house has been up to."

● ● ● ◉ ● ● ●

9 Vult

However much energy she had, there were still civilities and practical matters to deal with. Ashi couldn't just march up to the viceroys of the dragonmarked houses that maintained enclaves in Rhukaan Draal. Some, like Pater d'Orien, she knew fairly well. Others, like the viceroys of Houses Vadalis and Sivis, she hardly knew at all. Not all of the viceroys were immediately

available. Redek operated from the large Deneith enclave at the Gathering Stone, two days' ride north of the city—it took time to summon him and for him to arrive. Nor was he in a talkative mood when he finally did. It took considerable charm to persuade him that she had a right to know what was happening with Deneith's resources.

The viceroys—and often their staffs—weren't her only obstacles. As much as she might disdain him, Ashi was sharply aware of Tariic's attention. He could put a stop to her investigations with a word, even if she claimed to be about the business of House Deneith. She could still only make her calls on the viceroys when Oraan was her escort. At least she was doing something, though. She woke up every day ready to face the wall of Tariic's ambition. If she didn't know whether Geth and the others had survived Midian's visit, she tried to believe that they had. After all, there was no sign of Midian, either.

The information that flowed to her was slow but sweet like honey. The problem was that it didn't fit together in any but the most obvious of ways.

Twelve days after Tariic had summoned her to the throne room, she pulled out her grandfather's sword and began to sharpen it. The bright blade never actually needed sharpening or polishing, but it had been her duty to do so as a child when the sword had belonged to her father, then huntmaster of the Bonetree Clan. The sound of the whetstone against the steel was like meditation. It kept her sane.

Senen and Dagii's assessment had been correct. Tariic was paying the dragonmarked houses with the tribute he exacted from the adoring clans of Darguun. A portion of that money went to House Deneith for the hiring of mercenaries—quite a reversal for the house that more typically made money by brokering the services of Darguul warriors. Squads of war wizards and battle-hardened warlocks had joined the hobgoblin troops that ranged along the border of Darguun and the Mournland. That was sensible, Ashi knew. The elves of Valenar

had an edge on the goblins of Darguun in both magic and mobility. The mercenary spellcasters provided by Deneith would even out one of those advantages.

Magebred horses purchased through House Vadalis would even the other. Ashi had seen some of the beautiful mounts for herself at Vadalis's small enclave on the outskirts of Rhukaan Draal. Kravin d'Vadalis assured her that they were very nearly the equal of Valenar warhorses.

Vadalis's dealings with Tariic had a more mundane side as well—magebred hogs and cattle, fat and meaty provisions on the hoof, passed along the roads of Darguun and out to supply bases. Other dragonmarked houses provided similarly mundane services. Tariic had hired stonespeakers from the gnomes of House Sivis and healers from the halflings of House Jorasco. Magewrights of House Cannith were in the field as well, providing maintenance for the arms and armor of Tariic's soldiers. Pater d'Orien was probably the busiest viceroy of all. His caravans ferried dragonmarked personnel and supplies to the places Tariic needed them.

Only House Lyrandar was absent—they'd thrown in their lot with Valenar by providing their raiders with flying transportation above the dangers of the Mournland. Ashi was confident none of the other houses would make that mistake. Any services they offered to Darguun would also be offered to Valenar in a nod to the neutrality of commerce.

There was no neutrality in Rhukaan Draal, though. Every viceroy Ashi had spoken with had the same look of admiration whenever they'd mentioned Tariic's name. She recognized the power of the Rod of Kings at work. If a matriarch or patriarch of one of the houses had chanced to visit Darguun, any illusion of neutrality would have vanished. For a while at least, the heads of the houses were content to keep their distance and collect the lhesh's money as he orchestrated a massive mobilization of troops aimed squarely at an enemy that had attacked Darguun once already.

THE TYRANNY OF GHOSTS

And just as Haruuc had foreseen, it seemed as if no one cared whether Darguun and Valenar—upstart nations carved out of human territory during the Last War—prepared to wipe each other from the map. So long as they kept things between themselves.

The problem was, as far as Ashi could tell, there was still no sign of Valenar response. The raiders Dagii had defeated seemed to have fled entirely. If there were Valenar lurking in the Mournland, they were staying very quiet. There were rumors that all of the elven warclans were gathering on the other side of the Mournland's deadly expanse, but nothing confirmed.

Tariic was preparing a strong defense. What was wrong with that?

Everything, Ashi told herself. And nothing.

Skiirrr, went the whetstone down one side of her sword, then *skiirrr* down the other.

The door opened and Oraan entered to start another evening's "guard duty." Ashi glanced up at him, then away. He would speak when he felt it was absolutely safe. Finally, he did. "Dagii has no news."

Skiirrr. "*Rond betch*," muttered Ashi, an old Bonetree curse. She put the whetstone aside and took up a piece of soft cloth. "Can you be more specific?"

"Tariic's still treating him like a hero. The Darguuls can't get enough of him—"

"Goblins like their heroes," Ashi commented.

"—but Tariic still isn't telling him anything. Dagii's worried that the Iron Fox company is turning into a ceremonial guard, so he's had Keraal slip some hard fighting into their daily training."

Ashi paused in her polishing. "He doesn't worry Tariic will notice?"

Oraan's ears twitched. "He has them fighting the Kech Shaarat. I think Tariic likes the conflict. The Iron Fox is in for a battle, though. Riila Dhakaan and Taak Dhakaan are settling a third contingent into the barracks tonight, and it's the biggest yet."

"Has there been any clue of where the last one was sent?" Ashi asked. The first Kech Shaarat to arrive in Rhukaan Draal had been worrying. To have a second and then a third pass through on their way to the border of the Mournland—that much they knew, though nothing specific—nagged at her.

Oraan shook his head.

Ashi grimaced. She gave her sword a final swipe with the polishing cloth, then slid the sword into its sheath. "We're missing something."

"Dagii said the same thing. But what?"

Ashi sat back. "We're stalking a mud pig." When Oraan looked at her quizzically, she shook her head. "It's something adults in the Shadow Marches do to get rid of children for a while—send them off to look for an animal that doesn't exist. It gives the adults some calm until the children give up, figure it out, or die trying."

Oraan's ears rose up high. Ashi shrugged. "It's a hard place. The game teaches children too. The mud pig is supposed to be able to move without making any noise and without leaving any tracks. The only way to catch one is to be just as quiet as it is, to act like it would, to think like it does—"

The insight that burst into her mind surprised even her. She sat up straight. "That's what we're missing," she said. "We need to think like Tariic. Like a hobgoblin."

"I have some experience in that sort of thing," Oraan pointed out. "And Dagii *is* a hobgoblin."

"But you're not a Darguul warlord, and Dagii's not the right kind of hobgoblin. He thinks about *atcha* and *muut*. He's too damn noble. We need someone who has Tariic's kind of ambition and guile."

"Aguus of Traakuum," said Oraan. "Or Daavn of Marhaan. But they belong to Tariic. We couldn't ask them without him finding out."

"I have someone else in mind," Ashi said. She stood and grabbed a cloak. With the year turning toward mid-winter, even

THE TYRANNY OF GHOSTS

Rhukaan Draal was becoming cold by night. "We're going for a walk."

◦ ◦ ◦ ◉ ◦ ◦ ◦

The guards at the gates of Khaar Mbar'ost let her and Oraan pass without comment. If there was one good thing about living in a fortress with creatures as comfortable by night as by day, Ashi thought, it was that no one paid much attention to when you came or went.

She led Oraan in the direction of the *Khaari Batuuvk*, the Bloody Market. It was quieter by night than by day, though even more dangerous with only desperate or particularly unsavory merchants remaining open through the late watches. Ashi turned aside before the street opened onto the market and its maze of stalls, though. For a city founded only thirty years before, this area of Rhukaan Draal was relatively old—some of the first structures built, after Haruuc had more or less razed the Cyran market town that had once stood on the site, had been built here. Haruuc himself had made one of the early buildings his base of power while Khaar Mbar'ost was built. Tradition held strong, and while there were better parts of Rhukaan Draal, the warlords of some of the largest and most powerful clans still kept their city seats there.

A banner with a crest depicting a fanged maw wreathed in flames hung on the house where she stopped. A hobgoblin guard stood before the door. "Ashi d'Deneith will see Munta the Gray of Gantii Vus," she told him in Goblin.

The guard looked her over, a glimmer of recognition in his eye, but his ears flicked back. "Munta sees no one," he said. He sounded a little sad about it.

"Announce me," said Ashi. "Munta will speak to me."

"He sees no one. By his command, he is to be left alone."

Ashi held down a growl of frustration and stepped a few paces back from the front of the building. The house had been built

183

like a miniature fortress with the windows small and high above the street. Many windows still showed light, though, including one that was slightly larger than the rest and commanded a view of the Bloody Market. Ashi cupped her hands around her mouth and bellowed up, "Munta! Ashi d'Deneith wants to talk to you. Get your nose out of your cup and let me in!"

She was no *duur'kala*, but she could still summon up an impressive shout. Her call echoed along the street. The guard looked startled, uncertain of how to handle this challenge. Oraan just looked nervous. He swept the street with his gaze as if checking who might have heard.

Up in the window, a fat figure moved. Ashi called again, this time more respectfully. "Elder warrior, speak to me. I need your experience!"

She lowered her hands and waited. After a long moment, she thought she heard someone shout a command inside the house. A few moments more and the door of the house opened. A goblin servant stuck his head out. "Munta will speak with you," he said, and stood aside to let them in.

By human standards, the city house of the Gantii Vus was barren, but after weeks among Darguuls, Ashi could recognize signs of the clan's proud history in the weapons hung on walls and the carvings of battle and triumph on the sparse furnishings. There was a fine layer of dust over everything, though, a sense of wear to edges and corners, as if the clan—or its warlord—had lost some of that ancient pride.

Munta met them in a room hung with trophies—more weapons, pieces of armor, a few grislier relics of past fights. The room smelled strongly of old sweat and alcohol. Ashi guessed that this was where Munta had been spending most of his time recently. The old warlord who had been Haruuc's first ally waited for them by the window. When Ashi had first met him, she'd seen a hobgoblin well past his prime but still vigorous and keen-eyed, his remaining muscle hidden behind a padding of fat. She hadn't seen Munta since the day of their failed assassination of

THE TYRANNY OF GHOSTS

Tariic. The change in him was sad. He truly looked old. If there were muscles left behind his fat, they were slack and weak. His eyes were dull and bloodshot.

"*Saa*, Ashi," he said. He gestured with a cup, a simple pewter tumbler, to the flagon that stood on a table. "*Korluaat?*"

She shook her head at the offer of the fiery liquor. Munta shrugged and drained his cup, then looked at Oraan. "Who are you?"

"Oraan of Rhukaan Taash." Oraan thumped his chest in a salute.

"My escort," said Ashi. "Tariic wants to be sure I'm protected."

"Tariic?" A little life returned to Munta's face. "You're still in favor with him. Could you pass a message to him? Tell him I want to serve. Ask him to put me out in the field. I may not be as strong as I used to be, but my mind is still sharp."

"I'll tell him," Ashi promised.

Munta smiled and nodded. Wrinkled old ears twitched. "I think the lhesh doubts my loyalty," he said. "When he first took the throne, I spoke harshly of his decision to exclude me from the battle with the Valenar. Then when the traitors tried to kill him, I failed to capture that *taat* Geth. Lhesh Tariic needs to know that I only want to serve him. I need to be useful."

The insidious influence of the Rod of Kings on a proud warlord made Ashi grind her teeth in anger. She remembered standing with Munta in the hall of honor and listening to his complaints before Tariic had gotten his hands on the rod. The lord of the Gantii Vus had been angry, not mewling and servile. That was as compelling a reason as any to block Tariic's plans!

"Tariic doesn't invite you to court?" she asked.

"He invited me to stay away," Munta said bitterly. "I've been set aside, an 'honor' for my service to Haruuc. I haven't seen the lhesh in weeks."

"Good." Ashi reached out, laid a hand on Munta's arm, and drew on the power of her dragonmark. It flashed hot across her

skin, then passed into Munta. He drew a sharp breath, as if he'd been plunged into icy water, and stumbled. Ashi caught his arm and held him up. "Munta?"

"*Maabet*!" he cursed. He blinked as if waking from a dream. "What was that?"

"My dragonmark shielding you. How do you feel?" She looked at him closely. "How do you feel about Tariic?"

"Tariic? I . . . he . . ." Munta frowned. "Why do I want to drop down on my knees before him?"

"Oraan, watch the door," said Ashi. "Make sure no one disturbs us. Munta, you need to sit down."

She told him the story of the Rod of Kings as quickly and briefly as she could. Haruuc's fall under the rod's curse and Tariic's discovery of its power. The truth of their attempt to kill Tariic before he could take possession of the rod. Their failure. Tariic's utter dominance of the warlords—including him. "The protection of my dragonmark will only last for a day," she said. "If you want to stay free of the rod's power, you need to leave Rhukaan Draal and avoid Tariic."

Munta bared teeth that were yellowed but still sharp. "I'll be leaving," he said. "Tariic has earned an enemy in the Gantii Vus!"

"Don't defy him," said Ashi. "He has all the power. He could destroy your clan without hesitating—I know that he would." She'd left Oraan's true identity and Dagii's most recent involvement out of her story, just in case Munta fell under Tariic's influence again after all. She hoped it wouldn't happen, but Tariic seemed to have a way of defying hope itself.

Munta nodded. "We'll join the Silent Clans and go into hiding if we have to." He looked at her, though, his eyes glittering with his old cunning. "But you didn't free me just to give me a warning, did you? You could have done that weeks ago. What do you want from me?"

"What I said in the street. Your experience." She rose from a crouch beside him and paced the room. "Tariic is building up

THE TYRANNY OF GHOSTS

an army along the border of the Mournland, but that doesn't make sense. I know I'm missing something. Tariic says it's all to counter the Valenar, but there's been no Valenar activity since Dagii defeated them at Zarrthec. Tariic has been buying the services of dragonmarked houses too. He's got troops and supplies and hirelings pouring into the Darguul towns and villages closest to the Mournland." She ticked off on her fingers the destinations of Orien caravans that she'd learned from Pater. "Zarrthec, Olkhaan, Skullreave, Gorgonhorn—"

"Wait." Munta stopped her with a wave of his hand. "Skullreave?" She nodded. "That doesn't make sense."

"Why not?" Ashi tried to remember what Pater had said of the place. "It's halfway between Olkhaan and Gorgonhorn."

"And just as far from the Mournland as it is from either of them." Munta hauled himself out of his chair and went to a shelf on the wall. Sorting through several rolls of paper, he selected one and unrolled it on the table. It was a map of Darguun and the surrounding regions, Ashi saw. Not terribly recent, but recent enough. Munta pointed at the location marked Olkhaan, northeast of Rhukaan Draal. "Less than a day's march to the border of the Mournland."

His finger moved to Gorgonhorn in the extreme north and east of the country. "Right on the border," he said. His finger went to Skullreave, midway between the other two locations—but much father west. "Nearly a week's march," Munta said. "Useless if you're fighting anything coming out of the Mournland."

"But relatively safe from Valenar attacking across the border. That makes it a perfect supply base." Ashi looked up from the map to see tension in Munta's face. "Doesn't it?"

"It *looks* like the perfect supply base," the old warlord said somberly. "Haruuc thought the same thing twenty years ago. I helped him with the plans."

"Plans for defense against the Valenar?" Ashi asked, then realized her mistake. "No, twenty years ago there was no

Mournland. The Last War was still raging. Haruuc was planning a defense against reconquest by Cyre."

"A good guess," said Munta, "and that's what outsiders were intended to assume. But the defense against Cyre was a ruse. The plans were for attack." He put his finger back on Skullreave and moved it again, this time northwest around the end of the Seawall Mountains—and into Breland.

CHAPTER THIRTEEN

13 Vult

The stone arch that had once been the gate of Suud Anshaar still stood, even though large sections of the wall to either side of it had collapsed into a heap of rubble. "*Daashor* work," said Tenquis.

Ekhaas stepped up to the arch—somehow it felt more proper to enter this ancient site through the gate than through one of the gaps in the wall—and inspected what lay beyond. Anything made of wood had decayed long ago in the pervasive damp of the Khraal. Structures that had depended on wooden supports had fallen. What remained standing was a testament to the skill of Dhakaani craftsmen, masons, and, yes, *daashor*. Pillars and walls, flying buttresses and broken towers, vaults and more arches. More of Suud Anshaar lay sprawled across the ground than rose above it, but what did rise moved her. This had been a mighty fortress of Dhakaan. She could almost picture it in its glory—

The wail that rose above the ruins ended her reverie. The sound had been unnerving before. Up close it made her skin crawl and her ears go flat. None of them had put away their weapons. They brought them up as one and turned to put their backs together, each of them staring out into the gathering dusk. Ekhaas peered again through the arch, searching for any sign of movement beyond.

There was nothing. The wail could have condensed like rain out of the heavy air itself.

Marrow's fur had risen in thick tufts along her spine. She swung her head back and forth, snuffling at the air, then gave a strange whine. "She doesn't smell anything," Chetiin translated.

Ekhaas thought of the legends of Tasaam Draet. "If the wail is the ghosts of Draet's victims, there's probably nothing to smell."

"No," Chetiin said with a frown. "She doesn't smell *anything*. There's nothing alive here. Nothing."

"That's impossible," said Tenquis, but Ekhaas could tell he didn't believe his own words. The evidence was in front of them—rocks and rubble bare of even the hardiest grass.

The stories said the Dhakaani travelers who had first discovered Suud Anshaar's fate had found the fortress utterly empty of life. Her hand tightened on the hilt of her sword.

"Where do we start?" asked Geth. "Do you think there are lower levels? The fragments of the shield could have been stored in a vault."

"Remember what the Stela of Rewards said," Ekhaas reminded him. "Tasaam Draet was 'given the care of the symbols of *muut* forfeited by those lords whose treachery he has ended' as if that was some kind of reward. Legends also depict Draet as arrogant in his power. Someone like that would want to show off his reward. I think the fragments of the shield would have been displayed somewhere public."

She looked at the ruins again and pointed to a distant shell of nearly intact walls and soaring arches that lay among them like an egg in a cradle. "Dhakaani builders usually put throne rooms at the heart of a palace. The seat of a great lord would be in a similar hall. That's the place to start."

"That sounds good," said Geth. He stepped into the mouth of the gate.

"What? Wait!" said Tooth. The bugbear had been quieter than Chetiin, but his eyes went wide with fear. "We're going in tonight? Shouldn't we wait until the sun rises?"

"The moons give enough light. Do *you* want to sleep here?" Geth asked.

THE TYRANNY OF GHOSTS

Tooth's big ears twitched down a bit. "You can stay outside the gates, Tooth," Ekhaas told him. "You don't have to come in. That was our agreement."

Somewhere in the distance, the shriek of a varag rose over the jungle. Tooth's ears sagged a little more.

"*Maabet*," he cursed—and lifted his grinders. "Fight a wolf, fight the pack. I'm coming."

⊙ ⊙ ⊙ ◉ ⊙ ⊙ ⊙

The way through the ruins was slow. Suud Anshaar hadn't just been a single fortress—it had been a complex and a large one at that. The rubble of buildings blocked their way, forcing them over or around heaps of stones that sometimes seemed dangerously unstable. Chetiin moved with ease, but the rest of them had to pick their way. The lack of plant life was something of a blessing, if an unnerving one. The shadows cast by the ruins in the moonlight were deceptive and their sightlines already uncomfortably short. Ekhaas was glad she didn't have to worry about pushing through trees and bushes as well. She still found herself peering into every corner and behind every crumbling column, waiting for the attack she knew in her gut was coming.

Maybe that was why she was the first to see the skeleton.

She spotted it almost out of the corner of her eye, a silhouette framed within a stone window against the night sky. Visions of the undead, of dry bones to accompany bodiless, howling ghosts burst over her. She grabbed Geth and pointed—silently. The thing hadn't moved. Maybe it hadn't seen them.

Ekhaas felt Geth stiffen under her hand, then he hissed to get the attention of the others. Tenquis almost jumped. Tooth and Marrow both froze motionless like the hunters they were. Chetiin, however, glanced once at the skeleton, then burst into motion. Like an independent shadow, he darted across the ground, paused beneath the wall in which the window frame was set, then swarmed up the stones and through the frame. Ekhaas

saw the brief glint of moonlight on steel—then Chetiin paused, as still as the skeleton. After a moment, he lowered his knife, reached out, and touched the skeleton.

It still didn't move. Balanced on the window frame, the goblin turned and gestured for them all to join him.

"What is this?" Geth growled, but he followed as Ekhaas moved out under the window. Up above, Chetiin was examining the skeleton closely. Keeping one leg on the windowsill, he stretched the other across and rested it on the skeleton's bony hip, then reached up and heaved at the thing's skull.

It came off in his hands with an audible crack. The shock must have broken whatever balance kept the rest of the skeleton together, because it crumbled suddenly. Chetiin hopped back to the windowsill as the bones clattered down behind the wall like a small avalanche. Ekhaas's ears flicked.

"That sounded heavy for bones," she said.

"It did," Geth agreed.

"They're not bones," Chetiin called softly from above. "Geth, catch this. Be careful." He held out the skull with both hands. Geth caught it with a grunt. Ekhaas heard it scrape against the metal of his gauntlet and stepped up for a closer look as Geth held it into a shaft of moonlight.

It wasn't bone at all, but dark, slightly glittering stone. And yet it was a perfect, if weathered, copy of a hobgoblin skull. The finer details had been erased by time and exposure, but all of the ridges, all of the crevices that Ekhaas would have expected to find in a real skull were there. Even the jaw was properly jointed, though it broke away as Geth attempted to move it. He cursed like a child caught damaging something precious, but Ekhaas took it from him and inspected the interior surface. More protected from the weather, it retained every line and pockmark.

Tenquis stared over her shoulder. "If that's *daashor* work, it's like nothing I've ever seen."

"Dhakaani sculpture was never this realistic," said Ekhaas.

"I don't think it was a sculpture," Chetiin said as he came

spidering down the wall. "There were stone ligaments holding it together. I think it was a real skeleton that had been changed to stone."

"*Khaavolaar*," breathed Ekhaas.

"Could it have been done by a medusa?" asked Tooth. "Or a basilisk? No hunter has ever seen one in these parts, but this is old."

"Medusas and basilisks change living flesh to stone," Tenquis said. "Their victims look like statues. I've seen them. Magic might change a skeleton to stone." He looked back up to the window. "But why pose one like that?"

A yip from Marrow brought them around. The worg crouched beside another collapsed wall, pawing at something. Geth handed the skull to Ekhaas and went over. He bent down and brushed away dry dirt, then shifted a rock. His teeth flashed as he bared them. "There's another one here. Crushed. I think the wall fell on it." He picked something out of the ground and held it up. It was a battered and corroded metal greave. "This one was wearing armor."

Tenquis examined it. "Dhakaani design," he said.

Ekhaas shivered and set skull and jaw down on the ground. A frightening suspicion was growing in her. "Stay close, but look around," she said. "See if you can see any more."

Geth looked up at her. "You think these were the people of Suud Anshaar? But the stories don't mention this."

"I'm starting to understand that sometimes the stories aren't completely right."

They found four more skeletons nearby, some more weathered than others, most preserved only by some coincidence of shelter. Two stood in a hidden niche, entwined in an eternal embrace, yet also curiously apart. Tenquis slid a hand among the frozen bones. "If they were posed like this," he said, "why aren't the two skeletons actually touching each other?"

"I'm not sure they were skeletons when they died," said Ekhaas. She held her arm in a position similar to that of one

skeleton, then took Tenquis's arm and pressed it to hers, matching the other skeleton. "Imagine the gap between our bones," she said, her mouth dry, "separated by the thickness of flesh."

Tenquis jerked away from her. "Something turned their bones to stone?"

Geth considered the skeletons, his face grim. "It happened fast, then. I don't think they had any warning."

"Maybe they didn't," said Chetiin. The old goblin stood in a ruined doorway. "But you need to see this."

Beyond the doorway, two sturdy walls preserved a section of corridor no more than ten paces long, both ends open. Two stone skeletons stood in the corridor. Unlike the other skeletons they'd seen, these were posed in attitudes of panic. One was precariously balanced in a sprinting position—fleeing from something, Ekhaas guessed. The other was on its back on the floor, twisted around, and staring back with empty eye sockets. The person it had been must have fallen and looked around to see his—or her—doom bearing down.

The skeletons were different in two other significant ways from the others they'd found. They were clad in the ragged remains of clothing—and they were human.

"You said the last time someone came looking for Suud Anshaar was about thirty years ago?" Ekhaas asked Tooth. The hunter nodded, his eyes fixed on the black and glittering skeletons.

"Those are Cyran clothes," said Chetiin. "I think we've found the last people who came here." He walked up to the skeletons, paused a short distance away, and pointed at a faint dark stain on the floor around them. "That's what's left when flesh rots and liquefies."

"Do you think—" Ekhaas hesitated, words catching in her mouth before she forced them out. "Do you think whatever did this killed them? Or did they—?"

The words caught again, but this time Chetiin anticipated the question. "If I had to guess," he said, "I think they might still have been alive after it happened."

THE TYRANNY OF GHOSTS

Ekhaas's stomach rose. She had to clench her teeth and fight it down. Tenquis shuddered and closed his golden eyes. Even Geth and Tooth looked a little bit green. Marrow whined and curled her tail low. Chetiin turned away from the skeletons—

—just as the wail broke over the ruins for a third time. Once again it was strangely sourceless, but in Ekhaas's imagination it seemed closer than before.

"Tiger's blood," murmured Geth. "Whatever that is, I don't think it's a ghost."

Tooth's broad face had gone from green to pale. "It can't be the same thing that killed Suud Anshaar, can it? Why wouldn't your stories mention something like this?"

"I don't know. Maybe the empire suppressed what really happened before the story could circulate," Ekhaas said.

"I would," said Chetiin. He'd drawn both of his daggers, the one from his left arm sheath with the nasty curved blade and the one from his right arm sheath with the blue-black crystal that winked like an eye from its ugly straight blade. He looked at Ekhaas and Geth. "What do we do?"

Ekhaas exchanged a sharp glance with the shifter. His jaw tightened and he nodded. Ekhaas put her ears back. "We go on," she said. "We keep looking for the shield fragments. We watch, and if whatever is making that noise shows itself, we try our best to kill it."

"If it can be killed!" said Tooth. There was an edge of madness to his voice. "What if it can't? How—"

Tenquis reached out and slapped him hard. "We'll fight it," he said harshly, "when we fight it."

Tooth stared at him. Tenquis slid his wand into a pocket and calmly readied his crossbow. "You're harder than you look," said Tooth.

"I'm a tiefling," said Tenquis, "and I want my revenge on Tariic. I'm as hard as I need to be." He looked to Ekhaas. "How do we get to that hall?"

"This way, I think," she said. She led the way out of the other door in the ruined corridor, trying hard not to look at the remains of the last expedition to come this way.

Since she had become aware of them, Ekhaas spotted more of the skeletons as she climbed through the ruins. A few were whole or almost whole, blending into the shadows. Some were just weathered heaps of bones, collapsed over time just like the fortress. Others were no more than broken bits of glittering black stone tumbled among fallen rock. Not all were hobgoblin. Ekhaas recognized goblins and bugbears, a pair of dogs, varags—how many of them had wandered onto the Wailing Hill before they learned their lesson?—even the fragile skeletons of birds, hollow bones broken as if they'd fallen out of the sky.

If not even birds on the wing could escape the curse of Suud Anshaar, did they really have a chance?

No, she reminded herself, they weren't dumb animals, and they wouldn't be taken by surprise. Whatever waited in the ruins, they'd fought and survived worse. They *would* find the shield fragments. They *would* escape the fortress. The fragments of the shattered shield *would* provide the key to destroying the Rod of Kings.

Because if they didn't, this journey would have been for nothing.

She started to sing. Quietly, just loud enough that the others could hear her, and not a magical song, but a Dhakaani battle hymn invoking the strength of *muut* in combat and the glory of *atcha* in victory. It was an old song, as old as the long and wondrous middle years of Dhakaan, when the emperor's power spanned a continent. The same song might have echoed in Suud Anshaar. Tasaam Draet might have listened to and been inspired by it.

She felt some of her fear slip away. The others stood straighter and scanned the shadows with eyes that were brighter and more alert. They moved with greater confidence. Even Marrow seemed to beat her tail in time to the song. And when the wail inevitably

THE TYRANNY OF GHOSTS

came again, Ekhaas raised her voice just a little to challenge its power. For a moment, the wail seemed a little less terrifying—even if it did seem to have taken on a more directional quality.

Chetiin pointed across the ruins. "Somewhere over there."

"I think I felt it through the ground," said Tenquis.

Ekhaas let the song die away, the better to hear any movement among the stones. Geth's hand had stolen up to touch his collar of black stones. Faint wisps of vapor escaped between his fingers into the warm night air; he'd said in the past that the collar turned cold to warn of unnatural creatures.

"Geth?" she asked softly.

"Keep moving," he said.

They moved. The deeper they penetrated into the remains of the fortress, the better preserved the structure seemed to be. Walls, doorways, and pillars remained in place—with the result that their line of sight to the area around them was constantly changing and being cut off. Worse, the surviving corridors were often half-filled with debris. There was no running here. Moving too quickly sent loose stones sliding and might plunge a foot into a crevice. Marrow had real difficulty scrambling up and down the slopes. Heading around one steep heap, Tooth had to catch and brace her with his shoulder. The worg snapped and growled at him. Ekhaas couldn't tell if it was an expression of gratitude or a warning not to touch her.

Still, they went as fast as they could, sticking close together. Ekhaas took the lead, though she was only guessing the way and hoping she didn't lead them all into a dead end. With every mound of rubble they climbed or skirted, she half-expected to find her chosen path blocked.

It never was. Ekhaas crawled under a pair of columns that had fallen against each other and stood to find herself facing a high, double-arched doorway with angular Goblin characters carved over it.

TASAAM DRAET GOVERNS SUUD ANSHAAR BY THE WILL OF GIIS PUULTA, MARHU OF DHAKAAN. KNOW *MUUT* YOU WHO ENTER.

She whirled and called back under the columns, "We're here! This is the great hall."

Tenquis was just crawling through. Ekhaas helped him up, then stood out of the way as Marrow came squirming and wriggling through the gap. Chetiin followed, then Tooth. Geth came last, his face drawn hard and taut.

The collar around his neck was white with frost. She drew air between her teeth. "Is it bad?" she asked.

"Bad enough." He took her arm and pulled her toward the arched doorway. "Get inside. If there's going to be a fight, I want space around us."

Beyond the doorway, though, the great hall wasn't in as good a shape as Ekhaas had hoped when she'd seen it in the distance. The long stone spans that had once supported the ceiling still stood, but in many places the vaults between them had crumbled. Moonlight fell onto more rubble. The walls were cracked and looked as if a hard push would bring them down. Other doors were either choked with fallen stones or opened directly onto the night.

Aside from rubble and moonlight, the hall was completely empty.

Tenquis turned to her. "What now? What are we looking for?"

Ekhaas stared around the devastated hall. "I don't know. A shrine? Something ostentatious."

"Under the rubble?"

"Maybe," said Chetiin, "the shield fragments aren't here at all. Maybe they are in a vault somewhere."

"They're here," Geth said.

There was a strange wonder in his voice. Ekhaas started to turn to look at him but the shifter was already pushing past her. Feet crunching on gravel, he paced down the length of the hall, slowly sweeping Wrath before him.

"*Maabet*," rasped Tooth. "He's lost it."

"No," said Ekhaas. "He hasn't. Stay with him!" She jogged

THE TYRANNY OF GHOSTS

after Geth, catching up to him. "You feel the fragments through the sword, don't you?" she asked. "Just like you felt the Rod of Kings. The connection *is* there!"

Geth shook his head. "It's different. When *duur'kala* songs woke the connection between Wrath and the rod, all I had to do was hold out Wrath, and I knew where the rod was. This is more like a lodestone being drawn to steel."

"The shield has been shattered. It's bound to feel different—"

The wail rose again. This time there was no doubt that its source was close and coming closer—from the very direction they'd just come.

Tooth whirled at the sound. "It's tracking us!"

"Stay calm and keep watch," said Ekhaas. "Geth . . ."

"Here." He stopped, sword pointing at a thin scattering of rubble across the floor. "They're here!"

"You're sure?" Ekhaas asked. They'd almost reached the end of the hall. A low dais rose no more than a double handspan above the floor. It seemed a strange place to display relics given by the emperor as a reward. A fearful thought struck her. "They're not underground from here, are they? Not in some buried vault?"

"No. They're close." He dropped to his knees, set Wrath down, and started tossing fallen stones aside.

The first stones he moved revealed part of a Goblin inscription carved into the floor. It was only a single word, but it made Ekhaas's heart jump.

Shattered.

"Tenquis, help us!" She bent down beside Geth and swept more rubble away. The tiefling crouched on Geth's other side. It took only moments to clear the rest of the inscription.

LOOK ON SHATTERED *MUUT* AND BE HUMBLED.

The top of the inscription lay toward the dais. Anyone kneeling before the lord of Suud Anshaar would have had no choice but to read the words. "The fallen nobles," said Ekhaas. "He was reminding the fallen nobles of what they'd lost." She

scrambled past the words to rake at the remaining rubble. Her breath came fast. Her heartbeat echoed in her ears.

Purple byeshk flashed under moonlight. Ekhaas got down on her knees, stretched out her arm, and used it to sweep away the last fragments of stone.

Her heart fell. She sat back, her ears folding flat.

Set into the stone were three toothed metal disks. Three *shaari'mal* forged from byeshk. She looked up at Geth and Tenquis. "I don't understand," she said. "What are these?"

Geth picked up Wrath and brought it close to the embedded disks. "These are what I was feeling," he said. "These were forged from the same byeshk as the sword and the rod."

"But they're *shaari'mal*. They're not pieces of a shield. Unless"—she glanced at Tenquis—"could they have been reforged?"

The tiefling shook his head. "You don't just reforge an artifact, even one that was broken."

Ekhaas reached out and touched one of the disks. Strange runes had been carved into the smooth surface. They weren't Goblin or any other language she knew, but she had seen them, or runes very much like them, before—etched into the Sword of Heroes and the Rod of Kings.

The Stela of Rewards in Volaar Draal had shown an engraving of three *shaari'mal*. Were these what the emperor had given Tasaam Draet? Were they meant to be a symbol of Dhakaan? She couldn't deny that they seemed to be related to the rod and the sword, but what *were* they? She rubbed her head with dusty fingers—and froze as the wail came yet again, so close she felt it through the floor. So close it made the weakened walls of the hall groan.

"Geth! Ekhaas!" said Chetiin sharply. Ekhaas twisted around. Chetiin, Tooth, and Marrow faced the end of the hall where they'd entered. Beyond the arched doorway, the crossed pillars they'd all crawled under were trembling as if something strained against the other side.

THE TYRANNY OF GHOSTS

Ekhaas made a decision. "We're taking these with us," she said. "Geth, look for the best way out."

He nodded and jumped to his feet, snatching up Wrath and darting to the nearest open doorway in the walls. Ekhaas pulled a knife from her belt and tried to force the tip in between one of the *shaari'mal* and the stone that held it.

Tenquis brushed her hand aside. "Let me," he said. "A *daashor* set this here." Grabbing a pinch of dust from the ground, he narrowed his eyes, whispered a word, and let the dust sift over the stone around the disk.

Where the dust fell, stone crumbled like dry sand. The indentation it left was small, but it was enough. Tenquis hooked thick fingernails under the byeshk disk and lifted it free. He held it out to Ekhaas, but she shook her head.

"Do the other ones, then put them in one of your pockets. Keep them safe." She stood—

—just as the pillars fell in a crash of stone. Dust billowed up in a thick cloud, and the reverberations of the crash brought more dust sifting down from the ceiling of the hall. There was a second crash from behind her, accompanied by a curse from Geth. Ekhaas turned briefly to see the shifter leaping away from a doorway that had become just another heap of rubble—but a new noise brought her attention back to the drifting dust cloud. A slow grinding noise like millstones turning. She heard Tenquis whispering frantically over the remaining *shaari'mal*, then that was drowned out by another wail.

A shape emerged from the dust cloud. Or rather, seemed to absorb the cloud as it advanced. Marrow whined and eased back a few steps.

The creature . . . the *thing* . . . towered twice as tall as a bugbear. It had the obscenely thick body of a massive serpent, bigger around than Ekhaas could have encircled with her arms. Instead of rising to a serpent's head, though, that body became a woman's leanly muscular torso and arms. The thing's face was narrow, with a fine jaw, knife-edge cheekbones—and a smooth

expanse where eyes should have been. Above that blank brow, thick tendrils longer than arms, with sharp pointed tips took the place of hair, writhing with an independent motion.

But for all that it moved like something alive, Ekhaas knew that it wasn't. Its face was a statue, stiff and unemotional. Its skin was as black and glittering as the transformed bones of the skeletons that littered Suud Anshaar. The millstone noise that ground against Ekhaas's ears was, she realized, the sound of its great body slithering forward, accompanied by the fine grating of its twining tendril hair. The thing was stone given mobility, a construct like a golem or a warforged, but more finely crafted and surely far older than any Ekhaas had heard told of in any tale. As it slithered into a patch of moonlight, she saw the scars of millennia on its surface—

Something about the flash of moonlight on that stone made her vision blur, and when she blinked, the weathered scars were gone and the stone was smooth and flawless. She blinked again, and the scars were back. The black stone crumbled into dust with every movement, only to drift across a new patch of stone and resurface it. Just looking at the creature made Ekhaas's head spin and ache. It was as if time and space had only the loosest grip on the ancient thing. For all that it made her nauseated, though, the strange play of dust to stone and back again was captivating, the cycle of ages collapsed into moments . . .

"Look away from it! Everyone look away from it!"

Geth's hand was suddenly on Ekhaas's shoulder, shaking her. She wrenched her gaze away from the construct and staggered as reality crashed back around her. Geth caught her, held her up as she regained her balance, then turned her loose. Around them, she saw the others were also twitching and stumbling as if waking from sleep. Only Geth seemed fully alert.

The collar of stones around the shifter's neck was so cold it steamed in the humid air. The gift of the Gatekeepers had saved them all.

THE TYRANNY OF GHOSTS

As if realizing that its prey had broken free of its influence, the construct opened its stony mouth and let loose another terrible wail. It came slithering into the hall amidst a pattering rain of dust and masonry.

"Rat!" roared Geth over the wail. "How do we fight that?"

A bit of stone fell past Ekhaas's eyes and bounced off her arm. She twisted her head and looked back to Tenquis. The tiefling was on his feet, drawing his hand out of a bulging pocket. Ekhaas couldn't hear him, but his lips formed a word, and she saw the lines of embroidery on his long vest shift. The bulge of his pocket vanished. In the ground at his feet were three empty holes in the shape of *shaari'mal*.

Ekhaas grabbed Geth and shouted in his ear. "Get everyone out of the hall!" She shoved him in the direction of one of the last unblocked doorways but didn't wait to see if he obeyed. The construct was advancing with the unrelenting patience of centuries. Ekhaas raised her eyes to the leaping spans and trembling vaults over its head, filled her lungs, and threw all of her will into the magic of the song.

Dissonant cacophony exploded among the age-weakened stone, as loud as the construct's wails but more focused. Mortar that had endured for millennia burst. Stone cracked with a report like a lighting strike and started to slide.

Nature's laws took over. With a roar that punched all the way into Ekhaas's belly, the ceiling of Suud Anshaar's great hall came crashing down. The construct scarcely seemed to notice. It was still slithering toward her when the first blocks slammed into it.

Walls followed ceiling, but Ekhaas was already turning and sprinting in the direction she'd pushed Geth. Chips and chunks of stone flew around her. She ducked her head and ran. The doorway was close—and through it she could see Tenquis, the fingers of one hand tight around his artificer's wand, the fingers of the other splayed and trembling as if they supported an invisible weight. Ekhaas threw herself through the arch. She caught

a glimpse of pained release on Tenquis's face, then he dropped his hand.

The doorway crumbled just as her feet cleared it. The ground hit her hard, and for a brief instant, it was all she could do to catch her breath. Hands took her arms. Geth and Tooth hauled her to her feet. Ekhaas turned to look back at the heap of rubble she'd made. Dust swirled above it in the moonlight.

Then was sucked back down among the toppled stones. Rocks shifted and clattered as the thing underneath the heap moved. A muffled wail filtered into the night.

"*Khaavolaar!*" cursed Ekhaas. "We need to—"

The wail went silent. The movement beneath the heap stopped. Instinctively, Ekhaas froze for just an instant. They all did.

In that instant, a long, glittering black tentacle stabbed out of the rubble. It lashed through the air like a whip in the moonlight, so close Ekhaas could feel the knife-edge wind of its passing.

Tooth was the one who took the blow, however. His arm snapped up as if he could block the tentacle's attack, but it just wrapped around his forearm and pulled. The hunter screamed.

CHAPTER FOURTEEN

13 Vult

When the shrieks and howls of hunting varags had broken over the Khraal the previous afternoon, Midian had looked to Makka and asked, "Is there anything in this bloody jungle besides Geth and the others that would bring out that many varags?"

Makka had grinned at him. "Us."

Whatever the shifter and his group had done to provoke the varags' hunt—and Midian had a feeling it wouldn't have taken much—it had left the way clear for the pair of them to follow without fear. Every varag in the area seemed to have been drawn into the chase. They'd found the Dhakaani road, and even the need to track their quarry had been eliminated. When Makka had offered prayers of thanks to the Fury, Midian had been almost tempted to join in.

Then dusk had come and with it a terrible wail like nothing Midian had ever heard before. Moments later, Makka had frozen for an instant, ears cocked, then leaped for the nearest tree and climbed it like a squirrel. Midian hadn't stopped to ask why, but simply followed the bugbear's lead.

He'd barely reached a hidden branch before a flood of frightened varags came pouring along the road and through the undergrowth.

When they'd passed, he and Makka had descended and continued on their way. More wails had drifted through the

205

darkening jungle. The barren hill and its crown of ruins at the end of the road had been a surprise, but not much of one. They'd known their elusive prey was heading somewhere.

"Do we follow them in?" Makka asked, eyeing the ruins under the moonlight.

Yet another wail rolled out. "I don't think so," Midian had said. "They'll come out again—or they won't." He found a comfortable perch in a tree with a good view of the ruins and settled in to wait, with Makka crouched below.

After that, it was just a matter of patience.

※ ※ ※ ※ ※ ※ ※

Geth acted without thinking, roaring and swinging Wrath in a flashing arc. The byeshk blade jerked in his hand as it hit the black tentacle that held Tooth, but smashed through it with a crack like splitting stone.

The cut tentacle collapsed into a long line of glittering black dust.

Tooth didn't stop screaming, though. Ekhaas's voice joined his, shouting at him to stay still. Geth spun around. Ekhaas had the bugbear's arm in her grasp, struggling to hold it immobile as she beat at something black and squirming on his forearm. For an instant, Geth couldn't help but wonder how Tooth had come to have a swarm of tiny insects on his arm—then he realized what the black stuff really was. Just like the rest of the tentacle, the end that had grabbed Tooth had turned into dust.

But it hadn't stopped moving or released the hunter. The dust curled around his hairy arm as if it were a single unit, sifting back together where Ekhaas tried to scrub it away. None of it clung to her fingers. The curling thread flowed under Tooth's skin through a bloody hole made by the sharp tip of the tentacle.

"I can't move my fingers! By Balinor, just kill me. Kill me!" Tooth shrieked, and Geth remembered the skeletons with bones

THE TYRANNY OF GHOSTS

of glittering black stone. He clenched his teeth and made a decision.

"Ekhaas, stand clear," he said.

The *duur'kala* looked up. Something of what he intended must have showed in his face, because her ears flicked up, and she stepped toward Tooth's immobile hand, gripping it hard. Maybe Tooth saw it, too, because he tugged back the other way, probably more afraid than anything else. Between them, they pulled the arm straight—or at least as straight as was possible. The elbow no longer flexed.

Geth aimed higher as he brought Wrath down through skin and flesh and bone. No longer supported, Tooth staggered and fell, his scream finally ending. Blood gushed out of the stump of the bugbear's arm. "Ekhaas! Tenquis! Try to stop the bleeding!" Geth ordered.

Ekhaas let the severed arm drop to the ground as she went to Tooth's side. Geth knew the sound of falling limbs. He'd attended infirmary tents in the aftermath of battle. When a ruined limb had to be amputated, it fell with a meaty thump. It did not fall with a thud as if the bones within it were suddenly far heavier than they should have been. For a moment, Geth felt an urge to check the severed end, to see if the cut bone was white or black beneath the sheen of blood.

"Geth," said Chetiin quietly, "look." He pointed.

The thick line of dust that had been the tentacle was flowing back into the heap of rubble. Just beneath the sounds of Ekhaas's healing song and Tenquis's muttered words as he applied liquids and powders, Geth could hear a low sigh like running sand.

A sigh that grew into a slow grinding. He whirled around. "Get Tooth up! We need to get away from here."

Tenquis looked up. His brown skin was ashen; his golden eyes seemed dulled. "The wound won't stay closed. He needs bandages—"

"We'll stop when no more tentacles can reach us." He sheathed Wrath, squatted down, and slid his head and shoulders

under Tooth's remaining arm. The bugbear was groaning and only barely conscious. "Tooth," Geth said as calmly as he could manage, "can you walk?"

Tooth's head lolled in what Geth hoped was a nod. He stood up, taking most of Tooth's weight, and started away from the rubble of the great hall. The hunter must have been at least a little bit aware of the danger—he managed to put one foot in front of the other.

"Chetiin, Marrow," said Geth, "we need the fastest, easiest way out of here."

"The gates are on the other side of Suud Anshaar," Ekhaas pointed out.

"It's a ruin. The gates are wherever there's a hole in the wall. Chetiin, go!"

The old goblin nodded and darted into the shadows along with Marrow. Moments later, he reappeared atop a broken wall, waving them onward.

Behind Geth, a stone shifted and slid as the thing beneath the rubble started to struggle once more. Tenquis and Ekhaas glanced back, wand and sword raised. Geth didn't look but just concentrated on the uneven ground ahead. "A little faster, Tooth?" he asked.

Tooth's head lolled again.

An easy way through the ruins was impossible, but Chetiin and Marrow did their best, guiding them around the worst blockages. They moved faster, though, knowing that the worst danger of Suud Anshaar lay trapped behind them, at least temporarily. The stone skeletons held no more interest. Every muffled wail, every creak of stone brought a new clutching fear. Adolan's collar of stones didn't warm up in the slightest.

Tenquis stayed on Tooth's other side, keeping an eye on the bugbear's terrible wound. They'd covered perhaps half the distance to the outer wall when he hissed sharply and pressed an already bloody rag to the stump. "It's open again. Geth, we need to stop and bandage it properly."

THE TYRANNY OF GHOSTS

Geth looked ahead, then behind. The rubble of the great hall was out of sight behind the broken base of a tower. He ground his teeth together. There was no point in having saved Tooth from the construct's terrible power just to have him bleed to death. "Work fast," he told Tenquis and guided Tooth to the shelter of a solid-looking patch of wall.

Not until he'd lowered Tooth into a seated position and had drawn away to allow Tenquis and Ekhaas room to work did he realize how much blood had poured down over his arm. The sleeve of his shirt was drenched. He snarled under his breath and tore the fabric away.

"You've stopped." Chetiin's voice came out of the shadows so suddenly that Geth jerked around and drew Wrath halfway before he stopped himself. He slammed the ancient sword back down.

"We'll follow again as soon as Ekhaas and Tenquis have taken care of Tooth."

"Take a longer rest if you need it. The way is easier from here." The *shaarat'khesh* elder squatted down where he stood. Sharp eyes looked up at Geth from his parchment-skinned face. "You made the right choice," he said.

"I hope Tooth agrees with you." Geth settled down as well. "I couldn't let him die like the people of Suud Anshaar."

"I was thinking more that we'd need him to get out of the Khraal and back to Arthuun," said Chetiin. "But even so, an arm in exchange for his life seems a reasonable bargain. And it will make his tale of a trip to Suud Anshaar that much more believable." His smile was so thin that Geth couldn't tell if he was trying to be lighthearted or simply stating the facts as he saw them.

Even that thin smile disappeared, though, as the goblin added, "What about the *shaari'mal?*"

Geth looked to Tenquis again as the tiefling folded a piece of clean cloth into a long bandage. "I don't know. Wrath recognizes them." He looked for the words to describe what he'd felt

through the sword when the byeshk disks had been revealed. "Have you ever seen dogs from the same litter greet each other, even after they've been separated for years? It's like that."

"Perhaps Taruuzh forged more artifacts from the byeshk ore of Khaar Vanon," said Chetiin.

"But everything we found pointed to the shattered pieces of the Shield of Nobles, even the inscription in the floor." Geth rubbed his hands through his hair. "I don't understand."

Tenquis and Ekhaas rose from Tooth's side and joined them. "We've done everything we can," said Ekhaas. "He needs rest and a real healer. If we had the luxury, I'd say we should camp for the night, but he'll last until we have a chance to stop again."

"Then sit down for a rest yourself. We need it too." Geth repeated what Chetiin had said about the way ahead, then glanced at Tenquis. "Let me see one of the disks."

The tiefling nodded and whispered a word. The embroidered lines of his long vest shifted, the bulging pocket with the *shaari'mal* reappearing. Tenquis extracted one of them and passed it over. Geth weighed it in his hand, examining it closely. There was no sign that it had ever been part of a larger, shattered whole. The purple byeshk was heavier than might be expected, but Wrath was the same. The symbols carved into the disk were similar to those on Wrath too. There would have been no denying the relationship between them even if he hadn't felt the sword's sense of familiarity.

Maybe, he thought, there was a deeper similarity. The sword had a memory and a kind of awareness. The Rod of Kings certainly did. Maybe there was an awareness in the disk as well. He frowned and concentrated on it. *Hello?* he thought at it.

"What are you doing?" asked Tenquis.

He felt his face grow warm. "Trying to connect with it the same way I connect with Wrath," he said. He shook his head. "I don't feel anything, though."

"You couldn't feel anything when you held the Rod of Kings either," Ekhaas reminded him. "Maybe Wrath blocks the

shaari'mal the same way it does the rod." She held out her hand. "Give it to me."

He twitched it back. "Are you sure that's a good idea? Tariic only held the rod for a moment the first time, and he was lost to it."

"I've already touched one of the *shaari'mal*," said Ekhaas. "Before we got them out of the floor. I didn't feel anything then, but maybe it needs more."

Geth looked around at the others, then held out the byeshk disk. Ekhaas took it and wrapped her hands around its notched edge. Her face creased in concentration. A moment later, the creases grew deeper. Geth felt a flicker of worry. "Ekhaas?"

She opened her eyes. "Nothing."

"There's magic in the disks," Tenquis said. "I know there is. If I had time to study—"

From the ruins behind them came a sudden crash, like a heap of rubble thrown aside. The muted wail that had faded into the background of Geth's awareness rose again with shocking, angry clarity. The shifter sprang to his feet and vaulted up to the top of an unsteady wall. Back toward the center of Suud Anshaar, a column of dust had risen in the moonlight.

Had risen and was being sucked back down. Geth cursed and leaped to the ground. "We don't have time for anything," he said. Ekhaas nodded and tried to return the disk to Tenquis, but the tiefling was already sealing the pockets of his vest again. She stuffed it into a large pouch at her belt. Geth hurried over to Tooth. The hunter's eyes were open, though clouded with pain and staring in the direction of the wail.

Geth ducked under his arm and heaved him to his feet again. "Ready for another run?" he asked.

"Geth," Tooth said weakly, "you saved—"

The shifter bared his teeth. "Don't thank me yet."

They set off at the fastest pace Tooth could manage, which wasn't very fast to begin with and rapidly grew slower. The hunter's breath was a hard rasping; Geth felt the rise and fall

of Tooth's chest against his side. The hunter's face was hard with determination though. A rock turned under his feet, and the bandaged remains of his arm banged into an age-pocked column. His face turned pale instantly, but he didn't cry out.

"Just keep going," Geth urged him and started watching the ground ahead with greater care, trying to put the wails that echoed through the ruins out of his mind.

Ekhaas and Tenquis strode to either side of them—Chetiin had run ahead once more. Ekhaas looked back frequently, then finally said, "I think I could stop it again."

"No," said Geth flatly.

"I know a spell that makes the ground slippery. If I could cast it over a wide area, that construct wouldn't be able to get any traction. It wouldn't be able to move—"

"No!" Geth glanced up at her. "You took it by surprise. You can't risk doing that a second time. I don't want anyone getting within range of those tentacles again, unless we're forced to stand and fight."

Ekhaas's ears flicked, but she nodded.

"Chetiin's back," said Tenquis.

Geth turned his head the other way and found the goblin emerging from a relatively clear path that might once have been a road within the fortress complex. "Tell me something good!" he called to him.

"You're close," said Chetiin, falling into step beside them. "You've covered more than half the distance from where we stopped."

A wail from the pursuing construct broke the night, and in its aftermath, Geth thought he could hear the grinding of its movement. "How much ground do you think our friend has made up?"

"I saw it from on top of a wall on the way back. It's found the spot where we stopped."

Geth grimaced. Chetiin shook his head. "It's worse. The varags are back. Marrow caught their scent."

"Where are they?" asked Geth. "Have they figured out where we're headed?"

"Marrow says it smells like they're gathered over by the road where we entered. If we'd come back through the gates, they'd be waiting for us."

"Grandfather Rat's naked tail," Geth muttered. He hadn't thought much beyond escaping Suud Anshaar and the black construct, but returning to the road and getting out of varag territory had definitely been in his mind.

"Stay downwind of them," wheezed Tooth. "Varags track by scent."

His words turned into a ragged gasp. "Save your breath," said Geth. "It's going to be a race to get out of here. Ekhaas, can you sing that traveling song again?"

The *duur'kala* looked at Tooth draped over Geth's shoulder, and shook her head. "I don't think Tooth would be able to take the strain."

Geth cursed under his breath. At his side, Tooth struggled to speak again. Geth could guess what he was trying to say. "No," he told the bugbear, "we're not leaving you. You're staying with us."

"No," Tooth managed, but any further words were lost in a gurgle of pain as Tenquis forced himself under the bandaged stump of the bugbear's arm.

"Sorry, Tooth," Tenquis said between his teeth. His arm wrapped across Tooth's broad back, overlapping Geth's. He looked around the hunter's body at Geth. "If we're going to move faster, someone needs to help you."

"It's not going to work. Without an arm across your shoulders—"

Tenquis glared at him. "Do you have a better idea?"

He didn't. Geth shut his mouth and tried to ignore Tooth's moans of pain as he and Tenquis hurried him along. He caught a whisper of song and glimpsed Ekhaas's hand reach up from behind to stroke the bugbear's head. His whimpering eased.

"He still feels it," she said, "but it's distant and more manageable. Just be careful with him."

"We'll be as careful as we can," Tenquis said.

The tiefling was already breathing hard and struggling to keep his grip on Tooth's torso. Geth took a good grip on the arm that was draped across his shoulders, then shifted his hand on Tooth's back and grabbed Tenquis's arm. "Hold mine," he ordered. He couldn't see Tenquis around Tooth, but he felt his rough, thick-nailed hand clamp around his forearm. He squeezed. Tenquis squeezed back.

Chetiin kept himself a few paces ahead of them, hopping frequently up onto mounds and low walls to look both ahead and behind. Geth didn't like the way he was starting to look behind more often than ahead. He knew for certain that he could hear the grinding of the construct's advance. "How are we doing, Chetiin?" he asked.

"It's going to be close," Chetiin said tersely.

Ekhaas looked up at him. "Is the construct following our path?"

He nodded—and Geth saw Ekhaas spin around and dart back. "Ekhaas!" he shouted after her. "Don't!"

His sudden twist threw Tenquis off balance. "Careful!" the tiefling yelped, and for a moment all of Geth's attention was on keeping himself and Tooth upright.

When he looked up again, he saw the outer wall of Suud Anshaar ahead, a wide gap in its dark length shining like a beacon in the moonlight.

Ekhaas's song rose up somewhere behind them. A wail from the thing that pursued them rose to greet it.

He ground his teeth together and made for the wall. Chetiin dropped down and ran ahead of them. Ekhaas's song faded—

—and a moment later, footsteps came racing up behind them. Geth stared as Ekhaas slowed to a quick walk alongside him. She flicked her ears.

"I didn't get close," she said before he could speak. "I just put an obstacle in its path."

THE TYRANNY OF GHOSTS

A new note of confusion and fury entered the construct's wail. Geth heard the crash of stones and imagined the thing struggling to advance on ground that was suddenly slippery. "How long will the spell hold it back?" he asked.

"That depends on how long it takes for it figure out it can go around—"

The wail stopped. Ekhaas cursed. Geth guessed that she'd bought them maybe fifteen or twenty extra paces. He hoped it was enough. The ground between them and the wall was blessedly clear of rubble. He moved as quickly as he dared. Tenquis matched his pace. The gap in the wall drew closer . . . closer . . .

The wail burst out again. Geth turned his head just a little and saw a tentacle-crowned head rise above a mound. Stones fell and walls toppled in the construct's wake as it sped forward.

"Watch your feet!" said Ekhaas. Loose rubble filled the base of the gap. Geth clambered up onto it, dragging Tooth with him. Tenquis followed. Ekhaas put a shoulder against Tooth's lower back and pushed. The bugbear stumbled and fell. Geth cursed.

"Lift!" he ordered. He released Tenquis's arm and flipped Tooth around so that he could get his hands under his shoulders. Tenquis and Ekhaas took the hunter's legs and together they staggered to the top of the rubble heap.

The construct surged into the open space before the wall. Moonlight flashed on its glittering hide and the sharp tips of its stone tentacles. Its grinding and its wails merged into a single horrible noise. Geth's stomach rose. They were on the downward slope of the rubble, just barely beyond the walls. Even if the construct was bound to Suud Anshaar, those tentacles could still reach them.

"Keep moving." A small, lithe form darted past him. Chetiin raced up the rubble, up the broken edge of the wall, to prance before the construct. "Here!" he shouted as best as his strained voice would allow. "Here!"

Geth forced himself to keep moving, step after step away from the wall. "A little farther," he growled, "a little farther." He

spoke encouragement to Ekhaas and Tenquis, but he knew in his gut that he was really talking to himself. He couldn't pull his eyes away from the scene above as Chetiin bounced and danced, making a target of himself.

And the construct took the bait. It struck like a snake, whipping its entire body forward. Tentacles stabbed at Chetiin. The old goblin tumbled over one, whirled past another, ducked under a third, and spun back to face the construct—just as a fourth tentacle lanced directly at him. Geth's breath caught.

The tentacle chipped and skittered against stone. Chetiin was simply . . . gone.

A heartbeat later, he burst out of the shadows at the base of the ruined wall and came racing down the hill. Silence fell on the night. Stomach churning, Geth looked back up at the ruin.

The construct filled the gap, staring down at them, its tentacles calmed to a sluggish, almost inaudible writhing. Then, with an inhuman abruptness, it turned and slithered away as if it knew it couldn't reach them and that they were therefore unworthy of its attention.

Geth eased Tooth to the ground, then sank down into a squat himself. It took a long moment before he could do anything but suck in great gulps of the hot night air. Finally he looked up Chetiin. "How—?" he asked.

"A secret of the *shaarat'khesh*," Chetiin said. For the first time Geth could remember, Chetiin sounded winded. "Although that isn't exactly the way it's normally used."

A shadow broke away from the dark line of the jungle's edge and came trotting toward them across the barren hill. Marrow gave a soft, excited yip. Chetiin smiled. "The varags are running!" he said. "It sounds like whatever rage they worked up to come back and try to ambush us didn't survive actually getting a look at the construct. I don't think they'll be coming near the ruins again any time soon."

"Thank the sorcerer-kings," groaned Tenquis.

Geth took another deep breath, then stood up. Or tried to.

THE TYRANNY OF GHOSTS

The muscles in his legs spasmed as he rose, and he almost fell over before he found Tenquis's shoulder for support. His arms and hands were trembling too—but then again, they'd all risen early that morning, hiked through jungle, fought and fled from the varags, then fled again from the construct of Suud Anshaar. It was small wonder he was trembling and exhausted. And it was probably a good thing the varags had run away. He couldn't have managed more than a dozen strokes with Wrath before the sword fell from his hands.

"Geth?" asked Ekhaas.

"I'll be fine," he said. He glanced around at the others. They all looked as tired as he felt, even Marrow. His lips twitched and he smiled, then laughed. Tenquis turned to stare at him.

"Have you snapped?" he asked.

Geth shook his head, pushed away from the tiefling, and wiped at his eyes with hands that were sticky with blood and dust. "Before we went into the ruins, I asked Tooth if he'd want to sleep here." He nodded toward the jungle. "Let's get under cover, then find a place to rest. Even if that construct starts wailing again, I'm going to sleep like the dead."

* * * * * * *

The heat of sunlight on his face drew Geth slowly back toward wakefulness in the little clearing they'd found in the jungle. Vague memories of dreams clung to him—skeletal black serpents that chased after him while notched disks rolled across the night sky in place of moons. He shook the memories off, rising into a place of calm and well-being, where Ekhaas sang lullabies that shook buildings to ruins, Chetiin rode Marrow through shadows, and Tooth swung his grinders with both hands. They'd escaped Suud Anshaar. The varags had fled. It was good. He tried to will himself back down into sleep.

"Geth."

Sleep evaded him. Tenquis was there, mouthing words that

Geth couldn't quite hear. Geth tried to answer, but his words wouldn't come out either.

"Geth, wake up."

Tenquis slid away. A shadow passed between Geth and the sun. Something cold burned across his throat. Adolan's collar? No, it was too thin. Too sharp. He felt a sickening sensation of danger.

Any sense of calm vanished. His eyes opened wide to sunlight filtered through the canopy of the jungle. Instantly a hand pressed against his forehead. "Move," said a rich, calm voice from somewhere above his head, "and you'll cut your own throat."

Sudden waking blurred his thoughts. He knew that voice, but it was so utterly out of place that he couldn't identify it. He knew it was telling the truth, though. The cold at his throat was the edge of a knife. Geth forced his body to lie still and rolled his eyes back as far as he could to try and see who held him.

Midian Mit Davandi leaned into his field of vision. "Good morning," he said.

CHAPTER FIFTEEN

14 Vult

There was no immediate response from Geth. "I hope you slept well," Midian added. "It looks like you had an eventful night."

"What are you doing here?" the shifter growled.

"Lhesh Tariic sends his greetings," Midian told him with a smile. "And before you say anything else, shift your eyes to your right."

Geth looked—and his eyes widened slightly as he saw Makka with his trident poised over Ekhaas's chest. The hobgoblin's eyes were also open and hard. Midian had made a point of waking her first with a very specific warning. Any hint of a song and Makka would push his weapon home.

Two of their quarry neutralized and with them a third. Geth looked up and found Chetiin on his feet, waiting. The old goblin's face was blank. His hands were loose at his sides, but Midian didn't doubt that they could produce hidden blades in an instant. He knew he didn't have to warn Chetiin that whichever of his friends he tried to save, the other one would die—he and the *shaarat'khesh* elder were too much alike. That made Chetiin the most dangerous of the group.

"There's rope beside Tenquis," Midian told Chetiin. "Wake him up and have him bind you. Then have him muzzle and bind the worg. Make sure it doesn't resist him."

Chetiin's eyes narrowed. "Her name is Marrow."

"How precious," said Midian. "Rope."

So many weeks of racing after their prey, and it was over surprisingly quickly. Midian almost felt a little disappointed. Tenquis's face blazed with hatred, but he was quick to bind Chetiin and his worg, then Geth and Ekhaas. The bugbear hunter that the group had hired as a guide proved a little more difficult if only because Tenquis seemed confused on how to tie up someone who had only one arm.

"Feet together, then just tie his good arm to his side," Midian advised.

"Leave Tooth alone, Midian," Geth said. "Let him go."

"Please, I'm no monster." Midian went over to inspect the knots as Tenquis tied them. He bent down to touch the hunter's head. His skin was hot, and of all the group he was the only one who had actually resisted waking. Midian stood up. "He's not getting out of here on his own. Letting him go, that would just be cruel. What happened to him?"

"Nothing that isn't going to happen to you!" snarled Geth.

The butt of Makka's trident cracked across the shifter's skull, knocking him back onto the ground. Makka glared at Midian. "I don't like this," he said. "We should just start killing them. Tariic wants them dead."

"If we were in Volaar Draal, they'd already be dead," said Midian. "But I think Tariic would also like to know why his enemies traveled across Darguun to risk their lives in a ruin in the middle of the Khraal." He sheathed his knife and checked the bonds of the others as well, then turned back to Tenquis, still standing beside Tooth. "Strip off their weapons and any pouches. Bring me their packs."

The tiefling raised his head defiantly. "If you're just going to kill us, why should I?"

There was a reason Midian had chosen to leave him free. "Do you remember having your tail flayed and cut apart while you watched, Tenquis?" Midian asked him. "Tariic's torturer wasn't the only one capable of doing that. You only need one hand for what I ask. Don't make me ask you again."

THE TYRANNY OF GHOSTS

Tenquis trembled and went pale, but he didn't move. Midian raised an eyebrow in silent challenge.

"Do it, Tenquis," said Ekhaas.

Makka whirled on her. "What did we tell you about keeping quiet?" he roared. His trident rose.

Ekhaas looked up at him calmly. "You didn't. You told me not to sing."

"Let her talk, Makka. One of them is going to have to." Midian glanced at Tenquis again. The tiefling's eyes were on Ekhaas. She gave him a slow nod. Tenquis seemed to sag, but he moved to Chetiin and slid the daggers from his forearm sheaths.

"Watch him," Midian ordered Makka, then went over to Ekhaas. "You're trying to think of a way to escape."

Her ears flicked. "Of course I am. Wouldn't you?"

He studied her for a moment, then smiled. Drawing information out of a subject, matching wit against wit, was a fight to savor. He crouched down in front of her. "Yes, I would," he said. "And I would start by trying to distract my captors so a friend who is free might have a chance to loosen the bonds of my other friends, but that's not going to work."

Ekhaas inclined her head. "It's so obvious I wouldn't have tried." She looked back at him. "Senen Dhakaan mentioned in a report to Volaar Draal that you'd popped back up at Tariic's side. The last time I saw you, you were trying to get away from his mob. Now you and Makka are working together and hunting his enemies. You were captured, weren't you, Midian? Tariic used the Rod of Kings on you."

The memories that had haunted him at Senen Dhakaan's punishment came creeping back like roaches in the dark. He could see Tariic in them, holding out the Rod of Kings. He could hear Tariic's voice. He could hear a screaming worse than the wails of the creature that haunted Suud Anshaar. His screaming.

He ground his teeth together. "I serve Tariic," he said.

"You serve Zilargo."

221

"I. Serve. Tariic," the gnome said, biting off each word. He rose so that he stood over Ekhaas. "And Senen won't be spreading lies anymore."

That struck at Ekhaas. Her ears pulled back, and her eyes narrowed. "What have you done?"

"I didn't do anything, but when Tariic discovered that the Kech Volaar had been hiding you, he punished Senen as any traitor should be punished." He pinched his tongue between thumb and forefinger, stretching it out and miming a slicing action. Ekhaas's ears went all the way back. Midian rubbed saliva from his fingers and smiled again, all the dark memories banished once more.

"But let's talk about what you're doing here," he said. He gestured to the shriveled scalp that still hung from Makka's belt. "We happened to run into one of the Kech Volaar scouts who escorted you out of their territory. He was very helpful—told us about your disgrace, the incident in the vaults of Volaar Draal, which way you went when you were shown the gate of the city. We picked up your trail and missed you by just this much"—he held two fingers together—"in Arthuun. And now we find you here exploring some fascinating Dhakaani ruins." He folded his arms and propped his chin on his fist. "Let's start with something easy. Does this place have a name?"

He could see her weighing the wisdom of answering with the truth or with a lie. After a few moments, she said, "Suud Anshaar."

It was the truth. He knew it not just from her voice but from the hiss and groan that Geth made. Midian glanced over at the shifter. "You're not helping," he said.

Geth glared at him around Tenquis as the tiefling removed his sword belt. "You're a bastard, Midian."

"And the only reason you're not dead already is because I convinced Makka you might have something useful to tell us, so close your mouth before I decide I was wrong."

Makka snorted at that and set the tines of his trident against

THE TYRANNY OF GHOSTS

the back of the shifter's neck. Geth glowered and tried to twitch away, but Makka pressed the points close, following his movements and slowly forcing him forward until Geth bent over with his face almost in the dirt.

"Midian, stop him," said Ekhaas. Her voice was strained. "Please."

Midian glanced at Makka. "Let him be."

"The Fury has promised me my vengeance," the bugbear said.

"Your vengeance can wait a little bit longer," said Midian.

Makka scowled but pulled back his trident and stepped away. Geth sat up slowly, his face hard. From where he sat, trussed up like a goose ready for the oven, Chetiin said, "You'll regret this, Midian."

"I doubt that." Midian turned back to Ekhaas. "So—Suud Anshaar." He had to search his memory for the reference, but he dredged it up. "The fortress of Tasaam Draet, grand inquisitor of the Puulta after the Rebellion of Lords, abandoned as cursed after its population vanished. Dare I guess that the thing that chased you out of the ruins had something to do with the alleged curse?"

Tenquis stood nearby, head down, waiting his turn to take Ekhaas's weapon and gear. Midian flicked a finger for him to proceed. The tiefling move to her side and removed her sword belt, then started unbuckling the belt that held her pouches. Ekhaas kept her head raised, ignoring him and focusing on Midian.

"It was some sort of daelkyr construct," she said. "Possibly the original one that destroyed Suud Anshaar. The population didn't vanish. They died after their bones were turned to stone."

The scholar in him perked up. "Fascinating. But I don't think that's why you came here is it? What really brought you to Suud Ansh—"

If he hadn't been watching, he might not have caught Tenquis's sudden start as Ekhaas's belt came off. The tiefling

grabbed for the largest pouch as though it contained something particularly heavy. Tenquis glanced at Ekhaas and Midian saw her eyes dart to the tiefling's for an instant before returning to him.

"What brought us to Suud Anshaar?" she asked, a little too quickly. "That's a long story—"

Midian ignored her and thrust out his hand. "Tenquis, give me that pouch."

Tenquis hesitated. His arm tensed, and he looked to the jungle as if he were considering hurling the belt and the pouch away into the undergrowth. Midian jumped and snatched it from him. Tenquis yelped and tried to grab it back, but Midian simply twisted away and kicked him hard in the back of one knee. The tiefling fell forward.

"Makka, keep him down." The large pouch on the belt was indeed strangely heavy. Something inside strained the leather. Midian pulled the pouch open.

Purple byeshk winked at him.

He drew the notched disk out and threw the pouch aside. "Makka."

The bugbear looked over and snorted. "That's a poor weapon."

"It's not a weapon. It's a symbol of Dhakaan, a *shaari'mal*." His instincts as a scholar had truly come alive. The disk was unquestionably of original Dhakaani craftsmanship, far finer than anything even the modern Dhakaani clans produced, but it was also remarkably preserved for something so ancient. He held it up before Ekhaas. "What is this?"

Her ears flicked rapidly. "We found it in the ruins. We don't know what it is."

"Liar." He caressed the metallic surface of the disk and turned it into the sunlight to examine the symbols carved on it. "A *shaari'mal* forged from byeshk—when the Sword of Heroes and the Rod of Kings also happen to be forged from byeshk."

Ekhaas bared her teeth at him. "That's just a coincidence. It has nothing to do with the sword or the rod."

THE TYRANNY OF GHOSTS

"And yet the markings are similar." Midian felt giddy. Tariic was going to want to see this.

"They're not," Ekhaas insisted. There was a tension in her voice that she was trying hard to conceal. The others were reacting too. Geth was cursing. Chetiin had sat up sharply. Tenquis had squirmed around so he could see what was happening. Even Marrow's red eyes were darting around.

Midian smiled at the *duur'kala*. "Well, it's fortunate we have something to compare them against, isn't it?" He turned to where Geth's sword lay waiting on the ground. "The Sword of Heroes, conveniently to hand." He went to the sword and reached for it—then paused and stood up again.

Geth growled at him. "Go ahead, Midian. Pick it up. Draw it."

"Close your mouth!" barked Makka. The bugbear glared at Midian. "What's the problem?"

Midian chewed his lip for a moment. "The Sword of Heroes won't bear the touch of a coward," he said. He might have dismissed such a warning as an absurdity, a myth that had grown up around the ancient sword, except that he'd seen it himself. He looked down at Tenquis. "You. Draw the sword. Makka, let him up."

Tenquis's eyes went to Geth, then to Ekhaas, then he started to sit up.

"*Maabet*!" Makka said. The bugbear planted a foot in the middle of Tenquis's chest and shoved him back down. "You don't need him. Give me that."

A sense of danger ran along Midian's limbs. "Makka, don't be—"

But two quick strides brought Makka to the sword. He jabbed his trident into the ground, scooped up the blade, and yanked it from its sheath.

The crack of thunder split the air the instant Makka's hand closed on the hilt. Lightning writhed up his arm. He howled in shock and pain, the sudden contraction of his muscles more than

anything completing the action of drawing the weapon. Geth's sword flew from his hand to land blade down in the jungle soil.

Midian snatched his knife from his belt and whirled on Ekhaas.

He was too slow. The air itself seemed to tremble as the *duur'kala* opened her mouth and sang a single harsh note—

◦ ◦ ◦ ◉ ◦ ◦ ◦

Ekhaas felt the weight in her belt pouch shift the moment she sat up after Tenquis had finished tying her. At first, she cursed herself for cramming the lone *shaari'mal* into the pouch the night before, when the others were safe in Tenquis's hidden pocket. Then she cursed the *shaari'mal* for being a mysterious, useless piece of . . . whatever it was . . . instead of the fragment of the Shield of Nobles that they'd come looking for.

And then, as Makka bashed Geth without a second thought and Midian strode around like a bully, ordering Tenquis to take their weapons and pouches, she thought of a use for the thing.

Whatever its true connection to the Sword of Heroes and the Rod of Kings, the *shaari'mal* made ideal bait. A puzzle for Midian's arrogance. A lure for Makka's recklessness.

The paired duet of Wrath's anger and Makka's pain as the bugbear ignored Midian's warning and tried to draw the sword was like sweet music. All of the anxious triumph that Ekhaas had struggled to conceal under Midian's questioning rose up inside her.

The gnome turned on her, knife in hand. His face was wild with fury.

Ekhaas was ready for him. Every bit of her triumph poured into a song so tightly focused it shook the air and raised loose dirt from the jungle floor. The magic slapped Midian like an invisible hand, lifting him up and sending him flying back. The *shaari'mal* dropped from his grip and bounced across the ground until it hit her own discarded sword.

THE TYRANNY OF GHOSTS

Midian kept hold of the knife, though. Somehow he even managed to twist in midair, landing in a crouch like a cat. His eyes flashed like a cat's too—then narrowed. Makka, shaking his head to clear it, looked around. His eyes went wide. "No!"

Ekhaas felt another flush of triumph. To one side of her, Chetiin was wriggling like something without bones. Ropes that Ekhaas had watched Midian test—twice—slid from his arms and legs. To the other side, Tenquis had scrambled over to Geth. The labyrinthine patterns of his vest coiled and changed, then the tiefling was pulling a knife out of a pocket and slicing at Geth's bonds. Geth glared at Makka, growling like an animal. Ekhaas saw the shifting come over him, saw his hair grow wild and thick, heard his growl drop even deeper in his throat.

"You want me?" he roared. "You want me? Come and fight!"

"The Fury grants me your life!" Makka bellowed back. He seized his trident and leaped at Geth.

The final strands of rope parted. Tenquis ducked away, but Geth threw himself forward, rolling under Makka's leap. He came to his feet beside Wrath, pulled the twilight blade from the ground, and dropped into a crouch as Makka twisted around.

"The Fury," said Geth, "will need to come and take it herself."

CHAPTER SIXTEEN

14 Vult

The shifter sprang for Makka. The two met in a crashing whirl of blades and bodies. On the other side of the clearing, Chetiin swept up the ropes that had bound him and flung them at Midian. In the instant that it took for the gnome to bat them aside, the *shaarat'khesh* elder was on him.

Tenquis dropped down at Ekhaas's side, first slashing the ropes around her ankles, then moving behind her to saw at those on her wrist. "Ekhaas," he said quickly, "I'm sorry I did what Midian ordered, but when he said he'd cut off my hand—"

"You don't have anything to be sorry for. I couldn't have done what I needed to if you hadn't." Ekhaas forced her wrists apart as far as she could, straining the ropes so that they'd be easier to cut. She kept her eyes on Geth and Makka, Chetiin and Midian.

As they struggled, they were too close for her to use a song against an enemy without also striking down a friend, but at least the pairs were evenly matched. Shifter and bugbear roared and hammered at each other, catching blows on gauntlet and trident shaft as they surged back and forth across the little clearing. Both were already bleeding, trickles of red running from shallow gashes. In contrast, the gnome and the goblin fought in near silence, never moving far from where their duel had started. Midian's knife flashed, and Chetiin slid out of the way, responding with a stiff-fingered strike that Midian deflected with his free hand. Neither had been injured that she could see,

but Ekhaas knew in her gut that their battle would be decided with a single blow.

Beyond them, Marrow whined and writhed against her bonds. Tooth lay still, but his eyes—fever bright—were open and watching everything. Ekhaas's ears went back. Sooner or later, Midian was going to remember that he still had two hostages to hold against them. "Tenquis," she said over her shoulder, "we have to free Marrow and Tooth."

The tiefling's knife worked faster. The ropes fell away. Tenquis seized her hand and pulled her to her feet. Ekhaas grabbed for her sword, tore it free of scabbard and belt, then snatched up the fallen *shaari'mal* with her other hand—

Something had changed.

For a moment, the battle seemed to recede as she stared down at the notched disk in her hand. Byeshk that had felt heavy and cold before had a kind of lightness and warmth to it. It . . . pulsed against her touch, even though her fingers and palm told her it was just as solid and rigid as ever. She felt a sense of purpose push at her, not a compulsion, but just a feeling that there was something she was meant to do.

"Ekhaas!" hissed Tenquis.

The crash and surge of the fight rushed back over her. The sense of the *shaari'mal* in her hand didn't go away, though. If anything, it was stronger. She raised her head and looked across the clearing.

Shadows seemed to cling to Makka and Midian—especially Midian. The bugbear trailed shadows, but the gnome was wrapped in them like a shroud. As if he felt her gaze, he glanced away from Chetiin to look at her. His eyes narrowed.

Tariic stared out from those eyes. Ekhaas's stomach churned. Her grip on the *shaari'mal* tightened.

And for the briefest instant, the shadows parted. Just a bit.

THE TYRANNY OF GHOSTS

Midian met Ekhaas's eyes—and doubt tickled the edge of his mind. Not the doubt he would have expected, of whether he and Makka would be able to win this fight with two more enemies ready to enter combat. He'd already considered that, and if either of them could finish off their opponent in the next few moments, the *duur'kala* and the artificer wouldn't stand a chance.

No, the question that slid like a worm into his head was whether he should be fighting at all.

His jaw clenched, and he tried to beat back the doubt, but it wrapped itself around him. Why fight? Why put himself in danger? What was so important?

Tariic was important, he told himself. Tariic Kurar'taarn, his lhesh and master, wanted Ekhaas and Tenquis and the others dead.

But did he want them dead right away?

Midian tore his gaze away from Ekhaas as Chetiin sent another kick at his head. Midian ducked under and feinted with his free fist at the goblin's groin. Chetiin curled out of an instinct to protect himself, turning away as he landed. That gave Midian the instant he needed to step back and survey the clearing.

His eyes came to rest on Tooth.

Maybe Geth and his allies didn't need to die immediately. He was getting tired of this open fight anyway.

Chetiin's crouched landing turned into a leg sweep. Midian vaulted over it, not back or simply up, but forward. His free hand and all of his weight came down on Chetiin's shoulder, shoving the goblin to the ground as Midian thrust off once more, tumbled through the air, and came down right beside Tooth. He heard Tenquis shout in alarm, but he ignored the tiefling. His knife plunged down—and stopped just above the sweat-slick skin of the stricken bugbear's neck.

"Nobody move!" he commanded.

Ekhaas froze. So did Tenquis. Chetiin whirled and raised empty hands, but moved no closer. Geth and Makka's fight crashed on. Midian raised his voice. "Geth! Makka!"

He saw Geth react to his name. The shifter's eyes widened as he took in the threat to Tooth, and he tried to pull away. Makka wouldn't let him go, though. The bugbear slammed his trident against Geth's raised gauntlet again and again, every blow driving Geth back a step.

"*Makka!*"

"No!" roared the bugbear. "I swore revenge, and I will not be denied again. Tariic can keep you from me, but he can't keep them. He promised them to me. The Fury promised them to me!" He bashed Geth again, forcing the shifter back once more.

Anger flashed through Midian—anger followed by a cold chill of fear. He glanced around at Chetiin, Tenquis, and Ekhaas. For the moment, they were all keeping their distance. Tenquis and Chetiin's eyes were darting between him and the ongoing battle. Ekhaas, though, seemed to be looking only at him. He felt sweat roll down his back. "Makka, don't be stupid!"

"Run if you want to," Makka growled. "When they're dead, Tariic's command of alliance ends, and I will come for you." He thrust his trident into the air. "Fury strike through me! I give my all!"

The symbol carved into his chest seemed to writhe. Dark radiance like black fire shot through with flashes of color flared around his weapon. Teeth bared, Geth brought up his sword, crossing it over his gauntlet. Makka whirled around, both hands on the trident shaft, and drove the triple points directly at him, all of his weight and power behind the blow.

At the last instant, Geth dropped his guard and turned, offering no resistance. Makka's strike skimmed past the shifter, leaving tongues of black fire smoldering in his shirt and hair. Geth's right hand seized the trident just below its blazing head—more fire licked up his gauntlet—and held it.

His sword slashed up under the trident's shaft in a powerful backhand stroke.

THE TYRANNY OF GHOSTS

The flames along the weapon vanished.

Makka's black eyes opened wide with shock. For a moment, he just stood there, his mouth working. Nothing came out except for bubbling blood.

When he finally fell, he toppled backward, hands sliding off the trident. The wound from Geth's sword stretched from his left hip to his right breast.

Bloodied and smoldering, Geth hurled the trident down on top of him. "That's for Vounn," he spat, then looked up at Midian and raised his sword.

It took willpower to keep the knife at Tooth's throat steady. "That's enough," Midian said. He looked around at all of them. "Well played."

"You're not going to get away this time, Midian," Geth growled.

"I think I will." He flicked the knife, drawing a bead of blood to remind them all of what was at risk. Tooth gave a little whimper. "This isn't over."

"You're not going to surprise us again."

"I won't surprise you as easily," Midian corrected him. "I don't need Makka. Tariic wants you dead. You've only delayed it." He glanced around at them all. At Geth, at Chetiin, at Tenquis, and especially at . . . Ekhaas?

The hobgoblin was still staring at him, as intent as if he'd sprouted a pig's nose. Was that pity in her gaze? His anger rose again. Maybe Tariic's enemies had won this round, but he could still hurt them. In her left hand Ekhaas held the Dhakaani disk, fingers clenched tight around it. Midian held out his hand. "Give me the *shaari'mal*."

She blinked and sudden alarm replaced pity in her eyes. Her ears flicked back. "No."

Midian pressed the tip of his knife to Tooth's broad throat again and smiled at her. "I think Tariic is going to want to see it," he said, "and I don't want to take the chance that you'll try to hide it before we catch you again. Give it to me."

Ekhaas bared her teeth and clutched the disk close. Midian let his grin grow.

Tenquis's golden eyes darted between them, then he blurted, "Do you really think Tariic will want it?" The tiefling plunged a hand deep into a large pocket in his vest that must have been magically concealed. Midian was certain there'd been no pocket there before. "Because if he does, I think he'd really want these."

He pulled out two more *shaari'mal*.

Midian actually felt his heart skip in surprise. Ekhaas hissed sharply. "Tenquis, don't!"

The tiefling flipped the two disks so that he held one in each hand and lifted them up, wiggling them on either side of his head. "How about it, Midian? Does Tariic want these?"

Rage burned cold in Midian's gut. "Give those to me, Tenquis."

The tiefling's face tightened. "Go and get them." His hands snapped forward and the *shaari'mal* skimmed through the air. Midian's head jerked up as he followed them.

It was no random throw; he saw that in an instant. One disk went to Geth, the other to Chetiin. Midian twisted back around in time to see Tenquis thrust his suddenly empty hands out in the gestures of a spell. Magic rippled through the air, trying to wrap itself around Tooth like some sort of shield. The tiefling was quick, but not quick enough. Midian stabbed down through the still gathering force—

◦ ◦ ◦ ◉ ◦ ◦ ◦

Ekhaas saw Tenquis reach into his pocket and knew what he was doing before he'd even pulled out the other two *shaari'mal*. Fear raced through her. Before, when the disks had seemed like nothing more than hunks of metal, she'd been willing to use one as a distraction. But with one pulsing softly in her hand, the thought of tempting Midian with them was just wrong.

THE TYRANNY OF GHOSTS

How could the tiefling not feel the power in the disks? "Tenquis," she said, "don't!"

He already had them raised beside his head. "How about it, Midian? Does Tariic want these?"

The gnome's face twisted. "Give those to me, Tenquis."

"Go and get them." He flung the disks away—to Geth and Chetiin. For an instant, all Ekhaas felt was a sense of relief, even if she already knew in the back of her mind that Tenquis's defiance had doomed Tooth.

Then Chetiin's hand closed on the flying *shaari'mal*.

☉ ☉ ☉ ◉ ☉ ☉ ☉

—and the tickle at the edge of Midian's mind tore wide open. Hard-edged clarity rose up from inside him and shattered into a hundred jagged, conflicting emotions.

Tariic was his master.

Tariic had stood over him with the Rod of Kings and commanded him to rip open his own belly.

He'd do anything to please Tariic.

Tariic wanted him dead.

He served his lhesh and Darguun.

His soul belonged to Zilargo. He'd killed for his country. He'd killed one king for Zilargo and tried to kill another.

Hurled stones found him as he tried to flee. An agent of the Trust, brought down by a mob. When he returned to consciousness, it was already too late for him. Tariic raised the rod. "Sit still and be quiet." He had no choice. The power that had once belonged to the emperors of Dhakaan gripped like a wolf's jaws. He sat still and was quiet.

Later, in the privacy of his chambers with only Pradoor to watch and cackle and Ashi d'Deneith to stare in horror, Tariic tore Midian's mind to pieces—and put it back together again in a way that pleased him.

Midian screamed until his new master commanded him to stop.

He screamed again and fell back away from Tooth as

the work of the Rod of Kings unraveled. Every memory of that tortured night came rushing back over him. Irresistible. Undeniable.

※ ※ ※ ※ ※ ※ ※

The warmth and power that Ekhaas felt in her *shaari'mal* exploded the moment that Chetiin took hold of his. The sense of purpose became an unwavering certainty—not of the *shaari'mal* telling her what to do, but of it telling her to do what she knew she had to.

Telling her to follow her *muut*.

Understanding came between one blink and the next.

Geth had said that the Sword of Heroes showed him memories of those who'd wielded it before, guiding him along their path. The quality of heroes was wrath. *Aram*. The Rod of Kings, Ekhaas knew, taught its holder to rule with the uncompromising power of the emperors of Dhakaan. The quality of kings was strength. *Guulen*.

Heroes inspired. Kings commanded. And nobles . . . served. They did their duty. Their *muut*.

But *muut* had two sides, didn't it? Tuura Dhakaan had said she had *muut* to the Kech Volaar, that she led them and protected them "as it had been since the Age of Dhakaan." And what had Senen Dhakaan once said of the Shield of Nobles when she'd told the tale of the three artifacts? That the ancient *daashor* Taruuzh had given it into the care of the lords and ladies of Dhakaan, that it represented both the fealty that the nobles owed to the emperor and the protection that was their responsibility to the people.

Muut wasn't something that could rest in the hands of just one person.

There'd never been an actual Shield of Nobles in the way there was a Sword of Heroes and a Rod of Kings, Ekhaas realized abruptly. There had never been fragments for them to find.

THE TYRANNY OF GHOSTS

The shield, the protection that the nobles owed to the people of Dhakaan, had shattered because the nobles had failed in their duty. But *muut* couldn't truly be destroyed—though it could be forgotten, just as stories could be confused and misinterpreted.

Like stories of what Taruuzh had created for the nobles of Dhakaan and what they had lost to Tasaam Draet. The Dhakaani had known at least some of the truth. Giis Puulta had carved three *shaari'mal* into his Reward Stela. Maybe later emperors had deliberately let memories of the Shield of Nobles, of Muut, fade, just as they let Suud Anshaar lie abandoned. Maybe as the empire slid toward the Desperate Times, the emperors didn't like the idea of a shield standing between their power and the people.

A shield between their power and the people.

The disk in her hands shifted at that thought, and a feeling of clarity flooded through her. She remembered the sense of Tariic's eyes staring out from behind Midian's.

Ekhaas met Chetiin's gaze and knew that he'd felt the same thing she had. Why didn't Geth? Why hadn't Tenquis? Maybe because they weren't *dar*. Maybe because they didn't live with *muut* as the Dhakaani had. She raised the *shaari'mal*, the ancient symbol of Dhakaan that Taruuzh had chosen to represent the collective *muut* of the empire's nobles, and opened herself up to it. Chetiin did the same.

The shadows shrouding Midian flickered—and vanished. The gnome stiffened, the knife in his hand stopping just above Tooth's throat. For a heartbeat there was silence.

Then Midian started screaming.

Geth and Tenquis stared between him, her, and Chetiin. "What just happened?" Geth demanded.

Ekhaas lowered her fragment of Muut. The *shaari'mal* was cold again, but she could feel its power lurking under the rune-carved surface of the byeshk. Her heart was racing in her chest.

"We've found our shield," she said, "and our weapon against Tariic." She looked up at Geth. "It's time to go back to Rhukaan Draal."

CHAPTER SEVENTEEN

19 Vult

Ashi looked at herself in the polished surface of a shield. For the first time since Senen's exile, she was wearing her formal outfit of trim trousers and cropped jacket. Her boots were freshly polished, her hair was pulled back, and her eyes were once again highlighted with Vounn's cosmetics. The clothes and cosmetics were her tools. Her weapons.

And she needed all the weapons she had. She forced a smile onto her face. Her reflection smiled back at her.

"Are you ready?" asked Oraan quietly.

She answered without looking over her shoulder at him—although it was tempting, because he'd dressed formally as well, in light armor with a red sash around his waist. "I'm ready."

"Did you eat well today?"

Her smile became less forced. "Very well."

"Good."

They turned into the antechamber outside Tariic's throne room—and were engulfed in a crowd of junior warriors, minor functionaries, and merchants of little consequence. Oraan stepped around her and walked ahead, clearing a path with his shoulders and elbows. Ashi followed close behind, hand on her sword, the subject of a few disdainful glances but of many more jealous glares. Anyone in the antechamber was there because they hadn't been invited into the throne room.

And with the entire throne room turned into a feast hall, if those in the antechamber hadn't been invited, they really were unimportant.

Near the top of the stairs, a line of guards held back the uninvited. Razu, the mistress of rituals, waved Ashi to the top of the steps. She gave Oraan a disparaging look, but Ashi's invitation to the feast had specified that she be accompanied by one of her guards. The old hobgoblin stepped into the doorway of the throne room, rapped her staff of office on the floor, and announced, "Special Envoy of House Deneith, Ashi d'Deneith, shares the celebration of Darguun's birth!"

Ashi strode up the last few stairs and down into the seething chaos of the feast.

The mood here was different than it had been at the ill-fated feast in the hall of honor, not least because it was simply larger. That feast had been in honor of the arrival of Riila and Taak of the Kech Shaarat. This, as Razu announced with every new arrival to the hall, celebrated Darguun's birth. Or at least what Tariic claimed to be Darguun's birth. Vounn had taught her that Haruuc had declared Darguun's independence from Cyre after a summer campaign in 969 YK.

No one seemed to mind the contradiction. True or not, it was a reason for Tariic to hold a feast big enough to reward the warlords who'd been most supportive of him, to show the dragonmarked houses that he still had the wealth to pay them, and to reassure the ambassadors of the Five Nations that he had interests beyond preparing his nation for conflict with the Valenar.

A feast big enough, fortunately, to provide Ashi and Oraan the opportunity they needed to find proof of tariic's true plans to attack Breland.

◈ ◈ ◈ ◈ ◈ ◈ ◈

Munta had started them along the path to the truth. The difficulty was in getting anyone to listen. Wearing the face of a

THE TYRANNY OF GHOSTS

dwarf merchant, Oraan had approached Laren Roole, the ambassador of Breland to the court of Darguun—and returned shaken.

"I didn't even try to mention it to him," he reported. "I could see his eyes fade as soon as I started discussing the buildup of forces. Tariic has gotten to him. He probably has Laren reporting back to King Boranel that everything is just fine in Darguun."

The results were the same, no matter whom they tried talking to. Tariic had subverted every ambassador from beyond Darguun's borders, along with their diplomatic staffs, just as he'd subverted the dragonmarked envoys. Some, like Laren Roole, were deeper in thrall to the lhesh than others, but none of them seemed interested in any danger that might befall Breland. At worst, they simply declared anything Oraan told them a hoax.

"Tariic can't have used the Rod of Kings directly on everyone, but its power is insidious," he said, returning from another failed attempt. "Anyone who has heard him speak adores him."

"You said that other nations have spies in Rhukaan Draal," Ashi said. "What about them?"

"They'd have the same trouble getting a message out."

"What about smuggling a message to someone you know outside of Darguun? A coded letter sent by Orien post."

Oraan grunted. "The problem is proof. We don't have details. Even if I get a message out and it reaches the right people in time, what do we tell them? All we've got is the suggestion that Tariic's plans for fighting the Valenar are suspiciously similar to a decades-old plan for an invasion of Breland." He sat down in a chair and looked at her. "Ashi, maybe we should wait. If we give him time, Tariic may braid enough rope to hang himself. The Brelish border isn't undefended. Rogue Darguul clans raid across it all the time, and Breland stops them."

"Are border defenses that catch raiders enough to handle a full army?" demanded Ashi. "Tariic has planned ahead. I think he'll have thought of that. Oraan, even if he succeeds, the backlash will devastate Darguun."

"There are a lot of Brelish who wouldn't see that as a bad thing."

She glared at him. "Are you one of them?"

He met her gaze, then after a moment, shook his head. "No."

"Then we need to find evidence that people will pay attention to. We need the details of what he's planning."

Oraan sat back in his chair. "That's not exactly the sort of thing anyone leaves lying around. I've looked in Khaar Mbar'ost's map room and council chambers just to be sure. I don't think Tariic is even using them. He's keeping his plans very closely guarded. We might find something in his chambers, but that's risky. You might not have noticed, but he's there a lot. I'd need to find a time when I could be sure he wouldn't interrupt me."

"*We'd* need to find a time," Ashi said. "If you're doing this, I'm going with you." He raised his ears, but she just raised her head stubbornly. "If you're captured, Tariic will know I was involved anyway. He'll ask, and you'll have to answer."

His ears flicked, and he nodded. "Fine. But we still need to find the right time to get in."

Ashi smiled and held out the invitation she'd received that day.

◦ ◦ ◦ ◉ ◦ ◦ ◦

They moved through the crowded throne room, Ashi with a goblet of wine in her hand, Oraan a pace behind her, glaring like the guard he was supposed to be. For all that the crowd was composed mostly of hobgoblins with a few goblins and bugbears among them, it wasn't that much different than a feast in Sentinel Tower. Various warlords approached her, seeking favor or contracts with House Deneith. Dragonmarked envoys—Pater d'Orien, Kravin d'Vadalis, and others—stopped to chat. Ashi's efforts to find out what Tariic was up to had inevitably made her more friends than she really wanted. She followed the lessons Vounn had taught her, though, and kept

THE TYRANNY OF GHOSTS

herself moving around the room, waiting for Tariic's entrance and the beginning of the feast.

She did encounter one person who she hadn't expected to see. Or at least who she hadn't expected to see up close. As the crowd shifted, Ashi found herself face to face with Dagii.

The young warlord stiffened immediately. "Lady Ashi," he said formally. His eyes darted around as he looked for somewhere to get away from her.

Ashi glanced around. It was a sign of her distraction that she hadn't noticed him—Dagii wore the battered ancestral armor of a warlord of Mur Talaan, the distinctive tall tribex horns mounted on his back and shoulders standing out above the crowd as they would have stood out above a battlefield. No one who she knew to be particularly close to Tariic was nearby, though. Before Dagii could move away, she said quickly, "We're friends, Dagii. No one is going to notice if we spend a few moments talking in the middle of a crowd."

He didn't relax. "Your guard," he growled under his breath.

She realized that he didn't know Oraan's true identity. Although the changeling met with him often, it was always as Aruget. She looked back at Oraan and twitched her head. Obediently, he moved a few paces away.

Dagii's ears flicked back, and his eyes narrowed. "Tariic allows you that much control over your guards?"

"Let's say that he doesn't know my guards as well as he thinks he does," Ashi said. "Have you heard anything from Ekhaas yet?" She had told him, through Aruget, of Tariic's lie that the *duur'kala* was dead. She still held out hope, however, that Ekhaas might try to contact Dagii, that maybe some message from her had come in the last few days.

He shook his head, then asked in return, "Has there been any sign of Midian?"

She shook her head too. Dagii's ears bent back, then flicked nervously. "There is something," he said quietly. "I was going to send word the next time I met with Aruget. Tariic has decided

the Iron Fox company has done all it can in Rhukaan Draal. We're going to be sent to the border of the Mournland sometime next week." His voice dropped even lower. "We're being posted to Skullreave."

Ashi tried to cover her shock with a sip from her goblet. She felt as if he'd just slapped her. They'd shared what they'd discovered from Munta with Dagii. He knew as well as they did what a posting to Skullreave might mean. "You—no," she said. "He can't do that."

"He can," Dagii said. "He's the lhesh. It's our *muut* to obey." He nodded toward the tables that had been set up on the dais. "I'm sitting at the high table as a hero of Darguun, but the commanders of other companies are there tonight as well. I think we're all leaving Rhukaan Draal soon." His ears flicked again as he looked back to her. "I will send information to you if I can. Great glory, Ashi."

The formulaic response caught in her throat—and before she could force it out, Oraan was at her elbow. "Lady Ashi," he said, "we should find your seat. Lhesh Tariic is about to enter."

Ashi looked back to Dagii, but he had already turned to head to the high table. She curled a hand into a fist and let Oraan lead her away. The entire crowd was in motion as people looked for their places. Fortunately, they already knew where Ashi would be sitting—Oraan had found that out a few days ago. In fact, it was key to how they would be able to both attend Tariic's feast and use the opportunity to break into his chambers.

Razu appeared on the dais and rapped her staff against the floor. "Lhesh Tariic Kurar'taarn comes!"

The voices of the crowd rose as Tariic entered, striking in tigerskin cloak and spiked crown. He gestured with the rod, acknowledging the crowd and silencing it. "On this night," he called out, "we celebrate the night that Haruuc of Rhukaan Taash met with his closest allies to plan a grand strategy that would carve out a homeland for the *dar*. Because of that night, Haruuc of Rhukaan Taash became Lhesh Haruuc Shaarat'kor.

THE TYRANNY OF GHOSTS

Because of that night, we stand as Darguuls." He raised the rod as if in blessing. "Eat, drink, and celebrate the birth of Darguun!"

Once again, voices rose. Tariic let the adulation of the crowd wash over him briefly, then turned and took his place behind the high table. At that signal, servants entered the throne room carrying dishes and platters, bowls and tall pitchers. The feasters took their places on long benches, chatting with those around them and helping themselves as food was placed on the table. Unlike the feasts and formal dinners of the Five Nations, there was no waiting until everyone had been served.

Ashi's nearby table companions were people she knew only in passing: a couple of lesser warlords, the chief of a small but disciplined clan, another human who was an apprentice to the viceroy of House Cannith, a goblin with one eye who had served as a scout under Haruuc. She recognized the choice of seating as a deliberate slight. By rights, she should have been seated closer to the high table or at least with people of higher standing. It was easy to imagine that at other tables, people would be gossiping about her.

She didn't care. It didn't really matter where she was sitting because she wouldn't be there long. Ashi fell into the small talk of the table with an ease instilled by Vounn's training. She knew several warriors from the chief's clan had been placed with Deneith mercenary units, and praised them accordingly. She discussed hunting with the goblin scout, weapons with the warlords, and events across Khorvaire—such as she was aware of them—with the Cannith apprentice. All the while, servants brought their burdens to the table. Pale, slightly sour hobgoblin wine. Small cups of *korluaat*. Starchy *noon* prepared in a variety of ways, from small balls in sauce to big steamed dumplings stuffed with bits of meat. Chewy sausages pickled with bitter herbs. Meat and fowl of various kinds, roasted and stewed and smoked.

Ashi ate—and especially drank—sparingly. Vounn had shown her the art of making it seem like she was keeping up

with those around her, when in fact very little was passing her lips. She didn't feel a particular need to gorge herself on Tariic's bounty. For one thing, she had, as Oraan had confirmed, already eaten well and wasn't hungry. For another, she was watching for a particular dish to make it to the table.

It was good that she was watching, too, because when the dish appeared, the clan chief's eyes lit up, and he reached for the bowl. "Black *noon* with mushrooms and *braak* greens! Lhesh Tariic feeds us well."

Ashi beat him to the bowl. "Allow me," she said and scooped a generous helping of *noon* balls threaded with black mold, pale straw mushrooms, and limp, dark green leaves onto his plate before taking some for herself. It looked unpleasant at best, but she had to admit that it did smell very appetizing. She offered the bowl to the Cannith apprentice, who looked at it dubiously but relented when Ashi insisted it was a Darguul delicacy.

The goblin scout declined to partake, but the two warlords finished off most of the bowl before it made its way farther down the table. Ashi glanced at Oraan. If he noticed her, he gave no sign of it. Bracing herself, Ashi picked up her spoon and dug into the mess.

It didn't take long before the Cannith apprentice started looking distinctly pale. Ashi felt it too—a nauseating roiling in her belly accompanied by an uncomfortable swollen sensation. A belch forced its way up her throat and escaped from her mouth to leave a foul taste on her tongue and a pungent odor in the air. A light sweat shone on the face of the clan chief. He pushed his plate away and started to rise. "*Miin eshoora*," he said in Goblin, excusing himself from the table.

It was someone else from farther down the table, one of the last to eat the black *noon*, who vomited first, however. A goblin in merchant's robes turned suddenly away from the table and, without even rising, was noisily sick on the floor. The clan chief made a noise halfway between a burp and a gurgle, and fled. It was too much for the Cannith apprentice. She jumped up from

THE TYRANNY OF GHOSTS

the table and ran for the wall, huddling down to try and conceal her shame. Ashi might have grinned at the way Oraan leaped to get out of her way if she hadn't been concentrating on not throwing up herself.

Heads all over the throne room were turning to look at their table as feasters cleared away from those being sick. Another feaster down the table fled for the door, though he didn't make it quite so far as the clan chief had. The two warlords looked at each other in alarm. Both of them were starting to sweat. Ashi clamped down on her teeth, trying hard to keep her stomach from rising as servants raced in with empty buckets.

The goblin scout pulled the Cannith apprentice's plate over and inspected what was left of her meal. He sniffed at it, then pushed it back. "The black *noon* is off," he said calmly.

Across the throne room, plates scraped as feasters shoved them away. A servant reached Ashi with an empty bucket that smelled like it had recently held mop water. She ignored the smell and buried her head in it.

When she looked up, Tariic's eyes were on her. She nodded at him politely. One of the seats at the high table was empty. Tariic's lackey Daavn was down on the throne room floor talking to the viceroy of House Medani. The half-elf rose and came over to her table. He held out his hand, and the dragonmark that patterned the back of it seemed to flash brighter for a moment. He swept his hand across the table, pausing over the Cannith apprentice's plate.

"There's no poison," he said. "The *noon* in this dish was simply spoiled."

The goblin scout muttered something under his breath as the Medani walked away. Tariic gave Ashi another long look, then made a dismissive gesture. Razu came trotting over to the table. "Those who are ill may leave the feast."

Ashi cleared her mouth and spit into the reeking bucket once more, then handed it back to the servant. She rose, nodded again to Tariic, and, along with the others who'd eaten the tainted dish,

walked out of the throne room with all the dignity she could manage. The noise of the feast returned, and the last she saw of Tariic, he had turned back to his conversation.

* * * ● * * *

As soon as they were alone on the stairs leading back to the upper floors of Khaar Mbar'ost, Oraan slipped a vial into her hand. Ashi pulled the cork from it and swallowed the liquid inside in a single gulp.

Her queasiness vanished instantly. Her stomach settled, and even the bad taste in her mouth vanished, replaced with a sweet flavor vaguely reminiscent of cherries. *"Rond betch,"* she said. "That was unpleasant."

"But necessary," said Oraan. "If you'd been the only one to claim illness—"

"I know." Tariic would have been suspicious. He might not have allowed her to leave the feast at all. And while no one who hadn't eaten from the dish at her table would actually fall ill, the remains of a lone vat of spoiled black *noon* in the fortress kitchens would back up events. A cook might be beaten for carelessly preparing the tainted dish, but Ashi suspected that he or she had, along with the servant who'd brought it to the table, been very well compensated for their trouble.

They reached the floor where Ashi's chambers were located and turned onto it, but didn't stop. At the end of the corridor, a smaller servant's staircase gave more discreet access to the levels of Khaar Mbar'ost. They climbed again until they reached the floor with Tariic's quarters.

"Will there be guards?" Ashi asked.

Aruget—Oraan had changed faces again as they climbed—shook his head. "Not tonight. Tariic generously sent word for the guards on duty to relax and join in the celebration, so long as they're back before he returns from the feast."

"Did he really?"

THE TYRANNY OF GHOSTS

The changeling snorted. "Of course not."

"Won't he find out what happened?"

"You think Tariic actually talks to his guards?"

The corridor before the lhesh's quarters was empty. His door, predictably, was locked, but Aruget produced a pair of lockpicks and had it open in moments. The hinges swung in near silence. They slipped through, and he closed the door behind them.

Tariic's chambers were luxurious. Thick Riedran carpets muffled their steps. The furniture was carved with fine details of vines and flowers—Ashi recognized work from the Eldeen Reaches—and tables and shelves displayed objects of art from across Khorvaire. Light came from everbright lanterns, their harsh illumination filtered through screens of milky glass. Ashi had always known that Tariic had a taste for what the world beyond Darguun had to offer, but she hadn't realized he'd managed to accumulate so much of it.

And yet there was something in the way it was all displayed that made her think uncomfortably of the trophies of battle, as if the rooms were a monument to conquest to come.

"Where do we look?" she asked softly.

Aruget scanned the room they stood in, then nodded toward a doorway. The room beyond was somewhat more functional than the first, with a broad table and shelves of books. A richly illuminated map of Khorvaire hung on one wall, innocent in itself—Baron Breven d'Deneith owned one very similar, Ashi knew—but again, she found the sight of it vaguely chilling. A chair had been positioned, its back to the room's window, so that someone sitting in it could gaze upon the map. She could imagine Tariic sitting there with all of Khorvaire laid out before him.

"Here." Aruget stood before a tall cabinet. Unlike the furniture in the other room, it wasn't Eldeen work. The heavy doors were carved with mountain scenes while thick bands of bronze supported an elaborate latch and lock. Aruget wrinkled his nose. "House Kundarak made this. I wish we had Tenquis here. An artificer would be helpful."

"You can't unlock it?"

"I can unlock it—but locks probably aren't the only thing protecting it." Aruget dipped into the sash around his waist and produced a small silk packet from the folds. He unwrapped it, and glittering dust spilled into his palm. Blowing lightly, he sent the dust wafting over the cabinet.

It settled into gently glowing lines, a web of magic centered around the lock. "A ward," said Aruget. He studied the lines, then drew out a twist of fine silver wire that he bent carefully into a wide hexagram. He warmed a small bit of wax between his fingers, pinched it in two and stuck it to the back of the wire. "Stand back," he warned Ashi. She stepped away, and he gently set the bent wire around the cabinet's lock, pressing the wax against the bronze so the hexagram would stay in place.

The glowing lines shimmered and faded.

"Good." Moving quickly, Aruget set to work with his lockpicks again. It took longer to open the cabinet than it had to open the door of Tariic's chambers, but when he was done, Aruget let out a hissing sigh of relief. He picked the silver wire away from the cabinet, flipped the latch, and pulled open the doors.

The interior of the cabinet was a series of drawers, large and small. Aruget went straight for the largest drawer, opening it to reveal rolled and folded papers. His fingers hovered over them for a moment, then he plucked out a roll about the length of his forearm, dirty and ragged edged. Ashi glanced into the drawer skeptically. There were other papers that were larger, brighter, and seemed more likely to be important.

Aruget caught her look. "If you're looking for important information, look for what your mark handles most often. Chances are it's something near and dear to them." He held the paper up to the light and unrolled it. "Ah," he said.

Ashi moved around him. The paper was a map of Darguun. The writing on it was in Goblin—and there was a lot of writing. Notes and scribbles, arrows and lines. The map had been used

and reused many times, but Ashi recognized the essence of it quickly. Troop movements from Rhukaan Draal to the border of the Mournland, then back to Skullreave. Then across into Breland.

Just as Munta had suggested. She breathed a curse.

"It's not enough," said Aruget. "We need more." He rolled the map up again and set it on the table. "Be careful with these. We need to put them back as close as possible to the way we found them, or Tariic will know someone has been here."

"Won't he know that when he finds out the magic on the door is gone?"

"It should reweave itself once the doors are closed again. I know what I'm doing." He took more papers from the drawer, scanning each one, then discarding it on the table. Ashi caught glimpses of more maps, of lists, of ledgers. Aruget's ears flicked, and his mouth grew tighter as he glanced at them. "Here," he said finally. He put another map down on the table, then slipped a piece of folded paper, a miniature pot of ink, and a stubby pen out of his sash. "Copy that as best you can. No need to worry much about the details inside Darguun. Focus on the border with Breland."

Ashi studied the map and drew a slow, hissing breath. The plan sketched out in rough on the first, dirty map had been refined. Two broad arrows struck across the Brelish border from Skullreave. One went almost directly north to a place named Kennrun. Ashi recognized the name as a Brelish fortress that guarded a stretch of Orien trade road running parallel to the border. The other arrow curved northwest around the end of the Seawall Mountains until it met the trade road west of Kennrun. With the fortress and its soldiers bottled up by one of the armies from Skullreave, the second force would have an easy march along the trade road—straight to the town of New Cyre.

Ashi knew that name too. New Cyre was the settlement that Breland's king had granted to Cyran refugees who had been away from their home nation on the day it had been transformed

into the Mournland. It was a growing town, the heart of the region—and founded in the aftermath of the Last War, only lightly defended. If Tariic could take it, and maybe Kennrun as well, he would effectively extend Darguun's territory across the mountains and establish a new base for further expansion.

She dipped Aruget's pen into the ink pot and started sketching. There were names beside the two arrows, companies and units to be included in the attack, presumably. Some she recognized as clan names. The Kech Shaarat stood at the head of the companies attacking Kennrun. She scribbled them all down. "Aruget, see if you can find troop numbers. I have company names. Black Tongue. Devil Hand. Red Moon. Iron—" Her tongue stumbled as she read the first name on the list of companies attacking New Cyre. Iron Fox.

"I have them," said Aruget. His voice sounded grim. She turned to look at him.

He had a ledger book in his hand, maybe showing the troop numbers. Open across the pages of the book, however, was a letter. He flipped it around and handed it to her.

It was in her handwriting.

To Breven, patriarch of Deneith, on the 28th day of Vult, 999 YK—

By your message commanding that I remain in the court of Lhesh Tariic Kurar'taarn, you show that House Deneith turns away from me. Now I turn away from House Deneith.

You tell me that the mercenaries hired to Deneith by the lhesh of Darguun are worth more than the life of any member of your house, including that of a bearer of the Siberys Mark of Sentinel. I tell you to see what one who bears the Siberys Mark can do.

You said that Lhesh Tariic is more understanding than you if he accepts my continued presence in his court. Know that Lhesh Tariic has done more than welcome my presence. He has accepted and forgiven me. On this day, Darguul troops enter Breland. They are aware of every Deneith mercenary between

THE TYRANNY OF GHOSTS

Kennrun and New Cyre. I made them aware. They have been trained to fight Deneith's soldiers. I taught them.

I defy your threat of excoriation. As Tariic conquers Breland, I swear I will conquer Deneith.

—Ashi

She stared at the letter in shock. "I didn't write this."

"Sivis scribes are capable of amazing forgeries," Aruget said. "All he would have needed was a sample of your writing."

"This letter will destroy me. Breven will go insane!"

"That's probably the idea. Tariic wants to hurt you. At least we know the date of the attack, though. Nine days from now." He reached to take the letter back from her.

She twitched it away and tore it in two, shredding those pieces into smaller pieces.

"Ashi!" Aruget said sharply, but she cut off his reprimand.

"Tariic will *not* do that to me. I won't let him."

He grabbed her wrists. "But now he'll know we were here!"

Shadows fell across the doorway of the room. "Perhaps," said a cackling voice, "he already does."

Ashi and Aruget both looked up. Pradoor stood between them and the outer room. Behind her stood Tariic's three deaf bugbear servants.

CHAPTER EIGHTEEN

19 Vult

Aruget reacted instantly, vaulting over the table and slamming the door of the room in Pradoor's face. Ashi heard the old goblin priestess yelp in pain. Aruget put his back to the door and pointed at the table. "Get that over here!"

Ashi dropped the torn pieces of Tariic's false letter and heaved against the table. Papers went flying. Aruget hopped up out of the way, and she rammed the table against the door just as something—a bugbear's shoulder, probably—struck from the other side. The door shuddered, but the table held it closed. Aruget joined Ashi, and together they threw the table up on its end so the heavy top leaned against the door.

The silent door of Tariic's chambers. The thick, muffling carpets in the outer room—the same things that had hidden their entry, Ashi realized, had let Pradoor and the bugbears sneak up on them. How had she known they were there, though? Ashi glared at Aruget. "You set off that ward on the cabinet after all!"

"I didn't!"

"The Six hear our secrets," Pradoor called from the other side of the door, "and I hear you. Do you think Lhesh Tariic would keep his plans behind just one ward? The Keeper commands that both inner and outer doors be guarded."

A second ward inside the cabinet. Ashi ground her teeth together and Aruget cursed. "What now?" she asked him.

DON BASSINGTHWAITE

He looked around at the scattered papers, then scooped up both the folded paper she'd written on and the rolled map she'd copied from. He thrust the folded paper at her and stuffed the map through his belt. "We fight. Whoever gets out has to get this information to someone who can warn Breland."

Ashi's mouth went dry as she took the paper and slid it into her jacket. "What about stopping Tariic before he can attack?"

Aruget looked at her and shook his head. "That's not going to happen. I'm sorry, Ashi, but this could be the end for Darguun. The Five Nations will crush Tariic."

Another blow rocked the door and shifted the heavy table back by a handspan. Ashi jumped away from it and drew her sword. Aruget drew his as well and shifted around to the side of the door. When the next blow came, the door burst open, and a bugbear pushed his head and shoulders through. Aruget lunged.

His hobgoblin sword wasn't made for thrusting. The broad end of it, though sharp, left only a shallow cut in the bugbear's shoulder. The bugbear yelped and just jerked back. Aruget cursed. "Useless bloody—"

With a roar, the bugbear hit the door again. This time it flew wide, the table toppling over, and the bugbear surged into the room. Aruget leaped for him—and Ashi heard Pradoor's voice crack in prayer, invoking the power of the Dark Six. "See the glory of the Mockery!"

Aruget stiffened before he could land a blow. His eyes went wide with unnatural fear, and he leaped away. The bugbear lumbered after him, but the changeling pressed himself back toward the farthest corner of the room.

Ashi reached out and grabbed his arm. She focused her will, and heat spread through her dragonmark. Aruget sucked in a breath and the fear faded from his face.

"You're welcome," said Ashi. No further tricks of the mind lurking in Pradoor's prayers would touch either of them anymore. She ducked past Aruget and slashed at the first of the bugbears.

THE TYRANNY OF GHOSTS

The bright Deneith honor blade flashed and the big *dar* reeled back, clutching the gaping wound across its belly.

The other two bugbears pushed it out of the way, almost filling the room with their bulk. They were armed too. One carried an axe, the other a heavy hammer. Tariic might have had them deafened, but that hadn't taken away any of their battle skills. Both swung their weapons in easy circles. Ashi backed up a pace. She didn't even notice that Pradoor had also crept through the door until the priestess flung an arm toward her. "The Fury scours your soul!"

Black fire tinged with licking colors seemed to rush up around Ashi, feeling as if it were burning all the way through her. It vanished in an instant, but it left her gasping, and this time it was Aruget who ducked past to cover her. He wouldn't stand long against the two bugbears, though. Ashi sucked in her breath, pushed the pain of the fire away, and joined him. The hammer swung down at his unprotected side, but she caught the blow with her sword and deflected it.

The hammer's wielder bared his teeth and turned all of his attention to her. Crouched down low, she moved to the side, searching for an opening.

Beyond the two armed bugbears, Pradoor crept toward the one Ashi had wounded. She moved with eerie confidence for a blind woman, hand going directly to his wound. Ashi didn't hear the prayer she spoke, but she saw its effects—the bugbear jerked at her touch and sat upright. The wound across its belly was gone.

"Just run, Ashi!" snapped Aruget. He led the way, slipping around his opponent and sprinting through the shattered door into the outer room. Ashi feinted at the hammer-wielding bugbear, then slid to his other side as he reacted.

The bugbear Pradoor had just healed thrust himself to his feet and lunged for her. Ashi skipped aside, and the bugbear's arms swept wide, but so did her blow. Pradoor cackled with glee. Ashi plunged on through the shattered door after Aruget. The

changeling was almost across the outer room, almost at the door to the corridor—

"I call the teeth of the Devourer!" Pradoor shouted.

Whirling white blades burst out of the air between Aruget and the door. He tried to stop, but he slid half in among them. The blades seemed to close on him like a school of fish caught in a feeding frenzy. Aruget screamed and scrambled away. His left arm emerged torn and bloody from the attack. The white blades spread back across the door, cutting off escape.

Ashi caught up to him. "Aruget—"

"I'm fine," he said in a voice tight with pain.

"No," she said. "The map."

Tucked into the changeling's belt at his left side, it had plunged with him into the spinning blades. Pradoor's spell had chewed it to tatters.

Aruget looked up at her, and his face hardened. "Keep your paper safe then," he said—and shoved past her, charging back at the bugbears and Pradoor as they emerged into the outer room. He snatched a heavy vessel of Aundairian glass from a shelf as he raced by and hurled it ahead of him at the old priestess.

For once, Pradoor's strange senses seemed to fail her. The glass vessel struck her right between the eyes, and she pitched over backward. She hit the floor, and the barrier of blades vanished.

And the bugbear with the hammer hit Aruget. The weapon swung high, slamming into his chest and halting his charge. The changeling's legs flew out from under him and he crashed down onto his back. The other armed bugbear raised his axe. Ashi saw Aruget's eyes open wide. He flung himself aside and the axe chopped through the thick carpet deep into the floor. The bugbear jerked at the axe, trying to pull it loose, but the other two bugbears were already on Aruget, the unarmed one kicking at his head with heavy boots, the other raising his hammer for another blow.

There was no need. Between Tariic's servants, Ashi saw Aruget's face run like wax. The coarse features, ruddy tones, and long mobile ears of Aruget melted into a pale, delicate visage

THE TYRANNY OF GHOSTS

surrounded by short-cropped, silver hair. The bugbear froze in surprise.

Ashi had never seen Aruget's true face. Changelings didn't revert to their natural face in sleep or when they lost consciousness, only when they willed it. Or when they died.

Rage settled over Ashi. In her head, she knew that she should be running—out the door, down the stairs, and out into Rhukaan Draal in search of some way to get her information out of Darguun. Her heart told her she should be doing something very different.

Even though the bugbears couldn't hear it, she raised her voice in the fluting battle cry of the Bonetree Clan and flung herself at them. The first barely had a chance to look up from his buried axe. Ashi leaped off of a carved table and plunged her sword, with all of her weight behind it, deep into his back. The bugbear collapsed under her. She rolled off him, snatched back her sword, and whirled to face the others.

The unarmed one had seen her. He pointed, and the hammer wielder spun around, his weapon still raised over his head. Ashi thrust her sword up under his ribcage, then yanked it sharply out again. His mouth opened in a groan that never came, and he slumped backward.

The last bugbear, the one she had originally wounded, snatched up Aruget's fallen sword. He backed away from her with fear in his eyes, sword held low to protect his belly from another blow. Ashi stalked after him, then lunged suddenly. Her first attack bashed the sword out of his hand. Her second pierced his right leg and he toppled over, screeching his pain. She reversed her sword, raised it—

—and a voice like the creaking of a door called out, "The Six curse you, Ashi of Deneith!"

Pain shot through her, as if someone had gathered all of her nerves in a fist and pulled hard on them. It ripped a scream from her, and she almost fell. She forced herself to stay on her feet, though, as she turned to face Pradoor.

DON BASSINGTHWAITE

The goblin priestess was on her knees, blood running in a dark red ribbon between her eyes. The expression on her face, however, was rapturous. "You try to defy Tariic," Pradoor said. "You try to defy the will of the Six. But you won't. You can't. Tariic will bring in a new age, and Darguun will follow the power of the Six once more!"

It hurt to draw breath, but Ashi managed it. "The only power Tariic will allow in Darguun is him, Pradoor," she spat. She dragged herself closer to the old goblin, raising her sword with shaking hands.

"Fool," said Pradoor. "Tariic knows and fears the power of the Six—as should you!" She flung out a hand. Shadows flowed from the gesture.

The pain that shook Ashi seemed to intensify, sucking the strength from her limbs and driving her to the ground. Incredible weakness pressed against her. She couldn't stay upright. She could barely breathe. She sank down against the soft carpet, her eyes level with Aruget's.

The changeling looked disappointed in her.

Shuffling footsteps scuffed across the carpet behind her. Ashi tried to lift her head but couldn't. Groping hands touched her shoulders, located her skull. Pradoor gasped with effort.

And something hard and heavy drove thought out of Ashi's head.

* * * * * * *

A slap in the face woke her up.

Ashi started and opened her eyes to bright light. Shock rolled through her, and the habit she'd cultivated for weeks drove fear into her. It was morning. The sun had risen, and she hadn't renewed the protection of her dragonmark—

No. She blinked and the light came into focus—an everbright lamp. She was lying on a cold, hard floor with the lantern close beside her, and someone was holding her arms up above her

THE TYRANNY OF GHOSTS

throbbing head. An open window in one wall showed the darkness of night beyond. Relief replaced shock. It wasn't morning yet.

Then another slap hit her, and she saw who was striking her. Tariic stood over her, still in his tigerskin cloak, still wearing the spiked crown of Darguun, still carrying the Rod of Kings. He smelled of wine and meat as if he'd come straight from his feast.

The events of the night rushed over her. Tariic raised his hand for a third time.

"Do it," Ashi said, "and I'll bite you."

He stomped down on her belly instead. Ashi convulsed and retched. Tariic stepped away from her. "You're almost more trouble than you're worth," he growled. "Oraan is missing. I assume that changeling was him?"

Ashi twisted her neck to follow him. She wasn't in his chambers anymore, that was certain. The room was small and cold. She could hear the night noises of the Rhukaan Draal, but they seemed distant. A room in one of Khaar Mbar'ost's towers, she guessed. She lifted her head a little and looked down toward her feet.

Pradoor stood there. And Dagii.

Anger darkened the face of the young warlord of Mur Talaan, but he stood still and silent as Tariic paced the room. Ashi tipped her head back to see who held her. The last of Tariic's three deaf bugbears bared his teeth at her.

Tariic's foot thumped into her side, forcing a gasp out of her. "I asked you a question."

She glared at him. "Yes," she said.

"Was he Aruget?"

"Yes."

"And you found out what I plan for Breland."

She didn't answer that. Tariic's words had an effect on Dagii though. His face darkened even further, and his ears lay flat. "You have no honor," he snarled at Tariic.

Ashi felt a moment of surprise. Dagii wasn't under the control of the rod? What was he doing here, then?

He was there, she realized suddenly, because of her. Tariic didn't need the rod to command Dagii right then. All he needed was her as his captive.

Tariic flipped Dagii a piece of paper. Ashi recognized the paper—no longer folded—that had been in her jacket. "The copy is terrible," Tariic said, "but you should be able to make it out."

Dagii bared his teeth as he scanned her roughly drawn map. He looked up at Tariic. "This is a violation of the Treaty of Thronehold—"

Tariic turned on him. "First," he said, "don't pretend you don't already know." He pointed at Ashi. "If Oraan was Aruget, then she hasn't been as isolated as I thought she was. And if she wasn't isolated, she was going to friends for help. Senen Dhakaan. You." Dagii stiffened. Tariic sneered at him. "You should never lie, Dagii. You don't have the talent for it."

"Second," he added, "you need to get used to the idea, because you're leading the attack on New Cyre."

Dagii's ears flicked. "I won't."

"Your lhesh commands it." Dagii said nothing. Tariic's sneer returned. "At the feast tonight, you accepted my request to lead the Iron Fox out of Skullreave. If you already suspected that the defense against Valenar raiders was only an excuse, then why did you accept? You were willing to do your duty then. You swore an oath to do it."

Dagii met his gaze. "I deny my oath."

Tariic laughed. "You? Dagii, son of Fenic of Mur Talaan? You're not capable of it." He looked at Ashi. "Any more than Ashi here seems capable of placing any value in her own life."

Some of Ashi's own anger came back. "All your bracelets have done is keep me in Rhukaan Draal and my hands from your throat, Tariic," she said.

Tariic flicked his finger, and the bugbear holding her arms gave them a sharp tug. The pain made her gasp. Tariic smiled again. "True," he said. "That's why I think I need new leverage against you. Against both of you." He pointed the Rod of Kings

THE TYRANNY OF GHOSTS

at Ashi. "You are going to remain my prisoner, though not in the comfortable surroundings you have been enjoying."

He pointed his other hand at Dagii. "You will command the assault on New Cyre, the hero of the Battle of Zarrthec at the head of my armies. If either of you disobeys me, the other dies." His ears twitched and rose. "Is that simple enough?"

Dagii thrust out his chest. "Command me with the rod. You'll have my obedience then!"

"You don't understand, Dagii." Tariic's words rasped between his teeth. "I can *command* anyone. I command the Ghaal'dar clans. I command the Kech Shaarat who dared to come before me. I command the envoys of the dragonmarked houses and the ambassadors of the Five Nations. But that isn't true power. That's not how the emperors of Dhakaan truly ruled." He held up the rod. "This is a crutch. Unless I put care into my orders, my power doesn't extend beyond those who see and hear me. To rule an empire requires servants who serve because they want to"—he lowered the rod—"or because they have to."

He waited.

Dagii looked down at Ashi, then his ears drooped, and he lowered his head. His fist rose to rap his chest. "I will command the assault, lhesh."

"Dagii—" Ashi said, but the instant her lips moved, the bugbear jerked on her arms again. Her words vanished in another gasp.

Tariic ignored her. "Serve me well, and you'll be rewarded," he said. He gestured toward the door. "Now go, and remember what you have to lose."

Dagii walked out the door like a broken man. Tariic closed it behind him, then turned his gaze back to Ashi, gesturing for the bugbear to ease his grip on her arms.

"I know you don't care about risking your own life," he said. "How do you feel about risking Dagii's?"

Ashi glared at him. "I saw the letter that you had forged. It doesn't matter what Dagii does. You always intended to destroy me."

He drew his foot back to kick her again. Ashi braced herself, but the kick never came. Tariic lowered his foot. "Not always," he said. "But I knew that in the aftermath of my attack on Breland there was a chance Breven might relent and ask you to return to Karrlakton. I couldn't let that happen. You do know my secret—and my 'crutch' is very convenient." He turned the rod in his hands. "I didn't so much intend to destroy you as to make certain that no one outside of Darguun would want anything to do with you."

"Why not just kill me, then?"

He smiled at her. "Because I don't need to." He stepped back. "I saw that you tore up my letter. There really wasn't much point to that. I can have another one made. In fact, you've given me the chance to send Breven an even more impressive gesture of your disdain for Deneith."

He gestured, and Pradoor dragged out something she'd been hiding behind her back. Ashi's bright honor blade. "In the new letter," said Tariic, "you'll be sending it back." He took the sword from Pradoor.

Ashi started to struggle, but her bugbear captor renewed the pressure on her arms. She forced herself to relax. She glared at Tariic.

"I'll stop you, Tariic. I swear I will."

"I don't see how," said Tariic. "Dagii is gone. Aruget is gone. Senen is gone. You're out of allies. I'd suggest focusing on behaving yourself and keeping Dagii alive. His life is in your hands now."

He turned to the door. "Pradoor," he said. "Hold her."

The goblin priestess murmured a prayer, and once again pain burned through Ashi's body. While she writhed, the bugbear released her and lumbered to his feet, taking the lantern with him. By the time she could breathe again, Tariic, the bugbear, and Pradoor were all at the door. Tariic clapped the bugbear on the shoulder. "You already know your new jailer," he said. "Don't bother screaming. Nobody is going to be coming for you."

THE TYRANNY OF GHOSTS

She managed to raise her voice. "The dragonmarked envoys will miss me."

"No," said Tariic. He lifted the Rod of Kings. "They won't."

The door closed. The room plunged into darkness. Ashi heard the rasp of a bolt being slid home on the other side of the door. Two bolts. And a key in a lock.

She sat up slowly, utterly alone in the cold darkness.

CHAPTER NINETEEN

24 Vult

The riverboat drew in its oars and glided into an empty berth along the docks of Rhukaan Draal. Thick hawsers flew over the side, were caught by dockmen and made fast. A few moments later, the gangplank slid out.

Ekhaas and the others were down it as soon as the lower end touched the dock. "Good luck to you," the captain called after them. "Find your fortune and live to spend it!"

"We'll hire you a better cook for your galley," Ekhaas shouted back with false levity, then turned away and said to the others, "Let's get off the docks and find out what's going on." Her fingers touched the reassuring weight of the *shaari'mal* within her pouch, a habit of the last ten days.

They'd slipped out of the varags' territory as quickly as they could. Fortunately, the savage creatures were still cowed by what had happened at Suud Anshaar—they heard the varags' shrieks in the distance but didn't so much as catch a glimpse of them. If the ancient construct that lurked in the Dhakaani ruins still wailed, they didn't hear it.

The power of the Shield of Nobles was a revelation. Ekhaas had barely been able to sleep. She'd lain awake, listening to the jungle and imagining what they could do. One *shaari'mal* had weakened the hold of the Rod of Kings on Midian. Two had shattered it. They had three of the disks. What effect would waking all three have? Who would they

give the third disk, the one Tenquis carried hidden in his vest, to?

Dagii's gray-eyed face had risen in her memories.

Tooth, restored by rest and more healing magic, led them north out of the jungle. Several days later, they'd arrived at the town of Rheklor and the mouth of the Ghaal River, where boats traveled upstream to Rhukaan Draal in a constant flow of river traffic.

Unlike Arthuun in the south, they'd found the town alive with excitement over Tariic's plans for defense against the Valenar. The news had given them a convenient excuse for traveling to Rhukaan Draal—when they'd approached a boat's captain to arrange transportation, they claimed to be mercenaries looking to take Lhesh Tariic's coin—at the same time as it had made Ekhaas's stomach tighten with fear. A few inquiries established that no Valenar had been seen since Dagii's triumph at the Battle of Zarrthec. What was Tariic up to? What had happened to Dagii and Ashi?

They'd also bid farewell to friends at Rheklor. Tooth wanted more rest before he made the journey back to Arthuun. Marrow refused to board a boat or enter Rhukaan Draal. She would return to her pack across country. They'd said good-bye and boarded their boat a party of five once more. Ekhaas. Geth. Tenquis. Chetiin.

And Midian.

After he'd stopped screaming, the gnome had begged for the chance to take his revenge against Tariic. He'd poured out a story that, coming from anyone else, would have roused Ekhaas's pity. Coming from Midian, it only made her glad of his suffering. At the same time, though, they all agreed on two things. First, that freed of the influence of the Rod of Kings, Midian hated Tariic as much as any of them did.

Second, that they would need all the allies they could find. They had a shield against the rod's power, but Tariic still had an army to throw at them.

THE TYRANNY OF GHOSTS

◎ ◎ ◎ ◎ ◎ ◎ ◎

Beyond the docks, the streets of the city were strangely empty.

"It was like this when Haruuc died," Tenquis said. "Everyone went to watch him be laid to rest."

"I guess it would be too much to hope that Tariic has died, then," said Chetiin.

"I'd be disappointed if he had," growled Geth. The shifter adjusted his cloak and cowl. Of all of them, he was the most recognizable, having held the throne of Darguun as Haruuc's *shava* after the old lhesh's death. "I'd miss the chance to bring him down."

Ekhaas spotted a figure moving on the street ahead—a scruffy hobgoblin staggering along as if he'd just left a tavern. "Wait here," she said. "I'll see if I can find out what's happening." She had her answer quickly enough and returned to the others. "Everyone who can has gathered at the arena," she said.

"The arena?" Geth asked. "Are there games?"

"Not exactly." Ekhaas put her ears back. "Tariic gives blessings to the commanders of his army. They ride out today to take charge of the defense against the Valenar."

Geth grunted. "More soldiers riding to the border of the Mournland leaves fewer soldiers in Rhukaan Draal for Tariic to command. That helps us."

"Not when one of those commanders is Dagii," said Ekhaas. They'd made loose plans on the journey upriver, not knowing exactly what they'd find in Rhukaan Draal. Most had involved slipping into Khaar Mbar'ost—with Chetiin's and Midian's skills it would be relatively easy—and freeing Ashi, but all had involved gathering allies before they confronted the lhesh. Dagii had always been at the top of that list.

Chetiin looked to Midian. "What are Tariic's intentions for him?"

"I don't know," said the gnome. "I've been away from Rhukaan Draal almost as long as you, and Tariic didn't discuss

everything around me. I was his slave, not his adviser. It's surprising, though. While I was here, Tariic was keeping Dagii away from the action. He was using him as a figurehead, the hero of Zarrthec."

"Maybe that's what he's doing now," said Tenquis. "Sending him to repeat his victory against the Valenar."

"If there are Valenar," Ekhaas said. She tried to put her feelings for Dagii aside. "We can use this chance to get into Khaar Mbar'ost more easily. We'll find other allies. Munta the Gray could help us."

Geth bared his teeth. "Dagii hasn't left Rhukaan Draal yet," he said. "We can still intercept him and get the *shaari'mal* into his hands. There's no one else I'd want to have as part of the shield—especially if Tariic has made him one of the commanders of Darguun's army. I say we go to the arena."

Ekhaas's ears rose. "Tariic will be there. Are we ready to face him?"

No one answered her. No one had to.

The great arena lay on the other side of the city. If a crowd had already gathered, they needed to hurry. Dagii wouldn't waste any time beginning his march north after receiving Tariic's blessing. She pointed along one of Rhukaan Draal's crooked streets. "This way."

* * * * * * *

The window of Ashi's tower room looked out over the wide square before Khaar Mbar'ost, too high up to think of climbing down, but more than high enough to offer a spectacular vista of Rhukaan Draal. She wondered if Tariic had chosen the view deliberately. The square was where she and the others had tried and failed to kill him. Vounn had died down there. Ashi almost had too.

When Ashi saw troops parading in the square, she was certain the view was deliberate. Even from the tower window,

THE TYRANNY OF GHOSTS

she could make out the standard of the Iron Fox company. Tariic was taunting both her and Dagii. She could see the arch of the bridge over the Ghaal River as well. When Dagii led his troops north, she would be able to see them leave.

The Iron Fox wasn't the only company to parade before Khaar Mbar'ost. Ashi recognized the precision of the Kech Shaarat too. They'd been first on the list of companies for the assault of Kennrun. If Dagii was leading the attack on New Cyre, presumably Riila Dhakaan—or more likely Taak—would be leading the attack on the fortress. Ashi felt a flash of hatred for the two Kech Shaarat, over and above what she felt for their role in Senen's mutilation. She'd almost challenged Taak to a duel in the hall of honor. She wished that she had.

Her deaf jailer brought her food and water once a day, Pradoor waiting behind him with a prayer on her lips in case Ashi tried anything. Her days passed slowly and her nights, cold on the hard floor, even more so. Marks on the wall, scraped into the stone with the buckle of her belt, counted the days ahead to 28 Vult. The day of Tariic's attack on unsuspecting Breland.

Maybe the Brelish weren't so unsuspecting as she feared—but she doubted it. Tariic seemed awfully confident that his false aggression toward the Valenar, together with whatever misinformation he was providing through the ambassadors of the Five Nations, had fooled everyone.

Maybe the lhesh had been lulled into overconfidence by the Rod of Kings. Maybe the Valenar had gone to the lords of the Five Nations to tell them they had no intention of attacking Darguun again. Maybe Brelish scouts had slipped into northern Darguun and worked out Tariic's plans on their own. Maybe Aruget had somehow survived, returning to his natural form to lull Pradoor and Tariic into a false sense of security before escaping from the castle and fleeing to Breland to warn his masters in the King's Citadel . . .

"Maybe" could have driven her mad.

On the fifth day of her captivity, Ashi woke, watched the sun rise, and, for the first time since Vounn's death, did not shield herself with her dragonmark. After so many days of invoking its protection, it felt odd. Her mark tingled as if it wanted to be used. The world beyond her window seemed a little less bright and sharp without its clarity. Ashi felt a bit more relaxed, though. There was little need for the mark. Tariic hadn't come to see her since that first night, and even if he did come today, she could draw on her mark in an instant.

The irony of Tariic's forged letter, she reflected as she watched the sun climb into the sky, was that the core of it was true. She would never betray House Deneith, but she certainly didn't feel welcomed by it anymore. If Breven could turn his back on her, she could turn her back on Deneith. If she escaped Tariic's trap, maybe she would. There was a lot of Khorvaire she had yet to explore. If she went back to Deneith, Sentinel Tower was all she was likely to see. She'd be more comfortable than in her tower prison, but no freer.

Movement in the courtyard below caught her eye. She leaned over the stone sill to watch as a parade of figures streamed out of the fortress and into the streets of Rhukaan Draal. Sunlight flashed on armor—not just the plain armor of guards but the fantastic, ornate armor of the warlords of Darguun. In their midst rode a figure in a bright tigerskin cloak.

Ashi wrinkled her forehead. Where was Tariic going? Out in the street, a crowd had gathered, the sound of their cheers reaching up to her window. She saw Tariic wave in response. As the end of the procession passed out of the gates, the crowd spilled along the street in its wake.

She looked at her scratchings on the wall, crossed one more off and counted them. It was 24 Vult. If the attack on Breland was to take place on 28 Vult, Dagii needed to leave Rhukaan Draal very soon to reach Skullreave in time. That very day probably.

Tariic would be riding to give Dagii his blessing before the young warlord departed.

THE TYRANNY OF GHOSTS

Ashi closed her eyes and exhaled slowly. Tariic had put her in this room so she could see the Iron Fox ride over the Ghaal as they left the city. It was almost tempting to spite him by not watching—but by not watching, she would miss her last glimpse, however distant, of Dagii and his company.

She leaned against the wall to wait. The sun crept another handspan across the cool blue of the sky—

—and a sudden shout from beyond the door of her prison brought her jerking upright. There was a strange rattling, then the clash of falling metal. Another shout, cut short in a kind of wet grunt.

Ashi reached for the power of her dragonmark, feeling its heat flash across her skin and the clarity of its protection settle over her mind, before she realized that anyone who fought her guard was probably an ally. Still, she dashed quickly across the room and settled into a defensive stance at the side of the door, ready for whoever or whatever came through. Bolts and lock rattled. Ashi drew back her arm to strike. The door opened.

"Lady Ashi," said a voice with a heavy Goblin accent, "I'm going to enter. Hold your blow."

The speaker waited for a moment, long enough for her to grasp his message, then stepped through the door. Ashi let her arm fall. "Keraal?"

Dagii's lieutenant thumped a fist against his chest in a salute. The chain that was his weapon rattled. "Dagii sends his greetings and asks you to come with us. There is little time." He stepped aside, and three more hobgoblins entered, carrying the corpse of the dead bugbear between them. None of them wore a crest, but Ashi thought she recognized them as members of the Iron Fox.

"How—?" she began, then looked back up at Keraal. "Did Dagii tell you Tariic threatened to have him killed if I escape?"

She wouldn't have put it past the warlord to keep that bit of information from his men, but Keraal nodded. "He expects the attempt will come from one of the Kech Shaarat, but he doesn't

intend to be around the Sword Bearers for long. He is turning his back on Tariic." Keraal's ears flicked. "Dagii also told me that you will be killed if he defies Tariic. That's why you're coming with us."

Ashi's head whirled. Had Tariic anticipated this? Without her, he had no hold over Dagii once the Iron Fox was beyond Rhukaan Draal—unless he wanted to come chasing after them with the Rod of Kings. But there was another problem. She held out her wrists, displaying the silver cuffs Tariic had forced on her. "I can't leave Rhukaan Draal with these on," she said.

"What Cannith made, Cannith can defeat," said Keraal. He produced a pouch and opened it to show her three vials of pale blue milky liquid in its carefully padded interior. "Dagii procured these. They'll help you resist the cold. Cannith magewrights travel with the Iron Fox. Once we're beyond Rhukaan Draal and before we leave Tariic's service, one of them will be made to remove the cuffs." He put the pouch in her hands.

She stared at it for an instant. Keraal's ears flicked, and he gave a thin smile.

"Dagii thinks in strategy," he said. "Come." He pulled her out of the door. In the room beyond, the other soldiers of the Iron Fox were cleaning up blood spilled in her jailer's death. Bloody rags were thrown into the cell, and the door closed, bolted, and locked. Until that door was opened, there was no sign that the jailer hadn't simply walked away from his post, leaving her safely locked up.

Keraal sent his chain wrapping around his torso with a quick flip of his wrist, then pulled on a bulky coat discarded outside the door of the outer room to cover the weapon. Another soldier whirled a cloak over Ashi. "Suspicious," said Keraal, "but it will have to do."

Ashi pulled a hood up over her head. "Where are we going? I saw Tariic riding out to give his blessing to Dagii."

"The blessing takes place at the arena. We'll join the Iron Fox there. You'll be carried out of Rhukaan Draal in one of our

THE TYRANNY OF GHOSTS

weapons carts. While the Iron Fox receives Tariic's blessing, though, there's something you need to do."

From a pocket of his coat, he took a familiar folded paper and handed it to Ashi. "Dagii instructs you to find Pater d'Orien. You won't have difficulty—Tariic hasn't bothered instructing his guards to watch for you, and all of the envoys will sit together in the arena. Once you find Pater, use your dragonmark to free him from the influence of the Rod of Kings. Tell him to use *his* dragonmark to leave Rhukaan Draal immediately and carry this warning to Breland. Once you've done that, return to us and hide. Faalo"—he gestured to one of the other soldiers—"will be waiting with the cart to hide you."

Once again, Ashi found herself staring at what Keraal had put in her hands, then she looked up at him. "I would have thought you'd welcome an attack by Darguun on Breland. You rebelled against Haruuc because he held the warlords back."

Keraal's face darkened a little at the reminder. "I don't have any love for Breland," he said, "but Dagii has shown me why Tariic's war will only bring disaster for Darguun. Now hurry. I know the passages that a man condemned to the arena walks. We'll go that way to avoid the crowds, but it will still take time." Keraal turned for the stairs that led down. "Dagii's strategy has a schedule. There's no room for delays or errors."

◈ ◈ ◈ ◈ ◈ ◈ ◈

The people of Rhukaan Draal were packed into the streets around the arena. Ekhaas couldn't remember seeing so many, even during the funerary games for Haruuc. Fortunately, they didn't have to try and fight their way through. Geth led them to one of the monuments the old lhesh had erected around the city and indicated a heavy door behind a barred gate that was built into its base. "Open that."

Chetiin set to work. In the few moments that it took him to open first the gate, then the door, Ekhaas looked up at the

monument. It depicted a hobgoblin warrior carrying a sword and a wide shield—and wearing the horn-adorned ancestral armor of the warlord of the Mur Talaan clan. Geth followed her gaze. "Fenic," he said. "Haruuc's first *shava*. Dagii's father."

The door creaked open onto tightly curled stairs going down into darkness. "Will we need light?" Ekhaas asked.

"No." Geth started down the stairs. "Haruuc had a tunnel built, a way to bring prisoners from Khaar Mbar'ost if they're too hated to transport through the streets. And a way to leave the arena discreetly or in an emergency. I used it a couple of times during his funerary games. There are everbright lanterns lighting it."

The tunnel was cramped, just wide enough for two people to slide past each other, barely high enough for a bugbear to stand upright. The lanterns were few and widely spaced, giving just enough light to pass along the tunnel. In the midpoint between one and the next, the darkness was complete, even to goblin eyes. Distant sound—the roar of a crowd, the stomping of feet—carried along the corridor.

They'd just passed into the second of the deep shadows, well away from the stairs, when they heard footsteps behind them. All of them froze instantly. Ekhaas recognized the sound of boots coming on at a brisk pace. Through the gloom, she could just make out half-a-dozen figures hurrying along the tunnel. They were armed. She found Geth's arm and whispered in his ear. "Are there other ways out?"

"Only into the arena."

"I could take them," Midian murmured.

"We'd have to deal with bodies," said Geth. "Stay quiet and keep ahead of them. The arena isn't far."

They moved on, staying to the shadows, darting through the light only when those behind them were also under lanterns. Unfortunately, their pursuers weren't as concerned with stealth as they were and gained ground rapidly. Ekhaas looked ahead and saw a rectangle of brighter light. The exit into the arena—she hoped.

THE TYRANNY OF GHOSTS

Then the footsteps behind them paused abruptly and she knew they'd been spotted.

"Run!" snarled Geth at the same moment a voice from behind rasped in Goblin, "Don't let them escape!"

Boots thundered along the tunnel.

Ekhaas's ears flicked back. "Keep going! I'll slow them down!" She whirled, stepped to one side, as Tenquis, then Midian and Chetiin, sped past. She was under a light, their pursuers momentarily lost in darkness. That was perfect. She called to mind the spell of glittering dust that had blinded the varags and drew breath to sing.

A voice—a human voice—rolled out of the shadow. "Stop! *Stop*! That's Ekhaas!"

Some of the running footsteps stumbled to a halt. Others continued, the figures of hobgoblin warriors looming out of the shadows until the goblin voice ordered, "Halt!" Ekhaas's song had already caught in her throat, though. She knew both voices.

"Ashi? Keraal?"

Somewhere behind her, Ekhaas heard Geth curse in surprise and slow his flight as well, but her eyes were on the dragonmarked woman who came charging out of the darkness. Ashi flung her arms around her, and Ekhaas even returned the human gesture before she pushed her friend back a pace. "Ashi, what are you—?"

Ashi didn't let her finish. "Escaping," she said, lips peeling back from her teeth. "Keraal got me out of Khaar Mbar'ost. Dagii leaves Rhukaan Draal today. Tariic is sending him to attack Breland!"

"Explain as we move," said Keraal. Dagii's lieutenant came striding into the light with three warriors who Ekhaas recognized as members of the Iron Fox company behind him. He took Ashi's arm firmly, hurrying her along. He nodded curtly. "This is unexpected, Ekhaas *duur'kala*. Dagii didn't plan for you."

"We only just arrived in Rhukaan Draal." She turned, hurrying to keep up with his pace. Geth, Tenquis, and Chetiin

came trotting back. Ashi greeted each of them with an embrace as she kept walking. Then she jerked back suddenly, pulling out of Keraal's grip.

Midian stood waiting for them.

"What's he doing here?" Ashi turned to her. "Tariic sent him to kill you!"

"We know," said Ekhaas. "Ashi, we found something that can counter the Rod of Kings. Midian's working with us." She looked at Keraal. "We need to talk to Dagii."

"He's waiting with the Iron Fox." Keraal's ears twitched back. "Our timing is already close. You may be able to speak with him before we enter Tariic's presence, or you may not."

"We have to."

The end of the tunnel was barred by another heavy gate, though this one had been left unlocked. Deliberately, Ekhaas guessed. Keraal paused, hand on the gate. "Dagii plans to rebel against Tariic after he leaves Rhukaan Draal. If you don't have a chance to speak to him before we enter the arena, come with us. Ekhaas, you and Chetiin should be able to conceal yourselves among the Iron Fox." He glanced at Geth, Tenquis, and Midian. "There is a weapon cart we're hiding Ashi in. If you're close, you might all fit."

"I can disguise them with a spell," said Ekhaas. She turned to Geth. His face wrinkled as he thought, then he nodded.

"We can plan Tariic's downfall from outside Rhukaan Draal as well as we can from within it," he said. "Take us to Dagii."

"*Mazo.*" Keraal pushed open the gate, and they stepped into an empty, curving corridor. The sound of the crowd was even louder than before. It surged suddenly to an almost deafening level before sinking back. Keraal's face tightened. "There are ceremonial duels before the blessing," he said. "One just ended. Hopefully it wasn't the last."

He pointed along the corridor. "Ashi, your way lies there. You'll find stairs to the upper levels and out into the stands. When you're done, return to the ground level of the arena,

THE TYRANNY OF GHOSTS

and turn left. You'll find our mounts and Faalo waiting with the weapons cart. You have to be back before the blessing is finished."

Ashi nodded and slipped past. Ekhaas held her back for a moment. "What are you doing?"

"Warning Breland that Tariic is planning to attack. I have to get to Pater d'Orien in the stands so he can carry the message."

Midian stepped forward. "I'll go with her. I know the back ways through the arena and if there are problems with the guards, I can get her past them." They all looked at him. "I am still the royal historian," he said.

"No," spat Ashi. "I don't want you near me."

"I'm coming anyway."

Keraal put his ears back flat. "Just go!" he snarled. "You have no time to argue!"

Ashi glared at Midian, then nodded to Ekhaas and dashed away along the corridor. "I should follow them," murmured Chetiin.

Ekhaas hesitated, then said, "No. Stay with us. You should be close in case we need to use the *shaari'mal*."

Chetiin's big ears twitched, but he nodded slowly. Keraal gestured to the rest of them. "This way."

He led them the opposite way along the corridor, then up to what must have been a staging area for the arena. Sand spilled through from the other side of a pair of tall doors, currently closed, but shaking with the sound of the crowd in the stands above. Ekhaas could smell old blood and animal odors.

Lined up before the doors in parade formation was the Iron Fox, armor and weapons polished. Standing at the company's head in his scarred battle armor, helmet in his hands, was Dagii. The young warlord's gray eyes turned as they entered—then widened as he saw her.

Ekhaas's blood seemed to thunder in her ears at the sight of him as well. She was vaguely aware of Keraal urging them forward as he and his men moved to where junior warriors waited

to help them don their armor. Ekhaas tried to force her emotions back, but they resisted her. She walked to Dagii with Chetiin to one side of her and Geth and Tenquis to the other. "*Ruuska'te,*" she said. Tiger man.

He stared at her, not shifting from his parade position, though his ears were trembling. "*Taarka'nu.*" Wolf woman. She saw him swallow. "I'm about to swear a false oath before my lhesh and then rebel against his command. *Gath'muut. Gath'atcha.*"

No duty. No honor. Ekhaas knew that it was probably as close to an admission of fear as he was ever likely to come. She shook her head. "*Ta muut'rhu,*" she said. "You have a greater duty. Dagii, we've found a way to block the power of the Rod of Kings. We're going to come with you. We can fight Tariic."

His eyes widened and finally broke away from her to glance at Geth and the others. Ekhaas turned to Tenquis. "Give me the *shaari'mal.*" The tiefling nodded and murmured the word that revealed the pockets of his long vest.

Beyond the door, the crowd in the arena went suddenly silent.

Tenquis froze, hand reaching for his pocket. Dagii stiffened, his ears pressing flat along his head. "No!" he said sharply. "Get back—"

Tariic's voice echoed through the arena. "Let my commanders enter!"

The throb of drums and drone of war pipes rose. The great doors began to open. Dagii snapped around to face them as sunlight fell on him. Suddenly Keraal was beside Ekhaas and the others. "Your spell of disguise!" he said. "Use it now!"

Ekhaas blinked and sang more out of instinct than conscious thought. Picking four warriors of the Iron Fox, she held their images in her mind as the magic took shape. Illusion wove itself around Geth and Tenquis—and her and Chetiin too. One of the four warriors glanced away from the opening doors at the rippling sound of her song, and Ekhaas saw his ears rise at the sight of his own double.

THE TYRANNY OF GHOSTS

Keraal cursed and said, "Try not to draw attention to yourselves." He shoved them toward the Iron Fox and barked an order. The warriors shifted in their ranks and four places opened up. Ekhaas and the others stepped into formation just as the doors opened fully, and Dagii led his company out onto the sands of the arena.

◦ ◦ ◦ ◉ ◦ ◦ ◦

Ashi found the stairs to the stands and raced up them, not bothering to look back and see if Midian had kept pace with her. In fact, she hoped that he hadn't. Discovering that Ekhaas, Geth, and the others had made it back to Rhukaan Draal was exhilarating. Finding out that Midian was still alive—and had even become an ally once more—sickened her.

She knew where the dragonmarked envoys would be sitting in the stands. The envoys and their diplomat counterparts from the Five Nations always took the same seats, outsiders banding together in the sea of Darguuls. She paused outside the entrance to the stands, slipped off the hood of her cloak, and pushed the enveloping folds back. The disguise would do more harm than good as she joined the other dragonmarked, but she wanted to keep it available in case Tariic happened to be looking up this way.

A hobgoblin guard was standing just inside the entrance. He held up a hand as she tried to pass. "You don't belong here," he said in Goblin.

Ashi gave him a haughty glare. "I am Lady Ashi d'Deneith," she said in the same language. "I have every right to sit in this section."

He looked her up and down, and she realized what he was seeing. Compared to the other envoys and diplomats, she had the appearance of a pauper. Clothes dirty from days of captivity, hair and body unwashed—she certainly didn't *look* like she belonged here.

She hesitated and considered calling for one of the other envoys to verify her identity.

The crowd fell silent. The guard turned away. Ashi craned her neck to look past him.

In the raised box where he sat surrounded by Darguun's most prominent warlords, Tariic rose to his feet and held up the Rod of Kings. "Let my commanders enter!"

The big doors on either side of the arena opened, and two companies of hobgoblin soldiers entered. From the right came Dagii and the Iron Fox—Ashi didn't see Ekhaas or the others but Keraal was there so they had to be close. From the left came ranks of Kech Shaarat. She recognized both Taak Dhakaan and Riila Dhakaan at their head.

The throbbing sound of big goblin drums and the dissonant drone of war pipes filled the arena. The crowd remained silent, watching with fascination and respect, as the companies made a brisk parade and took their places. Ashi searched the stands in front of her and found the back of Pater d'Orien's broad shoulders only a few rows from the edge of the section. She clenched her teeth and tried the guard again. "Let me through."

He turned to glare at her, but his gaze shifted to someone behind her. Ashi looked back and saw Midian. In his travel-stained clothes, his small crossbow hidden beneath his stripped-off jacket, the gnome was only a little less disheveled than she was, but he stared up at the guard with a confidence much larger than his stature. "You stand in the way of Lhesh Tariic's guest," he said. "She's missing this great event. I am Tariic's historian. Have you seen me in Khaar Mbar'ost? Move or Tariic will hear about this!"

The guard's eyes darted between them—and he stepped aside. Below, the two companies had fallen into formation. They stood still, warriors looking straight ahead, commanders looking up at Tariic. The lhesh lowered his rod, and the drums and pipes faded. "Taak Dhakaan of Kech Shaarat," he said in Goblin. "Riila Dhakaan of Kech Shaarat. Dagii of Mur Talaan. You go to meet the enemies of Darguun—"

THE TYRANNY OF GHOSTS

The blessing had begun. Ashi walked past the hobgoblin guard, looked down at Midian, and gave him a nod of thanks. He wasn't even looking at her. His gaze was on Tariic, his eyes intent.

Ashi felt a sudden flicker of unease. Ekhaas said they had a way to counter the rod, but she wondered how permanent that way was. Could Midian have fallen under Tariic's power again just by seeing him with the rod? "Midian," she whispered as they walked down the stairs of the stand together, "are you still with us?"

"Don't worry, Ashi," he said. "Tariic's never going to have a hold on me again."

His eyes stayed on the lhesh. Ashi's unease didn't go away.

They were at the bench behind Pater. "Wait for me," she said. Keeping her head down and praying that Tariic kept his attention on the Iron Fox and the Kech Shaarat, she pushed her way along.

"—Do you accept the challenges that I set before you? Do you follow the will of your lhesh for the glory of Darguun?" asked Tariic.

"—Be careful!" said Dannel d'Cannith.

"—I can't see!" complained Esmyssa Entar ir'Korran.

"—I accept your challenge!" roared Taak.

"Ashi, sit down," ordered Laren Roole. The ambassador of Breland pushed her aside. "This could be an historic moment."

Ashi ground her teeth together. She took out the folded paper with Tariic's plans on it with one hand and reached for Pater's shoulder with the other. The viceroy of House Orien saw her and started to turn.

"Tariic!"

Ashi's head snapped around at Midian's scream. She looked up just in time to catch the flicker of movement as he jumped onto the rail at the edge of the stands, his crossbow steady in his hands. Everyone else looked up, too, including Tariic.

Midian loosed his bolt.

CHAPTER TWENTY

24 Vult

"Do you accept the challenges that I set before you? Do you follow the will of your lhesh for the glory of Darguun?"

Taak Dhakaan drew his sword and raised it high. "I accept your challenge!"

Geth struggled to stand as still as the hobgoblins around him, facing forward, eyes fixed on the air in front of him. It wasn't in the nature of shifters. His gaze switched from the Kech Shaarat beside them on the sand; to Dagii, standing with unbelievable control; to Tariic in the raised box above, acting like the emperor he wished he were. Geth's hand curled on the hilt of Wrath. Just wait, he told himself. Just wait a little longer. Tariic will gives his blessing and we'll all leave—

"*Tariic!*"

He whirled. Glimpsed Midian perched on the railing high above. Saw Ashi's face behind him. Recognized the madness in Midian's eyes. Spun back around and heard the hiss of the gnome's loosed bolt as he did.

At Tariic's side, Pradoor leaned forward suddenly, her hand swiping the air as her withered lips moved in prayer.

Midian's crossbow bolt dropped as if it had been slapped aside, clattering against the stone of the box just in front of Tariic. The lhesh's face twisted into something hard and vicious as he stared at the gnome and Ashi.

Geth felt his gut twist too. Midian had betrayed them again! Maybe out of madness rather than malice, but he'd betrayed them.

"Midian," whispered the Iron Fox warrior who was Ekhaas, "you fool!"

Tariic's voice rose. "*Icegaunt*!" he howled, and up on the stands Ashi cried out, clutched her arms, and fell back against startled dragonmarked viceroys and Five Nations ambassadors. Tariic thrust out the Rod of Kings. "Midian Mit Davandi—jump!"

Midian stiffened on the railing high above and turned slowly to face Tariic. The crossbow hung loose in his hands. On the tier of stands below, goblins, hobgoblins, and bugbears stared up, then scrambled over each other to get out of the way. Midian leaned forward—

"No!" shouted Ekhaas. Her disguise as an Iron Fox warrior unraveled as she moved, plunging a hand into her pouch and ripping out her *shaari'mal*. She turned around and held the byeshk disk high, a look of concentration on her face.

It seemed to Geth that he felt a tremor pass through Wrath. Up on the railing, Midian blinked and jerked back, the color draining from his face. A shout turned the gnome around—guards had appeared on the stairs. Geth saw a look of almost feral cunning come over Midian. He flung the crossbow at the guards and plunged in among the spectators still in the stands.

Chaos spread through the arena. Spectators in the stands were yelling and shouting and—incredibly—still cheering as if the unfolding events were mere spectacle. In the raised box, warlords had surrounded Tariic, maybe out of a desire to protect him, maybe to ask what was happening. Pradoor screamed for the wrath of the Dark Six to fall on Tariic's assassins. The Kech Shaarat warriors had drawn back, weapons ready for whatever might happen next.

Dagii spun around. "Iron Fox, shield line ahead and behind!" he ordered, and the warriors of his company moved with swift precision, locking their shields into overlapping barriers. One

THE TYRANNY OF GHOSTS

shield wall faced the potential threat of the Kech Shaarat, the other guarded their rear and the still open door through which they'd entered the arena.

Left between the two lines were Ekhaas—the *shaari'mal* still raised—Dagii, Chetiin, and Tenquis. Ekhaas's hadn't been the only disguise to unravel. Tenquis held his wand at the ready, golden eyes staring around in a mix of confusion and anger. "Geth . . ." he said, sharp teeth bared.

"Back to back," Geth told him. He drew Wrath, stepped in close to Tenquis, and looked up to Tariic.

The lhesh ignored the madness around him and stared down at them all. "You!" he bellowed over the noise that filled the arena. His eyes flicked to the *shaari'mal* Ekhaas held. "What is this?"

"Your undoing!" Ekhaas spat back.

Tariic's eyes narrowed. His ears went back. He pointed the Rod of Kings at Dagii. "Kill her," he ordered. "Kill all of them!"

Dagii's eyes opened wide as the command seized him. His helmet dropped from his grasp, and he reached for his sword. Caught in the rod's power, some of the Iron Fox abandoned the shield walls and turned as well. Ekhaas swung the *shaari'mal* first toward Dagii, then toward the advancing warriors. "No!" she said. "You can resist him!"

Another tremor shook Wrath as the power of the shield clashed with the power of the rod. Tariic held his attention on Dagii, though. The young warlord kept moving, drawing his sword and raising it high as he turned on Ekhaas. The *duur'kala*'s ears trembled. Geth saw fear and terrible loss in her eyes. Gut clenched, he tightened his grip on Wrath, ready to fight one friend to save another—

Then the tremor in the ancient sword became a charge like lightning as Chetiin stepped up beside Ekhaas and held out the second *shaari'mal*.

Geth felt the power of Muut form, throwing back the influence of the Rod of Kings. Dagii and his warriors stumbled, then

287

looked up with clear eyes. Up in his box, Tariic stumbled, too, staggering backward into the warlords around him. His face was slack with shock.

"It's not possible," he said. "It's not—" He glared at the warlords who were looking at him, then swiped the rod through the air in front of them, pointing down into the arena. "Get them!"

Zealous exaltation lit up the faces of the warlords, and they vanished from the box. A few came swarming down over the wall in their eagerness to carry out Tariic's command. Ekhaas and Chetiin turned the *shaari'mal* on them, but the tremor Geth felt this time was nothing like it had been before. One of the warlords hesitated, but the others kept coming.

"Horns of Ohr Kaluun," said Tenquis. "That's not good!"

Across the sand, Geth saw Taak Dhakaan and Riila Dhakaan glance at each other, then Taak roared, "For glory! Kech Shaarat, *itaa!*"

⦿ ⦿ ⦿ ⦿ ⦿ ⦿ ⦿

"*Icegaunt!*"

Cold burned through Ashi's wrists worse than it ever had before. Her world narrowed to that terrible, numbing pain. Instinctively, she jerked her arms close to her body, as if that would keep them warm, but it only brought the cold to her chest. She felt herself topple backward into bodies and heard Laren Roole yelp at her cold, shivering touch.

In her left hand, she could see the folded paper with Tariic's plans. It trembled as her fingers shook, threatening to slide away. Hold onto it, she told herself. Hold it!

Her fingers closed tight. Somewhere in the distance, there seemed to be a lot of shouting and movement, but Ashi tried to ignore it. She forced her other hand toward her belt and the pouch of vials Keraal had given her. Movement came in spasms. She got her hand to the pouch and hooked her fingers—she

THE TYRANNY OF GHOSTS

couldn't feel them—around the flap, but her first attempt to get the pouch open only jarred one of the vials loose. It flew up, and Ashi heard someone gasp in surprise, then the vial dropped and rolled away somewhere underfoot. *No!*

A hand closed on her arm and held it steady. Ashi looked up and saw Pater d'Orien's round face as he winced at the touch of magical cold. "You want one of these, Ashi?" he asked. Thick, rough fingers fished the remaining two vials from her pouch. "Someone open one of these!"

Another hand, she didn't know whose, reached past him and took both vials, then returned one to him opened. Pater put it to her lips and tipped it with surprising gentleness. Ashi slurped at the milky, pale blue liquid.

A kind of warmth spread through her. No, not warmth exactly—she was still cold, but she no longer felt it. She pushed Pater's hand away and thrust herself upright. Viceroys and ambassadors were gathered around her. Behind them, the arena was a seething mass of confusion as Darguuls moved around. On their tier, where arena guards rampaged through the stands as if they were looking for something, the spectators surged back and forth to avoid them. On the tiers above and below, it didn't appear as if the crowds were trying to escape at all, only to find the best view.

Pater's forehead wrinkled. "Ashi, what's going on?" he asked.

She grabbed his arm and drew on her dragonmark, sending its power through him. He gasped as the clarity of its protection settled on him. Ashi saw more questions form in his eyes, but she didn't give him the chance to ask them. "Tariic has been controlling you—all of you—with a secret power of the Rod of Kings," she said swiftly. "His defenses against the Valenar are really preparations for an attack on Breland that will take place in four days."

"What? That's ridiculous," said Roole. Ashi ignored him and thrust the folded paper into Pater's hand. Frost crinkled as the paper moved.

"Dagii has risked everything to get this to you," she said. "You need to get it to Breland *right now*. Do you understand?"

Pater blinked, then his face hardened into determination. "I understand." He heaved his bulk upright, drawing her up with him. "Ashi, I can take you with me if you want to come."

She shook her head and stepped back. "No, my friends need—"

"You!" The guard who had stopped her at the head of the stairs burst into their midst, grabbing for her. "You were with the assassin!"

Ashi tried to pull away, but someone's leg tangled with hers. She stumbled, tripping over a bench. The guard pushed past Roole and Kravin d'Vadalis to seize her.

Pater's meaty fist cracked into his jaw. His sleeve rode up, and Ashi glimpsed the dragonmark that curled across his wrist. The colors of the mark seemed to shimmer—and the guard vanished with the punch, reappearing and crashing into the stands half-a-dozen paces away. Pater stepped back with a look of satisfaction.

"Learned that trick on caravan guard duty." He checked the paper in his other hand and nodded to Ashi. "Thank you," he said. "I'll make sure Baron Breven hears about this." He closed his eyes, and a distant expression crossed his face, then he took a step and disappeared.

Laren Roole shot up and took his place. "This is intolerable," he said. "You're meddling in Brelish affairs, and I don't appreciate this fearmongering—"

Ashi pushed him back down and whirled around, trying to see what was happening. A battle cry drew her attention to the arena floor as the Kech Shaarat bore down on the Iron Fox. Other battle cries came as Darguun's warlords charged in through the arena's open doors to attack from the other side.

Ekhaas, Dagii, Geth, Tenquis, and Chetiin were right in the middle of it all.

And in his box above the combat, Tariic watched it like some kind of gloating puppetmaster with Pradoor at his side.

THE TYRANNY OF GHOSTS

Ashi turned back to the viceroys and ambassadors. "Where's Midian?"

"There," said Esmyssa.

Ashi looked where she pointed and realized what the guards had been hunting for. Midian hung in the grasp of two big bugbear guards as they came across the stands toward the group of diplomats. Other guards were converging on them as well.

"I think they saw what happened to the one Pater punched," said Roole. He looked around desperately. "If we give them Ashi—"

"Close your mouth, Roole," said Dannel d'Cannith. She looked at Ashi. "Is what you said about Tariic controlling us true?"

Ashi nodded. "I can't free you the way I did Pater, or I would, but it's true. He's been manipulating you since Vounn's murder. Some of you"—she glanced at Roole—"more than others. He had Midian under his control for a long time too. If Tariic wins here today, he won't let you get away."

"Then we'd better fight for ourselves if we want to get out of here," said Kravin. He slid a slim sword from a sheath at his hip. "Weapons?"

Esmyssa produced a pair of long needles from her thick hair. Dannel pulled off her belt and tossed it on the ground—Ashi watched segmented metal plates rearrange themselves and come to life as a steel serpent. Other viceroys and ambassadors drew more mundane weapons. The arena guards slowed their advance and spread out, suddenly wary.

"Go get Midian, Ashi," said Dannel. She handed Ashi the last of the potion vials, then hissed a command at her steel serpent. It slithered forward like a vanguard, the various diplomats following it.

Ashi crossed behind them and came up through the stands to cut off the guards holding Midian from the others. She wished briefly that she had gotten a sword from Keraal,

then realized she had something that was perhaps even more intimidating. Approaching the guards, she raised her hands, ready to strike.

Vapor from the cold of the wrist cuffs rose off them like eldritch smoke. When she swayed her hands through the air, the white mist left a short-lived trail behind. The guards backed off, eyes darting from her to the other guards who were trying to dodge Dannel's steel serpent as it glided among them. Ashi jumped forward and grabbed the bare flesh of a guard's arm, giving it a hard squeeze.

The trick worked. Shocked, if not actually hurt by the cold, the bugbear yelped, released his grip on Midian, and ran. The other guard hesitated only a moment longer before following. Midian dropped to the ground with a groan. Ashi dragged him up onto a bench, then slapped him lightly in an effort to wake him. "Come on, Midian," she murmured, cupping her frigid hands around the back of his neck.

He yelped and his eyes flew open, the slack leaving his face. He focused on her but Ashi had the feeling he didn't really see her. She jerked her hands away from his head just in time as he twisted and snapped at them with this teeth. He came up into a crouch, holding himself like a fighter but hunched and ready to spring like an animal.

"Don't touch me!" he snarled. "Nobody touches me!"

"Midian!"

"Ashi?" His stance softened, and he actually looked at her with recognition in his eyes. "Sage's quill, Ashi. They won't let me rest. They're always pulling at me."

"They? You mean, Tariic?"

Midian tensed up again. "Tariic. Zilargo. Darguun. Dhakaan. They all say I serve them, but I'm not going to play their game anymore. I'm not!" His eyes went wide, and his mouth spread into a mad, savage grin. "I'm going to kill them. They want me to kill. That's what I'm going to do. Let them see where my loyalty lies!"

THE TYRANNY OF GHOSTS

The tearing influence of the Rod of Kings had unhinged his mind. Ashi stood and took a step back, then glanced down into the arena and the chaos there. At Tariic and Pradoor, safely raised above the battle on the sands.

An idea came to her. Even if he had slipped into madness, there was one thing she thought she could count on from Midian. One of the fleeing guards had dropped his sword. She picked it up. "Come with me," she said to Midian. "I know where to start."

○ ○ ○ ◉ ○ ○ ○

The disciplined Kech Shaarat formed themselves into wedges as they charged. The rod-driven warlords who came streaming into the arena from the other side simply rushed the lines of the Iron Fox. In either case, the result was the same. With some of Dagii's men pulled out of place by Tariic's killing command, the shield wall was weakened. It buckled on both sides simultaneously.

"Back!" shouted Dagii. "Iron Fox, encampment formation!"

On the periphery of his vision, Geth saw the Iron Fox's shattered lines convulse and try to pull together, but he had his own problems. The warlords who'd been so caught up in Tariic's command that they simply dropped over the wall of the raised box were already inside the broken lines.

The shifter turned as Garaad of Vaniish Kai stalked around him, keeping the hobgoblin in his sight. He knew the warlord—lean and nasty as the spear he carried. And unlike Makka with his trident, Garaad wasn't going to sacrifice the reach of his weapon for the bloody joy of close combat. He stayed back, spearhead dancing and shifting.

"Geth," said Tenquis from his back, the tiefling turning as Geth turned. "More coming from this side!"

"Do what you can," Geth said tightly. He felt Tenquis move, arms rising as he worked his magic, and caught a whiff of acrid fumes. A warlord gasped, choked, and fell back. Geth kept his

eyes on Garaad's, waiting for the telltale shift that came before a strike...

Garaad's eyes twitched. His spear darted in. Geth met it with an upward sweep of Wrath, turning the blow aside, then spun along the length of the spear faster than Garaad could pull back. The warlord rocked away from Wrath's blade—right into the path of Geth's great gauntlet. He dropped like a pair of trousers trying to stand on their own. Geth raised his sword to finish him.

Dagii's voice rang across the arena. "No! Bring the warlords down, but don't kill them! They are our allies!"

The spectators still watching from the stands above jeered. Geth remembered something Haruuc had once told him. *Darguun wants blood. The people always want blood.*

It hadn't mattered if that blood had flowed from defeated rebels or the lhesh himself. It wouldn't matter if it came from Dagii or one of the warlords. Kings, traitors, nobles, heroes—they were all the same in the end. Geth ground his teeth together, gave Garaad a hard kick to make sure he stayed down, then turned away.

Tenquis fought ferociously, a shimmering field of force around him throwing back the blows of warlords with a sound like thunder, while the tiefling's wand spit short, crackling bolts of lightning. Nearby, Ekhaas fought with a grim determination, *shaari'mal* still in her hand, sword clashing with the weapon of a Kech Shaarat warrior, a song of determination and encouragement pouring from her throat. Chetiin darted across the field, his dagger flashing wherever an outthrust leg or exposed back presented itself. Keraal stood among the Iron Fox, swinging his chain to keep more warlords back.

They were holding their own. Barely.

Another warlord came at Geth. He met the hobgoblin with a snarl. Sword met sword in a bone-jarring crash. Across the arena, he heard Taak Dhakaan's voice rise in challenge.

"Dagii of Mur Talaan, fight me! The Kech Shaarat are no allies of yours!"

THE TYRANNY OF GHOSTS

Dagii's answer was a roar of fury. New clashing added to the clamor of battle. As Geth turned in his own fight, he caught glimpses of Dagii and Taak's duel. The young warlord charged and beat the Kech Shaarat warrior back a pace. Taak countered with a rain of blows that drove Dagii away. The armored figures closed again, struggling back and forth.

Geth smashed Wrath against his opponent's chest. The warlord's breastplate, bright steel chased with bright brass, creased under the blow. His face turned suddenly red as the bent metal crushed in against him, and he struggled to draw breath. Geth knocked his sword away and swept his legs out from under him, leaving the hobgoblin to struggle like an overturned turtle. He whirled back to Taak and Dagii—

—in time to see Taak break free and swing his sword around with all of his weight and strength behind it. He bellowed as he swung, his face as contorted as the demon visage on his armor.

Dagii rocked away. Taak's great blow passed just beyond his belly, dragging Taak around. Ears back, the warlord of the Mur Talaan stepped up and swept his own blade across Taak's shoulders with precision and control.

Taak Dhakaan's body fell to the sand, still tumbling from the power of his last blow. His head rolled free to stare up at Dagii.

"No!" Tariic's voice rang across the arena. "Pradoor! Stop them!"

Pradoor raised her head, and her milky eyes caught the light. "I call the teeth of the Devourer!"

Only a few paces from Geth, whirling white blades burst out of the air in the midst of a knot of Iron Fox warriors. The warriors screamed and broke formation, blood streaming from flesh that looked as if it hadn't been so much slashed as chewed. The Kech Shaarat they had been fighting cheered and fell on the scattered warriors.

Geth turned to Tenquis. "We have to get up there. Follow me!"

"Wait." The tiefling dug into a pouch and produced what looked like tiny glass rods. He flicked the rods into the air.

They vanished, but light streaked across the arena. In front of the raised box, the air shimmered, and stairs formed from planes of barely visible force.

Geth bared his teeth in a grin. Drawing Tenquis after him, he sprinted for the phantom stairs, bashing at anyone who tried to get in his way. Above, Tariic slammed the Rod of Kings down on the rail of the box. "Again, Pradoor. Call down the wrath of the Six. My enemies are their enemies!"

Anger crossed Pradoor's blind face. "The Six are not your lackeys, Tariic."

"Yes, they are." He thrust the rod at her. "Do it!"

Almost at the foot of the stairs, Geth froze as Pradoor's anger evaporated under the direct power of the Rod of Kings. Her arms rose stiffly. "Lords of the Dark Star!" she called, and Geth saw a kind of writhing darkness take shape around her as she spoke. "I invoke your—"

She never finished. A blur seemed to launch itself from the back of the box and smash into her. Pradoor hit the rail of the box. Her prayer ended in a moan, the writhing darkness vanishing. The blur became Midian. Putting one arm around the old goblin priestess's bony chest, he wrapped the other across her head and twisted with brutal efficiency.

◉ ◉ ◉ ◉ ◉ ◉ ◉

As she came through the back of the box, Ashi heard Pradoor's neck snap and part of her felt a rush of joy at the goblin's death. But Pradoor hadn't been their target.

She watched Midian drop Pradoor's body and turn to Tariic with death in his eyes.

Tariic brought up the rod. "Midian, stand where you are!"

The gnome stopped—for a moment. His face twisted. His hands squeezed tight, then spread into claws reaching for Tariic.

THE TYRANNY OF GHOSTS

And he took a heavy step forward. "I," he said between his teeth, "will not . . . be . . . controlled . . . again!"

Shock and rage flashed across Tariic's face. Ashi felt a sense of triumph. She lifted her sword and stepped forward, a demand for Tariic's surrender on her lips.

Then Tariic took two quick steps and slammed the Rod of Kings down on Midian's skull. Bone cracked. Midian staggered, and Tariic did it again. Midian went down, his head broken in.

The entire arena fell silent. The spectators who had cheered for blood stopped moving. Combat on the sands came to a halt. Tariic turned to the rail and glared out at those below and above him. "Who will defy the lhesh of Darguun? Who will challenge the emperor of Dhakaan Reborn?"

Mouth suddenly dry, Ashi moved forward and spoke. "Surrender Tariic. You're alone. This is over."

He looked at her with disdain. His free hand went to his belt and drew his sword. "Alone? I'm not alone. I command the largest army in Khorvaire." He looked back to the arena and raised the Rod of Kings, Midian's blood and hair dripping off it.

"Darguun," he shouted, "rise and destroy my enemies!"

● ● ● ◉ ● ● ●

"Darguun, rise and destroy my enemies!"

Fear stabbed through Ekhaas. Instantly, she thrust the *shaari'mal* into the air, concentrating all of her will on blocking Tariic's command. She saw Chetiin, his wrinkled face pale, do the same thing.

They might as well have tried to stop the tide with a bucket.

The power of the rod blasted through her, too strong to be held back. The shield of Muut muted some of it, but not enough. On the floor of the arena, Kech Shaarat, Iron Fox, and warlords alike staggered and fell, the shield allowing them to fight—if not entirely resist—Tariic's command. Above the arena floor, though . . . She twisted to look up into the stands.

DON BASSINGTHWAITE

All those who had remained in the arena to watch violence unfold were on their feet, eyes strangely blank. Ekhaas felt a crush of despair. Muut had failed them. Was this what had happened after the nobles of Dhakaan had abandoned their duty and the *shaari'mal* had been forgotten—

Hope sprang up inside her. She whirled around. Geth, protected by Wrath, still stood, his face twisting in anger as he stared at those writhing on the ground. One of them, right beside him, was Tenquis. Ekhaas saw Geth's fist tighten on his sword, saw him put his foot on the first step of the phantom stairs Tenquis had conjured.

"No!" she yelled. "Geth, the third *shaari'mal*! Get it to Dagii!"

From the raised box came the fluting battle cry of the Bonetree Clan as Ashi rushed at Tariic. The lhesh caught her blow on his sword, though, and slid past her easily. Ekhaas's gut twisted. Ashi might be able to prevail over Tariic, but if she didn't do it quickly, none of them would be able to take on Tariic's army.

She watched Geth look up at the sound of clashing swords, then down at Tenquis.

* * * * * * *

Every instinct told Geth to join Ashi against Tariic. Together, they'd be able to beat him.

In his hand, though, Wrath stirred with a life Geth had only felt a few times before. Memories of hobgoblin heroes, dead for thousands of years, flickered through his head. Memories of them performing great feats and defeating strange monsters, the tales of their exploits inspiring generations. The very reason that the Sword of Heroes had been created.

It was Wrath's way of telling him that this wasn't his fight. It belonged to someone else.

Geth bent down and reached into the pocket—fortunately still unsealed—where Tenquis had hidden the third *shaari'mal*.

THE TYRANNY OF GHOSTS

The tiefling's hand grabbed his wrist as he drew the disk out. Tenquis looked up at him, his eyes narrow with the effort of fighting Tariic's command.

The shifter eased his hand away. "I'll come back," he promised—then he sprinted across the sand.

Others in the arena had fallen to squirm on their sides or backs but Dagii had stayed on his knees, gripping his sword as he stared up at Tariic. Geth slid in the sand as he stopped beside the young warlord. "This is yours," he said. He pushed the *shaari'mal* at him.

Dagii stared at it for a heartbeat, then reached out and wrapped his fingers around it.

One disk held brought a tremor through Wrath. Two disks brought a lightning charge.

Three disks was like holding onto a storm. Geth felt as though he were gripping all of the great artifacts that Taruuzh had forged from the vein of byeshk called *Khaar Vanon*. He could feel the connection between them, feel the power and the destiny that they shared.

Power pulsed out through the arena in an invisible wave. On the sand, warriors and warlords stirred and sat up. In the stands, Darguuls seemed to draw a single, unified breath as the influence of the Rod of Kings was blasted away. In the raised box, Tariic screamed in rage. Geth's head jerked up, and he saw the lhesh batter Ashi with a blow that sent her sprawling one way and her sword spinning another.

Tariic didn't follow up on his advantage, though. He whirled to look out into the arena. "Who dares?" he bellowed in Goblin.

"I dare!" Beside Geth, Dagii rose to his feet and glared at Tariic. He held the *shaari'mal* high and gestured with his other hand to Ekhaas and Chetiin. "We dare."

"You can't!" Tariic thrust out the rod again. "Darguuls, obey me!"

Nothing happened. There was no new pulse of power. Geth felt no tremor through Wrath.

Dagii slowly lowered the *shaari'mal*. "We stand between you and them," he said, "as it was meant to be." He turned to look at the warlords on the sand and the people in the stands. "Tariic has manipulated you," he proclaimed. "He has placed Darguun in peril to satisfy his own ambition. He has forgotten his *muut*."

"I will lead Darguun to a new age of empire!" Tariic roared.

"You will destroy us!" Dagii shouted at him. "Haruuc realized it when he discovered the curse of the rod, but you were so caught up in the rod's power that you ignored the danger. Khorvaire is no longer the place it was when Dhakaan ruled. The Age of Dhakaan leaves its legacy, but an Age of Darguun, as Haruuc saw it, is the future."

He threw back his head, raising his face to Tariic. "It is the ancient right of a warrior to challenge his clan chief when he believes the chief has failed the clan. The lhesh is chief of the clan of Darguun. Tariic Kurar'taarn, lhesh of Darguun, I say that you have failed us, that you are without *atcha* and without *muut*. I am Dagii, warlord of Mur Talaan, commander of the Iron Fox, victor in the Battle of Zarrthec. Here and now, I challenge you!"

The arena was silent for a moment, then Ekhaas raised her voice. "I witness the challenge!"

Chetiin raised his strained voice as well. "I witness it!"

Tariic looked down at the warlords who had stood beside him in the box and who had rushed to fight at his command. Geth saw Garaad of Vaniish Kai, leaning on his spear, lift his head. "I witness it."

Tariic put his ears back and bared his teeth. "The challenge is accepted!" He raised the Rod of Kings. "But a chief who is challenged and wins has the right to take the life of his challenger."

"I expect nothing less," said Dagii.

Tariic swung his legs over the rail of the box and climbed down Tenquis's phantom stairs to the sand below. Those near the base of the steps pulled back to leave a clear space. Ekhaas, Chetiin, and Tenquis came to stand with Geth and Dagii,

THE TYRANNY OF GHOSTS

but there was no other movement. Kech Shaarat and Iron Fox remained intermingled. Tariic stood alone in the cleared space, waiting.

"Geth," said Dagii, "give me Wrath."

Geth didn't hesitate. He reversed the twilight blade and presented the hilt to him. Dagii took it. He looked at Ekhaas and nodded to her. She nodded in return, her ears standing high, then Dagii turned and stepped away.

Warlord and lhesh faced each other. They raised their swords, touching them together almost as if swearing an oath in the goblin fashion. Tariic sneered at Dagii. "You never understood power," he said.

Dagii's eyes narrowed, and his ears flicked back—

In that instant, Tariic dropped his sword and snatched at the *shaari'mal* held in Dagii's left hand. "Resist me without this!" he screamed.

Dagii's fingers tightened on the disk. His right arm raised Wrath and he struck.

At Tariic's left hand. At the Rod of Kings.

Geth knew what would happen. He'd felt it in that moment when Dagii had gripped the third *shaari'mal* and completed the Shield of Nobles. The artifacts of Khaar Vanon were connected. The destiny of one lay within the others.

Within the Shield of Nobles, the Sword of Heroes struck the Rod of Kings. *Muut, Aram, Guulen.*

The rod rang with a sound like a cracked bell and shattered. Shards of byeshk fell out of Tariic's hand. The lhesh gasped, let go of the *shaari'mal*, and staggered away. Dagii drew back Wrath.

"You never understood duty," he said—and swung.

CHAPTER TWENTY-ONE

28 Vult

The death of Lhesh Haruuc Shaarat'kor had been followed by a mourning period of ten days during which no fires burned in Rhukaan Draal, the streets were empty between dawn and dusk, and no one entered or left the city.

The death of Lhesh Tariic Kurar'taarn was followed by no mourning period at all.

It wasn't a case of spite. When Razu asked how Tariic's passing should be treated, Dagii had been willing to allow for a remembrance of tradition, but there was too much to be done too quickly. Messengers were dispatched into the north of Darguun with orders that the troops Tariic had put in place be demobilized. More messages were rushed to King Boranel of Breland advising him of the change in power in Darguun and of the nation's good will toward its neighbors. In addition, not everyone was convinced of Tariic's villainy. The power of the Rod of Kings had swayed many Darguuls, but many more had needed no greater persuasion than Tariic's promises of war and glory.

"His memory will haunt you," Chetiin had advised Dagii.

"It already does."

Geth stayed close to the young former warlord—the young lhesh. Someone had the idea that because he'd held the throne for two weeks after Haruuc's death, Geth was best suited to steer Dagii through his first days.

"The best advice I can give you is to keep your head down," the shifter told Dagii. "If it all gets to be too much, find a friend and duel for a while." He patted Wrath at his side. "That works for me."

Munta the Gray was summoned to Rhukaan Draal and installed as Dagii's chief advisor, which relieved Geth. The old warlord knew more about political maneuvering than Geth ever would.

When it came time to try and appease the dragonmarked houses, though, Ashi was Dagii's biggest help. The viceroys of the houses—and many of the ambassadors from the Five Nations—had a new respect for her. After the events at the arena, Dannel d'Cannith had personally seen to the removal of the icy cuffs Tariic had forced on her and promised an investigation into who in House Cannith had created such a device. If relations with the houses and nations beyond Darguun would take time to repair, the viceroys and ambassadors within Darguun were at least cordial. Most of them admitted to Ashi—sentiments she passed along quietly to Geth and the others—that they were embarrassed at having been manipulated by Tariic and suddenly faced a certain amount of suspicion from their monarchs and patriarchs.

The Kech Shaarat appeared to find themselves in a similar situation. When Riila Dhakaan appeared before Dagii to tell him formally that her clan's warriors would withdraw, she hinted that she would not have the warmest of welcomes from the warlord of her clan. Ruus Dhakaan seemed to feel that she'd fallen too much under Tariic's influence, the power of the Rod of Kings not withstanding. Dagii offered apologies for the death of Taak, but she shrugged them off. "He died with honor," she said. "Remember him as a strong opponent."

Messages of apology for the treatment of Senen Dhakaan were also sent to Volaar Draal, but there was no immediate response. Ekhaas admitted that she wasn't surprised. "The Kech Volaar are not a forgiving clan. It comes of having long memories."

THE TYRANNY OF GHOSTS

She hid her own sadness well. Geth, Tenquis, and Chetiin told the story of her exile from the Kech Volaar to Ashi, while Ekhaas told Dagii herself. Afterward, they'd come together and Ashi had tried to console Ekhaas. The *duur'kala* wouldn't allow her. "It makes it easier," she said.

"Easier?" Ashi looked ready to ride to Volaar Draal and threaten Tuura Dhakaan until she took Ekhaas back.

"Easier," said Dagii. "Normally marriage between a lord of the Ghaal'dar and a woman of a Dhakaani clan would force some kind of political alliance, but since Ekhaas is exiled—"

They hadn't let him finish before they were offering their congratulations. Ekhaas had shushed them all down. "There are still complications," she said. "Haruuc never married, so there was no need to figure out a female equivalent of lhesh."

"*Lhesh'nu*," said Dagii.

"Really?" asked Tenquis. "It sounds like you just made that up."

"I'm the lhesh. If I can't make up words, what can I do?"

There was one additional complication to the coronation—or rather, the wedding and double-coronation. On the third day after Tariic's death, shortly after the date of the coronation was announced, three hobgoblin priests of Dol Arrah, Dol Dorn, and Balinor, the gods of the Sovereign Host that Haruuc had revered, sought an audience with Dagii. They entered the throne room—where Tariic's crest had been removed and the crests of the clan were being restored—almost tentatively.

The priest of Dol Arrah took the lead. "We are concerned that you have chosen the day of 28 Vult for your coronation, lhesh."

"It's the day that Tariic would have attacked Breland," Dagii said. "It seems an appropriate day to begin a new reign."

Geth watched the priest search for the right words to respond. "We have heard that the servant of the Dark Six, Pradoor, was killed along with Tariic, so we hope that you do not intend to follow his support for her religion. Nonetheless,

305

we should point out that 28 Vult is the third Night of Long Shadows and sacred to followers of the Dark Six."

"I'm aware of that," said Dagii bluntly. "Are you trying to ask if I intend to include the rites of the Sovereign Host in my coronation?"

The priest looked relieved. "Yes, lhesh."

"No." He rose. "I respect the Host, but Tariic included one aspect in his reign that I will keep. The emperors of Dhakaan did not submit to religion and neither will I. I serve my people, not the gods." He nodded to the priests. "You are welcome in Darguun and in my court if you wish, but not beside my throne. *Saa'atcha*, Vassals of the Host."

"That was nicely done," said Geth as the priests retreated in some consternation.

"I'm beginning to get a feel for it," Dagii said, then turned to look at him. "Do you want to duel for a while?"

On the night of 28 Vult, the newly crowned lhesh and lhesh'nu of Darguun swept into the small chamber where Haruuc had once spoken in secret of finding an artifact called the Rod of Kings and where Geth and the others had once spoken of how to defeat it. Geth gave them the best bow that he could as he, Tenquis, Chetiin, and Ashi rose in greeting. "Your majesties," he said.

"Sit," said Ekhaas. "*Khaavolaar*, I wish I could." She poked at the stiff robes stitched with silver plates, a fanciful approximation of armor, that she wore. "I'd rather wear my real armor than this."

"Razu may not have been certain how to dress a lhesh'nu, but she knew no one would wear leather to a coronation," Dagii said. He tilted his head self-consciously, adjusting to the height and weight of the spiked crown of Darguun. "This is going to take getting used to." Ekhaas wore a smaller version, the rivets on it still bright. Both of them also carried a new addition to

THE TYRANNY OF GHOSTS

the regalia of the rulers of Darguun—two ancient *shaari'mal* forged of byeshk. With the Rod of Kings destroyed, the magic of the Shield of Nobles was gone—or at least pointless—but the *shaari'mal* remained potent symbols.

"The coronation ceremony was moving," said Ashi. Her mouth curved into a grin. "Even if it did lack the excitement of the last one."

"Where you got hit over your head, and I jumped out of a window," Geth pointed out.

"I like the formal name you've chosen," said Chetiin. "Lhesh Dagii Muuten'karda. The High Warlord Dagii of the Dutiful Throne."

Dagii bent his head in acknowledgment but admitted, "Ekhaas suggested it."

Ekhaas smiled at that, but it seemed to Geth that the smile was forced. "Grandfather Rat," he said, "get on with it. I told you I hate long good-byes."

The *duur'kala* snorted and flicked her ears. "Then it's just as well we can't stay long. Razu has us on a schedule tighter than an infantry drill. We just wanted to bring you together because we have gifts for you."

"I thought Tariic cleaned out the treasury."

Dagii's ears went back. "I see it as a chance to find ways of bringing wealth into Darguun other than by selling our warriors to Deneith as mercenaries. But these aren't those kinds of gifts, even if you deserve them."

He turned to Chetiin, but the goblin shook his head. "I have my reward," he said. "Exoneration in the assassination of Lhesh Haruuc and a *shaari'mal* of my own."

"I was going to say that the only other thing we can offer is our friendship." He gave the *shaarat'khesh* elder a deep nod. "I hope we can remain friends the way that you and Haruuc were. Consider the *shaari'mal* a bond between my clan and yours."

Chetiin twitched his ears, then returned the nod. Ekhaas took her turn, producing two items from behind her stiff skirts

and holding them out to Ashi. "These are for you."

"My grandfather's sword!" Ashi snatched it from her.

"We found it in Tariic's chambers."

Ashi drew the blade and inspected it, then looked at the other item in Ekhaas's hand. A silver horseshoe. Ashi frowned. "That was Midian's. It summons a pony."

"I took it to Dannel d'Cannith, and she examined it. It turns out it summons a horse the right size for whoever uses it. Dannel offered to buy it from us, but I told her no. I thought you could use it on your journeys."

Ashi flushed a bit, and Geth looked at her curiously. "Journeys?"

"I made a decision," Ashi said. "I'm not going back to House Deneith. At least not for a long while. Dagii cleared things up with Baron Breven, so I'm not under threat of excoriation if I leave Darguun, but I want to see more of Khorvaire. I'm not going to be treated as an asset of Deneith." She took the horseshoe. "This will be useful. Thank you."

Ekhaas turned to Tenquis. "We have something important to ask you," she said. This time it was Dagii who drew something out, presenting Tenquis with a bundle of roughly wrapped leather. The tiefling frowned and opened it.

Inside was a collection of byeshk shards. Tenquis drew a sharp breath. "The remains of the Rod of Kings?"

Ekhaas nodded. "We know you'll take care of them, and maybe you can learn something more about the *daashor*."

"I'm . . . honored." He folded the leather back together carefully. "I'll watch over them. I may not study them right away. If you don't mind me saying it, I need to leave the lore of Dhakaan behind for a while. Like Ashi is leaving Deneith."

"I understand," said Ekhaas. Finally both she and Dagii turned to Geth. He looked at both of them and felt an uncomfortable sense of familiarity with what he saw in their faces. Particularly in Dagii's. He crossed his arms.

"No," he said.

THE TYRANNY OF GHOSTS

Dagii blinked. Ekhaas said, "But you don't even know what we're—"

"I do. I saw the same look on Haruuc's face just before he rewarded me by making me his *shava*."

Dagii looked confused. "There's no greater honor. You wouldn't have to stay in Darguun. I wouldn't call on you."

"Haruuc made me that offer, too, and look where it took me."

"You're a hero," said Ekhaas.

Geth couldn't help smiling. "Maybe I am," he said, "but I took a rough road to get here. I've had enough of it. I've seen more than I wanted, done more than I wanted. I need a rest. I'm going home."

"Bull Hollow?" asked Ashi. He nodded.

"Where's that?" asked Tenquis.

"A little hamlet in the forest on the far side of the Eldeen Reaches," Geth said. He looked at the tiefling. "You should visit."

Tenquis smiled back. "Maybe I should. It sounds like the kind of place where not much happens."

"I don't know," said Geth. "Sometimes stories start there."

Raat shan gath'kal dor.

"The story stops but never ends."

— Traditional closing of hobgoblin legends.

RETURN TO A WORLD OF PERIL, DECEIT, AND INTRIGUE, A WORLD REBORN IN THE WAKE OF A GLOBAL WAR.

EBERRON

TIM WAGGONER'S
LADY RUIN

She dedicated her life to the nation of Karrnath. With the war ended, and the army asleep—waiting—in their crypts, Karrnath assigned her to a new project: find a way to harness the dark powers of the Plane of Madness.

REVEL IN THE RUIN
DECEMBER 2010

ALSO AVAILABLE AS AN E-BOOK!

EBERRON, DUNGEONS & DRAGONS, WIZARDS OF THE COAST, and their respective logos are trademarks of Wizards of the Coast LLC in the U.S.A. and other countries. ©2010 Wizards.

WELCOME TO THE DESERT WORLD
OF ATHAS, A LAND RULED BY A HARSH
AND UNFORGIVING CLIMATE, A LAND
GOVERNED BY THE ANCIENT AND
TYRANNICAL SORCERER KINGS.
THIS IS THE LAND OF

DARK·SUN WORLD

CITY UNDER THE SAND
Jeff Mariotte
OCTOBER 2010

*Sometimes lost knowledge is
knowledge best left unknown.*

FIND OUT WHAT YOU'RE MISSING IN THIS
BRAND NEW DARK SUN® ADVENTURE BY
THE AUTHOR OF *COLD BLACK HEARTS*.

ALSO AVAILABLE AS AN E-BOOK!

THE PRISM PENTAD
Troy Denning's classic DARK SUN
series revisited! Check out the great new editions of
The Verdant Passage, *The Crimson Legion*,
The Amber Enchantress, *The Obsidian Oracle*,
and *The Cerulean Storm*.

DARK SUN, DUNGEONS & DRAGONS, WIZARDS OF THE COAST, and their respective logos are trademarks of Wizards of the Coast LLC in the U.S.A. and other countries. ©2010 Wizards.

Dungeons & Dragons

From the Ruins of Fallen Empires, A New Age of Heroes Arises

It is a time of magic and monsters, a time when the world struggles against a rising tide of shadow. Only a few scattered points of light glow with stubborn determination in the deepening darkness.

It is a time where everything is new in an ancient and mysterious world.

Be There as the First Adventures Unfold.

The Mark of Nerath
Bill Slavicsek
August 2010

The Seal of Karga Kul
Alex Irvine
December 2010

The first two novels in a new line set in the evolving world of the Dungeons & Dragons® game setting. If you haven't played . . . or read D&D® in a while, your reintroduction starts in August!

ALSO AVAILABLE AS E-BOOKS!

Dungeons & Dragons, Wizards of the Coast, and their respective logos, and D&D are trademarks of Wizards of the Coast LLC in the U.S.A. and other countries. ©2010 Wizards.

FORGOTTEN REALMS

RICHARD LEE BYERS

BROTHERHOOD OF THE GRIFFON

NOBODY DARED TO CROSS CHESSENTA...

Book I
The Captive Flame

Book II
Whisper of Venom
February 2011

Book III
The Spectral Blaze
February 2012

...WHEN THE RED DRAGON WAS KING.

"This is Thay as it's never been shown before . . . Dark, sinister, foreboding and downright disturbing!"
—Alaundo, Candlekeep.com on Richard Byers's *Unclean*

ALSO AVAILABLE AS E-BOOKS!

Forgotten Realms, Dungeons & Dragons, Wizards of the Coast, and their respective logos are trademarks of Wizards of the Coast LLC in the U.S.A. and other countries. Other trademarks are property of their respective owners.
©2010 Wizards.

Don't wait until you're accepted into wizardry school to begin your career of adventure.

This go-to guide is filled with essential activities for wannabe wizards who want to start

RIGHT NOW!

Ever wonder how to:

Make a monster-catching net?
Improvise a wand?
Capture a werewolf?
Escape a griffon?
Check a room for traps?

Find step-by-step answers to these questions and many more in:

Young Wizards Handbook:

HOW TO TRAP A ZOMBIE, TRACK A VAMPIRE,
AND OTHER HANDS-ON ACTIVITIES FOR MONSTER HUNTERS

by A.R. Rotruck

DUNGEONS & DRAGONS, WIZARDS OF THE COAST, and their respective logos are trademarks of Wizards of the Coast LLC in the U.S.A. and other countries. ©2010 Wizards.

Books for Young Readers

EBERRON

LEGACY OF DHAKAAN
BY DON BASSINGTHWAITE

A new kingdom rises—and threatens to collapse—as Lhesh Haruuc, ruler of the goblin nation, unites his disparate peoples under the powers of the Rod of Kings. But when the artifact's charisma proves dangerous, it's down to a band of unlikely heroes to save the nation of goblins.

The Doom of Kings
Word of Traitors
The Tyranny of Ghosts

THORN OF BRELAND
BY KEITH BAKER

An agent of the Dark Lanterns, Thorn serves her country in the cold wars of the Five Nations. But during her missions, strange memories and powers are surfacing within Thorn: the memories and powers of an ancient, deadly dragon.

The Queen of Stone
The Son of Khyber
The Fading Dream
(October 2010)

THE DRACONIC PROPHECIES
BY JAMES WYATT

A once-proud hero fallen to disgrace and madness must learn to wield extraordinary powers to save those he loves, and to keep the world from sliding back into decades of warfare.

Storm Dragon
Dragon Forge
Dragon War

"Word...
... The story just keeps getting better and better. I'm eagerly awaiting the third novel."

—Dungeon's Master.com

Bassingthwaite skillfully balances the high adventure common to the DUNGEONS AND DRAGONS *novels with some tender and believable character moments. The grief over a lost sword-brother is given equal weight to intense battles, as is Ashi's frustration at the regimentation of her life amongst the Dragonmarked House of Deneith. My favourite touch however, was that rarity of rarities, a non-human culture that felt true without borrowing slavishly from an existing or ancient people of our own world.*

—Chadwick Ginther, writing for McNallyRobinson.com

LOOK ON SHATTERED *MUUT* AND BE HUMBLED.

The top of the inscription lay toward the dais. Anyone kneeling before the lord of Suud Anshaar would have had no choice but to read the words. "The fallen nobles," said Ekhaas. "He was reminding the fallen nobles of what they'd lost." She scrambled past the words to rake at the remaining rubble. Her breath came fast. Her heartbeat echoed in her ears.

Purple byeshk flashed under moonlight. Ekhaas got down on her knees, stretched out her arm, and used it to sweep away the last fragments of stone.

Her heart fell. She sat back, her ears folding flat.

Set into the stone were three toothed metal disks. Three *shaari'mal* forged from byeshk. She looked up at Geth and Tenquis. "I don't understand," she said. "What are these?"

Geth picked up Wrath and brought it close to the embedded disks. "These are what I was feeling," he said. "These were forged from the same byeshk as the sword and the rod."